The Rhise of Hope

Book Two of the Darkness Overcome Series

By Max B. Sternberg

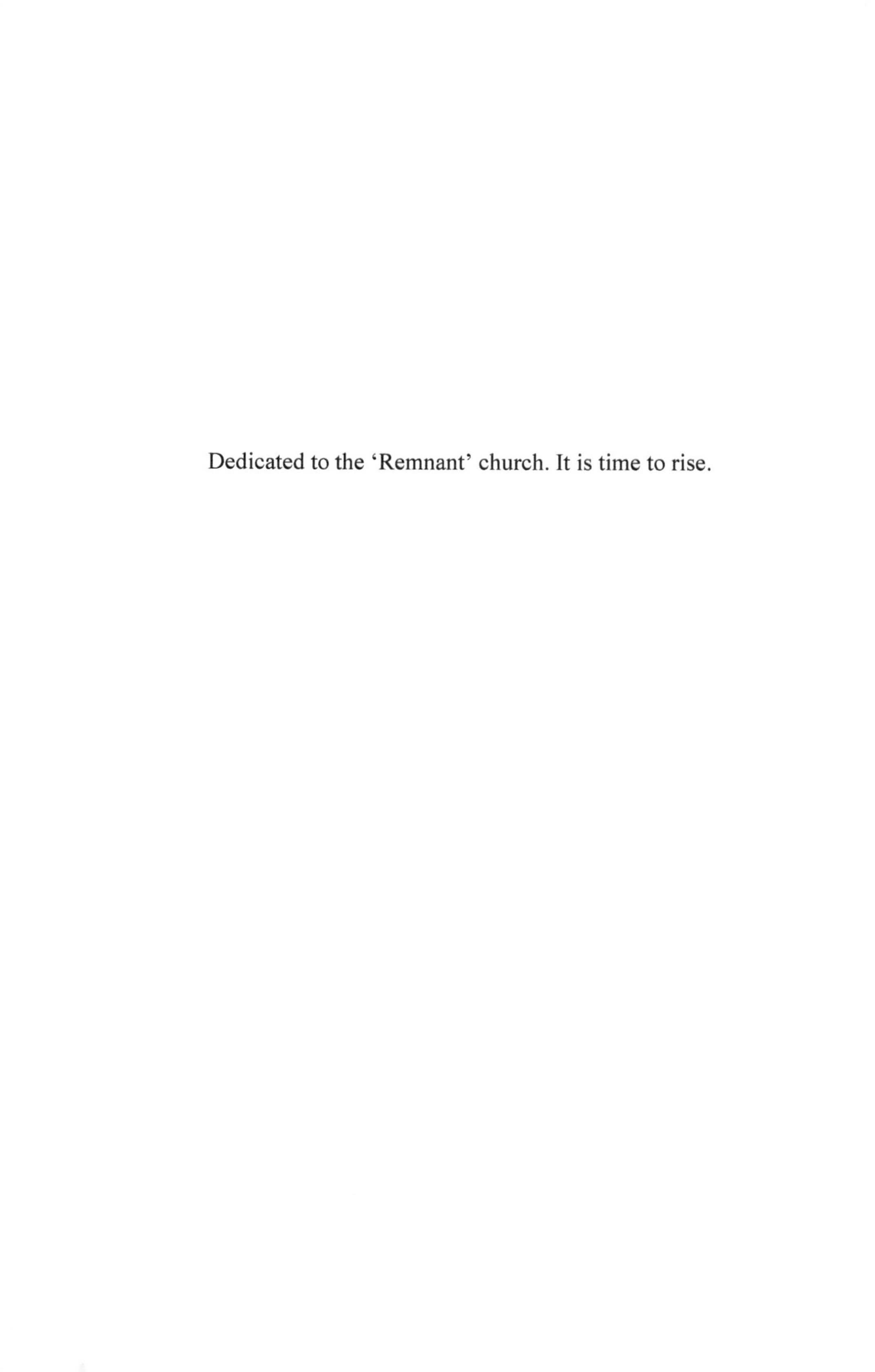

Dedicated to the ‘Remnant’ church. It is time to rise.

E-book ISBN: 978-1-7369989-3-9
Paperback ISBN: 978-1-7369989-4-6
Hardcover ISBN: 978-1-7369989-5-3

Front Cover Design by Nick Camilo
Map created using Inkarnate

FIRST EDITION

You can find more about the Darkness Overcome series and the author at:

www.maxbsternberg.com
https://www.facebook.com/maxbsternberg
https://mewe.com/i/maxbsternberg

Map of the Kingdom

Table of Contents

Prologue: The Survivor 2
Chapter 1: The Meeting 8
Chapter 2: The War 24
Chapter 3: The Golem 36
Chapter 4: The Council 49
Chapter 5: The Faith 60
Chapter 6: The Forest 70
Chapter 7: The Adversaries 84
Chapter 8: The Nephilim 97
Act Two: The Heretic 112
Chapter 9: The Sacrifice 113
Chapter 10: The Forgotten 126
Chapter 11: The Bridge 143
Chapter 12: The Trolls 160
Chapter 13: The Dwarves 170
Chapter 14: The Prisoner 184
Chapter 15: The Trial 198
Chapter 16: The Aeonyte 210
Act Three: The Hope 219
Chapter 17: The Idea 220
Chapter 18: The Groundwork 234
Chapter 19: The Attempt 247
Chapter 20: The Recovery 260

Chapter 21: The Assault 274
Chapter 22: The Defense 285
Chapter 23: The Star 294
Chapter 24: The Hidden 304
Epilogue: The Missing 312
Bible Verses 316
Acknowledgements 321
Author Bio 322

Part One: The Rescue

Arise, O Lord! Confront him, subdue him! Deliver my soul from the wicked by your sword. - Psalm 17:13 ESV

Prologue: The Survivor

One month ago…

Leon awoke in a cold sweat. His naval uniform was plastered to his clammy skin. The heirloom levigem necklace he wore was twisted awkwardly around, and painfully poked into his aching chest. He adjusted it and tucked the gem back into his shirt. Then he slowly sat up on the rough cot he found himself on. Everything hurt. Of course, that was likely from having walked for two days without food or water.

As he looked around, Leon discovered that of all the places he could have found himself, he had ended up in a dimly lit cell. Small, cramped, and damp, the air carried the stench of mold and rotting hay. A skin of water lay next to him and, feeling his parched throat, he grabbed for it and began to gulp its contents down with sheer desperation.

"Not too fast lad, or it'll just come back up an' out." A rough, weary voice sounded from outside the cell.

Surprise from hearing the familiar voice caused Leon to sputter a little. As he wiped the water from his mouth, he tried to get up from the cot. Exhausted, and still weak from his recent excursion, he only managed to move far enough to sit on its edge – though he did sit as straight as his tired muscles would allow.

An older grey-haired dwarf, with several gold studs on his lapel, entered the torchlight. He approached the cell and grasped its bars with one hand, while he drank from a flask with his other. The puff of long grey hair around his face resembled a lion's mane, yet somehow it blended well with the polished studded naval uniform he wore. The steely stare of Fleet Admiral Silverspine penetrated Leon as he said, "At ease, lad."

Leon relaxed, though only slightly, and cringed inwardly at his assumption of what would come next. Thoughts of what had occurred in the recent days flitted through his mind. Memories of what he had done. After swallowing another small sip of water, he croaked with a voice that hadn't spoken in days, "Where am I, sir?"

"In Agaprya, at tha naval yards. Ya slept tha whole way here. We had an apothecary feedin' ya, an' keepin' ya alive. Seems ta have worked. Now," Admiral Silverspine's leather gloves squeaked as he gripped the cool metal of the bars, and continued through gritted teeth, "Wot. Tha. Rust. Happened?"

Leon tried to fit the puzzle pieces of his ordeal together, and assemble them chronologically. Truth be told, he had a hard time remembering everything – though certain images would haunt his memory forever. So, without pretense, his words began to tumble out. Words that told the story of how the *Dawnfire* had crashed to the ground and impaled the dragon that had attacked it. How the injured Prince Gelan and he were the only survivors of the crash, and of the several days they spent making their way back to Agaprya on foot. Then he came to the point of their journey where the prince had succumbed to his wounds, though not before blaming Leon for the crash in his delirium induced haze.

When Leon arrived at the part of the story where he had been forced to decapitate the prince before he turned into an undead, the Admiral sighed and took a long pull from the flask he carried. Knowing that he had failed his mission of simply keeping the crown prince alive, Leon told of how he had been determined to at least bring the prince's remains back to the capital. Once he had completed that objective, his body finally collapsed. "And that's the last thing I remember before waking up here, sir."

The Admiral didn't respond for a long time. The guttural flicker of a low burning torch was the only sound that permeated the prison cell. All the dwarven leader could do was stare at Leon. His expression was unreadable through his mass of hair and beard. When he finally did speak, his voice was grave, "An' do ya have any proof o' wot ya are tellin' me?"

Of course, he doesn't believe me, Leon thought. He had delivered the final blow to the crown prince. His best efforts hadn't been good enough, and he hadn't been able to save him. By all accounts, the prince should have been here in Agaprya. All of the crew should have been here. All alive, and working to repair the flagship *Dawnfire* before setting out for the front again. The proof of his words was the crash itself – which would take days to verify.

A burst of inspiration suddenly struck amidst his thoughts. Leon reached into his pocket and pulled out the sharp, pale-yellow tooth he had carved from the dragon's corpse before he and Prince Gelan had left the wreckage. He tossed it to the admiral and explained where it had come from. The dwarf picked it up and examined it closely. Then Admiral Silverspine blew out a long breath. Leon could smell the stench of it even across the good distance that separated them. Rumors had always circled around the Naval Academy that the admiral had an on-again, off-again relationship with alcohol. When the admiral was sober he was a legendary tactician. However, when he took to overindulging in the drink held within his flask, his judgement became clouded.

The Admiral pocketed the tooth, and with a somewhat softened demeanor he nodded to Leon and said, "I'll be back." He then turned and exited abruptly. The squeak of the prison door hinges, and the slam of the door itself, was an ominous sign to Leon. He wondered how long it would take for the Admiral to come back.

Leon cradled his head in his hands for what seemed like hours. The sorrow of the situation served as his constant companion in the dank cell. A small piece of himself hoped that the Admiral would return and just chop his head off, then he wouldn't have to feel this pain anymore.

He wouldn't have to feel responsible for the fates of his crewmates. He would no longer feel anything at all.

To his astonishment, the dwarf eventually did return – and he was, in fact, armed. An elaborate double-bladed axe adorned his belt. It hung opposite of the flask that was attached to the other side. His gait seemed slower and more mournful. Each step made Leon's heart beat faster.

When the admiral reached the cell he once again greeted Leon with a penetrating stare – but this time there was also a curious glint in his eye. His voice was grave as he spoke, "Do me a favor laddie, an' take out tha necklace in yer shirt."

Leon knew that the dwarven race typically hated the Rhise family. Having met and interacted with the Admiral many times during training and his tenure as first mate on the flagship, he figured the visual reminder of who his family was might make it easier for the Admiral to kill him. Leon pulled out the necklace, gripped the cot's edge, and mentally prepared himself for the end.

"Boyo, by all accounts, yer a hero in my book. Not many can claim ta survive a airship crash, much less a dragon attack. Ya even brought back tha remains o' tha prince, so he could be buried proper." The admiral began to pace outside the cell, "But yer tha one who killed 'im, an' there are repercussions fer that." Leon noticed that as the Admiral spoke, his stare was not focused in his direction. It was almost as if he said these words for himself as well.

Another long silence ensued as the Admiral's hand drifted ever closer to the axe in his belt. Knowing that these were his last moments, Leon tried to make the best of them. "I am truly sorry, sir. I loved my captain like a brother at the end. He was the brother I never had, but always wanted. It… it was the hardest thing I ever had to do… to make sure he didn't turn."

"Ya told me before, that ya never got along with yer family, did ya?" The Admiral questioned.

"I joined the navy to get away from my father and brother, yes sir." Leon admitted.

The Admiral took a deep breath, his decision clearly made. Reaching to the table behind him, he picked up the keys to the cell. In their place he tossed down a small pouch that jingled slightly, as though it were filled with coins. He then unlocked the door, and it swung open on its rusty hinges. "Can ya get up lad?" The dwarf asked.

Confusion rolled through his mind, but he figured he might as well die on his feet, instead of on the edge of a cot. Leon slowly stood, stretched out his legs, and walked rigidly forward to stand at attention in the middle of the cell.

"Ya could've been tha best o' them, Leon Rhise. Ya were one o' tha finest airmen. Dedicated. Focused. Willing ta lay down yer life fer yer captain an' crew," The admiral started to say.

"Yes sir," Leon affirmed.

"Then ya are hereby dismissed from naval service. Consider that yer 'severance'," Admiral Silverspine continued, as he pointed at the coin purse and then out the door. "It's night outside, an' I made sure nobody is around. Yer pack an' belongin's are down tha hall. I left ya yer sword. Jus'..." The Admiral paused as he took the last sip from his flask, "Jus' don't go home. Start a new life fer yerself Leon. Now, go on."

Mixed emotions raged through Leon. They were like a sack of rats fighting over the last crumb in a ship's supply. While awestruck that he seemed to have gotten a stay of execution, Leon also reeled from the blow of not being able to continue his naval career.

What do I do now?

Where do I go?

"I– I don't understand." He stammered.

"I'm letting ya go, lad. Go live yer life, an' live it well an' in honor o' yer crew."

The roots of survivor's guilt dug deeper into Leon. Tears welled up in his eyes. He felt the need to honor the *Dawnfire* crew with more service, and tried to plead his case, "But sir, why can't I continue to serve in the navy?"

The admiral's answer was one that would push Leon Rhise into a spiral of depression and self-destruction for weeks.

"Boyo, nobody would ever want ta serve with tha lad who killed Prince Gelan."

Chapter 1: The Meeting

Present Day

Leon felt an abundance of energy in the early morning hours, long before any of his friends awoke. *Thank you Adonai,* he thought, because he knew he would need it shortly. He remembered his vision, and the instructions Rohiel had given him. There was a lot that he was supposed to accomplish in a short amount of time.

As he held the old spear, its blade shone with a pale yet brilliant light in the darkness of the small bedroom. Leon knew it was not yet sunrise, and with little time to waste he moved with purpose. He donned his well-crafted scale and plate armor that the dwarven smith had made. It served to mark his new identity: a Judge, a hero who hid the flawed man inside.

Leon stared at the helm in his hands. It was the final piece of the suit, and perhaps the most important. He couldn't take any chances; if he stepped out of the room without it, he might be recognized. There were a multitude of wanted posters throughout the city of Agaprya that accused Leon of theft, impersonating a noble, and crimes against the crown. Most of which, upon reflection, he had to admit were true.

He accepted the blame for having taken the spear from his father's manor when he left. Also, he had begrudgingly impersonated his pompous brother in order to gain entry to the city. Granted, he had only done so to save Miala from a harrowing situation. Leon was still not entirely sure why they were charging him with 'crimes against the crown'. He supposed one could easily argue that his act of beheading

Prince Gelan could've classified as such. The fly in the ointment was that technically, to the public, Leon Rhise was dead. So, unless his estranged father had changed his mind about not advertising the fact that Leon had struck the final blow to the prince, 'crimes against the crown' would remain a mystery.

The original lie that Lucien Rhise had spread by means of the Herald Guild – one that said all had perished in the *Dawnfire* crash – had been to save the respectability of their family name. So, his father must have been quite surprised when Leon unexpectedly showed up at home several weeks later. Shortly after his impromptu arrival, he found himself disowned and kicked out. All Leon had to show for being a 'former' Rhise was the mysterious spear he now carried, his levigem necklace, and a reward for either his capture or proof of his death.

Needless to say, he didn't feel comfortable making his identity known while those wanted posters were strewn about. Leon put on the helm that Duamé had fashioned (which also served as a mask), and quietly left the room that had been provided for him the previous night. Their group had been allowed to stay the night before at the behest of Princess Schalae. Using the leverage of her royal status, she had quite effectively maneuvered Head Archivist, Magnus, into a conversational corner. She single-handedly forced him to be hospitable to their ragtag crew. It had been an impressive feat, since not two hours before they had invaded the Archive's sealed off Judge's section, and destroyed the undead that were within it.

Leon now walked through the Archive, noting that only a few of the robed researchers were also awake at this early hour. They had already begun the day's process of packing up the facility. Moving the entirety of the Archive to its new location in Last Bastion was a monumental effort. It was especially daunting when one considered the countless types of knowledge housed within the old building. Leon couldn't fault those who wanted to get an early start, just as he did.

The two closest dark robed archivists stopped their work to simply stare at him. Their gazes held an intensity that caused Leon to become uncomfortable. He didn't really know what to expect from them. While he didn't recognize them from the prior day in the dim lighting of the early hour, Leon was certain that between the assistance they had requested to transport cannons downstairs, and the purging of undead that occurred in the Judge's section, the legend of the new Judge had grown significantly overnight. Rumors seemed to travel faster than a mail carrier airship. He considered himself a normal person, just like anyone else, and had no idea how to handle others being fascinated with him. If those who watched him wanted to gaze awkwardly in his direction, then by all means he was going to make them work for it.

"Good morning!" He called with a wave. "Did you two want to help me for a bit?"

Leon smiled under his helm as the now wide-eyed archivists pointed first at themselves, then each other – as if there was anyone else in the now empty main hall.

"Yeah! You two! I need to clear out some of the mess in the Judge's section. Wanna help?"

The Judge's section of the Archive had remained untouched, except for the removal of Anissa's body from where it had lain. In the back of Leon's mind, a small part of him still couldn't believe that she hadn't risen as an undead fiend. Such was the norm, the status quo. The recently deceased always rose again, with the sole purpose of killing the living. Yet, because Anissa had accepted Adonai as she lay dying, she hadn't turned. Much to everyone's amazement, her body was in repose, her soul and spirit were at rest. Once, a bitter rivalry had existed between mancers Anissa and Miala. The prior day's battle against the undead had seen that come to an end, with Anissa at peace in the aftermath.

Still, Leon wondered where exactly her body had gone.

Maybe Magnus will know. He mused to himself.

Once again in the forgotten depths of the Judges section of the Archive, Leon walked into that room with his two helpers, Zans and Ritz. The archivists genuinely seemed eager to help. The room was still lined with dry-rotted wooden shelves and detritus. What must have once been a trove of knowledge from Adonai and the former Judges, was now rubble that had been defaced and destroyed by the undead over the past two centuries.

The three of them got to work clearing away debris. The entire time they worked they couldn't help but wonder at what secrets would now stay hidden forever. First they removed the ruined books and scrolls, then they hauled out the deteriorated and damaged shelves themselves. They moved the mess out from the Judge's section and into the other larger, abandoned lower Archive rooms. Throughout the entire process his two surprisingly muscular helpers asked Leon questions about himself, and what it was like to be a Judge.

Leon was conscientious of his answers, and didn't reveal anything of his past, but instead talked to them about Adonai, and being a representative for Him. He described the attributes Rohiel had instructed him to embody, which had become a personal mantra that he strove to live by: Love. Joy. Peace. Patience. Kindness. Goodness. Faithfulness. Gentleness. Self-Control. He hoped Zans and Ritz would find value in them too.

The helpful archivists seemed to pay attention to what he said while they finished. Before they departed he thanked them for their help, and thought they seemed a bit star struck. He hoped they truly had focused their thoughts on what he said about Adonai, and not just on him being the Judge. Leon left the room completely bare, as he had been instructed to do in his dream. The only thing he hadn't touched was the stone table which stood in the middle of it.

Atop the table, positioned perfectly in its center, was the lump of mysterious metal that appeared to match the spearhead – which currently radiated light in Leon's hands. In his dream, one of the liches they had defeated referred to the metal as Aeonyte. He hoped either Gionna Gærheart or Duamé Onyxwill would know more about it.

Knowing that a couple of hours had passed, and that dawn was fast approaching, Leon headed upstairs to find a washroom to bathe in. While he was bathing the spearhead winked off. That signalled to him that dawn had arrived, and he was short on time. Once he dried off and got into his underclothes, Leon put the armor that Duamé created back on. He pulled on the scaled armor leggings and laced up the black leather steel-toed boots. Then, with a sigh of resignation, he put the helm back on. This was his identity now.

After having donned the helm, he once again exited his room, and was met by the multi-lensed glasses stare of the elderly gnome Gionna Gærheart. At a younger age she had invented the airship. It had been her war machines that allowed the kingdom of Xaelon to survive against the undead onslaught. Her intelligence was unrivaled, and despite her eccentricities she was quite interesting to be around.

"You are late, dearie." She stated.

"Sorry. I got up early and then came back to bathe and change. Is everyone already downstairs?" Leon asked.

"Princess Schalae hasn't arrived yet, but everyone else is waiting." Without another word she turned and walked away. Her purple and grey puffy ponytails swished in time with each step as her metallic cane rapped along the floor.

Leon hurried to accompany her, and they both descended the stone stairwell to the main hall of the half-empty Archive. Barrels and crates filled with books still lined portions of the walls, waiting to be transported to the Archive's new location. Workers of various races scuttled about in a valiant effort to safeguard the knowledge of their kingdom. Leon spotted Zans and Ritz talking to several of the other archivists, and they collectively stared at him as he waved to them. This seemed to be what the two archivists had been waiting for, because they suddenly seemed much more animated in the conversation they were engaged in.

The rest of Leon's companions stood at the bottom of the stairwell, next to one of the large pillars which flanked the grand room. They chatted quietly amongst themselves as they waited for everyone to arrive. The obligatory 'good mornings' were exchanged while they waited for the Princess of the Elvenwood to join them.

The gnomish head archivist, Magnus, ran down the stairs soon after Leon and Gionna arrived. He smoothed his white hair and beard, then took one look at their troupe and grunted. When they first arrived to clear out the forgotten section of the Archive the head archivist had looked panicked. This had been understandable since they would most likely die in their attempt. Now, he looked grumpy. He was probably more than a little irritated that the Princess had bullied him into hosting them. However, that didn't stop Magnus from waiting with them for her arrival – albeit at a distance.

"Where did Anissa's body go?" Leon asked Magnus, as the gnome looked away.

"What?" Miala asked, shuffling over to join their conversation.

Magnus' gaze fell over each member of the group and finally settled on his ex-wife Gionna, before he replied, "I respectfully had her body moved. She has been taken care of."

The fiery red-headed Miala Mytheriyn might as well have been physically on fire. Of course, as she was a pyromancer, such a thing would have been within her power. It would also have proven exceptionally dangerous for Magnus. "Where is her body?" Miala demanded, her voice laced with both fire and ice.

It seemed to Leon that Magnus tried very hard to be brave in the face of the enraged woman who stood double his height. He remained tight-lipped until Gionna walked over and tapped him with her cane. "Answer the question, Mags."

Under pressure from both Miala and Gionna, Magnus folded like a cheap tent. "I… I had her cremated."

At that moment the general process of packing that occurred within the Archive was moderately disrupted. Everyone who had been working stopped to watch as the strange group of assorted people began yelling in unison at the Head Archivist.

"Keep your voices down! I don't want the Mancer Academy to find out that she died here when she was supposed to simply unseal a section!" Magnus hissed quietly. The gnome looked around and yelled at all of the staff, "Get back to work!"

Leon issued a heavy sigh as he realized the only material evidence they had, which proved that accepting the forgiveness of Adonai would prevent you from turning undead, was gone. This would complicate things for him, and for spreading the word of Adonai throughout Xaelon. Upon reflection though, it would be a bit unsettling, and dishonoring, to display an unaltered decomposing body as evidence. *It is what it is.* Leon thought. Remembering Rohiel's request that he exercise patience, he tried to calm everyone down.

Leon didn't have to be patient for very long. Two elven warriors, one bulky male and one lithe female, soon entered the Archive. A giant sword was strapped to the male's back, while the woman had two knives at her thighs and a bow behind her. They looked like unusual elves. The male had a slightly longer neck than what was normal, and the woman had hair that grew from her head like a willow tree's branches. Their skin was like the color of tree bark, and in their hands they carried a few boxes and a couple small barrels.

The Princess stood between them. Her skin was a light brown, and she had tresses of hair the color of evergreen needles pulled back into a tightly braided ponytail. She no longer wore the black mourning gown from the night before. Instead, Princess Schalae looked ready for travel. She wore a fitted leather jerkin, and her medicinal bag was strapped to her side. Bracers that appeared to be made of a dark, thick tree bark adorned each of her arms. On the outside of her loose leather pants a quiver of arrows was strapped to her thigh – though Leon didn't see a bow on her. Instead, she had two short and straight staves behind her back.

"Good morning everyone!" Schalae exclaimed.

Their various responses seemed forced, due to both propriety and the early hour. Only Kelleren appeared to be as energetic as the Princess. The golden yellow dog all but jumped on her with his tail wagging.

"Oh, and hello to you too! How is my patient this morning?" Schalae asked, as she bent down to examine the bite wound she had treated on the dog's foreleg the previous night.

Miala answered for her companion, "He says that what you did worked, and that he feels as healthy as a pup. Thank you again."

Princess Schalae scratched Kelleren behind his ears, which caused one of his legs to thump against the ground. She stood and smiled, "He is coming along fine indeed. So," she clapped her hands together and rubbed them vigorously, "Who is hungry, and where shall we eat the breakfast we brought?"

Leon took that as his cue and stepped forward, "I prepared a place earlier this morning actually. If you would all please follow me back down to the Judge's section."

"Our resident Judge seems to have thought ahead! Lead on, good sir." Princess Schalae said, as she held out her arm. Leon knew, from his etiquette training, that he was meant to take it. He found himself taken slightly aback by her continued exuberance. Together they led the rest of their group down the many stairs. Magnus and Miala both lagged slightly behind the others.

The brick and mortar masonry of the Archive's above ground levels gave way to the huge, irregularly shaped stonework that managed to somehow fit perfectly together. They continued to descend the stairs until they reached the area outside of the Judge's section. The shelving and debris Leon had moved in the early morning crowded around the side of the entrance. The two cannons which had been used to wipe out much of the undead horde also lay nearby – next to the pile of bones, old weapons, and armor the skeletal warriors had possessed.

Seeing all the work that had been done, Gionna observed, "Well, you have been busy, haven't you, dearie?"

"We could've helped ya," Duamé chimed in.

Leon smiled as he felt the dull ache from that morning's exertion in his body. "It was no trouble, really. Besides, a couple of archivists helped. I was told to clear it out."

"By whom?" Princess Schalae asked, as she gripped Leon's arm slightly tighter. Leon happened to catch Miala watching her, and saw her eyes narrow ever so slightly.

"By Rohiel. He's a sort of teacher." Leon responded.

Leon's spear blade glowed brightly as they all made their way into the now empty Judge's section. The bright light allowed him to see as Princess Schalae's green brows rose in wonder at the spear. It also showed that the same large, monolithic stonework made up the room's walls, floor, and ceiling.

Leon gestured towards the table where the elven warriors placed the boxes they had been holding. The two silent elven warriors then bowed to their princess and took up positions behind her. "That is better. Now then, let's have some breakfast before we discuss business!" Schalae exclaimed.

She opened the boxes and began to take out various containers. Cheeses, vegetables, fruits, and nuts were displayed for everyone to partake of. However, it was the two small barrels with sloshing liquid inside that caught Duamé's attention.

"Is… is that wot I think it is?" Duamé asked, as he pointed at the barrels.

Schalae smiled radiantly at him, and poured a cup of dark liquid from one of the barrels. Wordlessly, she handed it to the dwarf. He sipped it, and shuddered.

"Ahhhh… It's been years since I've had a proper cup o' java," He sighed.

Gionna's eyes lit up behind her multi-lensed spectacles as she took a cup as well. Meanwhile, Leon cocked his head in confusion. "Java?"

"One of the primary exports of the Elvenwood. It gives energy to the tired body," Princess Schalae explained, as she handed everyone else, including her warriors, a cup.

Leon took a sip and though he found it to be slightly bitter, it was otherwise delicious. He could almost feel his drooping eyelids perk up as the liquid slid down his throat. He glanced at Miala, and noted that she also seemed to enjoy it. She even put her finger into the liquid and caused steam to emanate from the cup as she used her pyromancy to heat it up. Princess Schalae's eyes went wide at the sight, but she said nothing further.

Everyone made their introductions, save Leon, who only referred to himself as a Judge for the time being. He had no way to know whether the princess could be fully trusted yet. He begrudgingly knew that he would eventually have to reveal his identity to her. Of all people, she deserved to know the truth. From what Prince Gelan had said, she sounded as though she was a wonderful person, and truly gifted at all things medicinal. He had no idea if she knew the true story about Gelan's death though, or of his part in it. If his father, Lucien, really did have such extensive influence, there was no telling who he could have in his pocket. Even the elven princess.

"So, Judge, why would you come to a place such as this, hmm?" The Princess asked. "What exactly happened here?"

Under the watchful eyes of everyone present, Leon retold the events of what led them all to the Archive. How they came to the Judge's section to learn more about Adonai. As he heard himself explain the sequence of one improbable coincidence after another, like a tapestry of life which had knit them all together, he became aware of just how unlikely it was that they accidentally stumbled across each other. It had to be more than pure happenstance.

With occasional input from others in the group, Leon explained their assault on the fortified section of the Archive. Magnus tried to shed the best light possible on himself and the roll he played by admitting them. Meanwhile his ex-wife, Gionna, punctured whatever blown-up, self-important role he claimed. When she explained that he did everything other than bodily block them from entering the walled off section, the Princess glared at the elderly gnome. After that he didn't speak again for some time.

Once they had recapped the events to the point where Anissa died and did not rise again, Schalae stopped everyone and asked to do her own medical examination of the fallen aquamancer. She had the same reaction as everyone else when Magnus admitted he cremated Anissa. "Well I didn't know if she was going to rise as an undead later!" He exclaimed, in an effort to excuse his actions.

All who had been there attested to what they had seen, at which point Gionna pulled out two black robes and laid them on the table as she grabbed a handful of food. "I took these from the two liches that I found. Where was the third?" She asked Leon. "Didn't you kill it?"

"It was somehow made of shadow. The spear turned it into salt when I saw it." Leon replied. He then explained the spear and its powers to Schalae, who nodded as she took everything in.

"Why did ya take those robes?" Duamé asked Gionna as he peered at them.

Miala answered before Gionna could. "Because they are mancer robes."

Tapping the side of her spectacles, Gionna exclaimed, "Correct!" while the lenses on her glasses shifted around on their tiny mechanical gears. Leon knew from experience that those glasses could help the gnome see things that others could not. They helped her to be even more observant than she already was.

Gionna Gærheart explained her actions, "These robes are at least two centuries old, but they still have dimensional pockets! One each it looks like. I thought perhaps our resident pyromancer could take a look inside and see if they possess any clues."

Miala shrugged as everyone looked at her. She picked up the first dark robe and reached inside. Leon clearly saw as one moment her hand was there, and the next it wasn't! It didn't seem to bother her very much because she pulled out an unblemished hand shortly thereafter, with something held in its grasp. Everyone crowded around to see what it was.

She opened her hand to reveal a small clay statuette. It was painted black and looked to have different sized tentacle-like appendages, which extended in random places from an amorphous blob. Two tiny cut rubies served as its eyes.

"Well, that does not look very nice." Schalae commented.

Kelleren, close to Miala's hand, sniffed at the little statue and snarled viciously as he backed away. A moment later, Miala yelped and dropped the item. It clattered to the floor, but strangely it did not break as a clay statue should. "Leon! Stab it! Stab it now!"

Leon immediately reacted and brought the shimmering light of the spear blade down on the statue. As soon as the blade touched it, a screech came from it. The sound it emitted was like claws raking slowly across armor. It hurt their ears as it filled the room before the statue finally exploded into salt.

"Wot tha hematite was THAT?" Duamé yelled.

Miala shuddered as she kept wiping her hand on her robe. It was as if she was still trying to get it off her. "I don't know. Whatever it was, it was watching us, and listening to us. It was… aware."

Magnus piped in to Leon, "Good thing you destroyed it then! Well done!"

Miala shook her head, "I don't think you did. I think whatever it was is still alive but can't see us anymore." Steeling herself, she picked up the second robe before anyone could object. Her hand disappeared once again, and this time pulled out a small curved dagger. It looked simple, unadorned, but functional. This was evidenced by the dark stains that were dried on its blade.

"Who doesn't clean their weapons after they use them?" Miala asked in a disgusted tone.

Leon came to a conclusion that Gionna voiced before he could, "Someone who didn't care about blood on his blade anymore. Someone who probably died promptly after they used it."

The room was ominously silent as everyone thought about their discoveries thus far. The silence was only broken by Duamé audibly crunching on celery.

Leon suddenly felt that if he didn't get the truth out now, then he would never find the courage. He remembered the mistake he had made by not telling Miala and Duamé of his heritage, and knew he didn't want to struggle with the guilt of another lie of omission hanging over his head any longer than necessary. "Your Highness, I have a question if I may."

She flashed a radiant smile towards Leon, "Yes?"

Here we go, he thought. "How were you told Prince Gelan died?"

Her smile crashed just like the *Dawnfire* when it had carried Leon and the prince. Her eyes burned with a fierce intensity, "The official version I was told was that he died in the crash of the flagship. It took me almost the entire mourning period to figure out the truth – that a brave soul tried to bring him back to Agaprya."

Leon sighed, and regretted his earlier thoughts about her potentially being untrustworthy. At this point in his life, with wanted posters on display everywhere, he needed all the friends he could get. He lifted off the helm that Duamé had made for him, and pulled out the levigem necklace from his undershirt. "I was the person who brought him back, though I wouldn't describe myself as brave. I was disowned by my father for being the one who made sure he didn't rise as undead, among other reasons. I… I am so sorry that I couldn't save him."

Duamé threw up his hands, "Sure! Ask me ta make a mask an' start takin' it off everywhere ya go…"

With tear-filled eyes the Princess stepped closer to Leon. Uncomfortably close. She waved off the two guards that stood behind her and looked back into Leon's eyes before she suddenly closed the distance and…

…Hugged him.

"Thank you. Thank you for making every attempt to save him." She said, with her voice muffled into the shoulder of Leon's armor. Everyone around them shifted uncomfortably, Miala noticeably so. Flabbergasted, Leon broke the embrace. He also had tears in his eyes for his deceased prince and captain. While this certainly wasn't the reaction he had been expecting, it was welcome nonetheless.

Schalae looked more intently at the spear Leon held, as she picked up and sipped more of her java. "That is elvenwood, is it not? May I?" She asked, as she started to reach out.

"Unless ya can fire a bow from yer feet, ya really shouldn't lass. An Alukah who put hands on it got em charred ta ashes."

"Really? Wow!" Princess Schalae exclaimed, as she pulled her hands back and clasped them behind her back.

"Yes. It's elvenwood, and quite old. I don't know where it came from but," the iridescent spearhead tinked as Leon flicked it, "Recently, it was revealed to me that this metal is made of something called 'Aeonyte'?"

A cannon could have fired quieter than Duamé's reaction to that revelation. "WOT?!?"

"Dearie, why didn't you tell us?" Gionna chimed in.

Nobody else exclaimed in surprise, but with the potential to receive more answers Leon rushed to ask, "Do you two know something about it?"

They looked at each other, then each gestured for the other to go first, before Gionna finally took the lead, "It's a legendary metal. Incredibly rare, and just as good, if not better, at channeling energy than elvenwood!"

"Yeah, right! Aeonyte isn't supposed ta exist, boyo! No dwarf has ever found any vein o' it. Ever. It's a fairytale!" Duamé growled. "Who even told ya such nonsense?"

Leon sighed and hung his head slightly, "Rohiel showed me."

"An' ya always listen ta tha voices in yer head, right?" Duamé needled.

"Technically it's in his dreams," Miala interjected.

"And they haven't failed me yet." Leon finished.

"So, wait, that is Aeonyte too?" Gionna breathed softly, as she approached the table with the lump of metal in the center of it.

Without looking, Leon reached back and scooped the palm sized lump up. He handed it to Gionna, who cupped it in her hands like an egg. "You hang on to it and tell me," He said simply.

Then Leon closed his eyes. He hoped and prayed that as he turned around to face the table, he would see the other thing Rohiel had revealed to him in the directions from his dream last night. He opened his eyes again to see that the blob of what he knew to be Aeonyte, which he was also sure that the liches, skeletons, and whatever other undead creatures could never touch, had covered a small circular hole in the center of the table.

Miala walked up to the stone table and asked, "What's that?"

Everyone, even the silent elven guards and Magnus, approached the table and peered at the ordinary looking hole.

Leon smiled as he reached up and held the shaft of the spear to the opening, showing everyone that it was a perfect fit. "I think it's the key to more answers," Leon said, as the spear slid almost all the way into the table. The shaft was long enough that the diamond-shaped blade with the א Judge's symbol protruded from the top of the table.

The light that radiated from the spearhead seemed to retract into the blade, which caused it to become too bright to look at directly. A soft rumble began to vibrate beneath everyone's feet. The spear appeared to turn with the shaking. It continued to shift until the flat side of the blade faced parallel to the back wall.

A collective breath was held as the light spilled forth from the spear. A gaseous, luminescent fog began to roll down the table and towards the back wall. Leon's instructions hadn't included anything about this. He couldn't have guessed what would come next.

Duamé pulled a couple of hammers from his belt. The elven guards for Princess Schalae readied their weapons and pointed them at the now swirling, small circle of fog-emanating light. Gionna raised her metallic cane, pressed a button on the handle, and caused the length of the cane to split into three sections – a central shaft with two arms on either side. A cord secured at the end of those arms turned the gnome's cane into a functional crossbow. Lastly, Miala pulled out the two wands she had taken from Anissa's body and held them in front of her, their tips glowing red. Only Leon and Schalae seemed unperturbed, and watched the fog.

The swirling fog of light churned round and round as it rose into a column as tall as Leon. The light from the spearhead pulsed from the center of the table, which caused the fog to coalesce into a figure. One who now stood in front of the stone table and all those assembled.

The figure had large, bulky, curved armor that mirrored the blue sheen of the Aeonyte when it wasn't glowing. Around the edges of the armor was a gold trim, which was made up of tiny symbols. They were much like the symbol that was etched into the tip of the spear. The beautiful plate armor covered the being from its feet to its neck, and its radiant head shone bright enough to obscure all of its features. Though immense in stature, the being stood with loosely crossed arms, in a relaxed pose.

Rohiel, Leon thought. *He's here!*

The appearance of this figure, which until then had only shown itself in his dreams, was a surprise – but also a welcome relief to Leon. His friends' awestruck expressions were almost comical. Duamé's eyes bulged at the sight of the angel so much that it looked like he had tried to swallow an entire pineapple. *Is that what I must have looked like when I first saw him?*

"Fear not. I am Rohiel, angel of Adonai. Welcome to the Sanctuary, where you have all been brought to… Wait, is that java?"

Chapter 2: The War

The silence that met the angel was almost reverential. Leon seemed to be the only member of the group who could believe what he saw. A gauntleted hand held a cup of the bitter liquid. As Rohiel drank it, the cup disappeared into the light of his face, then reappeared less full. It seemed that it was up to Leon to respond to Rohiel.

"I have brought them, as instructed," Leon stated, hoping for some sort of acknowledgement.

"Do not seek the approval of others before the approval of Adonai, Judge."

"Sorry, Rohiel."

"You are forgiven, of course." The angel began to pace around the table, and the eyes of those who were assembled followed his movements through the empty space.

Leon spread his hands wide as he asked, "How… How is this possible?"

"All things are possible for those that believe," Replied the angel, as he grasped the edge of the table. "***Now, listen and learn.***"

The monolithic walls of the room seemed to expand outward without a sound. The floor and ceiling also seemed to stretch and fall rapidly away, which caused everyone to gasp in alarm. The only things that remained were the stone table, the shining spear set into it, and the remains of their breakfast.

"Have no fear."

Everyone present, with the exception of Leon and Rohiel, grasped the table as the room continued to expand beyond sight. It created a black expanse of nothingness – a void that stretched on forever. Then, the blue light of the spear blade changed to a rainbow-like hue.

The colors shifted and swirled all around the א in the middle of the blade. With a flash, light exploded from it as blazing beams shot forth. Where the beams ended, stars were formed. The expanse became filled with pinpoints of red, blue, yellow, and white. Large and small, near and far, lights innumerable grouped together and swirled around each other. Hundreds, thousands, Leon couldn't even count how many he saw. Color and light painted the blank space around them. The beauty of it stole his breath, and caused him to gaze around in wonder.

A small slurping sound came from Rohiel as he drank his java and broke the silence. ***"Adonai created everything. He still does. He loves to create. He loves all."***

Tears formed in Leon's eyes as he beheld the heavens from a proximity closer than he ever had. It was far better than even when he had been on an airship during a cloudless night. The starscape began to move and shift, and it felt as if they were traveling a great distance. Their table drew ever closer to one section of the beautiful light show. The sight was so incredible, that Leon almost missed Rohiel's words as his voice reverberated all around him and his friends.

"Some creations, however, sought higher stations than what they were made for. They defied their creator. Stepped away from His love."

Their journey drew them closer to one star that had spheres flying around it. As their table flew ever nearer to one of those spheres, Leon could see that it was blue and green in color. As it spun in place they saw a dense cloud of shooting stars fall to it. Iridescent balls of light surrounded them when they finally landed on its surface. Leon realized this sphere was their world, and they were at the very top of a snow capped mountain.

"Some of my brethren, my brothers and sisters, rebelled against Adonai. For that, they were cast out."

From where they stood at the peak of this mountain, they could look out and see miles of land that extended below them. Leon did not recognize the landscape, but he instinctively knew that what they were seeing had occured in the distant past. The balls of light that had fallen had scorched the earth like bolts of lightning upon their impact. Soon, all the balls began to gather together and move towards the mountain top. As they moved, their forms began to change.

What had shone as light turned into darkness. What once looked perfect and pristine was now marred. A grotesqueness started to pervert the images of Rohiel's brethren. The divine beings turned into something else – something unnatural.

The beings they saw had changed. They had been beautiful, but became ugly – with fanged maws, extra appendages, and bat-like wings that dripped shadow.

"They made a pact here, to teach forbidden knowledge. To become other 'gods' for creation to worship. To intermix with your kind, and taint Adonai's workmanship in order to achieve their own ends. They were outnumbered by Adonai's armies in the heavenlies, and they wanted... needed... more power. They sought to overthrow what cannot be overthrown. This is where they agreed to lead your world astray."

Leon knew that he was looking at a multitude of incredibly powerful beings, like Rohiel. The stone table they all held onto circled lazily around the assembled monstrosities. Their guide's voice took on an ominous, edged tone.

"Behold, the b'nei ha'elohim. The little gods. The Fallen."

Leon's mind reeled from the implications of what he was being shown and told. When he had first been charged with being a Judge, Rohiel had stated that Judges were chosen by Adonai to oppose the Fallen. These beings, however lovely or grotesque, were *gods*?

How could one contend against that? How could someone as insignificant as Leon be victorious against beings that had been deemed gods? As he looked at his companions, he saw expressions of awe splayed openly over their faces. They must have been wondering the same things, because Rohiel answered their unasked questions.

"As powerful as you may think they are, they are nothing compared to Adonai. Their power waxes and wanes. Adonai is the same yesterday, and today, and forever. He is the one true God."

After another sip of the heavenly java, Rohiel continued, ***"Over the centuries most have been imprisoned, some consigned to the very abyss. One however, has become an imminent threat to your world."***

The mountain, stars, and everything else faded around them into a familiar grey expanse. Everything except for one being.

Chills ran down Leon's spine as he saw the undulating shadowy form. It had inky black tendrils which stretched out all around and grasped at the air. Slits of red lantern-like eyes glowed with a familiar glow – one common to every undead being that Leon had destroyed. The miniature statue he had turned to salt earlier was of a similar likeness. It had not, however, even begun to capture the sense of sheer malevolence Leon felt as he stared at this Fallen.

Connections bridged in Leon's mind, and he made a guess. It was a name that he heard in his vision the night before. A name that had been chanted by the undead husks who had defended the Judge's section, or 'Sanctuary' as Rohiel called it, for two hundred years.

"Xhormas," Leon said aloud.

The angel sighed, ***"Yes. The b'nei ha'elohim of corrupted undeath."***

"He is bent on turning your world into his altar of worship. His aim is perversion. It is not the will of Adonai. Together, you have the power to thwart him."

"How?" Miala croaked.

"You have already started." The blazing light that came from Rohiel's head still obscured his features, but somehow Leon knew that the angel's gaze swept over each of them. ***"Each of you must align yourselves to Adonai's purposes in order to succeed. For He knows the plans He has for you… Plans for your welfare and not for evil, to give you a future and a hope."***

Rohiel stepped closer to the circular stone table, and the instant he set his empty cup onto it the room returned. It snapped back to normal as the illusion around them dissolved away. A few of the group gasped, while Magnus hugged the floor.

"Some of you have questions about Adonai. About the war. This is good. The beginning of knowledge is wisdom. The beginning of wisdom is awe of Adonai. Time is short. Ask."

Words tumbled forth from the others, while Gionna scribbled furiously on her notepad. It seemed as though her charcoal stick moved a mile a minute. "I– I have so many to choose from… Come back to me… WAIT!" She exclaimed, as she brandished the charcoal stick at the angel. "How does this Adonai stay the same in the past, present, and future?"

Rohiel held out a hand to the older gnome as he asked, ***"May I?"***

Everyone watched as Gionna nodded. Rohiel then picked the charcoal stick out of her hand and held it up. ***"Your life."*** He pointed at one end. ***"Your birth."*** Then he touched the other end. ***"Your bodily death."***

He then deposited the stick into the empty wooden cup which had held his java. ***"Think of the cup as Adonai, watching over your life. He is there… Ever present, all at once. He is at the beginning, and at the end. He exists outside of time. After all, He is the one who created it."*** Pushing the cup with the charcoal across to Gionna, he fell silent and unmoving at the other end of the table. The two elder gnomes, Gionna and Magnus, seemed to be the only ones who understood his explanation – confused looks abounded from everyone else.

Schalae pressed her hands on the table and leaned forward, "Can't this Adonai just fix everything if He is so all powerful? He could stop this Xhormas right now if He wanted to, right?"

"Who is to say that He has not already?" Rohiel countered, also leaning forward over the remnants of their breakfast. He picked up a leftover grape and set it at one end of the stone table. ***"Adonai sees all time, all at once, He sets His plans, which include our purposes, in***

motion." Flicking the grape, it rolled across the table until it slowed and stopped at the other end. ***"He sees the end before we do because He is already there. Already at the solution. Yet because we are not Him, we can only see the plan in motion. Your assumption that Adonai sees the world in the same way that you do would be incorrect."***

Leon was able to comprehend this explanation. How much had he not known about Adonai until now? Leon had thought that here, in the depths of the Archive, the very origin of the library itself, all of his sought after knowledge had been lost. He had figured that the undead destroyed any chance of learning more about the Judges and Adonai. Yet here was Rohiel – teaching them all about Adonai.

Nobody spoke a word. Whether it was speechlessness due to the shock, or perhaps awe from their experience, maybe it was due to their not knowing exactly what to say… Leon couldn't guess. It was at that moment, however, that Duamé stepped forward and squashed the grape with an open palm. "If yer God o' Love is so rustin' powerful, then can I have me daughter back?"

A sharp intake of breath came from several of those who were present, and was the only response to his question for a full minute. Rohiel stepped slowly around the table, and came to stand before the dwarven blacksmith who had lost his wife and child. Once, recently, the dwarf had unburdened himself about his past to Leon and Miala. He had shared how his wife died after a difficult childbirth. Then how his five-year-old daughter, Esperella, had succumbed to illness. Never had Leon encountered anyone who had suffered the kind of personal loss that Duamé had.

Upon discovering all that he had been through, Leon hadn't been surprised by his initial vehemence towards spreading the word of Adonai. It had been after Leon had learned about Duamé's past, that the other angel who frequented his dreams told him to have faith. She said that Adonai had a plan. Somehow, in that same lesson, she also taught him that he could jump really far. Lochemetel was kind of awesome.

Now, however, it had all come to a head. While Leon understood Duamé's frustration, he could never understand his pain. A pain so deep that it would drive him to ask an angel, whom he had just met, if Adonai could give his deceased daughter back to him.

Rohiel stood before the dwarf, and with a pronounced creak from his armor, got down on his knee to look Duamé directly in the eye. The radiant glow that came from the angel's head still obscured his facial expressions, but emotion came through the angel's voice as he responded.

"Duamé Onyxwill, it is not Adonai's will that any should suffer, but that all would come to Him. Your daughter is with Him, and with your help, and your acceptance of Adonai, countless other daughters and families can be saved."

"That's not… an answer… ta me question… Boyo," Duamé enunciated.

After their exchange, the angel became silent and withheld any further response. This seemed to only anger Duamé further. Soon enough the dwarven blacksmith cocked his arm back and flung his fist at the bright light of Rohiel's head.

The abruptness of the action was not lost on the angel. A gauntleted hand snapped up to close around the dwarf's fist. Everyone, including Kelleren, protested with shouts (and barks) of alarm.

The pressure of the angel's hand brought the dwarf to his knees, and Rohiel's shining head seemed to turn to Leon as he spoke.

"I will not be able to manifest like this again for some time. Judge Leon, take up Revelator."

The glowing spear hummed a pleasant tone and suddenly launched itself from the center of the table. Leon reached out and grasped the shaft of the spear while it was still in the air. He now knew the name of the mysterious weapon. As he looked back at Rohiel, the angel seemed to dissolve away into the air. Just like the images of the visions and memories when he dreamed. The angel's voice echoed around them as the pale blue gauntlet, which had held Duamé's fist in place, finally disappeared.

"Be sober-minded; be watchful. Your adversary Xhormas prowls around like a roaring lion, seeking to devour Adonai's creation. Make no mistake, he is aware of all of you, and has already set his plans into motion."

The hairs on the back of Leon's neck rose with the knowledge that a god was literally out to get him. Needless to say, this didn't sit comfortably with him.

"You have everything that you need. You must act. Now."

Duamé collapsed, and his fist struck the stone ground as he cried out in anger and frustration.

An elven archivist, known as Xieth, hurriedly entered the room. Her vapish demeanor from the day before was all but gone. Instead, a look of desperation and anxiety filled her face as she peered around the room. Her eyes settled on Princess Schalae as she composed herself. "Your highness, you must return home immediately! We have just received word that a massive horde of undead has been spotted invading the Chimera Lands to the west!"

All manner of decorum and reverence for what they had just experienced disappeared. Exclamations of surprise and alarm gave way to Magnus asking Xieth for further explanation.

The elven maiden's terseness from the prior day now worked in her favor, as she quickly informed them of the latest developments. "The Herald Guild spread the news that no undead had been sighted, and that no major attacks had occurred. With the lack of undead assaults against Bulwark Fortress, and the strange migratory patterns of the deceased, only some of the populace seem to be concerned, while most appear relieved. Their news signalled to many that the Kingdom may very well have survived the longstanding onslaught of undead. Celebrations are being held all around, while only a small contingent still hold onto their reservations."

As Xieth's report continued she explained that the undead seemed to have all gathered in one location and they had bypassed the cliffs of the fortress. She then told them that according to a newly-arrived appropriated mail carrier airship, a fast scouting ship if there ever was one, a collapse had occurred in the cliff face which had formed a natural staircase farther west. The undead had ascended that staircase and moved, en-masse, eastward towards the Chimera Lands.

This news presented its own set of problems. This use of strategy denoted an organized intelligence within the undead – one that up until their meeting with Rohiel, nobody could have known existed. Now, Leon knew better. This previously unknown being, this Xhormas, was most likely responsible.

They all listened to Xieth's report – asking only a few questions, and listening as the doom of the Kingdom was pronounced. If the undead army could not be stopped, it would mean the end of Xaelon and the living world.

"A council meeting has been called Master Magnus, and you are to report to the courts in haste, sir." Xieth finished.

"Yes, of course. I will be there presently." Magnus smoothed his white beard and turned to the princess. "Will you be joining me, your highness?"

After a deep calming breath, the elven princess shook her head. "No, I need to get back to the Elvenwood. A transport was already waiting for me today, and I must hurry to help with the defense."

Magnus nodded, as if he expected that to be her answer. "I will give the council your well wishes. It will certainly be an… interesting… meeting." He concluded, as he looked at the spear and to Leon.

"Will Lucien Rhise be there?" Leon asked, as he tucked his necklace back into his undershirt.

"Yes, of course. Along with the rest of the lords and the military leaders. Considering the dire situation, even King Garinth should attend this meeting!"

Leon knelt and looked the Head Archivist directly in his eyes, "I need to ask you to refrain from mentioning anything to him about me, about my being a Judge, and about what you saw here today."

Magnus patted Leon's pauldron, "I doubt anyone would believe me anyway. Besides, we can't have you arrested, right? You're the one on those wanted posters?"

Maybe Gionna hadn't been the only observant one in that relationship, Leon thought to himself. "I am. Although I assure you, I am not the criminal that the Herald Guild and Lord Rhise make me out to be."

Magnus huffed, "Judge, if I had to choose to trust Lucien Rhise, the Herald Guild, or an undead wretch offering me a back massage… I would get the incense, the lotion, and clear my schedule for an hour! Now, if you would excuse me…" As the gnome nodded his farewells, his gaze lingered on his ex-wife Gionna, before he finally followed Xieth out of the section.

His joke broke the solemnity for only a moment. Princess Schalae turned to the rest of the remaining group, "I humbly request any assistance you can give."

Leon had felt the stirrings in his heart, even while Xieth was still relaying what had happened. Stepping forward, he said, "I will go to the Elvenwood to assist you."

Gionna and Miala both stepped forward as well, "Us too."

Kelleren woofed.

Duamé, who had gotten up and watched the whole exchange, picked up the small partly-filled barrel of java with a frown on his face. It sloshed as he gulped the remnants down. He wiped his mouth and beard, then said, "Ya, alright. Wotever."

Glad he was still choosing to join them, Leon quietly asked, "Are you okay, Duamé?"

"I said I'm FINE, boyo. Let's get on with it an' bash some undead in!"

They made their way up and out of the Archive building to a remarkably different atmosphere. Those who walked about the thoroughfare outside were noticeably on edge. The princess and her bodyguards made their way to the airship yards at the naval academy, with Leon and the rest following. His helm and mask were back in place, as he couldn't risk his identity becoming more compromised.

As they reached the yards, they saw that the expansive grounds usually allowed for double the number of airships than were presently there. Something was off. Of course, it could be attributed to the looming army of undead that was headed their way. It could also be that Leon hadn't seen a decent battleship in the yard since he had initially gotten to Agaprya in the first place. If there had ever been a point in time that he wanted his "former" father to come to the rescue with a new assemblage of warships – it would be now.

When he had been thrown out of the house, Lord Lucien had basically admitted that he was going to build his own airships. He was even going so far as to marry Leon's sister off to a lumber baron, in order to do so. Liara's wedding to Halomir was only days away, and Leon couldn't imagine a worse fate for her.

The airship that they made their way to, was an older transport vessel. Lightly armed with three cannons on either side, what it lacked for armament it made up for in speed and cargo capacity. The slim airship was a single decker on the interior. It was larger than a mail carrier, but not able to be used as a full military ship. As they looked to the stern, where the small captain's cabin was, they saw a blocky figure painted on the side of the vessel. It was an artful rendition of a woman made of stone. *Golem* was written in cursive script above her. While Leon had never seen this vessel, he had heard tales of it.

Golem was supposedly the fastest transport in the Xaelon fleet. It also always seemed to have numerous accounts of narrow escapes and close calls. If such a thing as luck existed, then *Golem* had the worst of it. Or perhaps it had just enough luck to keep flying. Leon was an airship crash survivor – another mark of bad luck to have onboard an airship.

Duamé didn't help the situation at all as they watched the princess climb aboard with her guards. "Dwarves don't belong in tha air. We belong in tha earth." He muttered.

I once knew an Admiral who would strongly disagree with you, Leon thought.

Of course, Miala had to add her own jinx to things by reassuring the dwarf, "Don't worry Duamé, I'm sure that everything will be fine!"

Gionna sighed and shook her head, "Dearie, the phonetic pronunciation of 'everything will be fine' is in actuality a curse upon yourself in old gnomish. Best to never say that again." She tapped the side of her intricate glasses, surveying the ship they were about to board.

Leon groaned inwardly. If this was the transport taking them to the Northern Elvenwood, then he had good cause to wonder at what would befall them before they would arrive.

Chapter 3: The Golem

As they walked up to the ship after the princess boarded, they saw the captain of the vessel next to the docking ramp. She was a stocky orcish woman with short, dark hair that was tied back. It seemed to be pulled so tightly that it stretched her skin tight around her bony brow. This made her appear to have an expression of perpetual surprise. Her face was lined with thin scars, and some previous facial injury had torn off half of her upper lip. Due to that, her tusk on one side had been filed down to match the rest of her teeth.

"You're what all the fuss is about?" She looked at Leon and grunted in acknowledgement of how unimpressed she was.

"Ya, I know, I'm a pretty big deal. Still, I try ta be modest about it," Duamé quipped back at her. He then stuck out his hand to the orcish captain, "Duamé Onyxwill."

"Ashera Urk." The woman responded with a mangled grin, as she shook the dwarf's hand.

The rest of their group made their introductions, which left Leon to go last. He tried to get away with introducing himself as 'The Judge', but the captain shook her head, "Nobody gets on the Golem that I don't know. What's your actual name, big shot?"

Based on his previous actions, when he had entered Agaprya, Leon knew the consequences of lying. Even lies of omission. With a sigh he responded, "Leon."

Ashera barked out a laugh, "The wanted man with the ridiculous reward on his head is the Judge? Fine then. Don't tell me. Judge'll do.

Just don't get on my bad side. Judge or no, I'll toss you over if I think you are a danger to me or my crew. You got that?"

"Yes, Captain." Leon agreed. It was not his fault if the truth hadn't been believed. He had done his part and told it. Belief on the captain's part was not a requirement. Besides, Leon wanted to be on his best behavior. He knew of Ashera's reputation, and he had no doubt that without any hesitation she would make good on her threat. She was known to be quite abrasive, but also very protective of her crew.

As he climbed aboard, he saw that there were no other passengers. Leon surmised that since the Princess wouldn't be marrying Prince Gelan, it was no longer necessary to give her a royal send off. They were led to the guest quarters for those who traveled on the transport vessel. The captain then informed them, "Just scrubbed clean from the stench of the last dwarf who stayed here."

As the captain walked away Duamé promptly quipped back, "Aw that's just ta tear up our enemies' eyes, an' make it harder ta see us!"

They all stored their travel packs inside the small 'his and hers' rooms, then made their way back up to the deck. Captain Ashera's crew worked diligently to get the vessel ready for takeoff. Under her watchful eye, two small goblins worked feverishly on a pile of leather straps and metal hooks.

"You have ten seconds to get those untangled or I'll give your straps to them!" The captain hollered. This proved to be the motivation the goblins needed, and their thin fingers flew over the straps – barely managing to untangle the pile in time. Then she turned to look at the group of eight passengers. She carefully took in the appearances of Leon, Miala, Kelleren, Duamé, Gionna, Princess Schalae, and the princess's two silent guards. The two goblins began to outfit each of the passengers with the now untangled leather harnesses while Captain Urk launched into an explanation.

"You're going to want to familiarize yourselves with the metal eyelets that are around this ship. If I say the word, or we get into a scrap, or if I say the word, or we experience any turbulence, or IF. I. SAY. THE. WORD, you WILL latch the metal hooks attached to your harnesses onto the nearest eyelet. If you don't, and you fall off this ship, consider it your own fault, and I wish you the best of luck. Princess or no, I'll not come back for you." The captain looked at Kelleren and pointed to the dog, "Boys, do we have a dog harness?"

The goblins turned in sync towards their captain and shrugged silently, which caused her to announce, "I sincerely hope that whoever owns this dog has a collar and a leash. Otherwise, well, I'll not be held responsible if it tumbles off."

Something strange happened then. Miala turned to Kelleren and stared at him for a few moments, presumably to communicate with him mentally, as they often did. Leon assumed she was explaining the situation to him. Kelleren's hackles suddenly raised and he growled at her. Even stranger, he slowly backed away from her as she reached into her magical robe and pulled an odd looking collar from her pocket. It looked like a misshapen leather collar, with melted metal pieces all around it.

She spoke softly as she approached Kelleren with the collar and its corresponding leash gripped in one hand. She held both of her hands out in front of her, and spoke to her companion with a soothing voice, "It's okay, you won't be hurt anymore."

Still growling, Kelleren bore a wild eyed look as she fastened the damaged collar on him and scratched behind his ears. "You're okay. You're okay. As soon as we land it will come right off."

Everyone else fumbled with and tightened their own harnesses, making sure not to intrude on Miala and Kelleren's interaction. When it was over, and Kelleren was docile again, the Captain nodded and said, "Alright. Everybody secure themselves! We're about to go airborne!"

The group moved to the railings of the transport and Leon headed towards the bow. Memories of happier times danced across his mind as the ship prepared to take off.

✦✦✦✦✦

Four years ago…

"Petty Officer Leon, wot did ya ferget ta do?" Rear Admiral Silverspine asked wearily.

The drills that took place on the grounded airship at the Naval Academy were one of the final steps before graduation and assignment in the fleet. Due to this, the dwarf in charge of the academy's training oversaw the new recruits' exercises, to see who showed promise. Refusing to trade on his family name, Leon had worked hard over the past year. He wanted to pass conditioning completely on his own merits.

Coming out of his training without enough body fat to stay afloat in water, he was proud to hold the highest marks of his class. Only the Rear Admiral knew the true story of who he was. At first it had seemed to make the white-haired dwarf genuinely hate Leon. He had been pushed harder than all of the others in his class. The threat of being booted from the academy had constantly hung over his head, and he was given the harshest punishments for the slightest infractions. It took months for the Rear Admiral to realize that Leon was completely serious when he said he wanted nothing to do with his father.

By then, whether it was in swordsmanship, strategy, or skill, his peers viewed him as a natural leader – and a fellow no-name peasant. Silverspine's animosity turned into curiosity, which then turned into a commitment to help him. It was a commitment to help push him as far as he could go, and to help him distance himself from his father. When Petty Officers were chosen from among the training class, Leon was at the top of the list without contention. It seemed, however, that the promotion came hand in hand with Rear Admiral Silverspine critiquing his every move even more closely.

"Sir, I did not fasten my harness to the ship," Leon replied, standing at attention.

"Ya mean ya 'Didn't' fasten yer harness'! Every second counts in battle Leon, I don't need yer fancy drawn out talk!" The Rear Admiral barked at him in front of his smirking peers.

Still committing the abbreviations he had grown up avoiding to memory, Leon berated himself internally, and replied. "Sir, yes sir!"

Many of those who were assembled knew that the Rear Admiral was next in line to take over the Fleet Admiralty. Most thought that he was just being a stickler for rules and procedures, and was using Leon as a convenient source to pour his frustrations out. While the correction still stung, it was effective.

"I'll tell ya Leon, I'm goin' ta make ya or break ya – an' some days I don't know which one it'll be!" Admiral Silverspine lamented. "Run five laps around tha ship – an' maybe then you'll remember ta fasten yer harness before takeoff!"

Sixteen-year-old Leon saluted and ran to the gangplank, mindful of the lesson he was being taught. He ignored the smirk from Midshipman Dawes as he ran by and hustled off the ship. Leon resolved to beat his previous five-lap running time.

Leon smiled at the memory, as Geonna Gærheart joined him at the bow. She fastened her harness next to his, and asked, "First time back in an airship since the *Dawnfire,* dearie?"

Once again Leon marveled at the gnome's powers of observation. "Yes. It seems odd to not have any responsibility on board this ship. I find myself watching the others work, while restraining myself from joining them."

Gionna nodded, "Hpmh. Try designing them, and then improving that design, only to have the people in charge not listen! I see inefficiencies all over this vessel."

"What would you have done to improve them?" Leon asked, as he watched the last of the crewmembers fasten themselves in. From her perch at the wheel, Captain Ashera ran her gaze over the slim ship one final time before liftoff.

"Reinforce the hull with something that doesn't burn with dragon's fire. Find a way to increase speed, and counter their weight by adding more levigems. It's quality dearie, not the quantity of ships that will win this war. Well, that and your Adonai, apparently."

"Still thinking about our meeting with Rohiel?"

The pronounced glare of the elderly gnome distracted Leon from the change in his footing as the *Golem* lifted slightly off the ground. "It's not every day that you meet an extra-dimensional being who forces you to rethink almost all of your preconceived notions of how the world works. Unless you do that often?" She asked.

"That was a first for me while awake." Leon replied.

The *Golem* lurched forward slightly as the two long levigems on either side of the hull did their work. The transport ship rose higher into the sky and moved forward as the thick city walls of Agaprya passed under them. As they crossed over the top of the walls, a landscape of nearby farms could be seen abutting them. They also saw shantytowns outside of the gates that were brimming with the poor and infirm who were not allowed inside the capital. They started to pick up speed and crossed over the river that ran into the city. Guarded bridges stood atop thick grates that allowed water from the lake to flow through the city. Leon saw Ashera wave to the top of the large lookout tower on the northern side of the city as they angled westward over the lake.

Lake Xael was the natural center of the kingdom. Two rivers from the mountain ridge flowed into it, and another two rivers flowed out. It was at this crossroads, straddling the river Sigrit, that Agaprya, in all its real and imagined splendor, was located. The *Golem* stayed relatively close to the ground as it shifted forward and took off at incredible speeds, which were due in part to its slim frame and relatively light weight. The vessel glided over the lake, where a few fisher people could be seen trying to catch the even fewer live fish.

Leon looked over the railing, and could see the dark shapes that were housed within the lake. Dead shapes. Schools of unlife swam, ready to ravage any living creature stupid enough to go into the water. Before they had begun farming the fish, like they farmed crops, a meal had come at a high cost. Sometimes it still did. A quick end laid in those depths for any who had lost all sense of hope. It was known to happen sometimes, but was never talked about.

"Let me ask you… As a Judge you're supposed to be Adonai's representative, right?" Gionna queried.

"Suuure, let's go with that." Leon hedged.

The gnome's glasses shifted lenses as she tapped the arm on their side. It accentuated the skepticism that swirled in his direction from her. She held up her short fingers in front of Leon. "First, if you are, then you need to be more confident, dearie. Second, get ready for a list of questions I expect you to answer. I was blindsided before by that Rohiel character. I'll expect you to fill in the blanks before I make any sort of deitific commitment. Third, we all know Mr. Onyxwill and Ms. Mytheriyn's positions on Adonai… Have you thought to check in with the elves yet?"

Leon looked around, but couldn't see the elves above deck. They must have gone below before their departure. "You make a good point. I'll um… I'll circle back to those questions later."

Grasping the hook ends on his harness, Leon made his way around the ship with the maneuvers he had learned over the past five years. Hooking each eyelet with speed, he made his way along the railing to a stairwell that descended below decks. Kelleren seemed to be in a much better mood. His tongue had lolled out alongside the railing as he felt the wind blow on his face. Miala issued an apologetic smile as Leon stepped around her and her companion. The last thing he saw before he disappeared below decks was the expressions on the crew members' faces as they watched the Judge move along a flying airship with expertise. Perhaps the surprised look that registered on Captain Ashera's face was genuine this time.

As he descended below, the wind at his back eased. While Leon didn't need goggles, thanks to his helm, it had been almost two months since he had flown. The airflow was something he had forgotten about, and would have to get used to again. He walked between the crates and barrels of provisions as he made his way to the guest rooms. There he saw the two elven guards stationed outside of the women's quarters.

Leon decided to start by being friendly. Even bodyguards had feelings. "Hello there. I um, I didn't catch your names…"

They issued no response to him, but instead exchanged glances between themselves.

He heard some shuffling noises from inside the room, and then the Princess opened the door. "Um, they are Qas and Vyn," She said, as she gestured to the female and male elves in turn. "They have taken a vow of silence for a few years. Did you need something?" Schalae asked, as she adjusted her braided green hair.

Leon cleared his throat, suddenly nervous. "Well, I was just checking on all of you – seeing how you were faring after our… morning meeting."

The silent elves smiled broadly as the Princess stepped out of the room to join them in the hallway. "It was interesting to say the least. I have never met a deity, or an angel, before!" She replied.

"Well, a month ago neither had I." Leon admitted.

The Princess continued, her words tumbling over themselves. "I mean, trees know that they are created. We elves know that there is a delicate balance and design to everything. There is also a large relationship between trees and people. How could that just randomly happen? It couldn't! It was designed. We just do not really know who designed it all, or how it came about."

To Leon, it sounded like the Princess may at least be open to Adonai. However, he didn't want to 'push the parchment', so to speak. "Well, if you need to talk about it, I am open to questions. Gionna is drawing up a list of them!" Leon started to laugh before a sudden pain in his side made him clutch it.

The princess was quick to react as she waved off her guards and came closer. "What happened? Are you ok?"

Leon fought through the pain and shook his head, "It's nothing. When we fought the liches the other day, I may have broken a rib. I'll be fine."

The two silent elves winced as the eyes of the princess bulged. She stamped her foot and exclaimed, "Fine? Fine?! You stop that Judge Leon! 'Fine' my fir trees! That is perhaps one of the worst words in the living world! That's it! Take off that scale mail and let me have a look. You may be able to breathe shallowly to avoid the pain, but doing such a thing could eventually make you more sick."

Aghast at the prospect of undoing his armor in front of royalty, Leon started to protest, but was cut off by the headstrong elf. "Do not try to act chivalrous or modest! Goodness knows Prince Gelan had the absolute wrong ideas the first time he got injured too. Now, if you want my help, then let me see that rib!" She produced her rolled up medical kit with a flourish. It clinked as the glass vials and containers were carefully laid out on top of a crate.

Leon knew that he fought a losing battle, and that he couldn't refuse her royal command. He reasoned internally with himself that at least there were two other elven witnesses. For the sake of propriety, at least they weren't alone. He started to undo the fasteners and lifted the scale and plate mail off. It was set down on another crate, so that the א symbol, the Judge's mark, was on top. No rust stains dotted his undershirt yet, which was just another sign of the excellent metalwork that had crafted his new armor.

What happened next was a severely unfortunate happenstance. Upon reflection, Leon thought that perhaps it could be attributed to the *Golem,* and it's bad luck streak – if such a thing existed. As he pulled up his shirt to reveal his injury to the Princess, a loud cough sounded behind him. While the shirt covered his head, it did nothing to obscure Miala's voice as she said, "Well, excuuuuse me for intruding!"

If there was ever a worse time for the two other individuals in the room to be under a vow of silence, it was now. That just left Leon and

Princess Schalae to blurt excuses to Miala, who was already stomping back up the stairs to the top deck. Leon let out a heavy sigh as he pulled his shirt back down. "Sorry about that." He said.

The Princess waved her hand dismissively, almost as if she could fan away the awkwardness. "It is okay with me, but you had better go fix that. The worst misunderstandings are always the ones that are not resolved quickly. Here," Schalae pulled a vial of murky light blue liquid from her kit and held it out to Leon, "Drink this, and your rib fracture should heal faster. There is not much else that can be done."

"Thank you," Leon replied. His red-faced embarrassment at the situation was a stark contrast to the blue of the viscous liquid inside the tube. Unstoppering it, he gulped down the vial's contents and almost gagged at the chalk-like taste. As he started to put his armor back on, Leon wondered what else could possibly go wrong on this trip. He bade his farewells to the princess and her silent guards, then made his way upstairs to look for Miala.

Back on the top deck, he saw that they were already almost halfway to Hookvale. As the primary source of edible fish in the kingdom, the hatcheries that were housed there were closely protected. A proper wall, complete with guard towers, had been built around the village. Its defenses were unlike those he had encountered at Everbright; their town had not had any proper defenses, due in no small part to the alukah they had slain. He noted that the transport should pass over Hookvale shortly, as they traveled ever closer to the Northern Elvenwood.

Miala looked out across the expansive lake with Kelleren. Whatever she said to the dog was private, and only in their heads, but that didn't stop Leon from wanting to interrupt and solve the misunderstanding now. As he approached, hooking his way over to them, Kelleren looked at him and must have alerted Miala to his presence. Her gaze remained directed towards the Eye of Xael, a small island in the middle of the lake. As Leon began to say his piece, her eyes narrowed.

“Hey, Miala, um, nothing was happening down there. She was just checking an injury I got fro–”

“Sure, she was.” She snapped.

“She was! She gave me medicine and everything!” Leon exclaimed, as he held out the empty vial. Miala glanced down at it before she refocused her steely glare back on the lake.

“Well then, will you live?” Miala retorted.

“Um… yes? It’s just a fractured rib. She said it’ll heal on its own, so–”

“Great. Glad she could help.” Miala leveled a contemptuous glare at him. Her words were unbelievable due, in no small part, to her expression.

Leon felt as though this was going downhill fast. “Listen, there is no reason to be–”

“What? No reason to be – HEY!” She exclaimed, as Kelleren wrapped around Miala and Leon’s legs with his leash. It tangled them closer together, and he woofed. The companion then resumed putting his face over the railing of the airship, to let the wind blow over it.

The leash forced contact between the two of them, which Leon already knew made her vastly uncomfortable. They both grasped at the railing to help steady their footing, which caused their hands to touch as they reached for the same spot. Recoiling from that contact only served to make them lose their balance even further on the flying airship.

“Oh, come on! Really?” Miala complained to her dog. Leon thought it was wise to just stay silent. Kelleren seemed to think his point had been made, and he unwound himself from them. The dog then resumed his tongue lolling activity next to them once again.

Miala squinted at the island in the center of the lake which had held her attention before their entanglement. She yelled past Leon to the captain, “Something is happening over there!”

Captain Ashera Urk’s voice rose over the wind, “Scout Oaksap! What’s going on over at the Eye?”

The elven scout near the bow of the transport gazed back towards the central island in Lake Xael. It was known to be uninhabited, with only a few sparse trees on it, and the crew, as well as Leon and Miala, now looked towards it. Gionna twisted the handle of her cane and with a few clockwork whirs a spyglass appeared on it! She took a moment to steady the cane on the railing. Then she tapped her special glasses until a miniature compliment to the cane function extended from them, which connected the glasses and cane.

A small dark cloud appeared to churn above the small island. It folded over itself repeatedly, and quite unnaturally. It looked like a dark bread dough being kneaded and shaped all by itself. As it kept folding in, flattening and shaping itself, movement on the island became evident. Leon couldn't fathom this. No one could live there. The island was too small to have a sustainable village, and it was surrounded by the dangerous lake waters.

The scout peered through their spyglass and reported, "Undead skeletons on the island Captain! They are doing something under that cloud! Looks like they're… dancing?"

The captain had her first mate take the helm so she could look at the baffling report for herself. She pulled her glass from her side, and adjusted it as she peered through. Leon made his way towards her at the aft of the ship. He joined her as she stared open mouthed at the sight.

"May I see?" Leon asked, taking the spyglass she handed to him.

Looking through, he saw many skeletons that were stripped completely bare of flesh. They were bare of weapons as well. It appeared as though the only thing some of the various sized skeletons possessed were random bits of seaweed. *They must have traveled through the lake water. Why?* He thought.

Leon's answer was even more of a mystery. The skeletons did not seem to be dancing, per se, but were arranged in a circle – all facing inward towards the center. The grass inside the circle was gone, and in its place was barren earth that seemed to churn just like the dark cloud. The arms and hands of the skeletons were clasped together and outstretched, linking them each to one another. The red lantern light of their eyes lit the interior of the circle, and sparks of magic and elemental forces flew from some of them. Leon guessed that a number of the skeletons, if not all, were liches.

The strange sight didn't last long. Cold fear gripped Leon's heart when the skeletons all fell forward as one into the churning earth and disappeared. At that same moment, the dark cloud overhead streaked down to join the skeletons that had vanished. Shadow began to coalesce around the circle as the cloud collapsed, and something that burst through the ground in its place. It sped out of the spyglass frame too quickly for Leon to get a good look at it. Whatever it was caused gasps of alarm from practically everyone on board.

As he lowered the spyglass, Leon felt as though he was experiencing deja vu. He saw his recurring nightmare as it flew up from the island and turned sharply to wing its way towards the *Golem*. Somehow he had just witnessed a link between two different enemies – one that had been unknown before today. The initial cause of his recent trauma and downward spiral had become airborne once again. It was smaller than the previous one, and some sort of ichor dripped from its body, but it was no less deadly. Now, in a lighter armed airship, one commonly associated with bad luck, he watched as this new dragon flew towards them with a roar. Leon echoed Miala's words from earlier as he yelled his frustration.

"OH, COME ON! REALLY?"

Chapter 4: The Council

Meanwhile…

Lucien Rhise hid a sneer behind his smile as he entered the council chamber. It always smelled off to him – as if he could smell the body odor behind the masking perfumes of those assembled. His smile turned genuine as he reminded himself that the stench of Baron Halomir would not be present at the meeting.

As he walked in, with his son Laric close behind, they both knew to shake hands and nod their heads as they exchanged pleasantries with those who were already assembled. The circular chamber held a matching large, circular, dark wooden table, which made it easy to 'make their rounds'. Lucien made sure to talk with each noble and person present – even if only for a few moments. This action served to remind everyone in attendance of who truly held the power in the room.

The room was decorated much like his manor. Its walls were adorned with weapons and works of art. A large map, much like the one that hung in his study, filled the center of the table. This map was integral for many of the trade and warfare strategy discussions that occurred during these meetings. An assemblage of tokens and markers were scattered all around it which depicted the assembly's prior meetings. The doors to the council room opened behind Lucien once again, and the soldiers stationed around the room all straightened. Turning, Lord Rhise saw King Garinth.

The last time Lucien had seen the king was while Prince Gelan was still alive. He had been vibrant, energetic, and eager to start enjoying his upcoming retirement after he transferred the reins of the kingdom to his son. That had been almost two months ago.

Now the king looked thinner. Tired. Bags had developed under his eyes, and his crown looked as though it was too heavy for him. Long silver-grey hair kept the gold crown in place as he strode in with purpose. A thin purple robe, trimmed in gold, swished with its noisy fabric as the king stepped. His daughter, Princess Giselle, walked in behind him. She looked physically healthier, but no more vibrant.

The galvamancer bodyguard Exiosa made up the last of King Garinth's retinue as they strode wordlessly towards the head of the table. The dangerous mancer was dressed in the Xaelon blue and black, with thin strips of copper interwoven into her gloves and up her arms. Lord Rhise felt the hairs on his body raise slightly as the powerful mancer entered the room, and knew that many of the others felt the same sensation.

Lucien made sure to leave a space between himself and the princess for Laric to sit – which his son took full advantage of. Opposite Laric stood geomancer Clyborne and his… animal. The huge black bear was silent, and sat behind the Mancer Academy's Headmaster, eating from a large bowl full of mixed berries. Sitting across from Lucien himself was the bookish gnome archivist, Magnus. For some reason the gnome looked more on edge than normal.

Before the King arrived, Lucien had already passed instructions to Headherald Kazave and Admiral Schlymyel on what he wanted the outcome of the meeting to be. Their knowing nods to Lucien were not too obvious. The rest of the table was made up of various lords and ladies who served in the courts. At least Countess Serena gave Lucien a respectful greeting. After all, she was his neighbor in the Lord Gardens.

The seat next to Lucien was empty. Whether it was due to fear of being seen close to him, or because someone was missing from the meeting, he didn't care. King Garinth though, was quick to point out the absence. "Where is Baron Halomir?"

"I hope you will forgive him, your majesty. I got word just before the meeting that he will not be joining us. A terrible bout of indigestion apparently." Lucien explained. An imaginative explanation extrapolated from the simple parchment message he received from a mail carrier. In reality the message simply said, 'It is done', which left Lucien to scramble and come up with the excuse himself.

"Very well, let us begin." Replied the King, as he gathered his robe and they all sat. He gestured across the table, "Admiral Schlymyel, congratulations on your recent promotion. I hope that you can fill the hole Admiral Silverspine abruptly left us with. Please explain the situation."

The orcish admiral stood and pointed towards the border of the map. "The cliff face collapsed creating a natural stairwell. The hordes of undead amassed and climbed it, and according to the scouting report, their numbers are in the tens of thousands at least. They have marched towards, and invaded, the Chimera Lands. Once through them, they will go through the Elvenwood, and then move on to our lands beyond."

The King looked around the room again, and asked, "Princess Schalae is not here?"

The small old gnome, Magnus, stammered a response to the king's observation, "Your majesty, I invited her when I heard the news, but she instead left to defend her forest."

Small murmurs of conversation broke out around the table. Laric even leaned over and whispered to Lucien, "Foolish girl." Lucien quietly shushed him, even though he privately agreed.

"Has an overture of peace and assistance been offered to the Chimeras?" King Garinth asked after he sighed at the elven maiden's fate.

"They have kept to themselves so much, we would not even know who to talk to." Geomancer Clybourne remarked, staring at the forest on the map. "I doubt that after centuries of silence they would suddenly be willing to talk, much less let our armies invade their borders to protect Xaelon."

"We could offer to extend aid to Northern Elvenwood, and follow Princess Schalae!" Princess Giselle exclaimed. She seemed eager to help her late brother's fiancé.

The new orcish admiral glanced at Lucien before he responded. "Airships would be useless against ground forces in the forests. Besides, if the Chimera Lands fall, it will be too large of an area to try to defend. You are talking about an area that spans from the river line to Hookvale, and then swings back towards Bulwark. It is just too much ground to cover!"

The princess deflated as holes were punctured through her idea, which gave Laric the opportunity to speak reassuringly to her. *Good job, son!* Lucien thought to himself. His actions towards the princess would make this all the easier.

King Garinth stared at the map and the large number of tokens that represented the undead horde. He drummed his fingers on the intricately carved armrests of his chair. "What if we were to go to the Chimera Lands anyway? If I were in their position, I would not refuse the help."

An older woman in full plate armor rose from her seat. Her name was General Xiphos, and she was in command of King Garinth's ground forces. The General refused to even carry a conversation with Lucien. She was an unknown factor in this meeting, but Lord Rhise had hedged his bets well as she spoke. "It would be unwise, your majesty. An invasion into their lands at this stage would not just be met by undead, but also chimeras. Centaurs, satyrs, minotaurs, even giants walk those lands. Alive or dead, friend or foe, I would not risk our forces."

The King looked as if he was beginning to lose his patience, "Then what options DO we have?"

It was time for their meeting to truly begin. Lucien chose this time to speak up. "I may have a solution, your majesty."

“Your last material shipment for airships was lackluster at best Lord Rhise. I hope you have a good idea for me.” King Garinth warned.

Lucien flashed an ingratiating smile, and continued, “In order to increase productivity, Baron Halomir and I successfully assembled three new airships, which are already headed here to Agaprya.”

This news caused quite a stir amongst the lordly rabble at the table. It calmed slightly as Garinth spoke with an edged voice, “Why was I not informed of this?”

“Well, to be perfectly honest, Sire, you were a bit… preoccupied.” Lucien replied. He enjoyed seeing the King's face crash into misery. To rally the rest of the table to his side, he continued, “It was a confluence of convenience, really. I had hired many workers from the refugees who came for protection. That created excess people under my employ, who needed something to do. Halomir’s lumber route crosses my trade route, so to save time, we suddenly became shipbuilders.”

“You basically invalided the airship department at the Innovation Institute by doing that!” Admiral Schlymyel cried out in feigned outrage. A planned response to avoid the suspicion of collusion.

Lucien reached into his coat and immediately heard a loud crackle, which was accompanied by an odd smell that wafted through the air. Galvamancer Exiosa had reacted as soon as Lord Rhise placed his hand in his jacket. Small lines of electricity danced between the fingers of her hand and across the copper lining her gloves as she said in an even tone, “Let us all keep a level head. No offense to you Lord Rhise, but whatever you are about to reveal, do so slowly.”

Lucien acquiesced, and pulled out a folded parchment. The galvamancer relaxed, as did everyone else in the room. With a smile, Lucien opened it up and flattened it across the map for all to see. “I will acknowledge that it was a calculated risk, but one that bore fruit.”

Chairs scraped across the stone floor as those who were assembled rose to get a good look at the diagram. The King’s voice was barely a whisper as he asked, “What am I looking at here, Lucien?”

“A new class of ship, your majesty. We are calling it the ‘Dreadnought’ class. Twenty cannons to a side. Six bow chasers, and six Levigems per vessel to keep the speed of a battleship. There are three of these on their way here, and they will be more than a match for any undead horde that attacks Agaprya.”

A smattering of applause from the lords and ladies present punctuated Lord Rhise’s short summary of his project. This presented him with the boost of confidence that he needed to utter his next suggestion. “I am no military man, but it seems that they would be a good addition to our defenses should this horde reach our walls.”

Headherald Kazave chimed in, “This is fantastic! The heralds can spread the news of this... new hope… that Xaelon has!”

Almost everyone present looked at the new Admiral who, after studying the design for himself, nodded. “While we cannot come to the aid of the chimeras, this will most certainly help us ensure our sovereignty here. I do, however, propose that we evacuate Hookvale. If the horde cannot be stopped by the chimeras or elves, then Hookvale would be next in their path.”

“You are talking about consigning the elves to death.” King Garinth stated flatly. Lucien seethed internally that the king made no further comment on his dreadnoughts. Another slight to add amongst the many previous ones.

“With all due respect your majesty, the Elvenwood and Chimera Lands were doomed the moment that horde appeared.” General Xiphos commented. “I regretfully second the idea to evacuate Hookvale. We need to look to ourselves. Bulwark Fortress has been bypassed. The kingdom of Xaelon is in its final days if we cannot hold Agaprya.”

Countess Serena raised an old hand and piped into the conversation. “If we are talking along those lines, we should start evacuating those who cannot fight to Last Bastion. Just as a precaution mind you. Children and the like.”

It appeared to Lucien as though the elderly gnome, Magnus, seemed to wage an inner war of whether to speak up or not. One side clearly won, because the small gnome's voice resounded in the large council chamber. "Maybe the Judge can help the situation!"

The murmurings around the room quieted as the king held up a hand. "What did you say, Magnus?"

The gnome cleared his throat, suddenly nervous. "I said… maybe the Judge can help us. If we asked him."

Voices overlapped each other in the council room, ranging from awestruck to the ludicrously bemused.

Irritated, the King raised his voice, "Silence!" Those assembled quickly obeyed. "I must say I have not heard of such a rumor. Is there truly a Judge in Xaelon? After all these years?"

Lucien's ire rose as most of the attendees nodded their heads. This so-called Judge was a distraction. An aberration. An unknown in his plans. Lucien's ships were supposed to be the symbol of hope people would rally to. Not this person that was so puffed up as to call himself a 'Judge'.

Luckily for Lucien it seemed that King Garinth agreed with his opinion. "I do not like to go by hearsay, but what can any of you tell me about this Judge?" He asked the council.

"I have heard from multiple sources that he saved the village of Everbright from an alukah and its undead. Supposedly he defended the village from an attack, pursued it, and slayed it single handedly," General Xiphos explained.

Preposterous! Nobody has that kind of power. Lucien thought.

"I was told that he had some sort of fancy armor made locally here in Agaprya." A merchant lord opined.

"I heard that his weapon shines like the moon at night!" Countess Serena added.

"Yes. Yes! That's all true!" Magnus shouted, before he sat in his seat, looking like he had just swallowed a bug.

Princess Giselle cocked her head at the gnomish archivist. "Wait, have you SEEN him?"

Everyone, even Laric, leaned in towards the gnome. Lucien didn't see what the big deal was. One man couldn't destroy all of the undead in the world. Still, Magnus seemed oddly conflicted about talking about the Judge. "Please Magnus, elaborate." The King asked.

Magnus glanced up at Lucien and then down to his feet, "I… I think I did. He kept being referred to as a Judge by the others around him. And… and his spear did shine really brightly at night."

Lucien's heart skipped a beat, as Laric leapt out of his seat and yelled, "His WHAT shined?"

What was once disinterest became a feverish need to know more. The distraction in Lucien's plan now became a fire in the lumber pile. He yanked his son back down to his seat and whispered, "Be silent."

"His… his spear. It shined. It had this… blue metal on it and the symbol of the Judge's Mark. Making him the real thing!"

Lucien's heart resumed its normal rhythm, and Laric sighed in relief. He remembered that the blade Leon had taken was rusted through. There was nothing more to worry about. The king pressed the archivist, "Can we ask this Judge to come here? To assist us? Where is he?"

Magnus didn't lift his head as he replied, "I… I think he may have left with the princess to go to the Elvenwood."

A quiet pall fell over the table, as the unspoken implications of his statement simmered around the room.

After a heavy sigh, the king, and subsequently everyone else, stood at their chairs, "Well, we wish him all the luck in the world." Turning to Lucien, King Garinth added, "I thank you for your surprise gift Lucien. You were right. I was distracted, but am no longer. Evacuate Hookvale. Bring the forces at Bulwark back to Agaprya. Let us start using mail carriers and any other fast ships to evacuate those who cannot fight to Last Bastion. If this is the end of the living world then we will make our stand here. Let us get to work everyone."

Applause sounded around the table.

Princess Giselle's small voice made an off-hand comment to Laric, "I did not know about the fancy armor. I was told the Judge wore our naval armor… Um, my lords?"

Her eyes met Lucien and Laric's, who looked back at her in sheer panic.

Magnus assured Lucien repeatedly after the meeting that he had no more information on the Judge. As the little gnome hurried to leave, Lord Rhise wondered what his story would have been had he been in the presence of a discerner cube. Lucien knew he would have to corner Magnus at some point. With no discerner here at the council chamber, the lords were allowed their lies and mistruths. Otherwise, no real work would get done.

Now was not the time. Now, Lucien needed to calm his son down. "What are we going to do father?" Laric asked, as he wrung his hands.

"Stop sniveling and worrying for one thing!" Lucien responded. Speaking to each other in hushed tones, they made their way to grab something to eat. They paused their conversation any time someone came close to them. During the times when there was nobody nearby, Lucien continued to process his thoughts aloud. "I will meet with Headherald Kazave to spread the word of our narrative. The dreadnought ships will save this kingdom. We will save this kingdom. Not. Leon."

Laric pointed to one of the wanted posters for his brother, and lamented, "How did he become the Judge though father? Why?"

"It does not matter at this point. If he truly is headed towards the Northern Elvenwood, then he will die at the hands of that undead army. If he is elsewhere, then we will root him out." Lucien ripped the poster down and rolled it up. Lord Rhise then tapped Laric with it to emphasize his words, "Ten thousand gold alive. Five thousand gold dead. Enough money for people to pay attention… To find him."

"Father, I have seen our coffers the same as you have. That sum–"

Lucien finished for his son, "Will be paltry once our plans are complete. You let me worry about the funds. About the Heralds.

About getting word to Silas. About Leon. You only need to worry about one thing. Princess Giselle. Have you thought about tonight?"

Lucien's effort to distract his son with other matters seemed to do the job. Laric smirked, "There is this place I would like to try, father. Then I will bring some food back to her tonight, for a late dinner and conversation. Conversation is easier to swallow with good food."

Lucien snorted as he clapped Laric's shoulder with pride. "Good idea, even if you did sound a bit like Silas trying to be wise just now. Is that why you are leading me this way?"

"Indeed, father! Baron Halomir told me about this place. He recommended it. Hopefully he did not get his indigestion here!" Laric jested.

Lord Rhise chuckled with his son as they continued walking. Laric would never have to know. Never have to learn what Lucien did for his children whom he loved – the ones who obeyed him. Baron Halomir was merely a means to an end. A suggestion from Silas that, while useful, caused quite a stir. Especially when Lucien had agreed to the Baron's brazen proposal to cement their alliance with his daughter Liara's hand.

It had taken every ounce of willpower Lucien possessed to not spit in the odorous baron's face and strangle him on the spot at the suggestion. Instead, he smiled and agreed in public. In private, he knew he would never allow the marriage to occur. He had crossed lines before. Lines that he swore he would never pass over. In the end, arranging the Baron's demise had turned out to be a bit easier than he thought.

After having been assured that the baron would be handled, Lucien was subsequently informed that after he had thrown Leon out of the manor, he still managed to live. The truth of the matter was that after the crash, and the exorbitant amount that Lord Rhise paid to Headherald Kazave, Leon should have been a non-issue. Lucien had a plan, a timetable, and the many cogs working in his clock were counting down. Ordering the dwarf to kill the belligerent boy should have solved the problem. His appearance at the engagement party was a surprise to say the least. Maybe it was fate. Leon didn't seem to know certain critical details. A letter to the head foreman, a misunderstanding with a few workers, and the problem, once again, could have been solved.

While Lucien hated that Leon had not lost his misgivings regarding their relationship, he privately agreed with the boy on one thing: Liara did deserve better. Maybe that had influenced his decision to disown and cast him out, instead of the alternative. Well, that and the fact that his return during the party created too many witnesses. Still, Lucien didn't think Leon would persist to become such a problem.

"Father, we are here!" Laric exclaimed.

Lucien evaluated the three-story building. It seemed like a higher-class establishment than normal. It advertised lodging as well as indoor plumbing, which was quite impressive. He smiled as he saw another wanted poster next to the outdoor menu. What impressed him most though was the delicious smell that emanated from the building and made his mouth water. Hopefully the meal was as good as the aroma. If so, Laric's choice of dining establishment would be fine indeed. He looked forward to his meal at this Wise Guy's Inn and Tavern.

As Lucien reached for the door, Laric stared at the other poster and blurted, "Will everything be ok, father? With Leon, I mean."

Lucien grew slightly irritated, "Relax son! Remember to focus on your responsibilities. Besides, he is just one man! What can one man really do?"

Chapter 5: The Faith

"Dragon incoming! All hands! To your stations!" Shouted Captain Ashera Urk as she scrambled back to the ship's wheel and took control. She angled the craft away from the dragon as it gave chase.

Gionna, Duamé, Miala, and Kelleren slowly made their way towards Leon, while most of the crew descended to the ship's hold where the cannons were. A few crew members clambered towards a crate that was secured near the middle of the deck. The secured crate was quickly opened and several crossbow and bolt bundles could be seen inside. Most, including Duamé, took a bundle set, while Gionna only took a bundle of bolts.

The elves emerged from belowdecks, and the silent guards had their weapons in hand. Princess Schalae saw the dragon approaching from behind them and turned to give Leon a knowing look. She pulled the two short, different sized staves of wood from a harness at her back and held them end to end as she closed her eyes. The distinct sound of wood creaking and cracking filled the air. Leon watched as the wood grain shifted and fused together as one. The staves then bent backward at their ends, and a light green vine shot out from either side, which knotted together in the middle.

Prince Gelan had shared much with Leon about Princess Schalae during their trek back to Agaprya, before he had died. When he had spoken of her prowess as a warrior, he mentioned her weapon was very special to the elves. It even had a name: The Broken Bough. Leon had been dubious of all that Gelan claimed when he had described her weapon. He was less of a skeptic now.

It seemed that the *Golem* was capable of racing at a much faster pace than that of the *Dawnfire* when it had tried to escape a dragon. Even with their incredible speed though, the monster was quickly closing the gap between itself and the ship. The further they ran from it also caused a different problem – every second brought the dragon closer to the town of Hookvale. Leon didn't want to risk the lives of others, but he also remembered the *Dawnfire* attack all too clearly. A war began to rage within himself. One between self-preservation and the need to fulfill the role he had been charged with. His inner turmoil a few seconds before the late prince's words echoed through his head – 'Lead with love, because love conquers all.'

Leon needed to take the lead. He needed to protect the people of Hookvale, and those who were on the *Golem*. His new friends. This was not just another attack from a dragon, this was his second chance.

"What's your plan?" He asked the orcish Captain.

"Running away seems to be working for the moment." Ashera spat back.

"Are we not talkin' about wot just happened? How those skeletons SUMMONED a flintin' dragon?" Duamé railed at them.

Miala placed a hand on the dwarf's shoulder. "You heard Rohiel. The enemy is after us. I am just as shocked as you are but…"

"We have to angle away from Hookvale. We can't lead it towards the population!" Leon advised Ashera. This prompted her to give him an earful in return.

"I don't care if you're a Judge or not! I give the orders on this ship!" The captain then yelled, "CROSSBOWS TO THE AFT!"

A handful of crew members, as well as Duamé, scrambled to the back of the ship, and started to take potshots at the approaching dragon. The dragon was only a short distance away, and gaining rapidly. It winged and weaved slightly to avoid some of the more accurate shots. Few of the bolts found their marks on its sleek profile from their current distance.

At this point Gionna activated her metallic cane and it popped open into a functional crossbow. A slim red tinged monocle fell into place on her multi-lensed spectacles as she turned to Leon and shouted, "You had better come up with a plan fast, Judge!" She then clambered to the back of the ship and tried to find a spot her tiny frame would fit into to help assail the dragon. The bulk of the other crew members ceded little space, until she made her way to the very corner of the ship railing. She clipped her harness for security and began to fire on the dragon with careful aim.

What can I do? I've only got a spear! I can't throw the thing! Leon objected internally.

As he scrambled to find any sort of advantage against the dragon, he turned and asked the captain of the *Golem,* "Do... Do you have any canister shot aboard?"

Captain Ashera looked at him as if he asked her if she had a second head growing from her shoulder – and said head was the actual captain. "Two volleys worth. How'd you know about canister shot?"

"I know my way around airships!" Leon replied as he clambered closer to her. "The last dragon I faced took a round shot volley with ease, and it was bigger! If you use canister shot, you have a better chance of damaging the beast!"

The scarred orc woman looked back at the dragon that chased them as bolts fired from her crew and passengers. Most shots went wide or were ignored, until the dragon suddenly stopped chasing the airship and bellowed as it scrabbled at its snout with its foreclaws.

"HA! Aimed for the eye, but I'll take going up the nose!" Gionna cackled, as celebratory shouts from the crew congratulated her. Her shot bought the *Golem* several seconds and stretched the distance between the fleeing ship and its pursuer. The dragon exhaled a plume of flame that must have burnt up whatever had been lodged inside its nostril, because it immediately began to pursue the transport again. The dragon was more aerodynamic, and quickly began to gain on the *Golem*. It would soon be within crossbow range again. Leon knew that this attack was different from his prior experience, and that he was being given another chance to make things right. It was a chance to bring down a dragon before it could destroy more lives.

"Please Captain, the canister shot. It may be the only way." Leon pleaded.

The captain's attention left the dragon and turned to the Judge before her. "The canister shot, the way you move about my ship, you're a naval man – aren't you?"

If this was the way to gain the captain's trust, so be it. Leon thought. "Yes. I served on the *Dawnfire*. There was a cover-up, and suffice to say, the reason that I'm a wanted man is because there are those who want to keep what really happened a secret."

"REALLY, BOYO? Why'd ya go an' ask me ta make ya a mask if ya keep tellin' everyone WHO YA ARE?" Duamé raged at Leon from the firing line.

"Wait, you're serious? You were on the *Dawnfire*? You really are that wanted guy?" Captain Ashera exclaimed.

"I would listen to him, dearie!" Gionna yelled, before she fired another bolt at the approaching dragon.

"Why on earth were you telling the truth about that? Do you realize how much money you're worth? Dead or alive?" Her perpetual look of surprise once again seemed genuine.

Leon hoped the flat stare he gave her through the mask could be seen. "Is that really relevant right now?"

"Good point. CANNONS! SWITCH TO CANISTER AT STARBOARD!" Ashera Urk screamed down the nearby stairwell. They looked back towards the dragon again and saw that the elves had joined the crew with their crossbows. As they fired their arrows, aided by their better than normal sight, the dragon took more hits from arrows than bolts, and started to weave through the air. Occasionally a burst of fire was exhaled to destroy the projectiles that it couldn't weave away from. Overall, it seemed that the arrows and bolts were doing minimal damage to it. Their strategy wasn't working, and the dragon loomed ever closer.

Hope was fading from all present as the beast drew almost within range of the ship. The canister shot had to work. This airship, this crew, had to survive. Some of the crew, wide eyed, ran out of bolts and hurried back to the crate to refill. The crate also emptied quickly. Soon the only ones who still had any ammunition were Gionna, who used her bolts sparingly, and the elves who tried to make every shot count.

The seconds ticked by as they were chased within sight of Hookvale. The clamor that came from below decks conveyed that the crew went about their work of removing the round shot from the cannons before reloading them with the canister shots. A frantic crewmember yelled from the base of the stairwell below decks that they were ready to fire. Captain Ashera craned her neck to look ahead as she commented, "Well, it looks as if our demise is going to have an audience."

They looked and saw that the fishing village of Hookvale was not just close, but that they were almost upon it. Leon couldn't believe it! The chase had brought them exactly to where he didn't want to be. Now, not only was the *Golem* in danger, but all those in Hookvale were too. If their transport couldn't fell the dragon, then Hookvale would be doomed.

The pressure on Leon to dispatch the dragon increased as those without bolts or ammunition looked to him for answers. They looked to him for hope. He echoed words from the past, words that had once been spoken to him, and announced, "Prepare to turn hard to line up our volley. Have courage everyone, and we will see this through and bring home quite the story when all it is done."

The captain no longer seemed to mind that he gave the orders, as the crew strapped themselves into positions. Leon, and the rest of his group, made their way to the middle of the ship so they could see the cannons line up. All looked at him expectantly. They looked for him to save them.

The pressure of their hope weighed on Leon even more, and he tried to help them with the words that came unbidden, "Hope in

Adonai. If you have good hope and faith in Him, we shall be delivered from our enemy."

Where did that come from? He asked himself.

It seemed to be exactly what some of them needed, even though none of them had ever heard of Adonai. He just knew that it felt wrong for them to want to idolize the Judge himself. If anyone should get the glory of rescuing them from this situation, it should be Adonai. After all, they were just grapes rolling across His table.

The dragon was close enough to be within breathing distance of the ship now. As the frightened shouts from Hookvale came within earshot, and crowds of people could be seen cluttering the streets and walls of the village, Leon roared to the captain, "TURN!"

Captain Ashera Urk pulled hard on the wheel, which caused the *Golem* to turn starboard as the aft sharply swung in its new direction. Due to the speed of the vessel, most on board lost their balance – with the exception of the Captain, the elves, and Leon. The dragon roared and pulled its momentum back as it flew upright due to their sudden change in direction. Hovering next to the ship it reared back, and prepared to deliver a flaming death to them all.

Leon roared to the crew below decks, "FIRE!"

At such a close range, he could clearly see the cannons line up perfectly as one, two, and three successive blasts of canister shot in a row delivered their packages. Multiple two-inch sized iron balls from each canister peppered the dragon. The damage spread over its left wing, its belly, and its chest. A groan escaped from its maw as the beast dropped several feet and turned sharply to wing awkwardly away.

Cheers resounded throughout the ship and the village below, as the dragon retreated while it dripped its toxic blood over the lake. There were claps on the back and celebrations. Some of the crew disappeared into the hold to deliver the good news to the cannon crews and to help reload. Leon, though, felt slightly disheartened that the canister shots had not killed the beast. The feeling grew as he began to hear cries of alarm.

"It's coming back!" One of the crew members shouted.

Indeed, it was true. The enraged dragon, flapping one wing more heavily than the other, wheeled around, and began to approach the airship once again. Its draconic face held a murderous look: it wanted revenge. Many of the crew, and even Miala and Kelleren, hurried to the railing as the Captain screamed below decks for the crew to reload faster. However, with the speed that the dragon approached the airship, there would be scant time for the cannons to protect them once more.

As Leon started to lose heart, he heard the unmistakable voice of his sparring partner who existed in his dreamscapes. The millennia old Lochemetel was graceful and deadly with her spear, and had taught Leon many things in the short time he had known her. He had never heard her voice while awake before, but it sounded as clear as a bell. It was as if she stood right next to him and whispered. ***"Have faith, Leon."***

Faith?

The dragon winged ever closer to the airship as Leon remembered the lessons the warrior had taught him about faith. How faith was an assurance of things hoped for, and the conviction of things not seen. He wanted to believe that the dragon could be slain. However, with the exception of a few arrows, and an extremely fast cannon crew, there was no defense to be had against the threat that approached.

Unless...

Leon remembered another lesson as he yelled, "Make a hole!" He then stepped back until he touched the far railing in the middle of the ship. The crew and his friends looked back at him, and moved out of his way as their gazes returned to the dragon. Any who had remained at the ship's rail closest to the dragon, began to step back and stumble out of fear.

He grasped the spear and unlatched it from the strap on the back of his armor. The spearhead uncharacteristically winked on in the daytime. Not losing focus, he pulled off his necklace with his free hand. Leon wrapped the necklace around his hand and hoped against hope that this would work. It was one thing for it to happen in a dream, reality was quite a different matter.

Taking a step in faith, Leon began to run across the deck of the *Golem*. As he gained momentum he realized the dragon was still too far away to reach with a single leap. The beast was angled slightly upward, and about to inhale in preparation to unleash its deadly dragonfire. Leon would have to stop it at just the right moment.

Adonai help me, he prayed as he ran. When he came to the railing on the other end of the ship, he slammed his Levigem necklace into the elvenwood shaft of Revelator. The weightless feeling from his dream returned as he leapt from the rail – much farther than normal. Astonished stares and a lingering light from the spear were left in his wake.

With fierce determination, Leon yelled as he grasped the spear behind his head with both of his hands. The dragon's head was reared back, the fire held in its mouth ready to exhale. Just when Leon thought that he was about to be burnt to a crisp, an arrow from one of the elves behind him hit the side of the dragon's mouth. The fraction of a second they distracted the beast proved to be enough.

The shining blade of the spear impaled the dragon's throat as Leon continued to yell in righteous anger. He yelled in defiance of the dragons he had faced, and in response to the faith that it had taken to leap impossible lengths. There was a telltale flash in the throat wound of the dragon, and small flames of the volatile breath escaped the puncture. He held onto the spear for dear life, aware of the fatal distance to the ground. Leon felt the spear slicing further down the dragon as all around the wound its green scales turned white and granulated into salt.

As he heard the cry of his name from the ship, Leon looked back to see the awestruck faces of his friends and the ship's crew. One face in particular stood out to him. Her red hair whipped in the wind, and worry etched her features. Her arm was outstretched as she reached out to him across the huge distance. A distance that he had just managed to somehow cross.

As the dragon gurgled its death rattle Leon reached its stomach and the light from Revelator pulsed again. The dragon started to turn completely into salt. Its wings turned white and stopped beating, then the husk of the dragon began to fall towards the earth – with Leon still attached to it.

Using every muscle he had, he managed to place his feet against the salt chest of the falling dragon and propel himself forward with one more giant leap – this time back towards the *Golem.* Whether from the panic of falling, or the salt that had cracked under his footing, Leon instinctively knew that this supernatural leap wouldn't cover the needed distance. The Levigem and Revelator did their combined work, but this time, trying to jump upward, a small seed of doubt had crept in.

Leon felt himself slow at the apex of his jump, and he began to fall. He reached out for the ship's rail with the hand that held the necklace, but missed. Suddenly his fall stopped.

A hand had miraculously grabbed the tail end of the spear.

The last time another being had touched it was when he fought the alukah, Rhoxmas. This had caused the Revelator to emit a powerful tone, and then the false god's hands had charred and turned to ash. It had allowed Leon the moment and opening he needed to defeat the creature.

Now, Miala held the spear with one hand while she gripped the railing of the *Golem* with her other. The spear began to emit the same note, and Leon saw the frightened look in her eyes.

To their surprise, her hand didn't char or flake away.

Instead, the light that came from the Revelator's spearhead shined even brighter.

Through the almost blinding light, Leon felt himself being lifted as a string of crewmembers helped Duamé, who had grabbed a hold of Miala. Their combined effort brought him back over the railing and onto the floor of the *Golem.* The same tone that had resounded in the alukah's chamber continued to reverberate through the air around them as Leon and Miala both still grasped Revelator. When Miala released her grip, the light that emanated from the spear resumed its normal, metallic blue, daytime appearance. The sound also ceased, and the entirety of the *Golem* fell silent as they looked at Leon and Miala in awe.

Their silence allowed everyone on board to hear the cheers and cries of celebration from the residents of Hookvale.

Leon climbed to his feet, and found himself staring directly into Miala's piercing green eyes. Perilously close to her, with his heart racing, he took another leap as he whispered, "You told me to 'not get interested'. I confess that may not be possible."

Miala's emerald eyes grew wide as she stared at him through his mask. Tears started to form, giving her a glassy-eyed appearance. "Good, because I was afraid, I pushed you away."

All on board the *Golem* whooped, clapped, and cheered as Leon and Miala embraced and shared their first tender kiss.

Chapter 6: The Forest

As he replayed the events over and over in his mind, Leon walked in a sort of half daze. The crew, the captain, and his friends all peppered him with questions.

"How did you do that?"

"Did you see how that dragon turned white and shattered when it hit the ground?"

"Who was that Adonai you spoke of? Why should we hope in Him?"

"Are you ok, dearie?"

"Does this mean the curse on our ship is broken?"

"Shut your holes, and everyone get back to work!"

"Why haven't ya done that before, meat shield?"

"Can I have your autograph? Somebody get me a quill and ink!"

"You're the Judge, right? You're here to save us all!"

"Did you see that? He's a dragonslayer!"

Leon stumbled forward, towards the bow of the ship, as the adrenaline continued to pump through his veins. He collapsed at the nook in the bow and trembled from the excitement and exhaustion that fought within him. Faintly, he heard the captain shout that they were resuming course to the Elvenwood. The shouts and cheers from the town still echoed as the ship moved away with a burst of speed. The movement and sudden rush of wind caused Leon's back to gently bend forward before he rocked back and hit the bow railing.

That small movement jarred him enough to allow his tears to start flowing behind his mask. So many emotions coursed through him. Leon couldn't tell if he was crying because he felt that he had finally avenged his *Dawnfire* crew, or because, yet again, he had nearly died only to be saved by Miala. Maybe it was from relief that her hand hadn't charred off? Or perhaps the tears were due to their shared kiss?

Most of his friends slowly made their way towards him at the front of the ship. They had to maneuver around the crew members who busied themselves looking for more excuses to stare at the new celebrity in their midst. Gionna noticed their odd behavior and waved them off ferociously with her small cane and frame. "Give him some space! Don't you hooligans have a job to do somewhere?"

Even the silent elven warriors who followed their princess came over to Leon. Their silence wasn't reverential, but voluntary. Still, their eyes showed a respect that Leon hadn't picked up on before. They, as well as the rest of his group, sat down around him. Kelleren padded over to lay his head on Leon's lap, which prompted him to absently scratch behind the dog's ears.

That was when Leon noticed one of their members was missing. Hoping he hadn't done something wrong, he asked, "Where is Miala?"

Duamé grunted, "Preachin' bout yer Adonai ta tha yahoos on tha ship."

"Seriously! How did you do that dearie? You must have jumped the entire length of the airship!" Gionna exploded.

Leon held up the small necklace in his hand and told them about the vision he had with Lochemetel, and how he had leapt over the chasm in the dream. Then he shared how he had used the Levigem to break free from the gravimancer lich's powers when they assaulted the Archive. The whole time he spoke, Gionna took rapid notes in the little scrapbook she carried.

"What should we expect when we reach the Elvenwood?" Leon asked the Princess, as he tried to shift away from being the center of attention.

Princess Schalae sat down cross-legged, while her silent guardians stood behind her. She traced the grain of the wood planking on the *Golem* with her finger. "I will introduce you all to my mother and the others. The Grove will probably have changed drastically since the last time I saw it. I've only seen the trees in their defensive formation once before, but I am sure it will be quite the sight."

Miala walked up at that moment and smiled at Leon, which caused his heart to flutter. She stared at Kelleren for a few minutes, who presumably brought her up to speed because she then asked, "Defensive formation?"

The Princess gazed speculatively at Miala as she held up her fabled weapon. "There are some among the elves who can manipulate the woods themselves. They can suggest to the wood how it should be structured. You will see what I mean when we reach the Grove." There was a splintering sound, followed by a sharp crack, as the Broken Bough became two different lengths of straight wood once again. Leon noticed that the vine, which served as her bowstring, receded and wound itself tightly around one end of each piece of wood – creating a natural handle. She slipped them both behind her back as she continued.

"Is it a mancer power?" Miala asked, as she sat next to Kelleren and Leon.

"Nettles, no! It has never been formally recognized as such, but I guess you could say 'Hortimancy' would be as applicable a term as any other. Your powers though, may cause some distress amongst some in the Grove." Schalae warned.

Miala immediately became defensive, "What? I volunteered to come and help!"

"And I appreciate it. More than you know. However, the simple fact that you are a pyromancer may cause certain… prejudices… to come to light."

Miala's face fell as a look of hurt covered it. This was a woman who had been a hermit in her last village, a true outcast. She had been a fugitive just like Leon. When he rescued the villagers in Everbright, thanks in part to her help, he had promised to help find her a new place to live. He understood her plight. After all, Leon didn't truly have a home anymore either. Neither of them belonged anywhere.

"Relax. I'm not going to burn the forest down." She muttered.

"Oh fir trees, I know! Just, let me take the lead on this." Schalae replied.

It was much later in the day when the *Golem* finally flew over the forest, and Princess Schalae directed it towards the only 'city' in the Elvenwood: The Grove. In the setting sun, small plumes of smoke could be seen throughout the Chimera Lands which were located across the river Tesuephra. The forest was eerily silent. No birds chirped or insects buzzed anywhere. Leon watched as carrion birds circled over the forested Chimera lands on the far side of the river.

The crew was still wary of Leon. They recounted the flight and fight of the dragonslayer amongst them in an effort to keep it fresh in their minds. Leon remembered how accounts of their rescue of Everbright had been exaggerated to the point of fantasy. This had been due in part to Duamé starting an extraordinary rumor. Leon owned no white horses, and honestly didn't want any glory for himself. The only reason he had survived this long was due to Adonai and His angels taking the time to teach him.

His thoughts sent a small chill down his spine as he recalled the clear sound of Lochemetel's voice during the battle. Hadn't Rohiel told him that he wouldn't be able to contact Leon for some time?

Did that mean that Lochemetel could?

"Fear not."

Awestruck, Leon looked around himself and the airship, but couldn't see the armored angel. He withdrew to an isolated portion of the deck and asked aloud, "Um, Lochemetel?"

"I am here."

"Since WHEN?"

"Since you summoned us to the Sanctuary. Rohiel taught all of you, but could only manifest for a short time. I will advise you in this way, and thus will be able to stay longer."

Flabbergasted, Leon couldn't help but smile and silently thank Adonai before adding, "Welcome to the team! I am sure the others would love to meet you."

"Only you can hear me."

Though somewhat disappointed, Leon was still encouraged by the prospect of having the angel in his ear to help in the coming days. With a massive undead army to fight, he would need it. "Still, thank you."

"Dearie, who are you talking to?" Gionna asked, as she walked up behind him.

Leon explained the latest development while Gionna's eyes narrowed in multi-lensed skepticism.

"Do you realize the impossibility of what you are saying? How can only you hear her, if she is around us? Why can't we see her for that matter?"

Leon tried to explain the visions of when he saw the angels battling in their spiritual war. He then shared how Lochemetel defeated the Mazzikin swarm after they had purged the Archive's Judge's section. Halfway into his explanation Gionna began to write on her notepad, while muttering under her breath. When he was done, she gave him a pointed look and thumped him in the chest with her cane.

"Extra-dimensional beings interacting with our own kind is far-fetched when you consider the fact that no one has ever seen them, or even talked about them. No Judge has been around for centuries to explain all of this. Your Adonai was all but forgotten. That section of the Archive was sealed up, and given enough time no one would remember Him at all." She started to shuffle away before Leon called after her.

"What if that was the point?"

The old gnome stopped and slowly turned back to him with a quizzical look on her face. "Explain, dearie."

Leon tried to think about it from an adversarial perspective. "We saw the little statue and the knife, right? Those mancers must have wanted to go to that section for a reason. Maybe it was to deny access."

Speaking as the thoughts came to him, he continued, "We are talking about beings with thousands of years of existence under their belts. What if Xhormas' plan was always to make people forget about Adonai? Forget that He ever existed in the first place. You can't believe in, much less follow, a God you know nothing about."

A tense silence stretched between them as Gionna closed her eyes and shook her head. "Your world scares me. I can invent weapons and other things to protect the kingdom, but I have no idea how to protect myself against beings like what you describe."

"You protect yourself with Adonai. It's probably why they targeted Him in the first place." Leon stated.

"Destination sighted Captain!" A scout shouted from nearby.

Leon and his friends approached the front of the ship as a clearing where the *Golem* could land was revealed in the middle of the forested Grove. As the airship hovered over it, those who had never seen the Grove gasped in wonder.

It was beautiful. Exquisite even. Roughly the size of the village of Everbright, the elven homes appeared to be made entirely of trees.

Tall trees, short trees, trees with blooms of every hue. Even trees as wide as Gionna's house dotted the circular cityscape. Every structure appeared completely natural, no cut wood could be seen anywhere. A great number of the trees were wide and short, instead of tall. Doorways and window holes appeared to be sculpted from the trunks themselves. Colorful, blossoming trees of all types appeared to carpet the living city. Several tall redwood and sequoia trees bordered the city, and their tops served as watchtowers. The watchtower trees were interconnected with other densely packed trees. Their branches, and the vines near their bases, threaded together to form a living wall around the Grove. As they passed over it in the *Golem,* Leon could see that brambles and thorns provided another natural defense.

Even more breathtaking than the city, was the forest itself. The last time Leon had looked over the edge of the ship was when they had approached the outskirts of the forest. At that point it had looked like any other. Now that they were upon it, he saw that it was an obvious and veritable maze. The treetops stretched to dizzying heights, but their trunks and branches grew in tight dense lines. This allowed little to no room for wide formations of armies to march through. Concentric circles, and paths that seemed to lead nowhere, stretched off into the lush forest as far as his eyes could see.

All sorts of foliage peppered the cityscape. Enormous leaves provided shade from the rays of the setting sun. The circle of willow trees surrounded the apparent airship landing zone wafted gently in the wind. As Captain Ashera Urk lined the ship up to gently land on a grassy field within the clearing, she roared to the crew to ready the gangplank. Leon was thankful for the soft landing. If he were to be honest, he couldn't recall the last time he had experienced one.

Once the gangplank had been lowered, and the large red levigems on the sides of the ship faced straight up and down lengthwise, the captain rested the wheel with its control levigem, into its base. Then she took a nearby chain and securely locked it into place before pocketing its small key. Part of Ashera's responsibility as the captain was to ensure that the airship could only be flown by her. Leon could tell that she took her responsibility seriously.

Leon and his friends shouldered their possessions, and gathered with the crew members in preparation to descend the gangplank into the Grove. They were met by an elven delegation, an entourage of at least twenty elves in full battle attire stood at attention to greet them. They were lined up, ten elves on either side of one single person. These warriors had bows and curved blades sheathed either behind their backs, or on their legs. Their armor appeared to be made from dark wood and bark, and fit quite snugly. Different arrangements of painted stripes and lines adorned their armor and faces, which accentuated the seriousness of their features. These warriors were clearly battle-ready. They were elves prepared to defend their homes and their Queen.

The elven warriors, and for that matter all of the elves around them, had wide variations in their appearances. All of the adult elves that surrounded Leon showed characteristics of various trees. They had bark colored skin and hair tinged with the color of leaves or flowers. Some of the elves, though, looked quite different from what he had seen before. Their height also varied, and some stood a full head taller than others. Many elves even had outfits that could only be made in the forest. Hats were made of wide interwoven fronds, and vine-like dresses caressed the ankle high grass all around them.

Leon had never met the Queen of the Elves, but her matronly appearance didn't detract from the obvious resemblance to her daughter. While Schalae was lithe, her mother was of a more round and stocky build. Loose dark green hair fell from a wooden diadem, which looked to be made from whitish tree roots that branched through her tresses. She wore no armor, but instead was covered by a dress that appeared to be made entirely from cherry blossoms and leaves.

Princess Schalae all but ran to her mother, and they embraced as the Queen gently stroked her daughter's hair. A few whispered words were spoken between them, not to be heard by any of the others who were gathered. Leon surmised by Schalae's expression, and her mother's consoling demeanor, that the Queen was expressing sympathy over the Princess' loss of Prince Gelan.

After a few hushed moments Princess Schalae turned towards the crew and Leon's companions, to make introductions. "Everyone, may I present Queen Chlorae of the Northern Elvenwood."

Most of those present, with the exception of the elves, bowed or nodded respectfully, while the princess began to introduce her mother to each of those who had disembarked from the *Golem.* The last two to be introduced were Miala and Leon – both of whom shifted uncomfortably under the gaze of everyone that was assembled.

"This is Miss Miala, a powerful Pyromancer and my friend – and this is her companion Kelleren." The Princess said. The elven warriors were mostly successful at hiding the fact that their muscles tensed when her title had been revealed. Queen Chlorae didn't seem to mind, and instead thanked her for coming to the forest's defense. Kelleren also attempted to ease the tension by padding up to the Queen and greeting her in his own doggy way. She smiled at him and greeted him respectfully, before she turned back to Miala.

"I am grateful for your camaraderie with my daughter, and for your help in these dark times."

Miala nodded with respect once again, focusing on the Queen and not the mutterings that came from the nearby soldiers.

As the sun finally set over the horizon, Revelator's spearhead burst forth with brilliant light. It caused more than a few of the elves among them, as well as the crew of the *Golem*, to flinch back in surprise. Leon heard the collective intake of breath as the branches of the trees around him began to creak and lean in, as though they were attracted to the light of the spear. After a few reverential moments, the Queen herself broke the silence.

"Even the trees that rustle in the wind tell of a Judge who walks through Xaelon in our last days. I see now that they are not without merit. You must be the Judge who has promised to help us."

"In any way that I can." Leon replied simply. "That WE can," He quickly corrected himself.

Queen Chlorae smiled and gestured further into the wooden city, "I welcome all of you to the Grove. While I wish that we could have met under better circumstances, I can assure you that we appreciate everyone's aid. Please, follow me."

They had begun to make their way into the Grove when Captain Ashera tapped Leon's plate pauldron. Turning, he saw her try to shield her eyes from the brightness of the spear. With a hand held up to them, she said, "I can't thank you enough for saving the *Golem.* This is where we part ways. We are not a combat vessel, so will head back to Agaprya to resupply and get our next orders."

She clasped his hand and shook it with respect. "Good luck, and safe travels." Leon replied.

“You too.” She then turned and ushered her crew back onboard, “Come on you louts! This ain’t a sightseeing tour! Strap into positions for liftoff!”

Leon sighed with contentment as he saw the *Golem* off. Then he hurried to catch up to the others.

He found them in another small clearing not far away. It appeared to be some sort of meeting area. Several elves, as well as his friends, congregated around a large circular stone slab that had formerly served as the base of a fallen statue. The upper portion of the statue lay nearby, and appeared to have moss covered owl ears poking from the top of it. It was quite apparent that this idol had toppled long, long ago. It’s broken base now served as the perfect slab for a makeshift map.

Little twigs and berries, paired with a blue paste that cut through the large depiction, created an accurate representation of the Northern Elvenwood and its neighboring Chimera Lands. What Leon saw, as the light of Revelator illuminated the scene, was the representation of a grim situation.

The Chimera Lands were lost. There was no other word for it. The undead horde, represented by red berries, took up more than half of the Chimera forest. They had penetrated it from the small mountains and large hills to the west. Those who were assembled mused over the map as an elf who was dressed in ornate black wooden armor glanced at Leon, while he continued to speak.

“The undead horde grows with every slain chimera. They become more dangerous and will soon pass across the river that separates our lands. They have a vast numerical advantage and can cross the river from multiple points, while we can only defend a few. The situation is quite grim. Due to this, our shapers have used the Mycelium to wall off the river, and labyrinth the woods. The walls will serve to slow them down and divide them up.”

Gionna cleared her throat and raised her hand, “What is ‘the Mycelium’?”

The Queen smiled warmly at the gnome and answered, "An artifact of the elves. It connects to the forest, and allows us easier access to the trees and to shape their wood."

The Princess asked the commanding elf, "Thorne, is there a plan in place beyond mere defense?"

"We must protect our trees." The elf looked again at Leon and the others who were not from the Grove. "For… obvious reasons."

Gionna piped up at that, hauling herself up onto the stone slab. "Overwhelming odds and a large area to defend is not a good combination, dearie."

The intensity of the black armored elf increased as his voice became incensed, "Regardless! We must protect them! For all elves!"

Queen Chlorae, who had been content to listen and watch up until this point, raised her hand to quiet the murmurings and the elven commander. "I would like to hear what the Judge thinks about our situation."

All eyes turned to Leon, and Kelleren padded over to nestle his head into Leon's free hand for encouragement. Staring at the map after having listened to the commander, he reasoned through strategy and tactics aloud.

"The biggest obstacle that the undead have to overcome is the river. Even the simple act of climbing out of it will slow them down. If you hold them there, you could pick them off – depending on your supply of arrows. You are right though," Leon said, looking at the elven commander, "The situation is grim. This is a massive force of undead. One that I am sure is several times larger than our own. I don't think holding the forest can be a lasting option."

"A wise assessment." Lochmetel whispered in Leon's ear. He resisted the urge to jerk abruptly away at the unexpected input from the angel.

"Plus, to top it off, we saw a disturbing sight on the way here. The undead summoned a dragon." Miala added quickly.

Cries of concern laced the voices of the elves that were present. The Commander's voice spoke, sharp as a dagger, "What would you have us do against the horde then? Against a dragon? Retreat? To where?"

Leon bristled, "I don't know. You asked for my advice. Just because you don't like it doesn't mean it's inaccurate. This will be a hard battle."

"I would think that a fire-breathing dragon would be too volatile in a forest. They wouldn't want to burn down their own forces." Gionna speculated.

The elves grumbled amongst themselves, clearly agitated. Nobody would ever voluntarily choose to give up their home, but the anger they expressed seemed a bit overly dramatic to Leon.

Then again, he thought, *I didn't want to lose my home either.*

Queen Chlorae again motioned for silence as she emphasized, "We cannot give up our home. Our trees. Our lives. We must stand firm. I would ask that the shapers create more fortifications from the surrounding woods. Commander Thorne, any way to slow them down would give us an advantage. What options are there?"

Thorne nodded respectfully to his queen, "We will hold them at the river and draw them into the labyrinth only when necessary."

"Thank you, commander. Please see to it. We have several long days ahead of us. Everyone get some rest when you can."

He saluted and left with a large contingent of warriors. Some, who must have been tasked with the Queen's protection, remained along with Schalae's silent guardians.

"Are you hungry?" The Queen asked. Leon suddenly realized how famished he was. They were all hungry, but Kelleren was the most vocal about his plight. He howled before running up and showering the Queen with slobbery kisses and affection. Thankfully, she laughed at his antics along with the rest of them.

That evening they were treated to a meal of fruits, vegetables, and nuts. Duamé complained about the lack of meat, but that didn't stop him from having several helpings of honey coated nuts. When they were all full, and the exhaustion of the day weighed heavy, the Queen excused herself and Princess Schalae so they could catch up. Before they left, she directed a warrior to escort the visitors to the 'guest tree'.

As they walked through the Grove, they were led through massive trees that sprouted from the ankle-high grass. Most of the trees looked old and overgrown. Leon could see the elven families who occupied each tree through the open doorways and window holes in their massive trunks. Generations of families must have occupied them. The guest lodgings were in an enormous maple tree that smelled faintly sweet inside. Light, springy, oblong grass served as beds, which lined the inner trunk's outer walls. A squared off bench formed from the inner trunk itself served as seating opposite the beds. Spiral steps had been grown out of the inner wall, and led to a second level which held more beds. Everything inside this tree had been grown from the tree itself, there was not a single cut furnishing anywhere!

Exhausted from the day's events, Duamé clambered up the stairs without a word, and crashed on one of the beds. Gionna, Miala, and Kelleren took the three downstairs beds, which left Leon to also climb upstairs and claim the remaining bed. Too tired to bother taking off his armor, it nevertheless felt amazing to lay down on the grassy bed.

Leon was still in disbelief that they had slain a dragon earlier, and hoped that they were all prepared for the clash that was about to happen. Before falling into a dreamless slumber, he heard Lochemetel whisper to him.

"Men fight, but only Adonai gives victory."

Leon didn't know how long he slept, but when he awoke in the pale light of early morning it was not of his own accord. Instead, he was roused by a bone shaking, ear vibrating roar that split through the air.

"WOT WAS THAT?" Duamé yelled, as they bolted upright.

"The enemy approaches! Nachash Seraph is here!" Leon heard.

"Nachash Seraph?" Leon whispered, as he scrambled to get his helmet back on.

"A commander for Xhormas. The chief of serpents."

"Well, that's just great!" Leon lamented, as he clambered down the wooden stairwell.

"He is one of the Fallen, and very dangerous."

Hearing the dread in Lochemetel's voice caused a shiver to creep up Leon's spine. Lochemetel had been fighting a war against the Fallen for thousands of years. She always bested him in his dream training sessions. That she would warn him of the danger posed by this Nachash Seraph, caused a sense of unease to settle in his gut. He and Duamé ran down the stairs to find everyone awake and in a wide eyed state of panic and fear. Gionna looked out one of the tree's window holes, and motioned for everyone to come over.

Leon could see with certainty that this dragon was different. It was twice as large as the one that had crashed the *Dawnfire*. A long snake-like body undulated in the air as the massive wings near its head flapped. Its wings created gusts of wind, which caused swirls of new spring leaves and blossomed petals to fall from their trees. Instead of greenish scales, its body was covered in a dramatic explosion of shining, chromatic rainbow hues. It flew above the Grove in another circle, then landed on the westernmost redwood tree tower. While it had only two giant claws midway down its length, instead of four, they appeared to be oversized. One singular claw looked to be as large as a man. Its weight caused the tree to creak and snap in a useless protest, as the beast coiled around it. The largest dragon to have ever been seen would have been considered beautiful to the undiscerning.

A distinct red glow that came from its eyes showed to whom it had sworn allegiance.

It was at that moment, huddled together with his friends in the maple treehouse, Leon heard a dragon speak for the first time. Its serpentine voice drawled out in a throaty rumble:

"THISSS ISSS YOUR ONLY CHANCE TO SSSURRENDER. IN RECOMPENSSSE YOU WILL ALL BE ALLOWED TO DIE PAINLESSSLY."

Chapter 7: The Adversaries

The only sound that could be heard was the creaking of the redwood as it strained in useless protest under the weight of the dragon called Nachash Seraph. Fear permeated the Grove, and grew with every lazy flap of his enormous wings. Such a massive being had never been seen before. It was unbeatable. Unkillable. To battle against such a creature and his armies would be hopeless.

"Do not listen to the mazzikin."

Leon shook his head – as if that mere act would clear the defeated thoughts away. The dark-winged, shadowy shapes and beasts that flew unnoticed throughout the world were a huge problem. When Lochmetel wasn't occupied within his mind, she took it upon herself to hunt them.

Are there mazzikin around us right now? He questioned silently.

"These ones follow Nachash Seraph's orders. They sow fear, unease, and doubt. Should you choose to listen, the enemy will have an easier time influencing you."

The defeated feelings he felt from the sight of the awesome dragon gave way to an understanding of Lochemetel's words. The mazzikin caused him to remember a time, not too long ago, when he had been on the streets of the wharf area of Agaprya. A time when he had sat in alleyways or doorways near the docks, miserable and broken from the heartache generated by the cruel hand life had dealt him. Broken from his role in the mercy killing of Crown Prince Gelan. Miserable that he had to slay his undead crew members and friends. The guilt he felt had been forgiven by Adonai, and yet it still tried to rear its ugly head on occasion.

As he beat those feelings back down, Leon was struck by a sudden connection: the first night he cradled the spear in the tree by the road, he had thought about hurting himself. He had considered ending his life.

Have mazzikin been attacking me the entire time?

Lochemetel provided a cryptic answer, as she often did. ***"You are learning. Your minds often confound your own thoughts. The mazzikin attempt to lead you away from your true purposes. Faith in Adonai gives you resilience against their suggestions. That is not to say that you humans do not come up with your own flawed concepts. You are, however, highly susceptible to the beings you cannot see."***

After several minutes passed without response, Nachash Seraph beat his wings faster in clear agitation. His grating, reverberating voice echoed through the trees.

"DOESSS NO ONE SSSPEAK FOR ANY OF YOU?" He raged.

From the window hole of the tree everyone watched as the Queen and the Princess strode into the clearing, followed by a retinue of guards. While their steps were purposeful, they were also hesitant. Their retinue stayed close to a line of cherry blossom trees, and pink petals sprinkled them every time the dragon flapped its wings. At what they must have considered to be a safe distance, the guards huddled together with their bows and arrows pointed at Nachash Seraph. Leon noticed as the elves drew closer that they all were dressed in the same black bark-like armor the elven commander had worn the night before.

The Queen shouted in the sternest voice she could muster, "I am Queen Chlorae of the Elvenwood, and we will NOT accept your terms. Depart from our borders at once!"

Nachash Seraph's claws dug into the redwood, gouging holes in the old tower of a tree. Its massive head craned down to stare at the elven monarch and her retinue.

"YOU ARE DOOMED. YOU MUSSST KNOW THISSS. YOU CLING TO YOUR TREESSS FOR YOUR LIVESSS, BUT DEATH

IS NOT SSSOMETHING TO FEAR! IT IS SSSOMETHING TO EMBRACE." Wood snapped as one of the branches on the redwood broke off due to the constricting coils of the dragon.

The weight of his persuasive words fell on Queen Chlorae, causing her to close her eyes and look away. Many of the warriors near her shook with fear. Their bows could be seen quivering in the air.

Leon had enough. Much like the lich who had tried to talk them into surrendering during their struggle in the judge section of the archives, this Nachash Seraph was trying to convince the elves to give up. Sure, they faced overwhelming odds and the situation looked grim. Did that mean there was no hope? Was it perhaps that this serpent had a different agenda? Every elf that surrendered to death would be one less to fight for life. Every second spent here instead of preparing their defenses was another second wasted. Nachash Seraph was using intimidation as a weapon to unnerve his adversary.

Time to return the favor.

Leon moved past his friends and walked out of the tree. The others followed closely behind. Duamé muttered about the insanity of it all while Gionna reached into a pocket and pulled out a vial of clear liquid. *Maybe she's thirsty,* Leon thought.

After they walked into the clearing, Nachash Seraph swiveled his head and the red glow that came from his eyes grew brighter as they widened in surprise.

A rumble of, "UNEXPECTED. HOW AMUSSSING," escaped Nachash Seraph's maw, as the group joined the elves in solidarity.

"That's quite enough of that," Leon commanded in admonishment to the dragon.

"DO NOT SSSEEK TO TELL ME WHAT TO DO, MORSSSEL!" Growled the dragon.

"In the name of Adonai, I–" But Leon was interrupted as Nachash Seraph rumbled.

"WHAT DO YOU KNOW OF ADONAI, MORSSSEL? I HAVE KNOWN HIM SINCE THE BEGINNING OF TIME. HAVE YOU EVER HEARD HISSS VOICE? HAVE YOU SSSEEN HISSS

FACE?" The dragon's massive head inched closer towards a bewildered Leon. "I THOUGHT NOT. YOU CLAIM TO BE A JUDGE, YET ALL I SSSEE ISSS A SSSNACK."

Have I heard Adonai before? Leon asked himself. The peace in his heart unsettled slightly as he wondered at the dragon's words. With a reminder to himself that it was all a trick, he shook it off. Then he slammed the spear to the ground and shouted, "I do not need to hear His voice to follow Him, to know that He is real! I know what He has done for me!"

The dragon appeared to chuckle at this. Its coils constricted even more around the redwood it hung from, causing sharp creaks and cracks to punctuate every word, "YOU ARE INSSSIGNIFICANT, AND WILL NEVER BE GOOD ENOUGH FOR HIM. NO ONE ISSS. THAT ISSS WHY THERE ISSS NO POINT IN FOLLOWING HIM. YOU ARE A FOOL."

"Boyo! Don't upset tha dragon!" Duamé hissed in fear.

But Leon knew the feeling of peace that resided in his heart. He remembered the waves of light that washed over him in his visions. He never wanted to give that up or let it go. "I may be a fool… But if you have lived for thousands of years, and have seen His face, yet still fight against Adonai, then I am not the only fool here, Nachash Seraph."

The chief-of-serpents leaned closer, which caused the feathers that surrounded his head to ruffle. With his closer proximity a smell of rotten eggs also began to permeate the air. Then its serrated rows of teeth opened slightly, and its split serpentine tongue ran over their edges.

"I DID NOT GIVE MY NAME. WHO GAVE YOU SSSUCH KNOWLEDGE?"

Leon panicked slightly until he heard a small whisper, ***"Tell him."***

Summoning up a mask of contempt, Leon stared hard at the beast before declaring, "I have learned much from Lochemetel."

The dragon recoiled as if it had been struck, and roared so loudly that those who had free hands covered their ears. Its wings beat furiously, slapping against the ruined redwood tower. In its rage Leon watched as one multicolored wing became gouged on a stout branch, and a small amount of black blood oozed out.

"We have history." Lochemetel explained. Leon could hear her amusement at the dragon's temper tantrum.

Smoke escaped from Nachash Seraph's nostrils and the corners of its mouth while it hissed in vehemence, "I SSSHALL THOROUGHLY ENJOY ROASSSTING THAT WENCH'SSS PET!"

The dragon's serpentine body uncoiled from the tower as it reared back and lunged down. Its massive jaws were wide as it dived straight towards Leon and his group. A furnace of death rolled in its throat, which promised an untimely end. "Miala!" Gionna yelled, as she threw the vial that contained the clear liquid. It arched towards the dragon's head as a burst of flame shot from the tip of Miala Mytheriyn's wand. The flame connected with the vial, and exploded in a volatile reaction. The explosion connected with the head of Nachash Seraph. It recoiled from the airburst with its ruffled mane burned and singed.

"Focus on his wounded wing! Ground it!" Lochemetel yelled urgently.

While arrows from the many elven defenders peppered the dragon's face, Leon ran forward. He activated the Levigem against Revelator and immediately felt lighter of foot. With his focus on the bloody wing, Leon leaped and almost flew towards the wing that still rapped against the redwood. He had jumped absentmindedly across the distance towards the beast, and realized that he overshot the wing, and would arch over it.

Nachash Seraph also noticed his approach, and bent toward him with his jaws wide open. Leon shifted the spear's blade to angle down, and caught the top edge of the wing a few feet from where it met Nachash Seraph's body. The sudden resistance caused him to pivot behind the wing, on the opposite side of the dragon's approaching mouth.

The telltale light flashed from the spearhead as Leon dangled. A colored wing, which oozed black, was all that separated him from death. A soft hiss met his ears. He looked and saw a jagged line of white salt growing from the wound he had created. Scale, bone, and sinew all transformed into the granulated substance. Leon grit his teeth and sawed at the wing as he pulled down on the spear – tearing its flesh, tendons, and muscle.

A few distant and garbled shouts from both the elves and his friends preceded another roar from Nachash Seraph. This time it was a roar of pain. A shudder ran through its body as Leon successfully cut halfway down its wing. The smell of the dragon was terrible, but oddly the smell of salt helped to neutralize it. The white salt burned the flesh and dried the black blood of the dragon. Leon heard a growl from beneath him, and abruptly looked down. A red eye, as large as a wagon wheel, glared at him only inches from where he hung.

With a sudden surge of adrenaline, and at the urgings of Lochmetel, Leon sprung off the angry eye and wedged himself into the growing wound. Determined to accomplish his task, Leon continued to slice downward through the injured wing. Nachash Seraph blindly snapped his jaws where Leon had just been, roaring in both frustration and pain.

As the last bit of tendon and flesh gave way, the salted wing and Leon dropped a short distance to the ground below. Leon quickly leapt back towards the elves and his friends. The voice of the angel crooned in exultation, ***"He is permanently maimed! Even if he leaves your plane, he can never fly again!"***

The dragon undulated in shock. Its voice reverberated throughout the grove as it crawled away, now robbed of its flight. "SSSO BE IT! ALL WILL SSSUFFER ON YOUR ACCOUNT. I WILL REND YOU LIMB FROM LIMB WHEN WE MEET AGAIN!"

Leon turned and shouted in reply, "Then I'll make sure to have a plan, and not just 'WING' it!"

There were more than a few snorts and snickers behind him, and he even heard Duamé mutter, "Ooo, good one."

Leon turned around and was greeted by amazed stares and guarded stances against the retreating dragon.

"Well, that's one way to negotiate." The amused Queen said. By her side the Commander from the previous night, grinned from one pointed ear to the other.

"How often can you do that?" He asked.

"Witty comebacks? Fairly often if need be."

"Jumping like a grasshopper." Commander Thorne clarified.

Leon held up the spear. "As long as I hold faith in Adonai, and I use the gifts he's given me."

"Who is this 'Adonai'?" Queen Chlorae asked.

Leon smiled and began to explain as the adrenaline still coursed through him

✦✦✦✦✦

The elves were much more open to belief in Adonai than the villagers of Everbright had been. As Princess Schalae had explained on the *Golem*, elves had no qualms with the idea of creation, they just had no one to ascribe it to. Many of them bowed their heads and were overcome with emotion at the news of this 'God of Love' that they had lived without.

Leon explained about Adonai while the elves and the others geared up for war. After Nachash Seraph's unexpected visit that morning, the elves of the Grove didn't want to take any chances. They all donned the same dark bark armor, which covered their varied skin tones, and strapped quivers of arrows to their shins and forearms for easy access. Sharpened stakes and strung bows of all sizes were tested and readied.

What looked to be large ceremonial jars were carried out by the Princess and her two silent guards Qas and Vyn. Elves gathered around them and dipped their hands into the jars. When they pulled their hands back out their fingers were covered in paints of various colors. Reds, pinks, and blues began to appear in streaks across elven faces and limbs. "This is so we do not shoot each other in the forest."

The Princess explained, after the multitudes of warriors adorned themselves. She then reached into the assorted jars, and with the help of her silent partners they painted lines and symbols across Leon and his friends.

When the quiet Qas reached towards Duamé with a purple hand the dwarf backed up saying, "Don't you dare! I ain't gettin' no–"

Before he could protest further, Princess Schalae, who stood near him, reached out with a simple, "Boop," and placed a red dot right on the tip of his nose. He tried to rub it off with a harrumph, but this seemed to be no normal paint. His efforts just smeared it all across his face and hand. He growled at the princess again, while she smiled in amusement back at him.

Vyn put his two orange handprints on Leon's shoulders, then pointed at the א in the center of his armor and gave Leon a thumbs up.

"He believes." Lochemetel silently voiced.

Leon's smile was genuine as he clasped forearms with Vyn, and shook his hand as a fellow believer. It was at that moment they looked over and saw Miala.

Streaks of red paint ran across the chainmail shoulder armor that adorned her robe. Both were enchanted to withstand the high levels of heat she exuded. She had handed her three wands to the Queen, who held them bunched together. She closed her eyes and with a wrenching motion the wands began to shift and spiral together. Where there had been three separate wands, she now held a singular stout and inseparable rod.

This appeared to have been planned and overseen by both Miala and Gionna – as the elderly gnome then deposited the blob of aeonyte into Miala's hand.

"What are you doing?" Leon asked.

"An experiment, dearie!" Came Gionna's brisk reply, as Miala's hand began to brighten and grow hotter and hotter. Soon the heat impacted the aeonyte, and it changed from a pale blue color to white. It also appeared to have softened. After a nod from the pyromancer, Queen Chlorae carefully stuck one twisted end of the modified wand into the softened metal. Miala shaped the softened rare metal onto the rod's end with her hand. A small amount remained on the tip of the elvenwood wand, while the other half of the aeonyte glob was pinched off and remained separate.

Buckets crafted from single pieces of wood were then carried over by a few elves. The end of the recreated wand, and Miala's hand, were doused in them. The hiss of water along with the small clouds of steam built the anticipation of everyone who had participated, and they crowded around to see the final results.

Miala withdrew her newly braided wand which was now equipped with a spherical piece of aeonyte at the end. Satisfied with the result, she deposited the remaining half of the unused metal back into Gionna's eager hands.

"But will it still work?" Leon asked, his voice laced with concern.

"We will find out shortly I guess." Miala responded.

Kelleren sniffed at it and emitted a soft whine. Leon surmised it might be due to the dog also being concerned. Miala was quick to reassure him with a scratch behind his ears as she inspected the improvised black bark armor that had been fashioned for the dog. Due to his unwavering devotion to his mancer, he refused to remain behind during the fighting. The armor adorned his back and abdomen, and Miala expressed how grateful her companion was for their thoughtfulness and effort.

At this point Gionna walked up to the rest of the group, "I would love to help, but these old bones aren't made for long battles anymore. I will stay and help here in any way I can."

Queen Chlorae placed a friendly hand on the gnome inventor's shoulder. "You are certainly welcome here and you can observe your friends' progress through the Mycelium with me. Commander Thorne, is everyone prepared?"

Leon looked over the multitude of elves that were gathered in the clearing with the commander. There must have been at least a few thousand present. All of them wore the hard, black bark armor, and were outfitted with various weapons. A majority of their weaponry appeared to be bows and quivers full of arrows. The elves seemed prepared to defend the Grove with their very lives, if need be. Leon hoped it wouldn't come to that. The wounding and subsequent retreat of Nachash Seraph had been a good start to their day – and the morale boost that many needed.

After Thorne assessed his troops and deemed them ready, he helped the Queen up to the stone dais she had occupied the night before. She looked around and addressed all who were assembled, "We have many reasons to fight. For the Grove. For our futures. For our trees. For our loved ones. Even for the God whom we have not known about until today. I ask that whatever your reason to fight, you do so with every breath in your body. For the Grove!"

"For the Grove!" resounded in response. It echoed throughout the city and within the trees, with both elderly and children elves joining the call. Commander Thorne issued orders for the elves to march, and as one they turned towards a wall of dense trunks and marched off into the labyrinth of trees. A straight path opened before them, as the lush grasses and trees bowed away from it. Leon looked back beyond the army of elves and saw Duamé trying to keep up, as well as the worried looks of the elven children who watched as their family members went off to war. Gionna climbed onto the table next to the Queen and waved her cane at them in a solemn farewell. The last set of eyes that Leon saw were Queen Chlorae's. She watched in trepidation as her daughter, Princess Schalae, went to assist in the defense of the forest.

When the last elf exited the Grove, it seemed as though the forest came alive. The gap in the wall closed as the trees snapped and creaked back together. Branches and underbrush intertwined, which left no real entrance to the Grove at the end of the labyrinth. Thorns and brambles, designed to trip and snare the enemy, sprouted along the ground.

"Come!" Princess Schalae exclaimed as she rushed past. "My mother is using the Mycelium. She must seal up the maze as we head towards the river to attack the undead when they come across."

Wooden walls merged together behind them. Clinging weeds and gnarled roots sprouted along the paths as sources of defence, which complimented the living walls.

"Ya know, our plan is a little rough around tha 'hedges'…" Duamé quipped, as they ran on the heels of the elven army.

Miala and Schalae groaned in unison while Leon chuckled.

Miala said it was shortly after noon when they reached the river that provided the border between the Elvenwood and the Chimera lands. The water moved lazily across the expanse, a stark contrast to the rapid depopulation that was occurring across the way in the Chimera lands.

While no one had ever actually stepped foot in the Chimera Lands, and airships gave the land a wide berth, the distant ziggurat-like pyramid structures and totem towers spoke to their tribal and ritualistic culture. The inhabitants of those lands made no alliances, gave no gestures of friendship, and were generally hostile if encountered outside of their region.

Now, ominous pockets of smoke rose from within the forested landscape across the river. Occasional movement could be seen on the distant shore, but it stopped just as suddenly as it had begun. The defenders watched with muscles coiled, and eyes alert as they roved for signs of danger. The elves who held longer range bows cradled them horizontally from where they perched within the tree line, near the river's edge. They occupied the highest branches, and Leon wouldn't have known they were there had he not climbed the trees with them.

He occupied a lower branch, along with the other elves whose weapons had similar capabilities to his own. These elves had a mixture of short and medium range bows, and Princess Schalae was numbered among them. Within the tree line Miala, Kelleren, and Duamé stood on the ground with Commander Thorne and many other elves. They provided the necessary defense for the opening of the maze at a bottleneck point along the shore. The rest of the tree line was an impenetrable wall of thick trunks and twisted saplings.

Princess Schalae seemed to have the ability to connect here in the forest, one that had not been displayed in Agaprya. By keeping a hand pressed to the trunk of her tree, she could communicate with her mother. The Queen seemed to keep her updated on the other elven defenders who were spread throughout the forest, and on the progress of the undead at the other defensive hubs. So far, the elves had been able to keep a mixture of shamblers and wretches in check. Leon found himself in agreement with the Queen's relayed assessment: the fact that no chimeras had shown up at other locations, meant the main attack force had not yet come.

Questions raced through Leon's head. *What was the enemy's plan?* An undead horde planning tactical maneuvers was unfamiliar to Leon. The undead hordes he had fought while in the service, and as a Judge, relied purely on overwhelming numbers. They were undead – they didn't tire and they didn't stop. What would happen now that a dragon was at the helm? Or with the addition of undead chimeras to their fighting force? Would the undead attack in the same way?

"Of course not. Nachash Seraph is a cunning adversary." Lochemetel piped in with a whisper in Leon's ear.

"You said you had history?" Leon asked in barely a whisper.

"He and I have been adversaries for a long time. I ruined many of his plans back when he fought for dominion on his own."

Leon felt confused. "You mean he wasn't always the commander of Xhormas' armies?"

"If a house is divided against itself, it cannot stand. Infighting between the Fallen was common, much like your countries and kingdoms. It was when they aligned under Xhormas' banner that your world began to fall – one land after another."

Shaking his head with remorse, Leon wondered just how long ago things had started to turn for the worse in their world. Sure, the latest Dead Wars had kicked off two hundred years ago, but he wondered about the time prior to that. So much knowledge and history had been lost. When had the Fallen even come to this world?

When Leon asked Lochemetel, she replied, ***"Does it matter? Does knowing the exact time of rebellion change what happened? It happened, they rebelled against our Creator. It does not matter when so much as it matters why."***

"Alright then, why?" He asked aloud, garnering glances from other elves.

"Pride. They worshipped themselves instead of Adonai. Defiled creation by twisting it to their own purposes. Mixed creatures of different kinds to come up with their own creations – without caring how unnatural they were."

"You mean the chimeras?"

"Are you talking to me?" Princess Schalae asked, concern laced on her face.

Leon mouthed 'sorry' to the princess, and resolved to not look like such a madman in public.

Sudden realization hit Leon as he whispered, "Wait, how could an angel fight a being like Nachash Seraph if he was in our world, and you were… where you are normally?"

There was a long pause before she answered, ***"If you do not know the truth of a matter, then all you have are suppositions and lies. There is only one truth."***

Even more confusion ran through Leon's mind. "What does that mean?"

"And there is more than just one type of angel."

"Again, what is that supposed to–"

"THEY COME!"

Chapter 8: The Nephilim

After shouting Lochmetel's warning, it was confirmed by Princess Schalae, who echoed a warning from the Queen. A mass of movement occured in the brush, as bodies broke through the tree line on the opposite side of the river. Red eyes and flailing limbs became immersed in a frothy spray as the undead crashed into its waters and disappeared into its depths. A few archers launched arrows at the emerging mass, until Commander Thorne roared, "Save your arrows! Make every one count!"

The massive horde continued to exit the chimera forest, and the line of undead widened further and further as they entered the river. There were so many, and yet there was no sign of Nachash Seraph. Disturbances and eddies appeared on the river's surface, as the undead walked along the riverbed underneath – completely protected from arrows.

"How deep is that river?" Leon asked Princess Schalae.

"Too deep. Shooting in there would be useless!" She remarked.

Lochemetel chimed in, whispering a crazy thing for Leon to do.

"Uh, WHAT?" He asked aloud.

"I said it's too deep! Don't tell me you've got jitters before the battle!" Schalae said with dismay.

"No, not you! Just…" Leon listened to his invisible adviser again. "Tell the archers to get ready."

This time it was the princess' turn to say, "Uh, what?"

But Leon didn't respond. Instead, he felt quite silly as he wrapped the levigem necklace around his left wrist, and grasped the jewel in his hand. This was stupid. It made zero sense.

"It is better to be a fool for Adonai, than wise in your own eyes." Lochemetel chimed.

"Okay, here we go." Leon said, as he tapped the gem against Revelator, and immediately felt lighter. He angled his body just right, and leapt from the tree branch. The spearhead erupted into a light almost as bright as the sun. With a yell, Leon landed in the shallows of the river. At the moment of impact, while crouching down to absorb the muted shock of having jumped from such a great height, he brought the shining blade down into the water. He held it there, pointed towards the Chimera Lands, and the horde.

The impossible happened. Frothing water erupted around the blade, and it emitted the same hum as when he and Miala had touched the spear together. The tone that filled the air was loud, uncomfortably so. Then a massive, deep pulse came from the spear. As soon as the pulse went out, the sound ceased and the unbearably bright light faded.

A tidal wave formed in the wake of the pulse, which kept building and growing as it headed across the river. It seemed to collect every last drop of water on its journey. The wave pulsed and pushed as it expanded with a growing roar towards the other side. The receding water exposed the undead who had already entered the river and made it more than halfway across – leaving their limbs trapped ankle deep in mud and muck. They were frozen in place as the growing wave continued across to the other side. More and more of the river bed was revealed, and the air was filled with a familiar scent.

All of the undead within the depths of the river had been turned completely into salt.

They were statues, white and unmoving, stopped in their tracks by the power of Adonai.

A great cheer erupted from behind Leon as the water began to flow back into the dry riverbed that had been left in the tidal wave's wake.

The salt outlines of nightmarish undead figures were toppled over, and washed away in the current of the returning river.

A draconic roar that shook the air and vibrated the trees across the river echoed, as the maimed Nachash Seraph lost his temper again. More undead rushed into the returning current, and a trumpet blast of a voice resounded. "KILL THEM ALL! BRING ME THE JUDGE'SSS HEAD!"

"I think you made him angry!" Hollered an amused Commander Thorne.

"Well, I do have that effect on people!" Leon quipped back.

"So it seems… OPEN FIRE!"

The low water level appeared to slow the advance of the undead enough to allow a cloud of arrows to rain down upon them. Bodies jerked and fell as arrows of all sizes peppered them. Leon walked back to the lines of warriors, and stood next to Duamé and Commander Thorne – who seemed to have warmed up to Leon. He, along with several other elves, clapped him on the back with appreciation. Their levity proved to be short-lived as the undead horde that broke through the opposite tree line changed.

Their new foes were fast moving. A few strides was all it took the decomposing undead centaurs before they splashed into the shallow water, and advanced towards the elven line. Some held long, lance-like pikes, while others held bows and arrows of their own. More than a few of the undead creatures carried wretches on their backs who were armed with their own bows and arrows.

Elven arrows, which had flown only in one direction, began to be interspersed with a few arrows directed back at them. The undead started to truly retaliate.

Leon was filled with dread as he realized the tactical brilliance of Nachash Seraph. By firing at the slow-moving undead as they crossed the river, the archers had revealed their defensive positions. He had used them as bait, then sent the centaurs across the river to attack – knowing exactly where to aim their arrows. Still, the occasional undead arrow didn't prevent the elves from picking wretches off of the centaur backs, or from impaling their heads and joints.

A couple of red-eyed centaurs successfully galloped to the elven side of the river, though both had multiple arrows sticking out of them. They carried long lances which were pointed straight towards Leon. These undead advanced intending to impale and take him down.

Leon had trained with Lochmetel in dreams and visions for what seemed like hours. Though he had practiced while awake for weeks in Agaprya, this was a situation that was unfamiliar to him.

Though unfamiliar, it was something he was ready for.

Running forward, ahead of the line of elves, Leon knocked one lance aside and lacerated an undead centaur's leg, which caused it to fall off. A quick well-placed stab ended its existence as he turned to see the other centaur's head had disappeared. A smoking stump was all that remained as Miala held her new wand out and looked at it in amazement.

Other enemy forces moved across the river and slowly gained ground. The rising water level began to obscure some of the smaller foes that traversed its bed, and arrows continued to fly back and forth. Creatures with oversized wings and the intermingled features of bird and lion burst through the canopy of the chimera land's trees. These beings wheeled about in the air before setting their sights on the elven side of the river.

"Gryphons!" Commander Thorne shouted.

As the gryphons flew rapidly towards them, the archers' attention became divided. A few were felled, but many maneuvered away from the piercing arrows. Miala joined the archers, and her well aimed lances of white fire blasted holes in wings and torsos. The aerial assault drew away arrow fire which had originally been aimed at the river. This allowed the undead, both chimera and not, to successfully reach the elven side of the bank more frequently.

The line of elven ground forces began to move in order to meet the undead advance, and a general melee erupted. Vyn, carrying his two handed broadsword, rushed forward to hack down a kilted wretch who was armed with a short sword. Qas was still in the tree with the princess, and directing arrow fire toward the gryphons that had reached them. Even Kelleren was engaged in the battle. He pounced on a gnomish skeleton and broke it apart. A fast moving shambler was about to skewer him, until Duamé jumped in. He shattered the sword arm of the undead with one hammer and knocked its head off with another. Over the din of battle cries, and shouts from the elves, Leon heard the dwarf yell, "Git away from me dog!"

The chaos of battle continued as the undead poured over from both the river and the sky. The smell of undead putrescence was terrible. It mixed with the smell of sweat and grime, which caused Leon to struggle to keep his stomach under control. The chilling silence of the undead hoard was also disturbing to him. The screams, yells, and shouts of fervor and pain all came from the living – while the undead fought and perished in silence.

After turning another centaur to salt, Leon noticed that the elves who were in the trees ran along their branches, and back towards the general melee. The gryphons and arrows that flew at them had become too much to handle. Quite a few of the elven defenders could be seen unmoving within the trees. They had been maimed by their kinsmen in order to prevent their undead rise. Elves who fought on the ground seemed to hold their own a bit better due to the bottleneck created by the tall trees. While it still allowed a wide enough space for the line of defenders to fight, those who tired were able to switch places with others behind them. The elves that died, or received fatal wounds, were permanently dispatched by their fellows. Once their gruesome task was completed, the dispatching elves began their own assault on the undead force in front of them.

A wall of unmoving bodies was beginning to form from the corpses whose red eyes were no longer lit. The undead clambered over their fallen fellows; uncaring, and mindlessly driven to end the living. This caused Leon and the elven force to move slowly backward. They ceded ground to prevent the dead from being able to reach the tree branches around them and clamber towards the elven archers. During their slight withdrawal a large boulder sailed through the air towards them, which caused the elves to cry out in alarm and run. Some couldn't escape and were killed instantly, while others, who were not as lucky, were crushed as it rolled over them.

Leon barely heard as Princess Schalae screamed at them, "Giant! Retreat! Elves, to the forest! Back to the Grove!"

Leon cut down a wretch and then jumped up onto a high branch near the Princess. As he landed in the tree Schalae steadied him, and he looked at what she had alerted their defenses to.

The mass of undead still crossed the river. While the water had resumed its normal depth, an enormous, terrifying giant now walked across. Covered in intricate bronze armor, one of its hands carried a spear that must have been crafted from an entire tree. Its other hand had thrown the boulder that pulverized some of the elves. As it climbed up the embankment from the river, a wickedly curved sword could be seen at his back. Leon could also see more of the large lumbering shapes as they moved through the trees on the far side of the river.. More giants were approaching the battle. This one was close enough to see that its height was comparable to that of four men who stood on each other's shoulders. It had a bright orange-red mane of hair, a misshapen head, and large baleful eyes that were narrowed in concentration.

Its eyes were normal! No red light shone from them!

Something was very, very wrong here.

Lochemetel voiced her concern. ***"This Nephilim changes everything. You must pull back!"***

The Nephilim?

The last time he heard that term was when he saw Lochemetel battling a large, winged, shadowy beast in a vision. *Why would she use the same name now?*

Confusion mingled with the fog of war inside of Leon, as cries of alarm and despair echoed and faded into the forest. Groups of elves ran into the labyrinth and split apart onto different paths. They were followed by elves who ran along the treetops and branches, and fired upon the enemy with precision and grace. The undead horde followed behind them all.

Leon motioned to Schalae, and pointed out Duamé and Kelleren as they ran past below. The Princess waited until Qas fired her nocked arrow, then tapped her on the arm. They all jumped down near the dog and the dwarf, who reflexively swung his hammer at Leon due to the sudden movement. It clanged off a plate pauldron, and Leon exclaimed, "Hey!" before a flood of undead rushed around a leafy corner.

Shamblers and wretches were led by a fast-moving blur. They approached as Duamé yelled, "Sorry 'bout that!"

The kilted blur raced ahead of the other undead, and a raspy voice echoed in the corridor of the maze, *"Drop your weapons! Stand still! Let us kill you!"*

An alukah. Whether it was due to confidence, or annoyance at the mystery around the Nephilim, Leon didn't hesitate to rush and meet the creature with the Revelator. A sharp crack of wood sounded behind him, and Lochemetel voiced a suggestion in his head. When the alukah saw that its command hadn't worked, it snarled and brandished a deeply curved sickle. They ran at each other, and once the undead alukah was close enough, Leon shifted his hands back on the spear. He quickly lowered it to let his fast opponent trip itself over the blade.

Leon smirked as the alukah's feet disappeared with a flash. Once again, he got the satisfaction of punching an alukah in the face, as its momentum carried it forward. It flopped onto the ground with a scream and Leon exclaimed, "The light shines through your lies!" As he stabbed it in the head.

The other undead rushed up, and were met by Duamé, Schalae, Qas, and Kelleren. The princess had divided her Broken Bough, and the two curved wooden swords were as sharp as any blade that Leon had ever seen. Mail, leather, and dead flesh were all divided from her cutting blows. Qas and Schalae were both whirling dervishes.

Separating limbs and heads, they moved with their entire bodies and danced around sword thrusts and blows.

"Where is Vyn?" Schalae yelled as she attacked.

"I don't know. Where is Miala?" Leon responded.

Kelleren darted in between his feet and barked repeatedly. He seemed to have devised his own strategy, and went after the more skeletal undead creatures. The dog could easily separate bones that were held together by the thin threads of necrotic magic. The undead would become unbalanced and collapse, while Kelleren would growl and bite down on their bony necks. With one sharp jerk, the red glow from their eye sockets would wink out. Then he would repeat the process with his next bony opponent.

The fighting intensified as Kelleren kept barking. The unending tide of undead, both armed and not, pushed against Leon and the others as they retreated further back. The wall of trees and branches that were near them suddenly began to smoke and split open, which caused the adjacent trees to recoil.

Miala stepped through the new opening.

Her arms were both aflame, and wide arcs of fire burst forth from them. She walked amongst the undead, incinerating them and melting any weapons brought against her. Her dance, unlike the elves, was more brutal – more focused. Short blasts of fire dropped any undead that came against her. Once she charred those in her immediate vicinity, she turned and let loose a thin line of pure white fire from her new wand. It bisected torsos and limbs as it tore through the undead with its incinerating heat. The undead that hadn't been finished off were left to crawl across the ground, and easily dispatched.

Miala extinguished herself, and the red runic glow from her robe and chainmail faded. She breathed heavily as she ruffled Kelleren's fur and consoled him. Princess Schalae surveyed the smoldering remains and her eyes flicked back to the tree that had smoked at the pyromancer's entrance. A dark expression fell over her face as she looked at Miala, before she closed her eyes and breathed deeply.

"Thank you." She said. It looked as though she struggled to believe her own words.

"Is everyone alright?" Miala asked.

"We are still missing Vyn…" Schalae began. Qas silently pointed back in the direction they had come from as Vyn rounded a distant corner. He cut down two shamblers who were behind him with a flourish of his large blade, then continued to run towards their party. He smiled and gave a thumbs up, glad to have found them.

The ground rumbled as the giant they had seen before entered the maze behind Vyn. It too wore a kilt, like many of the undead they were fighting, and its gleaming bronze armor was now stained with red sprays of blood. The giant grinned wide with bloodlust as it laughed and ran towards them along the narrow corridor. Leon saw two disgusting rows of pointed teeth that filled its mouth. It hefted the large spear it carried, and licked its lips as it lunged forward. The bronze head of the weapon impaled Vyn from behind. A look of shock registered on his face as he was stopped in his tracks.

Qas fell to her knees, horrified, and the first sound Leon ever heard from her was a scream.

Princess Schalae yelled out as well, but her's was one of rage. Then she ran towards the laughing giant with her two wooden swords. The rest of their group hurried to support her. The giant dropped its spear, which still impaled their dead friend, to the ground. Reaching back, it drew its own two-handed bronze sword from its scabbard. As tall as a man, the blade boasted a sharp curve which looked like half of a circle, before it tapered to a point. The air audibly whooshed as the giant swung its sword in wide arcs and welcomed them into its range.

Princess Schalae leaped over a low horizontal slice, and as she landed she brought both of her swords against his arm. They clanged harmlessly off his wrist bracer. The giant retaliated by kicking her into a wall of greenery as the rest of them began to engage him. Duamé and Miala attacked from the edge of the maze wall on one side, while Leon went along the opposite edge, hoping to get close enough to attack. The giant laughed again as it chopped downward at Leon, completely ignoring the blows from Duamé's hammer against its shin armor. Even the bursts of flame Miala launched against his armor appeared to accomplish nothing. The spider-web script engraved in the bronze armor glowed with each fiery attack, just like the runes on Miala's cloak. Somehow the giant had come to possess enchanted armor, and a frustrated panic splayed across Miala's face.

Leon barely managed to avoid the deadly chops that kept coming at him. There was just no use, this giant was too well armored, and its strength and reach was too great. Its legs were as big as tree trunks, and the giant's midsection far out of reach. Even with the Revelator's extended range Leon couldn't make contact with it unless he was right under him. All of his concentration was spent avoiding the giant's wicked slices. He feared that blocking the heavy blade with Revelator would compromise its integrity, which left him to dodge, duck, and leap over the maniacal attacks of the laughing nephilim.

The laughing stopped as a loud agonized cry echoed through the straightaway of the maze. After his latest escape from the giant's sword, Leon saw the hulking figure stagger around the tight space. Dangling from one of his legs was Kelleren. The dog had gone unnoticed, and had crept behind the giant, to leap up and bite down on the backside of its leg. The dog had latched onto an unarmored section of flesh, and was fiercely clamped down on the giant's hamstring. Struggling to successfully turn in the small area, the giant found itself unable to twist around in his bulky armor and reach the dog attached to him.

Eventually the muscle in the injured leg couldn't support the giant's massive weight, and he fell to a knee as Kelleren jumped away. The giant was no longer laughing, but screamed in pain and anger with a look of murder in its eyes. It hefted the huge sword and was about to bring it down on them, when it became caught in a bundle of tree branches that hadn't been there before. Vines exploded from the branches and wrapped around both the sword, and the giant's hands. Other vines and roots snaked up and tangled around its feet and ankles, causing it to struggle against the binding greenery. Every thready brown cord it managed to snap was replaced by two more, constricting the giant as they multiplied.

Princess Schalae emerged from the forest wall she had been thrown into, one hand still held to the tree that the vines had grown from. They now wrapped around the giant's neck, and she mirrored the snarl the giant wore back at him. Elven blood, a color reminiscent of tree sap, oozed down her cheek as she growled, "My mother and I cannot hold him for long!"

Leon saw an arrow suddenly sprout from one of its eyes, which caused him to glance back. He saw Qas holding a bow with her face set in determination. She looked at Leon, gestured to Revelator, and nodded. As he turned back to the giant, Leon ran up and pierced the midsection of the creature.

Every time that Leon had struck one of Xhormas' creatures with Revelator's blade, to include the dragon from the airship and the fierce Nachash Seraph, it had turned the wound to salt. For a living being, salt in an open wound was agonizing. However, that wasn't the only thing the spear could do. When the alukah, Rhoxmas, had grabbed hold of the spear's shaft, it emitted a tone and turned that undead's hands to ash.

This giant chose to align itself with the undead army while still alive. It enjoyed the pain that it inflicted on those it deemed as lesser than itself. Leon clearly remembered the first vision Rohiel had shown him. Giants thought all other beings were beneath them. They were truly evil creatures.

Which is why Leon sincerely believed that Revelator reacted as it did. The now familiar sound emanated from the spear once again, and began to turn the surrounding flesh to salt. The symbols and sigils that spanned the giant's armor blackened as the armor itself disintegrated into ash. The huge giant twitched in place as it quickly dissolved into a pile of salt and ash. All the while the tone pulsed and reverberated through its body. Soon the sound faded, and the only evidence that remained of their evil foe was the mound of particulates that hadn't flaked away in the wind.

"Wot tha shale was that?" Duamé breathed, as they stared at the pile.

Qas and Princess Schalae both knelt next to Vyn, the silent partner they had spent so much time with. Amber tears flowed down Qas' cheeks as she cradled his face with a look of awe. The princess seemed to realize the same unspoken truth at that moment, and turned to Leon wide-eyed.

Vyn hadn't turned to undead.

"Judgement." Leon finally responded to Duamé.

After Qas carefully cradled Vyn's sword, they followed the princess through the twists and turns of the maze. They could still hear fighting in the distance, and Schalae informed them that Queen Chlorae was concentrating on walling off the undead army from the survivors. The Queen's order, that everyone make their way back to the Grove, stood.

Leon felt the eyes of the others on him as they hurried, exhausted as they were, through the maze. There were so many unanswered questions about Revelator, the giant, and the term 'Nephilim' – which seemed to address two completely different creatures.

He asked Lochemetel with a whisper, and she replied, ***"They are one and the same."***

Leon was tired of being kept in the dark, and slowed his pace so he could walk behind the group. Muttering aloud, he asked, "What do you mean?"

"It is a difficult concept to understand." She began, before Leon grew even more irritated.

"Please try." He said through gritted teeth.

"You are a being of three parts. Body, soul, and spirit."

Sounds simple enough to me, Leon thought. "And?"

"Your body is like the earth. Formed from it. The same materials. It houses your soul. Your blood. Your life."

"Um, ok?" Leon stated, a little more confused.

"Adonai chose to make people in His image. His Spirit. That is the eternal part of you. The part that will forever be with Him if you accept Him and follow Him."

Leon tried to understand and connect the dots together. "And if not, you become undead?"

"No. If you do not accept Adonai, and follow His ways for you, then you have made the decision to separate from Him. Away from Adonai's original purpose for you."

"What does that have to do with the giants? Or the Nephilim?" Leon asked a little louder. Kelleren's ears twitched and a few odd glances were cast his way.

"The Fallen intermixed with your people, remember? The giants, the Nephilim, are their children. Their progeny."

What?

This was starting to sound crazy to Leon. How could that even be possible? Yet the Fallen had rebelled against Adonai. If the people who had been created by Adonai could be destroyed or corrupted, then tactically it would be the equivalent of destroying an enemy's supply of resources in a war.

"You are learning. The Nephilim, the giants, are body, soul, and spirit as well. Their bodies are like the one that you and your friends have slain."

That was the toughest fight, and closest brush with death, that Leon and his friends had encountered thus far. Granted, that was also the biggest giant Leon had ever seen. There were a few other smaller ones, but still…

"The soul of the giant is wicked. Bent on evil. On rebellion. Their spirit however –"

Leon remembered the vision of Lochemetel battling the large shadowy figure outside Rhise Manor.

"The Fallen cannot go back to Adonai, most are imprisoned. The Nephilim who also choose to rebel are much the same, and their

spirits remain after their bodies and souls perish. They continue their war, persecuting the living."

Realization struck Leon as he narrowly avoided walking into a tree. He reoriented himself, and kept following the others. "They are like the Mazzikin."

"Only much more dangerous. They are trapped, with nowhere else to go. Living eternally, with a wealth of knowledge from their Fallen forefathers. They do not whisper influence to you, they try to possess. To take. Dominate. Demonize."

"They can control people?" Leon asked, shocked.

"Yes." Lochemetel replied.

"Do… Do I know anyone like that?" He asked, thinking of his father.

"Why do you ask questions, to which you already know the answers?"

Rust. Leon thought, taking a page from Duamé's book. "Can their influence be broken?"

"Yes."

Irritation flared again. "Anything else of vital importance that you are keeping from me?"

"Yes."

Taken aback by Lochemetel's honesty, Leon spluttered, "W–well? Tell me!"

"No."

"Why not?" He asked with frustration.

"Because you are not ready yet. You would make the wrong choices, and you would die."

"Isn't that my choice to make though?" Leon seethed.

"Your choices affect more than just you. You will learn when you must."

Lochemetel didn't respond to any more of Leon's probing after that, which left him to stew over the revelation that had been given to him.

After a few more fast paced hours, and the elimination of more than a handful of undead gryphons which flew overhead, Princess Schalae led their tired troupe through a quickly made opening and back into the Grove.

Inside the Grove, there was chaos.

Act Two: The Heretic

No weapon forged against you will prevail, and you will refute every tongue that accuses you. This is the heritage of the servants of the Lord, and this is their vindication from me," declares the Lord. - Isaiah 54:17 NIV

Chapter 9: The Sacrifice

Elves ran around in a hurried blur of browns and greens of all hues. Leon saw children, who were barely taller than Gionna, running around with quivers of arrows for the older, armored elves. Hundreds of elves walked and patrolled the wooden battlements that surrounded the Grove. A sense of desperation filled the air as occasional groups of elven survivors filtered through the protective wall from the river battle. Amber blood and wounds were visible on most of the worn out warriors.

An elf in dark wooden armor hurried towards their group, and it took Leon a moment to realize that it was Commander Thorne. An ugly gash ran down one side of his face, and his corresponding eye was missing. A thin bandage, made of a long leaf, covered most of the injury. Although the wound was a grievous one, Thorne didn't display any outward signs of pain.

"You're all alive!" He exclaimed.

"What is the situation? How is mother?" Princess Schalae asked with urgency.

Thorne glanced towards the clearing where they had all met the night before. "She has strained herself too hard. We had to all but force her from the Mycelium. It took that brash gnome woman to berate her into submission. If her tongue was a sword it would be the sharpest in the Grove!"

"That sounds like Gærheart, make no mistake 'bout that!" Duamé admitted.

As they followed Schalae towards the clearing Commander Thorne asked, "Was Vyn not with you?"

Qas' steps faltered. She collapsed, and with silent sobs cradled Vyn's sword against her like a babe. Her reaction was all the answer the commander needed, and he hung his head with a sigh. Miala looked at Kelleren for a moment and nodded. With a quiet woof, the dog lagged behind and padded up to the grief stricken warrior elf on the ground. She kept crying as Kelleren shouldered up against her.

Leon turned back to follow the rest of his comrades, allowing the warrior some privacy in her time of grief. Many tired and weary warriors were gathered around the stone table. A bustle of activity surrounded them all, as those who weren't helping with the defenses rushed to quench the thirst of warriors with jugs of water and java. Even Leon was offered a cup of the dark liquid, which he gladly accepted. He savored the slightly bitter taste and let it rejuvenate his tired limbs.

"Where is mother? Where is the Queen?" Princess Schala demanded.

"I am here, dear child." Queen Clorae responded as she was escorted by Gionna into the meeting area. The two older women appeared to have formed a fast friendship. She was haggard in appearance and held onto Gionna for support with one hand, while her other held onto what must have been the fabled Mycelium.

The artifact looked like a hollow sphere formed from triangles. White threads that wove off the fist sized structure wafted slightly in the wind as the Queen held it in her grip. The Mycelium looked to be entirely made of those wafting white threads, which were constantly moving. They undulated all around and across the geometric shapes they formed.

"Are you alright mother?" Princess Schalae asked.

"I am concerned, my dear. I did the best that I could to protect us, but I fear it may all have been in vain. Commander Thorne, report."

"We have little less than half of our forces remaining. Fewer and fewer survivors have come back. Meanwhile, the undead are flooding through the maze. Soon, the Grove will be surrounded, and we will have to make our stand here."

"Yer as dense as dolomite if ya think ya should stay here, lad. Cut yer losses an' run!" Exclaimed Duamé.

Gionna rapped her cane on the stone table to get everyone's attention. "I agree with Mr. Onyxwill. The statistical likelihood of our survival is abysmally low, and the longer we remain the lower it becomes."

"Running is not an option! I will not abandon our trees!" Rebutted Commander Thorne.

"Why?" Blurted Leon.

Blank, unfriendly stares were his only reply until Leon continued, "Nachash Seraph said that you needed the trees. You cling to them, and it is obvious to anyone who's not an elf that there is somehow, in some unspoken way, a relationship there. So why do you feel the need to stay?"

Gionna waved a dismissive hand, "They won't answer you, dearie. I've lived for a long time, and no elf will share that secret."

Frustration boiled within Leon, "Well then, I suppose that secret can die with them!"

Young and old, warrior or not, almost every elf jeered and voiced their discontent with the Judge.

"How dare you!"

"Outrageous!"

The dark glares and voices continued until a voice from behind Leon said, "Because our longevity is tied to the trees."

Shocked gasps, and cries of more outrage echoed as he turned and saw Qas, with Kelleren by her side. She held Vyn's sword in both her hands and looked squarely at Leon as she continued. "Our lives are tied to the trees that we bond to, that we make covenant with. Without them, we age faster. Just as humans do."

Commander Thorne laid a hand on his sheathed sword, and with a venomous voice retorted, "How dare you speak? How dare you turn your back on your oath!"

The words from the commander seemed to pierce her heart just as if she had been struck by an arrow, but Qas remained steadfast. "My Vyn is dead. I care not for oaths anymore."

"Leave her alone!" Declared the princess. "Can you not see she is grieving?"

Then arguments broke out all around the table. Elves yelled at Qas, while other elves yelled at the Commander. Even the Princess and Commander were yelling at each other – all while the Queen rose to her feet and shook her head in exhaustion. Leon stood in the center of it all, his anger growing. He slammed the butt of Revelator on the ground. A wooden echo sounded from its force, and the tree branches above them moved, creaking as they bent and swayed.

"Enough!" He shouted.

"Your squabbling over trivial matters needs to end now! There's an army of undead almost at your gates, and yet all you wish to do is argue? Over a secret to long life? Would you rather live no life at all?"

"You don't know what you're talking about, human." Growled Thorne as he stepped closer.

Leon matched Commander Thorne's steps and replied, "I know enough to understand that you would ultimately sacrifice your lives just to be able to live longer than the rest of the world! I know that you are selfish and prideful, and that we will all die soon if you don't listen!"

"You want to live longer? Then get this through your head: you MUST leave the Grove, or you will ALL die in the Grove!" Leon finished.

Something strange happened. Branches from the old trees that surrounded them creaked even more, and the light of the afternoon sun shone like a beam directly onto Leon. It was as if the trees themselves moved their canopies to allow the light to reach him.

The elven anger gave way to awe. Even those who hurried to set up defenses, stopped and watched the bright light as it followed Leon while he awkwardly tried to shuffle sideways out of its radiance.

"The trees, which are wise enough to listen, have spoken. We must listen to the Judge." Queen Chlorae spoke with solemn resolve. "We must leave the Grove."

She turned and whispered instructions to a few attendant elves. Too shocked to disagree or dispute her instructions, they left. Commander Thorne just shook his head in dismay.

"This is madness! Where will we go? Hookvale? Agaprya?" He pointed an accusing finger at Leon and Miala both, who stood close together. "Where were the humans and your King Garinth to help us? I saw no airships come to our defense! What makes you think they would not just turn us away?"

Leon approached the commander, the light overhead tracking his every step. "Agaprya has taken refugees for years! Why wouldn't you go there for protection? They will need all the help and defense they can get to battle this horde!"

Gionna piped up, "Begging your pardon dearies, but even if we left the forest at this point, we would still need to sleep. Rest. The undead have no such need, and will overtake us. We will be overrun before we even have a chance to get anywhere."

"You see?" Commander Thorne snorted, "It would make no sense to flee. We must stay. We must fight."

Run, fight, or hide. Remembering the lesson that he had been taught in the naval academy, Leon had implemented that principle throughout his career. It had served him thus far, and he wouldn't stop using it now. "We cannot hide from the undead onslaught, and we have seen what fighting this horde would result in. That leaves running."

"But how would you stall the undead? And where would we even run to?" Thorne shouted, inches from Leon's face.

Duamé, who had remained mostly silent, blurted out, "Masterwork Halls would take ya!"

The din of elven arguments quieted, as those who were assembled turned to the dreadlocked dwarf. "If ya can get ta Masterwork, an' ask fer ‘sanctuary’, they are obligated ta take ya in. Even if ya didn’t want ta live under tha mountain, they got plenty o’ space above it fer ya!”

The Queen, who until then had been directing and instructing elves, turned to Duamé with a warm smile. “Are you sure Mr. Onyxwill? I am inclined to agree with Commander Thorne in my displeasure at Agaprya’s missing aid, but I would not dare to impose upon Masterwork Halls and its council.”

Duamé grunted and replied with his hands on his hips, “If me pa is still alright, he’s one o’ tha council members. I can get him ta talk to ya, an’ from there maybe an audience with tha council itself. Tha elves an’ everyone will hafta ask fer citizenship.”

Princess Schalae’s sunny disposition seemed frayed to the point of unraveling. Leon could see that the battles, recent losses, and responsibility weighed heavily on her. That was probably why her outburst towards Duamé held such vitriol. “Citizenship? CITIZENSHIP? We don’t need it! We will return to the forest once this is all over and take it back!”

“Masterwork Halls has been strained in its resources ever since…” Duamé cast a furtive glance at Leon, “Ever since about twenty years ago. Everyone who stays there is asked ta contribute. Ta be useful. It is as simple as gettin’ a majority vote from tha Nonagint ta stay. That was tha case a few years ago, so it coulda changed, but if not, then be prepared fer it.”

After a tense silence, the Queen nodded her head, “Then it is decided, I have already instructed some to start the process of evacuation. We leave for Masterwork Halls within the hour.”

“That still does not solve the issue of the undead pursuing us!” Princess Schalae replied.

The entire time the others had been talking, Leon had been mulling over an idea. It was a contemplation so horrible that he dreaded proposing it. However, as he saw no other option, he begrudgingly said, “I can only think of one way to delay the undead.”

Questions and inquisitive looks peppered him while he turned with a sorrowful look to Miala, who stood next to him.

Confusion shone through her eyes as she looked back at him. Then her eyes widened as she realized what his unspoken request was. "No. NO! You cannot ask this of me! Not this!"

Gionna Gærheart muttered, "Clever. Horrendous… But clever."

Queen Chlorae sighed as she shook her head, "They would die anyway, and their judgement has not changed."

Duamé was still confused, "Wot? Wot is it?"

Miala screamed at Leon, "I WILL NOT BURN THE FOREST DOWN!"

It took the quick action of Queen Chlorae to calm all of those who were assembled down. She took a few steps back then slammed the geometric Mycelium into the soft earth. A green flash erupted from her, which caused the angry yells from the elves around them to subside.

"I have invested my energy into connecting with the trees and preparing them for what is to come. I decree that Princess Schalae is to make all royal decisions while I am incapacitated. Listen to her, and listen to the Judge."

She turned her eyes to her daughter and continued, "My dear, I would not wish this decision on anyone, but it is necessary for you to do this. The trees understand. I understand. You must understand. You are our hope for survival. I ask you to do this for all the elves. Do not waste this opportunity."

With that, the already tired Queen collapsed as another burst of green energy was emitted from the Mycelium. In tears, Princess Schalae rushed to catch her as she fell. Commander Thorne proved quicker than she, and caught the Queen before she hit the ground. Schalae put a hand to her mother's head and concentrated, worry crossed her green eyebrows. "She's alive, but barely."

"What do we do now?" Commander Thorne asked.

"We follow my mother's orders." Princess Schalae replied. Heartbroken, she turned to a trembling and crying Miala. "Please. Those may have been my mother's last words."

Miala shut her eyes and turned her back to everyone's stares. Kelleren nuzzled against her, and she asked, “What do I have to do?”

The bustle of activity in the Grove began to change. Where before elves were helping to bolster defenses, now they helped to gather everything that they could carry. As there was no cut wood to be found, jars and pots were carried through the use of vines and leather straps by those who were not warriors.

Five of the elves that the queen had spoken to before she collapsed returned with two ornate pots. Three others presented bundles of various branches. All were presented with reverence to the princess. After looking, she nodded her approval and turned to Leon. She gave him a neutral stare, and explained, “These are the seeds the trees have given us to regrow a forest, as well as our last reserves of harvested magical elvenwood. I hope that this plan of yours is not in vain.”

Without waiting for a response, she walked away and joined Commander Thorne in a whispered conversation. The Commander, and his jovial attitude toward Leon, had changed since the meeting. He now looked at the Judge with an almost open hatred.

Other elves seem to have changed their opinions about Leon as well. Even those who had listened to him, and to his knowledge had accepted Adonai, now looked at him with doubt and concern.

Did I make the right choice? He asked himself. *Could I have suggested anything different?*

Lochemetel had been silent for a while, but her words to him now were poignant. ***“Sometimes, Judge Leon, there are no easy choices. Only the right ones.”***

The creaking of the trees increased as their branches seemed to recede and shrink. It appeared that the trees were drying out at an accelerated pace. Meanwhile, hundreds of elves with their children, babies, and supplies strapped to them gathered in the central part of the

Grove. The warriors who had survived surrounded them to protect them.

Princess Schalae and a few others gathered together with the Mycelium. Using it like her mother had, with the aid of elves who formed a chain with their arms and hands, she concentrated, and the trees and tree roots separated on the eastern facing side of the Grove wall. It seemed to lessen the strain on her when others helped, but still looked to be an exhaustive effort nonetheless.

A mass of mournful elves followed commander Thorne and Duamé out of the Grove, towards Masterwork Halls. As they hauled their meager possessions, they trekked forth with tears in their eyes. Small physical wounds could be seen on the warriors, but their emotional wounds appeared to be much larger. They knew that their lives would be cut short no matter what option they chose, so they obeyed their Queen with the hope that their exodus would allow them to survive longer.

The elves, the ones the Queen called Shapers, used their Hortimancy to continue their work. A mass of tree roots and branches emerged from the ground then curled, smoothed, and wound together, cupping a small portion of the earth. The formation was the size of a washtub, and was filled partway with dirt. Within minutes, the elves had created a makeshift toboggan, in which they laid their Queen, the three jugs of seeds, and the elvenwood bundles.

It was then that they stopped using the Mycelium, and the elves who had participated paused to catch their breath. The Princess refused to allow her exhaustion to stop her. She stood and attempted to tend to the wounded and those who could not travel unaided. She reached back for her medicinal bag and gasped at what she found. Leon saw that all of her vials and stoppers were shattered.

"What happened?" Asked Leon.

"They must have broken when I was thrown into the trees by the giant!" She moaned as she inspected the bag. The sharp shards of glass poked at odd angles while the liquids and other ingredients had combined into a sticky dark ball. It occasionally fizzed and bubbled as medicinal smelling vapors escaped from it.

Schalae sighed in disgust as she dropped the bag to the ground and looked over at an injured elven woman who had a dressing formed of leaves and petals draped across her shoulder. The woman's breathing was ragged, and she weakly reached for the Princess, rasping, "It's okay, your Majesty, I have given my life to this Adonai the Judge spoke of. I… I am not afraid of the end."

The Princess laid a comforting and clinical hand on the injured woman's shoulder and responded, "I… I know…" Glancing at Leon who stood at a respectful distance. "I did too."

The sun's last rays fell over the horizon, which caused Revelator's blade to flick on. The light from it fell on the two elves, but another small glow also shined.

From Princess Schalae's hand.

Everyone present gaped at what they witnessed, as the glow began to slowly fade. The princess slumped over from exhaustion, and Leon rushed to catch her. She said, "I just… I just wanted… to…"

The glow faded from the shoulder of the injured elf as well, and Qas gently removed the dressing to find that the ragged gash of a wound was gone. Unblemished pale brown skin lay in its place, a stark contrast to the dried amber blood on the rags that had been used to cover the wound.

"...heal her." Princess Schalae whispered in exhaustion.

✦✦✦✦✦

Schalae insisted that they put off any discussion of the miraculous healing until a later time when they were all safe.

The rustling of undead and the clinking of weapons and armor was soon close enough to hear from outside the Grove. The Princess recovered enough strength to stand, and after a little java, she and Qas joined Leon and Miala at the top of a forest wall to look back towards the river behind them.

A sea of glowing red eyes met their view. It didn't even appear as though the undead were done crossing the river in the distance. Small and large eyes that glowed, as well as dark outlines of large shapes, moved toward them without pause. They were uncountable.

Princess Schalae's lips moved as she peered at the undead horde, until she found her voice. “More giants... centaurs... I can even make out a few minotaurs. Fir trees, they must have killed almost the entirety of the Chimera Lands!”

With a sigh, she turned to Leon and Miala. “You were right. There is no way that we could have beaten them. We must hope that... that destroying the forest will drastically impede their progress.”

They gathered next to the Queen and Gionna, who had taken it upon herself to tend to the elderly elven leader. A few other elven warriors remained as an honor guard to the queen, and as Princess Schalae once again picked up the Mycelium, she turned to Miala.

“I will activate it and connect it to the forest. It will be up to you to send flame through the Mycelium. Then we will need to rejoin the others. Quickly.”

Miala, silent and solemn, nodded numbly.

“Everyone else, get moving! We will be along shortly.”

Miala glanced at Leon before looking away again, as Kelleren padded over to her and received an absentminded scratch behind the ears. The elves, which now included the miraculously healed elven warrior, took up the braided vines at the front of the toboggan that held the Queen and Gionna. Then they began to pull them smoothly along, following the rest of the elves who were led by Qas.

When it was just Schalae, Miala, Kelleren and Leon, the Princess activated the Mycelium by bringing it to the ground. As it worked to connect to the forest, she spoke, “When an elf dies, the tree they bonded to receives a portion of their soul. The bond, the covenant between them, remains and empowers the wood. This empowerment causes it to channel energy. It becomes elvenwood.”

Leon never knew the process of how elvenwood was created. To his knowledge, nobody outside of the elves knew. It was a process that was never explained, and when asked, the elves would clam up and leave the conversation. He didn't realize the sacrifice that was required; the death that had to occur to make such a powerful object. It didn't seem worth it.

Schalae continued, “When a tree dies before the elf, our bond with the tree is broken. It is like… losing a loved one, a close member of the family that you had chosen to adopt. The progression of time continues for us at a faster rate, and our long lives are cut to the same measure as you humans.”

“I do not know if we will be able to replant a forest with those seeds, but I do know that I could not have healed that woman without Adonai. He has gotten us this far. If this is His will, He can get us further. He can give us a new forest if He wishes to.”

A loud crack sounded and started to repeat from the Grove wall that led back to the river. The undead army had arrived and had begun their assault. After a few more tense moments, with amber tears openly flowing, the Princess nodded and said, “Now! Miss Miala Mytheriyn! Ignite the Mycelium, and then we run!”

Miala, with tears brimming in her own eyes, made a fist that burst into flame. “May Adonai forgive me.” She said, as she brought the bright flame down to the Mycelium.

The white artifact of living threads burst into flame, and the flame seemed to spread out in a circle from it. The two women stepped back and Schalae shouted, “Run! Run for your lives! It will grow quickly!”

They rushed to the exit, and Leon looked back to see that the flame had bloomed like a low, squat mushroom. It exploded in a violent burst, and rapidly churned outward. It fed itself as it consumed everything around it. The nearby trees caught alight and the flame viciously jumped from branch to branch, and tree to tree.

They ran, as they tried to escape the growing forest fire.

Leon saw Miala start to stagger and reached out a hand, only for her to slap it away. “I'll be fine. Go!” She replied with anger. Leon trusted her word, and turned to Kelleren who bound along next to them, “Look after her.”

"Woof." Came Kelleren's reply, as he ran a little closer to his companion.

They joined the caravan of elves who pulled the Queen along at the forest's edge. Those elves, in turn, hurried to catch up to the elves who had outpaced them. Gionna asked what had happened, and was promptly informed by Princess Schalae, who had also been allowed to join them in the toboggan. She tried to heal and awaken Queen Chlorae under the light of Revelator, but was quickly frustrated when it wouldn't work as before.

An hour later they caught up to the rest of the elven survivors, who looked back towards the Grove and surrounding forest that had been their home. Many tears flowed and quiet sobs could be heard as Leon turned back for the first time since they had left.

The entire forest was on fire. It spread across the edge of the horizon, as far as the eye could see. Gold and orange hues lit the night, and no red eyes appeared to be drawing nearer. Homes, bonded trees, magical elvenwood, and forest creatures both alive and undead succumbed to the flames. The short, mushroom-like beginnings of the fire had grown to be a mighty pillar. It seemed, for the moment, that they were safe.

Safe, at a steep cost.

Chapter 10: The Forgotten

It was a long walk and a hard day for everyone. Throughout the day random pockets of elves would start to sigh, or break down in tears. A word of comfort or consolation from either the Princess or Commander Thorne would lift them from their temporary misery, as they continued to move eastward.

Leon caught dark stares that were cast at both Miala and himself on more than one occasion. The pyromancer stayed close to him, but when Leon reached for her hand to provide unspoken support she evaded it. "Don't. Just… don't." She said somberly. She seemed to be battling her own depressive thoughts regarding her actions, and every time she turned around she was reminded of them afresh.

The forest continued to burn behind them, evidenced by a great pillar of smoke that rose to the sky. No undead seemed to follow them through the blaze, but Miala wore a haunted look whenever Leon glanced at her.

As they walked, groups of elves harvested edible plants and weeds from along the path and its surrounding area. It reminded Leon of another recent journey that he had made on foot, only that one had been with a prince instead of refugees. They stored the edible greenery in clay jars and containers, then walked back to the main body of elves that surrounded the sled which bore their unconscious queen.

This is where Prince Gelan got it from. Leon thought to himself. *The knowledge of survival on scarce resources. The elven Princess taught him.*

The Princess once again tried to miraculously heal injured elves, with varying success. Some who she tended to had minor cuts and burns, others had abscesses or infections. She insisted that Leon come along with the spear, and while some were healed, others were not and had to continue to limp along as best they could. To Schalae the successful healing seemed random. Leon, however, saw that those who received healing were the same elves that were preoccupied with asking him questions about Adonai. With the aid of Lochemetel's disembodied direction, Leon tried to help the injured believe that they were already healed, so it could manifest. He tried to help them see that with Adonai's power their healing could happen either in an instant or progressively, but that faith for it was the primary requirement.

Some of the elves who were injured, like Commander Thorne, spent their time complaining to Leon rather than focusing on his attempt to help. Discontentment at leaving their forest, or the injuries sustained, became the dominant topics of their conversation. It overshadowed any discussion of what poultice or bandage could help them at that moment.

When Princess Schalae wasn't helping her people, she remained close to her mother and fretted over her still form. Leon and the others also stayed close to the sled, and he overheard Schalae's whispered words to her mother.

"Please get better. I am not ready to be queen."

"You would be a good queen, dearie. You seem to care for your people well enough." Gionna said from her seat next to her.

"Fir trees, no! She was always much better at it than me. I have to constantly remind myself that my actions are always under scrutiny. That everything that I say or do is critiqued and watched for error. For my mother, doing the right thing just comes naturally."

“Why do ya care wot other people think ‘bout ya?” Duamé asked from nearby.

The Princess spoke with a sigh, “I truly do not. I simply know that I will one day become queen. If I do not live up to my mother’s standard… then… I would let her down.”

Duamé blew out a sigh as he shook his head, “Take it from me lass, I don’t think ya could let ‘er down if ya tried.”

A wan smile was the response he received from the elven royalty. A faint shout came from Commander Thorne at the head of the elven mass, which signaled a halt for lunch. Sighs escaped the mouths of many of the elves as the warriors set a perimeter up around their massive group. This gave them a much needed moment to rest. The sled came to a halt and the sojourners sat right where they had stopped to eat what rations they had. A somber silence, punctuated with an occasional sob, filled the air.

In the end, it was Kelleren who momentarily lifted everyone’s spirits. He traveled all throughout the camp, and unspokenly enlisted the help of the youngest walking elves. Toddling elves were followed by those who were only slightly older, and began to chase the yellow haired dog through and around those that were assembled. Kelleren dodged this way and that, juked, and intentionally slowed down in order to then put on a burst of speed ahead of the growing number of children who joined the game.

“I have a question,” Leon asked Schalae as he observed the elven people. “Why do all the children look similar, but the adult elves look drastically different from each other?”

Schalae watched the game with a smile as she answered. “They have not bonded to trees yet. When an elven child reaches their thirteenth spring, they can choose which tree to covenant with. Their characteristics further develop at that point.”

“Is that why ya look different from yer ma?” Duamé asked from nearby.

Schalae chuckled as she responded, “I took after my father and chose an evergreen tree.”

The children smiled and laughed as they enjoyed their game of chasing the dog. This in turn made their parents laugh, and soon the entire camp was watching the game of chase with delight. At one point Kelleren relented and allowed the littlest elf to catch him – which caused the camp to erupt in a cheer. It was this exaltation that finally stirred the Queen, who weakly asked, "What is all the joyous noise about?"

The princess jumped to attention upon hearing her mother speak, and with the help of Gionna started to fuss over the still weary Queen Chlorae. The elves around them also noticed Queen Chlorae's awakening, and another cheer erupted, which spread even more positivity throughout the elves. After feeding her mother, and explaining their current situation, Princess Schalae felt the reassuring touch of her mother's hand as she said quietly, "That is good. You… you have done well. Very well, dear child."

Commander Thorne strode up to them at that point, and visibly relaxed when he saw his queen awake and responsive. "Your Majesty, how are you?"

The Queen arched her brow as she quipped, "I'll grow back like a weed – hopefully a thistle. Does anyone have some java?"

The dark liquid was produced and as the Queen sipped on its soothing warmth, she beckoned over the one person who had remained silent throughout the exchange. "Please, come here."

Miala approached the lounging Queen with shaky, hesitant steps and a stony expression. Once she was close enough, Chlorae's hand shot out from the sled and grasped the pyromancer's wrist with surprising speed. Her other hand patted the top of Miala's in a motherly gesture.

"I cannot imagine what you must be feeling, but I am thankful for what you did. When you have to make a hard choice between losing some or losing all, it is easy to feel only like you lost. It is harder to know what you have won."

Miala burst into tears. Leon and the others felt slightly uncomfortable watching the brave mancer break down. Elves turned away or shifted uncomfortably, having no trees to hide in or behind. The consolation was short lived, as Queen Chlorae pulled her hand away and announced, "Let it be known that Miala has done no wrong to us elves! That she is a friend to us – to my daughter, and to me!"

The demeanor towards Miala seemed to change in almost an instant. Elves went from shunning her to displaying curiosity. From staying away from her, to coming close. She might as well have been an elf herself. The only one who didn't openly share in the enthusiasm was Commander Thorne, but he kept his opinion silent.

Soon afterwards, they broke camp and continued into the day. Their spirits were much higher after their lunchtime reprieve. Kelleren got several ear scratches and belly rubs for his earlier antics. After he returned to Miala's side everyone praised him for his initiative – especially after his companion explained. "He knew exactly what he was doing. He just wanted to spread happiness. Laughter is usually the best way to do that."

"What's it like when he talks to you?" Gionna asked from the sled.

Miala grew more excited than she had been for a while as she explained. "He doesn't talk necessarily, it's more like a voice that pops into my head with different suggestions. They are not complex sentences, so it's pretty easy to tell when it's him and his ideas."

Princess Schalae joined in the conversation as she walked alongside with her mother, who was finally up and now stretching her legs. "How did you find each other? Mancers who have companions do not bond with just any animal, do they?"

Miala and Kelleren shared a look, and it seemed to Leon that they were having their own mental conversation. After they appeared to reach an agreement, Miala explained. "I was in Hookvale for… a period of time. Unfortunately, some of the entertainment there can be quite… vile. He was part of a litter that had been bred for dogfighting."

Various reactions of revulsion came from those who were close by and heard her. Kelleren leaned into Miala as she absently scratched his head. “He refused to fight. He didn’t want to hurt others. So he got hurt instead. At the time, I was passing by and… stopped it.”

“Ugh. A horrid thing to do to an animal.” Princess Schalae affirmed.

“The dogfighting ring happened to be close to the lake. I caught the ringmaster attempting to throw Kelleren into the lake alive. I emphatically convinced him not to.” She explained. “Kelleren spoke to me the next day. I never thought I would get a companion out of the whole experience.”

Her explanation brought a flash of insight as a painful memory resurfaced for Leon.

A month ago…

Sorrow. Guilt. Regret.

It’s all my fault.

Leon had wandered the streets for a few days after Admiral Silverspine released him. Overwhelmed by emotion, Leon waited until the hunger was unbearable before he ate, and his throat a dry husk before he drank. His self imposed penance consumed all of his thoughts until he could only sit in doorways, benches, and alleys – paralyzed by his misery.

Unkempt hair and beard had grown over the passing days, until one day he stared into a stagnant puddle and couldn’t even recognize himself. He had been bathing with the occasional rainfall, or open water barrel, and soon learned that life on the streets was uniquely challenging.

Opening the ‘severance pay’ that the admiral had given him, Leon discovered no copper crows at all, but mostly golden eagles and silver sparrows!

What kind of sick logic was this? Why should I have this kind of money after what I did? What I was miserably forced to do?

He considered throwing it away when he heard a raucous laughter coming from nearby. Looking up from his thoughts, he saw the glow of a tavern. More laughter came from inside and promised to be a temporary balm to his pain. Slowly, he moved towards the doors.

Hours later, brain in a fog, Leon burst from those same doors, his vision swimming and dizzy. He barely made it to a side alley before he retched into the small gutter on the side of the street. Collapsing due to muscle weakness, Leon blacked out. He was awakened in the same spot, by being poked and prodded.

"What's all this then?" A high pitched voice asked.

Leon looked up with blurry vision, and saw a small soldier who was jabbing him with the blunt end of his javelin.

"Oi! Ya drunk idiot! Git up an' outta 'ere!"

Through his pounding headache, he saw the blue tabard of the soldier was marked with Last Bastion's tower. It hung loosely over the prodding goblin's frame, who seemed to be the headache of his human counterpart.

"Sir, do you have any residence we can escort you to?" Asked the annoyed sounding guard who accompanied the goblin.

"N-no." Leon stammered. His throat felt awful and his breath was rancid.

"See, boss? He's a lout! A vagrant! He should throw hisself in th' lake!" The goblin yelled. His oversized head tilted slightly and he smiled a toothy, chilling grin.

The human guard's reaction was more tempered. "What? No! That's just… No!" He positioned himself in front of the goblin, still keeping a respectful distance from Leon. "Sorry sir. Field day for trainees out of the War College. Bazescraw here has plenty of… gumption."

The guard and Leon looked at the goblin trainee, who was currently using the javelin's pointy end to pick between his teeth. The goblin noticed their stares and pointed the sharp point of the javelin towards Leon this time. "It's a fine fer 'public int...intocka…'"

The unnamed guard tried to help, "Intoxication."

The older man proved to not need any help.

The leader of the gang was about to swing his knife down, when the robed man brought his skinny limb, armed with a fist, into the leader's eye. He then spun and connected his heel directly into another youth who was rushing at him with a club. He managed to somehow avoid a few blades aimed in his direction, before continuing to defend himself with fists and feet rather than weapons.

Even more impressive was the way he managed to just barely avoid each weapon as he retaliated. His blows landed in just the right places to knock down the gang members and render them unconscious. Elbows and knees flew as the old man bounced around eight people who were less than half his age. Not one person hit him. No one could touch him as he proved to be a step ahead of them every time.

Groans escaped from those who still were conscious until the old man put them to sleep with a strike. Leon was frozen to his spot, awestruck at the sight. The sheer folly of it defied all logic. All he could do was watch as the man tugged his sleeves back down, put his hood up, and began to walk away.

Then he stopped, turned, and looked right at Leon.

"Come forth, young man."

Leon came out from behind the pillar and shouldered his backpack. Feeling shameful for not helping the man, he slowly stepped towards him.

"Do not be afraid." The man encouraged, beckoning him forward.

When Leon was only a few strides away, the old man held up a hand to stop him.

"I am Calvin, and you are?"

Leon hesitated then started to speak, before Calvin interrupted him.

"Nice to meet you, Leon."

What? How did he...

"Oh, I did it again, didn't I? I can see it on your face. Please, pardon my interruption. Still working on patience. It's a life-long effort. You look like you have had a rough time lately. Well then, let's go get something to eat!"

Leon was thoroughly confused. "Uh, but I–"

"Are you hungry?" Calvin asked as he walked away.

Leon followed, noting that even the old man's gait was odd. One minute Calvin walked with purpose towards an undisclosed location, and the next he would pause, or walk with uncertainty, as if he wanted to go in two directions at once. It would have been comical if Leon hadn't still felt remorse and cowardice for not helping the old man fend off his attackers. The remorse bridged over to other recent events, which caused Leon's thoughts to spiral, and him to bump into Calvin's outstretched hand.

"Would you please stop your incessant whining? At least until we get there?" The man asked.

"I… I didn't even say anything!" Leon objected.

"Yes you did! At least three times now! It is not a reason to throw yourself into the lake, now is it?"

Mouth hanging ajar, Leon wondered if this individual was some sort of mind reader.

"No sonny, that would be a lot easier on the ol' noggin." Calvin emphasized by flicking his temple. "Come on, we could have already been there by now!"

They soon came to a small market stall where Calvin purchased two folded up pieces of bread, stuffed with meat and vegetables. Leon had never been here, and found it to be quite delicious. The robed man devoured his quickly, then requested another. Leon followed Calvin, fascinated by the man as they walked and ate.

Leon waited until Calvin took a bite of his second helping before asking, "So, are you some sort of mancer then?" He was relieved that he was able to get a full question out.

"Sonny, one day, when you possibly get to be as old as I am, I hope you have the privilege of speaking to a young buck, less than half your age, who is so ignorant that they ask inane questions with obvious answers."

"Wh–"

"Yes. And no, I don't want to elaborate, because I rarely leave my tower. I don't interact well with people. I have a hard time… sorting it all out. Most of the time I am just meditating you see. Trying to see more. How the strings connect and intertwine. How fragile it all is."

Leon wanted to state that he didn't understand at all, but a mischievous smile from Calvin gave Leon a feeling that the old man already knew.

"Well, then why were you there at the docks?"

"Ah. Well, you see, my latest meditation brought me to a series of events that are centered around one particular source. Before I go back to my tower and meditate further, I need to make sure that source heads in the right direction, you see. Otherwise it could prove quite disastrous. All the strings would break." Calvin seemed to enjoy being cryptic as he took another bite out of his meal. Leon started to speak before the old man interrupted him once again.

"Why would you ask that?" Calvin asked.

"Uh, what?"

"Why woul– oh, causality. You see? It's that easy to fall off course. Wait a moment, let me think."

With that, Calvin grabbed Leon's shoulder and closed his eyes. For a full minute the strange old man just stood there. Then, after mumbling to himself he spoke in a louder voice.

"Well, there's only one choice right now. I don't like it. You definitely won't like it. When you do finally remember, just know that it was necessary, Leon. Hopefully, we will meet again soon. Until then–"

Before Leon could process the man's confusing words, Calvin's leg swept behind Leon's knees, causing his legs to collapse. A pinch behind Leon's neck controlled his fall somewhat, until his kneecaps hit the cobblestone painfully. "Hey–" was all Leon was able to say before Calvin's other hand slapped against Leon's forehead, covering his eyes.

Feeling the breath of the old man against the side of his head, the last thing Leon heard before he blacked out was Calvin's voice in his ear.

"Go home, Leon. You need to go home."

Leon awoke with his head pounding and feeling quite disoriented. It pounded even more when something hard pressed against it.

"Ow!" He exclaimed.

"Oooh! You again! Didn't learn yer lesson the first time eh? Gonna fine ya more now!" An entirely too high pitched, but familiar, voice said.

Leon opened his eyes again to find the goblin, Bazescraw, once again poking him with his javelin. The human guard was there too, but this time he looked none too pleased with Leon instead of his companion.

"Sir, we told you once before sleeping in alleyways is no place to be. If you got in a fight with the wife–"

Leon waved them both off, knocking the blunt end of Basescraw's weapon aside in the process. "I'm… I'm not married. Sorry. It… it won't happen again."

The human guard helped Leon get up as Bazescraw stated, "That'll be three silver this time, or if ya like, ya can spend the time in the cell to sober up."

Sober up? Leon thought. *I don't remember drinking.*

In fact, Leon didn't remember much of anything. The last memory he had of the subject was a resolution to not to ever drink again. Other than that, Leon had the vague recollection of being in the wharf area before feeling the strong urge to go home to Rhise manor.

He paid the goblin, who eagerly took the coins and transferred them into his own pouch under the now ground-stained tabard. The human guard sighed before he asked, "Seriously sir, is there a home for you to go to? Perhaps we can take you to the shelter, or if you join up with the guard there is always a hot meal and a roof over your head."

Leon's thoughts focused only on one word the guard said. The rest were lost amongst the sea of confusion that the still groggy Leon swam through. "Home? I… I can go home."

Could I go home? It's been five years! He thought. There had been no communication from Rhise manor, or any letters of correspondence, in that entire time. *Would my family even recognize me? Would things change between father and myself?*

Worry poured over Leon as Bazescraw stepped on his foot. "Ow!" He yelped.

"Officer Smythe is talking to ya! Show some respect!" The goblin howled.

The human, Leon now knew to be called Smythe, was indeed talking through his introspection. "Sorry, trying to remember… which district I am in right now." He lamely explained.

The guards looked at each other, thin lips showed their skepticism. "You're in the Market District, close to the southern gate. Now go home sir, or we will toss you in lockup the next time we see you!" Smythe warned.

"Yeah, or the lake!" Bazescraw added.

"No Bazescraw, we never do that." Sighed Smythe patiently.

"Tch. Fine." Bazescraw the goblin then snapped at Leon, "Move along sir. Nothing to see here!"

Leon, dazed and confused, followed their instructions and thought that if nothing else, the four day journey to Rhise Manor would allow him plenty of time to rehearse what he was going to say to everyone when he saw them.

Present Day…

Awestruck at the memory that unlocked from its haze, Leon remembered the odd mancer for the first time since he had met him. Whatever Calvin had done to Leon, it had worn off. What remained now was a memory that prompted more questions about his past and what the old man meant. Their conversation, and what Calvin had done, had clearly set Leon on his path back home. Home… Where his whole world had been turned upside down.

The conversation around him continued, as Leon's companions intently watched the Queen inspect something small. "It is indeed from an elder tree. Older than mine if I dare guess. It's enchantment is all but faded, but even I cannot discern what it does. I can tell you it is not 'cursed' like you originally thought." She said, as she handed the ring they had carried since their battle with Rhoxmas back to Duamé.

"Ya know, I've just about had it with this." The dwarf grumbled. He then put the tip of his left leather glove in his teeth, pulled it off, and flexed his fingers.

"What, you're putting it on?" Leon asked.

"Oi, look who decided ta join tha conversation! Yes I'm puttin it on." Duamé stated, gesturing grandly as he pointed to those around him. "Ya have yer saltshakin' nightlight. Miala has her wand… thingy. Miss Gærheart has her contraptions. An' lest ya forget, I'm down one hammer. So, yeah boyo, I'm wearin' this."

With that, Duamé slipped the triple braided ring on his finger. A small static pop from the ring to his finger gave a telltale sign that the magic of the item took hold. Those assembled looked expectantly at the dwarf. Duamé looked expectant as well, then after a few moments… nothing happened.

"Do you feel any different?" Leon asked, as he tried desperately not to smile.

"No."

Gionna tried to be helpful, "Maybe you have to concentrate, dearie. Close your eyes and think about the ring."

After a few more minutes, with his broad bushy brows furrowed tightly, Duamé grunted in frustration and pulled on his leather glove over his hand and the ring. "Flint an' feldspar! Course I get tha broken item!" He stomped off ahead, making a beeline for Commander Thorne who led the elves at the front of the throng.

Leon glanced at Miala, and saw that she looked insecure again. He walked over to her, hoping to get some answers. "Hey."

She glanced at him but didn't say anything until Kelleren woofed at her. "Hey."

Leon decided to start simple. "Got a question for you."

Sigh. "Go ahead."

"At Mancer Academy, when you were there, was there an old man named… Calvin?"

Miala seemed taken aback by the question, "Um, not that I can recall."

"Are you sure?"

"The Academy has roughly three to four hundred students and faculty at any given time. It is smaller than you would think, so everyone pretty much knows everyone else after a while. What branch was he?" She asked, now curious.

Leon had no idea, but described his experience with the old man. The more he talked about the encounter, the more that Miala's eyes narrowed. When Leon finally ended his tale, she couldn't hide the suspicion from her voice. "Green fancy robe. Bald thin old man. Super lucky."

"Uh, yeah."

"Because what you are describing is a legend. A story told to new students to freak them out. Sometimes even get them in trouble or prank them."

"What do you mean?"

"Leon, there are multiple branches of mancey, and a tower at the Academy for each. All of them are occupied except for one, because there are no mancers for that branch anymore. Headmaster Clybourne used to go into it just to make sure that no one was there that wasn't supposed to be. Like new students on a dare." She explained.

Baffled, Leon asked, "What branch?"

She closed her eyes and trembled. "A horrifyingly powerful branch. I shudder to think what a lich with it could do. Yet, we used to always say there was one mancer there. Even a few teachers would say it, just to freak us out."

"Miala, what branch?" Leon restated.

"Chronomancy. The power over time."

Chapter 11: The Bridge

It was a day later when they noticed the obvious tracks in the ground. Large, six toed footprints penetrated into the soft grass. Other smaller tracks were all around it, but their origins were not discernible. Commander Thorne didn't slow their pace, but sent scouts out ahead of the main elven party. The last thing they needed was to escape from the undead horde only to run into another giant.

As time progressed the fire that consumed the forest behind them appeared to lessen somewhat. That, or they were far away enough that they couldn't see it as well as before. In place of the blaze that had created red hues in the night sky, a thick column of smoke rose and dissipated high in the air. The mood was still somber, and only the moon, stars, and Revelator shone any light into the darkness of the night instead of the burning forest behind them.

The third evening after their departure from the Elvenwood, while sitting huddled together, Leon noticed that Gionna was feverishly scribbling in the bundle of small parchment she kept with her. At one point she called Miala over, who provided whispered commentary with a few nods. After observing them for a few moments Miala met Leon's eyes, then went back to the area she had set up for herself opposite him.

Leon knew she had been avoiding him since they left the forest. He wasn't blind. What bothered him was her not talking to him about it. They had shared a kiss. It meant something. Now, she didn't want to talk to him at all? He concluded that women were confusing, and set his eyes on the eldest among them.

"What are you working on?" Leon asked.

"A modification of my turret back home which may prove fruitful. I'll say no more on the subject! I don't wish to put the cart before the horse." Gionna replied in an imperious tone.

"What, like the undead plow idea you had in the workshop? The one that wouldn't protect the horses pulling it?"

Gionna stared at Leon through her multiple lenses. "Yes. Exactly." Then studiously went back to her notes.

Seeing their conversation wasn't going anywhere, Leon decided to lay down and go to sleep when he heard Gionna say, "Would Adonai approve of… killing?"

"Wait, what?" Leon asked.

"I have been inventing weapons of destruction for all my life. New ways to crush, to burn, to kill. I say that I do it in defense of people. I have even sacrificed relationships along the way in pursuit of my career."

"Magnus?" Leon asked.

"Among others. It seemed like a curse. Either they were interested in stoking the fire of my imagination, or they married me for money, or for whatever the reason… There was always a reason other than the one I wanted."

Leon wasn't blind or deaf. He had even lived with the gnome for a few weeks. She was irritable, and prone to outbursts of both creativity and anger. Gionna's temper towards her lost loves seemed to have built a wall around her. A defense that trapped her in her work.

"I have tried to make other things." she continued. "Tried to create, and not destroy. A shield instead of a sword. It just wastes time, money, and effort dearie. I know what I am made for. I am made for war. I imagine Adonai would frown upon someone like that."

The lenses around her eyes magnified the tears that welled in them. They traversed down the well worn wrinkles on her face. Leon got up and repositioned himself next to the crying gnome before he spoke.

"I think what is in your heart is more important than what's in your head. If you are defending the innocent, those who can't defend themselves, then I don't think He would find fault with that."

She leaned against Leon and a rustling from Miala's tent made them both look up. Kelleren sleepily loped over to them and laid his head on Gionna's lap. His eyes gazed up to hers as she managed a slight smile.

"You don't know the things I have done, dearie. The thrill I get from explosions. From destruction."

"Look at it this way… your desk arson at the Institute led you to meet us. Whatever it was you threw at Nachash Seraph saved me, saved all of us. None of us would be here if it weren't for you and your 'thrills'."

She removed her glasses and wiped her face. "That was what I was working on while you were staying in the workshop. My one and only sample of a mixture I was trying to make. It would have been stronger than black powder. Now I have to start over."

"Well, speaking as the person whom you saved, I think it was well worth it."

They chuckled quietly as Kelleren blinked at them both.

The words flowed from Leon as he thought, "I was told once that Adonai is love and maybe it is just me, but I don't think that there is a limit to the one true God. So I don't think there is a limit to His love. Even how He loves – caring, defending, or tough love. If you were trying to fill the void from your husbands' failings with weapons and warfare and innovation, I don't think you'll ever feel completely satisfied. I think only Adonai could fill that emptiness."

"Young one, how could I possibly love someone I've never seen? Whom I have never met?"

"With everything you have." He repeated the words that had been whispered into his ears by another, more angelic voice moments before. Lochemetel had been silent for some time, but whether that was due to nothing needing to be said, or something else, Leon wasn't sure.

Gionna teared up again and Leon thought perhaps she was embracing the unknown for the first time, instead of seeking to understand it. For once, maybe things did not have to make sense for her. She stroked Kelleren's head as she asked Leon what to do next. What to say to Adonai in order to follow him.

After he led her to Adonai they went to bed, and Kelleren returned to Miala.

That night Leon dreamed for the first time in several days.

A grey expense filled the horizon. The sky was lighter but still colorless save for one feature. The shining ball in the sky was significantly larger than when he had last seen it, in the dream where Rohiel had told him what to do to activate the sanctuary. The light that came from the ball was warm and inviting as Leon basked in its peace and comfort.

As before, a flare of light escaped from it before it exploded outward and crashed over him like a wave. The feeling of being washed clean with the light of the expanse overwhelmed Leon, and filled him with humility and awe. As the light pulsed, it crossed his vision and in its wake stood two figures. Their aeonyte armor was detailed and complex, and had scrawling letters along the seams and ridges.

"Rohiel. Lochemetel."

"You have done well Leon. But my presence cannot remain with you anymore." Lochemetel stated.

"Thank you for lending me your wisdom through the difficult times." Leon conceded.

Rohiel piped into the conversation, ***"The days ahead will grow to become more difficult. Do not lose faith. Do not lose heart. Trust in Adonai, and He will never fail you."***

Leon had enjoyed Lochmetel's unseen presence as she helped him. Her presence, her counsel would be deeply missed. But he needed an answer before the dream ended. "Did we do it? Did we stop them when we destroyed the forest?"

There was nothing from them but silence.

Heart troubled, Leon persisted, "Can you stop being so cryptic and just give me a straight answer?"

"You dealt with but a fraction of the undead."

"Nachash Seraph is regrouping."

Leon reeled at the news. "Was this all for nothing? The forest burnt down for nothing? How many elves are lost and yet still the horde of undead is not destroyed! What else can be done?"

"One among you remains untouched by the light."

Duamé.

"I– I don't know how to talk to him. His daughter died… How– how can I help him through that?"

"Your hardest trials will come soon. You must be ready. You must learn."

"Ready for what? Learn what?"

"The answers. The choices. Be strong Leon. Be steadfast. Be the Judge that is needed."

A wave of peaceful light crashed through Leon and woke him from the dreamscape.

They traveled eastward for a few more days. Everyone became more nervous and irritable as time passed. Duamé began to become noticeably short tempered, claiming that Leon was giving him a persistent headache. When pressed, he gave the same response as everyone else who knew why nerves were running high.

They were all approaching the bridge.

It was widely accepted that everyone in Xaelon knew about the bridge and its inhabitants. Unlike the legend of Calvin at the Mancer Academy, this legend was common knowledge. After constant warfare, and years of infighting, the savage leader Argleo had banded all of the trolls together under his clan's banner. Since that time they had imposed exorbitant fees to cross the bridge. Everyone within their group knew that all the money in the kingdom wouldn't be enough to convince the trolls to allow the elves to cross. Therefore, they knew that while crossing the bridge, they would be subjected to horrendous mental assaults. Even though the four armed trolls who guarded the bridge were built solidly, they would not resort to physical violence. Unless attacked first, physical violence was not their way. Instead, they issued the worst, most vile insults imaginable. They would say things that would make your ears burn red, and your heart ache without a shred of mercy. They always knew just what areas to attack, to break down even the most steadfast beings.

Such was the tyranny and common practice of the Entyrnet troll clan.

Their bridge spanned a gorge which housed a fast moving river at its bottom. An enormous waterfall to the north, near the dwarven territory, fed its strong current. A small stairwell wound from each of the ends of the old stone bridge to a series of caves in the cliff faces. The caves provided homes for the Entyrnet trolls. They had everything they needed for both shelter and food, as the well stocked river kept them nourished. Their presence had been a mainstay at this bridge for years, and the military would never be able to root them all out. They were just too well fortified.

This made the menacing yells and battle shouts the advance scouts heard as they drew near extremely concerning.

Leon and his group members joined Commander Thorne and Princess Schalae near the front of the line as they crawled up the edge of a hill. The hill was a fair distance away from the bridge, but it provided an excellent vantage point to see that a battle was taking place.

The Entyrnet trolls were being assaulted by hundreds of satyrs and a giant. The chimeras, who had horns sprouting from their heads and the hooved legs of goats, were armed with spears and leaped around in their attacks. Their powerful legs granted them the ability to make large jumps, much like Leon could with the aid of Revelator and his necklace. They used this ability with expertise, while battling against the trolls who defended their home.

The giant that led them seemed slightly different than the other ones Leon had seen thus far. It also had short, curling horns that protruded from its orange-red hair. An intricately jeweled crown adorned his head, complimenting the horns. Instead of carrying a spear like the satyrs, it bore a wickedly curved and barbed halberd which cut down swaths of trolls.

"Well, this is unexpected." Thorne whispered.

"How did they get here?" Schalae asked.

"I suspect they must've fled the Chimera Lands and circled the Elvenwood. We certainly did not see them going through our territory." Replied Thorne.

Leon noticed that the Entyrnet trolls held most of the satyrs at the closest end of the bridge. Their four arms gave them a distinct advantage, and made them deadly in close quarters. Spears that were not immediately withdrawn by an attacking satyr, were methodically taken by the quick skills of the multi-armed trolls, allowing them to rapidly end the satyr's lives.

However, there were at least twice as many satyrs, plus the giant who led them. Even with all of their losses, the chimeras were gaining ground and winning, which Thorne commented on. "I don't see any red eyes. Perhaps the satyrs could be dealt with after they defeat the trolls. They would be tired from the battle, and might let us pass unmolested."

The nearby elves nodded their assent, which stood in direct opposition to Leon's conviction that it was wrong to wait. His inner thoughts were affirmed by Miala's hushed criticism, "We are just going to let the trolls get slaughtered?"

Thorne appeared to bite back a hot retort. After taking a deep breath he replied, "With all due respect Miss Mytheriyn, this has to do with military tactics. Which I have a vast array of experience in – what are you doing?" He hissed to Leon, who had raised his head up from their hiding place and pointed.

A short distance from the bridge assault, he spotted movement in a copse of trees along the gorge edge. The rustling of bushes and foliage soon revealed a fleeing pack of trolls. They were smaller in appearance, and led by a taller female troll who ushered them away from the battle and the hidden elves.

A mother and children. They were trying to escape the battle, and the mother kept glancing back towards the attacking satyrs, with worry written on her disproportionate warty face. The worry compounded into a yelp of alarm as three satyrs broke off from the attack to charge after them. Through a combination of their rapid gait, their ability to leap large distances, and the use of their spears to catapult themselves, they vaulted towards the terrified family, and would soon be upon them.

Leon didn't have to think. He stepped forward, towards the fleeing trolls, before Commander Thorne latched onto his ankle with a surprisingly strong grip. The elf hissed, "You will reveal our position! They are just trolls!"

Leon wrested his ankle away and hissed back, "They're children!" Then, sprinting to their defense, he reached back and pulled Revelator from his back, with the blade starting to glow.

The satyrs must have noticed Leon. One brayed as it peeled away from the other two which pursued the running troll and children. As it approached Leon, it launched itself into the air. As it reached the zenith of its leap, the satyr twisted and thrust its spear at him.

He knocked the incoming spear aside with Revelator, which ruined the satyr's attack. He then followed through, and used the butt end of Revelator to smash into the satyr's face and knock it down. A boot stomp snapped its knee, and it brayed in pain as Leon ran after its two comrades.

Seeing that the satyrs would reach the trolls before him, Leon fumbled with and yanked off his necklace. Securing a firm grasp on the gem, he slammed it into Revelator and made a lateral leap towards where he thought he could intercept them. The shock on his face from both his sudden acceleration, and the jarring of his spear blade as it pierced another satyr's midsection, was mirrored by the surprised expression on the satyr's face. A widening hole made of salt began to dissolve its midsection as Leon removed Revelator and turned to confront the final satyr. The trolls cowered nearby, mere steps away.

The chimera thrust its spear at him which he deftly blocked. Compared to Lochemetel, this beast was as slow as molasses. It stabbed at him again, only to have Leon turn slightly and trap the shaft of the spear under his arm. The satyr followed up with a kick from one of its furred legs, and its cloven hoof slammed into Leon's armored chest. While the move staggered him, Leon caught and held the back of the chimera's leg before he shoved forward and knocked the satyr off balance. At that moment, he struck it with Revelator, and dispatched him.

He looked back at the smaller trolls and their mother, and saw they were staring at him with terrified eyes – shocked by what they had just seen. Comprehending that they were all right, he rushed toward the battle to help in any other way he could. Looking ahead he saw that the dynamic of the battle had changed. Trolls were on one front, defending the bridge and holding their ground against forces who now had to split their focus. The satyrs were also now being forced to contend with a line of elves and archers, who had launched their own assault on the jumping creatures from behind.

The satyrs were caught in the middle between the two forces. A couple of them came dangerously close to the elven firing line, only to be enveloped by bursts of white-hot flame – evidence of Miala's preparedness. Leon also saw Duamé, Schalae, and several other elves rush forward from the line of archers with hammer and sword, to make sure that the felled satyrs did not turn. Duamé swung his hammers at their joints and weapons, shattering everything he connected with, and crippling any who came against him.

The horned giant, who had been occupied near the bridge, also noticed the change in circumstance. He ignored the stray arrows that bounced off his armor or stuck into his arms. With his massive weapon and imposing size, he defeated any who came against him up close. In the midst of cutting through huge swaths of trolls, with a speed that matched his oversized muscles, the horned giant reached down and plucked up one large troll who was adorned with precious stones and fine linen. He grasped the troll around its midsection, then jumped a great distance away from the front line he had been in, towards the attacking elves. He landed with a crash that Leon felt vibrate through the ground. Dropping his halberd onto a nearby elf, he reached down with a meaty hand and snatched up an elf who emitted a cry of pain.

The arrows that fired from the elven line ceased as they realized who struggled in the giant's grasp. Shouts of chagrin poured forth as the troll leader, held in one hand, was joined by Princess Schalae in the other. The giant squeezed slightly as he roared, "ENOUGH!"

The war cries died off as the satyrs bounded and hopped towards their horned leader. They provided a protective semicircle around the giant, as both the trolls and elves followed them. Though the trolls and elves severely outnumbered the satyrs, it didn't matter. All of the fighting stopped, and though weapons were pointed at each other, no "action" was taken due to fear of reprisal.

Holding both the Princess and the troll leader, Argleo, out like shields, the giant stood unmolested. It chuckled and surveyed the corpses splayed across the battlefield. The shocked and pained expression on Schalae's face was mirrored by the whole race of elves. Only the Queen's face remained resolute, as she stood with Miala and Gionna nearby. Locking eyes with them, Leon approached the back of the line of elves and trolls that faced down the giant and satyrs.

"WHO SPEAKS FOR YOU?" Rumbled the giant, as his fingers squeezed and tightened around the Princess causing her to writhe in pain. The Queen stepped forward, protected by an entourage of warrior elves, and piped up, "Stop it! I speak for the elves! Release her!"

"I GIVE THE ORDERS HERE! I CLAIM DOMINION OVER THIS BRIDGE! YOU WILL ALL SERVE ME NOW!"

The troll leader, Argleo, spat a few guttural trollish words, before he snapped, "Murdering, crazy mountaAAGH!" The giant squeezed the troll leader before yelling, "EVERYONE IS TO DROP THEIR WEAPONS! NOW!"

The satyrs remained armed with their spears as elves and trolls dropped their assorted armaments. There was a significant clatter of metal as the short, broad bladed swords of the trolls were piled in front of them. The elves reluctantly dropped their weapons as well, until the giant and satyr's gazes were left to linger on Leon, who stood unmoved between the trolls and elves.

The giant looked Leon over and laughed, handing his prisoners to the waiting satyrs who pointed their spears at them. He ran a hand down his arm and snapped off arrows that stuck from it – without even one wince of pain. The giant then heaved his barbed halberd onto his shoulder, and stated, "WHAT HILARITY. A JUDGE APPEARS AT THE END. JUST IN TIME TO SEE YOUR GOD FAIL."

Leon felt a small quiver in his legs from being addressed by the enormous giant. Rather than let the fear get to him, he decided to show bravado instead. "Adonai is ever assured of victory, nephilim."

"I AM THE REPHAIM MAHOMET. KING OF SATYRS. DO NOT TRY TO INTIMIDATE ME WORM. YOUR PREDECESSORS WERE FAR MORE IMPOSING THAN YOU. STILL..." The horned giant peered closer at Leon, "THIS CONFLICT DOES NOT SEEM TO INVOLVE YOU. YOU MAY CROSS MY BRIDGE. BE GRATEFUL THAT I AM LETTING YOU LIVE."

A difficult situation was now made more difficult. Leon knew he couldn't just leave the elves and trolls. He couldn't just walk away from his friends and responsibilities. With a shake of his head, Leon tried to think of a way out of this mess. "Why are you here? Don't you serve Xhormas?"

"HOW LITTLE YOU KNOW OF OUR WAYS. MY ULTIMATE GREAT UNCLE HAS HIS PLANS, I HOWEVER, CAME FROM ANOTHER. WE ARE PROGENY OF BAPHOMET."

This was a being that Leon hadn't heard of before. "Baphomet?"

"THE GOD OF PLEASURE. OF DOING WHAT YOU WANT WITH NO CONSEQUENCES." The giant pointed an enormous finger at Leon. "YOU CAN SET ASIDE THAT SPEAR AND FOLLOW HIM IF YOU WISH. I WOULD GIVE YOU A HIGH RANK WITHIN MY ARMY. YOU COULD HAVE WHATEVER YOU

WISHED OF THE FLESH HERE. ALL YOU WOULD NEED TO DO IS SERVE ME."

Sounds positively disgusting. Leon thought. He had dreamt of giants and their ideas of pleasure. He tried to keep the contents of his stomach down as he scrambled to think of a way out of this situation for himself and his friends. Trying to buy time, Leon replied, "I cannot abandon these people to their plight and serve you. Such a situation would prove to be EXPLOSIVE at their very next opportunity to rebel."

The leather wrapped around the hilt of his weapon creaked as the giant gripped it and smiled with rows of serrated teeth.

"I WOULD SIMPLY KILL DISSENTERS. ALL HERE IS MY PROPERTY. THE BRIDGE. THE FOOD. THE FEMALES. SUCH PROBLEMS ARE EASILY SOLVED WITH A FEW NIGHTS OF... ENTERTAINMENT."

Faces blanched and shudders abounded as goatlike guffaws came from the small army of satyrs. In the midst of the ring of satyr spears pointed at her, Princess Schalae's eyes grew wide as the giant appeared to look at her with unspeakable desires. Leon's righteous anger towards the giant sparked and was reflected in the spear blade that grew brighter as he responded.

"I would see you turned to ash before you touch any of them."

"AND YOU ARE IN NO POSITION TO MAKE DEMANDS. THIS IS YOUR LAST CHANCE, FOOL OF A JUDGE. JOIN ME, LEAVE, OR DIE."

Why is the rephaim giant so intent on me leaving or joining him? Leon asked himself. The giant king was four times the size of Leon, and he couldn't think of a reason why the giant would be so adverse to confronting him unless…

Unless he knew that Adonai was stronger than Baphomet. Unless the fact that Leon was a 'Judge' intimidated the giant. Feeling the need to clarify, and get a message across, Leon asked, "How do I know that you won't... burn me alive… or something, if I join you?"

The giant bellowed in laughter and a few elves made shocked noises. "YOU DO NOT. BUT YOU WOULD BE WISE TO DEPART FROM YOUR PRECIOUS ADONAI WHILE YOU CAN. HE DOES NOT SEEM TO CARE ABOUT THIS WORLD ANYMORE."

There was a lot of suffering occuring in the world right now. It was unnecessary, unjust, and unfair. Leon had certainly seen his share, and would undoubtedly see even more before this day was done. If he had free reign to do what he wanted, he would certainly try to make the world a better place. It would have to be on Adonai's terms though, and not his own. Which meant he could not compromise with Adonai's enemies.

Leon walked forward, towards the giant, and through the line of trolls and elves. The light of the spear remained unchanged in brightness, and seemed to convey a confirmation of sorts to the rephaim.

"IT IS THE SAME WITH ALL OF THEM. HE ALWAYS CHOOSES THE FLAWED AND THE BROKEN. THEN BREAKS THEM FURTHER BY GIVING THEM RULES TO FOLLOW. THAT IS WHY ADONAI WILL LOSE. WE DO NOT PLAY BY THE RULES."

The giant barked a few commands to the satyrs in an unknown language and ten of their heavily armored members ran and jumped towards him. What followed was a blur to Leon. He knocked spears aside and avoided being surrounded as much as he could. He stayed on the move. Fractions of seconds were all he was allotted to defend himself against the multiple attacking chimeras. Thankfully, fractions of seconds were what he was used to when he practiced with Lochemetel. When an opening provided itself, he used it to stab or slice against limbs, six-fingered hands, and hooves.

Leon was able to slay two of them before he felt a sharp cut run across his hip as he whirled away. The dwarven armor Duamé made absorbed some of the impact, but he felt the gash and hissed from the pain. Sparks flew as the satyr's spear grated across his armor. Leon reached out and grabbed the large nose ring of the offending satyr and pulled its head into the path of another incoming spear, eliminating that particular threat.

Two more satyrs worked in tandem, attempting to outmaneuver and outposition Leon. With so many adversaries to focus on in this fight, Leon found himself constantly backing away while knocking spears aside. So when one satyr jumped behind him, Leon was a little too slow. He felt the rough, six fingered hand of the satyr pull him backward and attempt to hold him in place. It bleated angrily as Leon twisted and flung an elbow behind him. It connected to the satyr's head, just under its curling horn, and dazed the creature enough to allow Leon to scramble behind it. He brought the shaft of Revelator to its throat and with a sharp twist and jerk, broke the satyr's neck before refocusing on the others.

All those who were held hostage watched. They groaned each time Leon took a solid hit, and cheered every time another satyr was downed. When he whittled down the number of his attackers to four, two fully goat headed satyrs worked together to sweep Leon onto his back, while another leapt high and came down with its blade aimed towards his chest. Leon rolled out from under the attack at the last second, bowling one attacker over, and whirled Revelator around on the ground to slice through its legs and spread salt where the furry appendages had just been. He then scrambled to his feet and stomped on one satyr's spear, breaking it in half, as he finished off two of their other, less ambulatory, allies.

The last two satyrs attacked with ferocity. Leon was forced to constantly defend until one gave into its goatish nature. Curled ram horns rushed toward Leon. He tapped his necklace against Revelator, and jumped to avoid the mindless creature. With Revelator's tip pointed down, it ran along the spine of the rushing satyr, killing it. As Leon descended, he knocked the last satyr's spear upward, exposing its vulnerable flesh. He landed and spun Revelator with a flourish, skewering it and turning its bray into a salty gurgle. Leon's eyes landed on King Mahomet as they stared daggers at each other.

The king snarled in hatred as he lifted his wicked looking polearm. Striking it against his large horns, he barked another command. It caused the numerous remaining satyrs to create a path for him. Leon was winded and spent from fighting the giant's 'children'. His side hurt where he had been cut, and as he breathed heavily, thoughts of his mortality ran through his head.

This is it.

Mahomet rumbled as he started to step forward, "I WILL EAT YOUR LIMBS WHILE YOU WATCH."

As he reached the front line of the satyrs, a red ball arched through the air and landed right below the giant's shoulder. The instant it hit, it blossomed into a fireball and then a cacophonous explosion as big as a house. It blew the surrounding satyrs apart, and knocked the giant to the ground as he was flung towards the cliff edge. There was a mass of confusion as trolls and elves retrieved their weapons amidst war cries and brays. Princess Schalae and the troll chieftain lashed out all around them, taking full advantage of the confusion.

Leon slammed his levigem against the spear one more time and launched himself at the burning giant as he slid to a stop. The stench of burnt flesh was a testament to their successful attack. The giant's gritted teeth and half wheezing rumble told of how extensive its injuries were. One of its arms was blackened to a crisp, while the bladed part of its halberd had broken off and must have tumbled down the gorge. Leon landed next to the giant, and before striking at the fallen king it rumbled, "THIS… CHANGES NOTHING. XHORMAS WILL… KILL YOU ALL."

Mahomet jerked toward Leon in one final attempt to kill him with his massive horns. Instead, Leon jabbed Revelator into the giant's head. A bright flash and loud bell sound rang as salt and ash formed and blew into the chasm. The distant sounds of battle rang from behind Leon, who had stayed and stared at the dissolving giant. He prayed silently to Adonai during the experience, and hoped that what Mahomet had spoken was nothing more than the rantings of a dying foe.

As he turned towards the quieting sounds of battle he saw that the satyrs were being routed by the combined elven and troll forces. With their leader dead, the remaining creatures fell into a mass of confusion. After a few minutes Leon grimaced, held his side, and stepped across to the safer side of the battle. He moved towards his friends who ran to meet him.

Gionna accompanied Queen Chlorae towards Princess Schalae, who was still on the front line of the battle and exacting revenge against her captors. Kelleren whined and padded over to Leon. He sniffed at the wound Leon bore before he rushed back to Duamé and Miala – who seemed to be quite upset with him for some reason.

"Will you STOP telling me to burn things?" She yelled.

Taken aback by her brazenness, Leon snapped back without thinking, "Well I'm glad you finally picked up on what I was trying to tell you!"

Duamé threw his fist in the air, "Ha, told ya he was speakin' in code!"

Miala threw her hands up in a similar gesture, but one of exasperation. "UGH! It was fairly easy to figure out!"

"Then what took so long?" Leon barked back.

"I had to hide it, and CHARGE it! Remember how long it took with Rhoxmas?!"

"Why are you YELLING AT ME?" He countered, stepping closer to her.

She shouted and pointed at the ash wafting in the air nearby. "Because you almost died! AGAIN! It seems to be a bad habit of yours!"

"Well, thanks for saving me! AGAIN!"

"YOU'RE WELCOME!"

"FINE!"

"FINE!"

Miala and Leon were a mere hair's breadth away from each other, and the heat of the moment between them changed in an instant. Before either of them even knew what was happening, they were wrapped in an embrace that lasted long enough to cause both Duamé and Kelleren to turn respectfully away… Miala suddenly broke away from the kiss they shared, "All I do is burn things down. Forests, relationships, people. Don't pursue this. Don't pursue me. That was the last time. That… was goodbye."

Then she walked away from Leon, back towards the victorious survivors. Once again out of his reach.

Chapter 12: The Trolls

Argelo was dead. His undead form had been pinned to the ground by several satyr spears until someone had finished him off. There were only a handful of trolls left alive. A mere fraction of their once formidable numbers. They managed to still be intimidating with their four muscular arms, blades, and the clubs that they wielded. However, only about a hundred of their population had survived the battle.

A certain mournful tension permeated the air among the elves and the trolls. The elves had lost warriors as well, however their princess had survived, while Argelo had not. Leon noticed that an animosity, a tension, began to take root between the two races. He worried that a fight might break out, until harsh guttural words were shouted towards the trolls from behind him.

He looked back and saw the female troll whom he had saved. She stomped brazenly up to the taller, more intimidating Entyrnet trolls and issued a harsh reprimand in an unrecognizable tongue. She pointed at Leon with her two left hands and in her trollish language berated the troll warriors until their posture became submissive and they wore downcast looks.

After some debate, the tallest troll was hastily given a golden torc around his neck. It had adorned the previous chief, and Leon was glad to see that at least they had managed to wipe the blood off of it before they gave it to its new owner. The tall troll sheathed his weapons, which signalled the other trolls to do so as well. It cleared it's throat and crossed both sets of arms before speaking in a broken low baritone, "I new leader Gezado. Hoppy Judge, burny mancer, cross bridge for free. Twiggy elves, big discount."

The female troll with the children barked at Gezado in trollish once again. He winced and furrowed his bushy brows. "Elves cross free too."

Low cheers arose from a few of the elves around them, as the procession of elvenwood survivors made their way across the bridge. It took time, and no small amount of parental guidance, to keep the younger children from peering over the edge of the bridge into the rushing waters of the chasm below. As the elven crossing progressed, the trolls gathered their dead into a pile and burned them. Commander Thorne also directed some of their warriors, who were not escorting others, to gather the slain elves for a pyre as well.

The odorous satyrs were gathered last. Gezado neatly picked the oversized golden crown from Mahomet's dust and ash pile before he barked a few commands to the other trolls who carried it away.

After a couple of hours, all but the royal elven retinue and Leon's friends had crossed the bridge. Gezado patted Leon on the shoulder as he said, "You go now."

Leon, numb from the experience of watching bodies burn, felt confused as he looked up at the tall troll. Not quite as tall as an ogre, Gezado's muscled physique was no less imposing. He looked as if he had been carved from rock. "Wait, you are staying here?"

"This home." Gezado replied.

Concern laced Leon's face as he relayed the information that the giant king had shared. With the undead horde still possibly posing a threat, the trolls could be overrun and consumed. Suspicion laced the faces of some, but others, like Queen Chlorae, were concerned by the news.

"What reason would the giant have to lie?" She asked of those assembled. When no one could give an answer, she turned to Duamé. "You asked us to make the journey to Masterwork Halls for refuge. For asylum. Would the Halls take the trolls as well, if they wanted to come along?"

Duamé, to his credit, restrained himself from shouting at the Queen, "I invited ya elves. I'm sure ya can remain above ground, an' make a home there. Ya can keep ta yerselves if need be, an' if there is still a horde o' undead still out there, it ain't gonna make much difference much longer."

Duamé jerked a thumb at the Entyrnet trolls that were watching the exchange. "I highly doubt there'll be a place fer that odorific lot!"

"What 'odorific'?" Gezado asked.

"Ya got four armpits, boyo! Figure it out!" Duamé exclaimed.

Grumbling sounded from the trolls, and a few barked in outrage as they communed amongst themselves. The female troll was outspoken once again, as she edged closer to Leon. She pointed at him emphatically and made grand gestures back towards where they had come from. She was a few heads taller than him, and wore several jewelled necklaces that reflected the afternoon sunlight. Her leather tunic and kilt were similarly adorned, and she looked as though she held a high rank in their culture. She caught Leon staring, and waved with one of her hands until he returned the gesture in confusion.

Finally, Gezado barked a few commands to the same two trolls who had carried away the crown. They must have hustled to where they stored it, because they returned with it and two hefty sacks. They then accompanied their leader as he walked up to Duamé. Gently, they placed the crown and sacks in front of the dwarf. Duamé opened the sacks with wide eyes, and shaking hands. The containers, that were a third of his height, were filled with golden eagles! While Duamé stared at the bags, Gezado announced, "Thur make point. We live if horde not come. We live if we go to Halls. We die if horde come, we stay. We maybe die if go to Halls, horde come. We more live chance if we go to Halls. We pay puny dwarf, let us go to Halls."

The treasure the trolls offered Duamé was easily as large as the treasure they had found in Rhoxmas' lair. The knowledge that this treasure was all his seemed to cross his mind, as he closed the sacks and put on his most accommodating face. "Well, I uh- suppose I could let'cha all tag along." Then he held both of his hands out, with his arms crossed. Gezado made a similar gesture, and they shook both hands. After they untangled themselves, the troll leader barked a few commands which prompted all the trolls to disappear into their caves underneath the bridge on the cliff. Before long they returned, and appeared to be carrying everything they had. The time they had taken to pack allowed Duamé to begrudgingly pay Miala to carry what he couldn't, in her mancer robes.

Leon noticed that the remaining trolls were carrying many more pieces of jewelry, and similarly adorned sacks of treasure. As he looked around, it seemed that a few of the others also took note of the fact that the trolls' vast accumulated wealth would be traveling with them. Less than an hour later, under Gezado's leadership, the Entyrnet trolls joined the elves and Leon's group on their exodus.

That night, after turning north towards the Halls, Miala's powers had returned enough to help Duamé mold his new fortune into his preferred gold bars. Several of the trolls found the process fascinating, which appeared to make Miala uncomfortable. Leon knew by now that she never really enjoyed being the center of attention. He watched from afar, granting her a respectful distance, even though he desperately wanted to be closer.

Deep down, he realized what his error had been. He had thought of her as a tactical asset, instead of as a woman, one too many times. She wasn't a military tool, but a person, who had feelings. Who had a heart. He had won her affections through showing interest, only to then push her away by using her. Remorse and regret over his actions filled his thoughts, but he couldn't think of another way they would have survived. *Maybe if I had worded the requests differently?* Leon lamented.

He probed at the tender and bruising side that the satyrs hit, but nothing seemed dire thankfully. Getting down to business, Leon set up his sleeping area and bag, then ate a few rations before he sat down to pray and talk to Adonai. He had started that habit a few days ago, and tried to make it a point to do it at least once a day. This evening Leon had his eyes closed, and thanked Adonai for getting him, and his friends, through the battle. He thought about his troubles, and asked Adonai for His help to solve them. As soon as that thought crossed his mind, a pungent odor caused him to quickly open his eyes.

The female troll, referred to as Thur by Gezado, stood only a few feet away, watching Leon. He smiled at her, and in the light of Revelator he could see her grin back. Her tusks poked through above and below her lips. She said something in trollish that Leon couldn't understand, then sighed in clear frustration. She gestured to herself saying, "Thur."

She must not know common speech. Leon surmised. He thought back and realized she hadn't spoken a word of common speech since he had met her. Trying to build bridges, Leon patted his own chest and said, "Leon."

"Leeunn." She said, sounding his name out.

"Close enough." Leon stated.

She grunted quizzically, then reached into a pouch and pulled out what appeared to be a leg from either a goat, or from one of the satyrs they had battled earlier. It had been through a fire, which had burnt away the fur, and while Leon was sure that she offered the food out of friendship, his stomach churned at the thought of where it might have come from. He patted his own stomach and stated, "No, thank you… I um, I ate earlier."

It took a few more attempts, with her continuing to offer him the leg, before she seemed to understand that he was full. She chewed on the leg herself, and mumbled in trollish with a full mouth.

Leon tried to be patient with her, thinking that she was just being friendly since he had saved her. When he excused himself to go to bed, he slid into his bag, only to see Thur begin to settle near him.

"Uh, wait… Woah what's going on?" Leon said as he clambered back out of his bag.

Duamé, who was close by and had been watching the whole time, burst out laughing. "HA! This is great! Oi, meat shield, yer in fer it now!"

"Can you tell me what she is doing, Duamé?"

“I could, but I won’t. This is far more entertainin’!” He said with mirth.

Thur looked at Leon with confusion, and said something in trollish again. Leon thought he heard her say something like, ‘Leeunn gozee,’ before inspiration hit him and he said, “Um, Thur?”

She looked at Leon attentively and grunted.

He gestured as he spoke, “Thur and Leon, go see Gezado?”

For a moment Leon thought that she would attack him, then she stalked off into the night, muttering in an angry trollish. Duamé seemed to find this even more hilarious, and collapsed into helpless laughter. “Of all tha things ya could have said! Oi, this is perfect!”

“I am so glad that you are amused at my expense. Now will you tell me what’s so funny?”

“I haven’t spoken ta a troll in years, meat shield. But seein’ how they are so close ta tha Halls, when I was there we tried ta at least have an understandin’.”

“So?”

Duamé cackled wildly, “So trolls are possessive by their nature. ‘Gozee’ means ‘my person’.”

Leon thought back to the confusing conversation. “I’m… her person?”

“So in tha troll culture, when their partner is killed they go inta mournin’, like everyone else. If someone takes revenge on tha killer, then tha partner has ta bond ta tha person. Like a marriage. Ya belong ta each other.”

“Wait, what?” Leon.

“She musta been Argelo’s gozee.”

Realization struck Leon like a club to the head. “We’re MARRIED?”

“What’s worse, tha word we use fer ‘and’ means ‘no’ in trollish. Before she stormed off, ya basically refused her, and told her ta go be with Gezado!”

Leon groaned and knew that the dwarf would never keep this to himself for long.

His assumption was confirmed in the morning when he awoke to nearby laughter. Stirring, he cracked an eye open to see Duamé recounting what had happened to his companions and a group of elves. Even Miala was doubled over with laughter next to Gionna, who in turn hugged Miala and clutched her cane to keep from falling over.

As Leon packed his bags, he kept seeing elves raise their mugs of morning java to him in wordless salutations.

Leon needed to find Gezado as soon as possible to sort this out. He walked up to Duamé who had his own cup of java, and said, "Now that you've had your fun, I need your help translating to Gezado."

"Yeah, alright. Don't want ta slay dragons an' giants only ta come ta an early end at tha hands of yer troll wife?" Duamé laughed.

He found the troll leader in an animated discussion with others of his kind. Leon didn't understand a word of their language, which consisted of barks and growls as well as certain similarities with the common tongue. Standing amongst the trolls who trailed behind the elven caravan, Leon felt he now knew what Duamé must feel constantly. Every troll was taller than him, and had enough muscle in their four arms to pull him apart if he offended them.

This seemed to be the common sentiment towards Leon this morning. Several trolls growled at him before Leon did as he was instructed by the dwarf, and crossed his arms in front of himself, hands extended towards Gezado. The troll leader did the same, and grasped his hands in what Leon was told was a traditional troll greeting before he rumbled, "What mean great offense towards trolls? Thur sad hoppy Judge reject her."

Leon kept glancing at Duamé, waiting for him to jump in to help. When the dwarf did nothing but smirk, Leon sighed in frustration and tried to be diplomatic. "It was not my intent to offend, Gezado. I didn't know that Thur would be promised to me if I killed Mahomet. I didn't know your culture."

It took a few moments before Gezado responded, "You come to bridge not knowing trolls? You not smart, Judge."

Rather than launch a normal smart retort, Leon felt it would be better to not argue the point around the muscular monsters. "Maybe not. I ask for your an–" he stopped himself before he said a word that might be lost in translation, "I ask for Gezado's forgiveness. For Thur's forgiveness."

A blank stare of incomprehension met Leon, and after a few mutters, Gezado asked, "What 'forgeevness'? Not troll word."

Leon was baffled by this, and his mind went blank trying to think of a response. Duamé then interjected something in a halting trollish. Whatever he said must have been effective, as comprehension dawned on their faces. Gezado placed a hand on Leon's shoulder and said, "We not know. You should have say something." The troll leader called forth another of his followers and spoke to him in trollish. Soon, Thur returned and talked with Gezado for a while. A look of what Leon hoped was shock came across her face. He hoped it wasn't rage. She clasped her hands together and bowed slightly to her chieftain, then she left and headed towards the younger trolls without casting a glance towards Leon.

"What… what was that about?" Leon asked Duamé as they headed back towards their own party.

"I solved yer problem."

"Okay, thanks, but how?"

"One second, boyo. I don't want ta hafta explain it twice." Duamé responded.

As they got back to everyone else, Duamé hollered out to their friends to gather around. Leon noticed Miala eying him warily as she hovered around the edge of their troupe.

"What is it, dearie?" Gionna asked.

"Right. So, ya know our Judge's little problem with tha troll widow?" Duamé began, as snickers that abounded that caused Leon grow red in the face.

Duamé continued, "Well, he asked me ta solve it an' I did. Cultural misunderstanding. He ain't with tha troll widow no more."

"Thank you, Duamé, but I still–" Leon began.

“Instead, if anyone asks, yer already married.” Duamé interrupted.

“Wait, what? To whom?” Leon asked.

“Ta Miala genius! Who’d ya think I meant? Yer God?” Duamé retorted.

“What? Why did you do that?” Leon exclaimed in disbelief.

“Well excuse me fer coming up with a foregone solution! Cause ya know ya make eyes at each other, an’ kissed an’ all! Plus, yer tha only two humans around here. It jus’ made sense.”

“I would like to have been consulted before the spreading of such a ridiculous rumor!” Miala’s eyes flashed in hot anger, and Leon felt the very air around him start to rise in temperature. Heat shimmers came off of her as he protested. “I didn’t know he was going to do this!”

Gionna chuckled with mirth, “Now dearies, you can’t take this too seriously! Goodness, this is just like the first time I got married to Mags! We spent so much time together, that eventually we decided to just dive right into matrimony!”

After much protesting from both Miala and Leon, they finally calmed down enough that Duamé, Gionna, and even Kelleren’s mental input, convinced them to not squash the idea outright. Duamé explained to them that Leon’s arms could be essentially ripped out of their sockets if the trolls were further offended. At that point Leon begrudgingly accepted the circumstances he found himself in with Miala, and she with him.

When it came time to settle in for the night, Leon casually observed the trolls join Thur and Gezado together in what Duamé told them was a marriage ceremony. Many elves looked on with curiosity as the Entyrnet Trolls appeared to ritualistically hurl insults at the two. The troll leader, and Thur in turn, bit back with increasingly vocal retorts. Soon the trolls were all practically screaming to be heard, but no one was listening as they were all too busy shouting. Even in a different language, everyone could tell that the most vile insults were being thrown, but it didn’t seem to phase Gezado and Thur. They just laughed it off.

“It’s an odd culture.” Duamé commented.

At some predetermined stopping point, the shouting ceased and turned into bellows and cheers. The trolls then began dancing and celebrating around a bonfire. Thur's trollish honor had somehow been redeemed. Their culture still baffled Leon. Even with the insults, extra armpits, and body odor, they had a simplistic, but appreciative, air about their ways. Still, the way Duamé had chosen to help was uncalled for. Leon knew the complex cost of a simple lie. It was on every wanted poster spread throughout Agaprya. Leon went to bed after a while, plotting the ways that he could humorously get back at Duamé.

Chapter 13: The Dwarves

The next morning, as they rounded a steep hill along the path, Leon's group, along with the caravan of elves and trolls, were greeted by quite the sight.

Hundreds of dwarves lined the road towards Masterwork Halls. They were hearty, well armored dwarves who bore crossbows, axes, and hammers. The dwarves stood in silence while a small rumble echoed from the top of the hill. Leon had thought the higher elevations were unoccupied, but then saw another multitude of dwarves. Every one of them pointed a staff with a crystal on its end towards their group. One dwarf moved out from among them, to the front of their forces. He walked with a slight swagger, and an impish grin distorted the short goatee that was on his face. He appeared to be younger than Duamé, and his dark hair reached to his shoulders. It just touched the brown leather duster coat that was draped around him. A small, white and black striped badger padded next to him and curled near his leg as he pulled an apple from his pocket.

"Sooo…" He drawled in a shout. He took a bite of the apple, chewing while he finished, "Wot's all this about?"

Queen Chlorae made her way towards the bottom of the hill with her retinue, as the loud dwarf continued, "Looks like ya got Entyrnet trolls with ya too! A ragtag invadin' bunch o' ragamuffins ya lot seem ta be!" He took another bite of his apple while the other dwarves remained unmoving. Their weapons were held at the ready for any hidden command. Leon looked closer and saw that the dwarves on the hill looked like their spokesperson. They looked exactly like him. Their clothes, faces, and weapons were all the same as they stood there unmoving.

Queen Chlorae continued to move slowly towards the base of the hill and the outspoken dwarf. "I am the Queen of the Northern Elvenwo– the northern elves and I humbly request an audience with the Nonagint to plead for sanctuary."

The sly dwarf's grin faltered as the badger at his feet tittered and squeaked. After taking another bite from the half eaten apple he dropped the rest down to the badger, and spoke in a slightly softer voice, "Tha smoke our scouts saw on tha horizon fer the last few days. That was the Elvenwood? Yer forest is gone?"

"Yes. The horde had to be stopped." The Queen responded with resignation.

"Jarosite!" The dwarf on the hill swore. "Ya burned it down on purpose?"

"Only ONE dwarf I know swears with THAT kind o' mineral!" A voice yelled from far back in the crowd of elves and trolls. Leon turned to see that tall figures were being pushed aside as Duamé barrelled through the crowd.

"Duamé?" The dwarf on the hill questioned.

"Jaq Copperchin!" Duamé called with open arms as he burst through the taller people at the front of the line.

"Ya limestone layabout!" Jaq laughed, as he scrambled down the steep hill and gripped Duamé in a bear hug. They clapped each other on the back and the younger dwarf turned and exclaimed, "It's alright lads! No fightin' today!"

The tension between the two forces visibly and audibly relaxed, as weapons were sheathed with sighs of relief. There were a few grumbles and groans of disappointment, but those were quickly shushed. The new troll leader, Gezado, was among those who sounded disappointed as he slung three axes back into their holsters. Duamé knocked the other dwarf, Jaq, in the stomach as he asked, "Wot are ya doin' leadin' this lot?"

Jaq's impish grin somehow widened as he said, "Well, wouldn't ya like ta know?" Looking around them, he continued, "Wot are ya doin' with THIS lot?"

Duamé took that opportunity to make introductions, and when he came to Leon he paused before saying, "This here, is a Judge."

"For real? A little tall fer a Judge, ain't ya?" Jaq asked.

"Aren't you a little short for a geomancer?" Leon quipped back.

"Ha! I like this one." Jaq commented to Duamé. "Wot's yer name?"

This could be a problem. Leon thought. He wouldn't lie, so he did the only thing he could, "I'm Leon."

"Woah, tha bandit? Crimes against tha King's court an' all?" Jaq asked.

Duamé smacked his palm against his face and groaned in frustration. His friend's voice was loud, and carried beyond their huddled group of friends and royalty.

"I assure you that I am not what the heralds make me out to be. The truth of the matter is that we are here to request asylum from the horde that is coming."

Jaq thought for a few moments before he blurted out, "I'm gonna call ya Lee! Always been a fan o' nicknames, like this fool here. Ya know, I used ta call him–"

"Oi! Shut it!" Duamé railed. Leon saw him try to stifle his laughter, and instead use that moment to change the topic of conversation. "An wot's with tha critter?"

Jaq exclaimed, "Oh!" Then he looked back up the hill and snapped his fingers. Another rumble occurred on the hill, and the statue-like figures all crumbled to the ground. The badger padded forward in the midst of the green and brown motes of energy that flowed back to Jaq. When she reached him, she nuzzled against Jaq's leg and stared at Kelleren.

"I found her after ya left. She stuck around like... well... Honey."

"You named your badger Honey?" Miala asked in disbelief.

After they spent the next few minutes filling Jaq in on the situation as it stood, he rallied a few of the dwarves that were under his command. He instructed them on how they were to escort the refugees back to Masterwork Halls. A few minutes more, and they were back on the road. Jaq led his dwarven ranks from the front, while the elves and then trolls followed behind.

It was late evening by the time they reached the base of the mountain that held the halls. One side of the road they walked the foothills that surrounded the mountain range were displayed with their sparsely dotted trees. A low roar had grown in Leon's ears as they approached the dwarven home, and as he looked towards the sound he saw a massive waterfall. It began halfway up the mountainside, and cascaded down its face before crashing into the chasm at the bottom. It then flowed into the river that sat to the other side of the road they had traversed.

A horn blast signalled them from the mountain as they approached. The dwarves who traveled with Jaq responded with their own horn blast. Soon, they reached a pair of massive stone doors. They were angular, and opened inward. As the dwarves filed in, Jaq fell back to find Leon and the others who were with the Queen. "Right. So, I would probably end up a head an' neck shorter if I brought all o' ya in there without talkin' ta tha Nonagint first. I can get ya a audience with them easily an' then ya will hafta petition them fer citizenship. But who's going?"

Queen Chlorae and Princess Schalae both stepped forward. Commander Thorne nodded his head in agreement, and volunteered to set up a camp for the elves near the entrance. Gezado rumbled his intent to enter, folding both sets of his arms. Then Leon and his friends also asked to enter. Jaq responded, "That'll probably be enough fer now… Now, I assume none o' ya except Mista Onyxwill have been here before?"

Queen Chlorae raised her hand with a smile and said, "I actually have." After a sharp look from Schalae, the Queen shrugged, "I wasn't always a queen."

"Fair enough. So, for tha unknowing, let me give ya tha condensed version." Jaq began as he patted the huge stone door with affection. Then he walked backward and beckoned them to follow him in. A long corridor with torches set into the mountain wall welcomed Leon as he entered. High vaulted ceilings gently curved to join each other at their peak. What appeared to be one long, carefully carved and polished picture ran along each of the walls. The carved scenes were mirrored images of each other on either side of the large long hallway. Jaq gestured to each scene as he began to speak, "Masterwork Halls, like yer humans Last Bastion, used ta be a home fer giants. Long ago, we dwarves were enslaved by 'em. With tha help of a Judge, we were able ta free ourselves."

Sure enough, a small figure stood out from the carved dwarven images, and was depicted rallying them against the larger giants. Leon couldn't be certain, but this figure looked as though he held high some sort of weapon. *It couldn't be a spear. Could it?* He thought. The image was too old and worn to be sure, but as he tore his eyes away from it he briefly met Jaq's eyes as the dwarf continued.

"After a short but bloody war, we got rid o' tha Amalekite, Jebusite, and Hittite tribes o' giants that lived here. Their towers were abandoned an' closed off. Nobody goes in em o' course. Haunted. Only a handful o' giants escaped, but we didn't care because we were free. Then we turned this place from a prison, ta a paradise."

Another portion of the wall showed the recently freed dwarves scurrying about. It depicted some making sculptures, while others planted and grew food. A third group was shown fishing, while the last group was shown organizing into ranks and arming themselves. Leon had a vague recollection of Duamé mentioning something about this once. He had spoken about the three guilds of the dwarves: Crafting, Commerce, and the Military.

"What ya are about ta see is our land. It ain't much, but it is home. An' no giant, no ore shortage, no horde is gonna change that."

They reached the end of the hallway and another pair of stone doors. The doors were still open from having admitted the dwarven army earlier, so they strode through and were greeted by a most unique and unparalleled sight.

The interior of the mountain appeared to be predominantly hollow. A single large pillar in the center of the massive chamber supported the top of the structure. An enormous carved dwarf that held a double bladed axe in its hands oversaw the halls. There were multitudes of stalactites in the cavern ceiling interspersed with sections that had been worn smooth. Jaq explained that the smooth areas were left after the geomancers removed stone to repurpose it.

Small crystals, that twinkled almost like stars in the night sky, were embedded everywhere. They reflected the sunlight that filtered through a massive opening in the cavern wall to their left. The waterfall that flowed down the exterior face of the mountain was on display as it divided and ran over the mouth of that opening. The water that fell into the cavern fed an interior lake that stretched across a good portion of the Halls. Throughout the cavern floor small glowing mushrooms lined their carved walkways.

It was beautiful.

"Never thought I'd be here again. Gettin' a headache just thinkin' about tha welcome I'm gonna get." Duamé said as he rubbed his temples.

In the distance, Leon could see three very large towers set into one of the cave walls. Their construction matched what he had seen in Rhoxmas' cave, and in the Judges section of the Archives. Huge monolithic stone blocks which all fit perfectly together at odd angles. The towers were different from the buildings and houses that the dwarves occupied throughout the cavern. Most of the dwarven structures appeared to be formed from hollowed out stalagmites. Some of the larger structures, however, had been cobbled together using immense stone blocks. Certain structures appeared to have been crafted with beauty in mind, while others seemed to be more functional. There also looked to be a massive fortress near the back of the cavern, which sat next to a slightly sloping amphitheatre.

Nearest to where they stood was a large area that had been converted into underground farmland. Potatoes, tubers, and mushrooms were all cultivated from carefully maintained earth just inside the mountain's opening.

"It's like you live in a giant hollowed out donut!" Miala exclaimed. Almost as an afterthought she added, "I promise we can eat soon, Kelleren."

Jaq sighed, "Ya know, there's always at least one who makes that comparison."

Duamé replied, "I think it's hilarious."

"In all my years…" Gionna breathed, as she looked around. She never bothered to finish her sentence, letting the picturesque home of the dwarves speak for itself.

They made their way past a few squat guard towers, and down a wide path of smooth stone towards the center of the Halls. Their whispered exclamations, as they pointed at interesting architecture, were occasionally punctuated by a drip of nearby moisture or the faint repeated ringing of hammers and metalwork from the small field of anvils where dwarves were working.

A multitude of beautiful sculptures lined the road they walked along. Some twisted, some tumbled, while others were abstract representations of random objects. All of them required an impressive amount of skill, and were made from various metallic materials. Leon hadn't the faintest clue what some of the art was. However, some pieces, like the slaying of a giant by many dwarves, or his father in chains, were fairly obvious.

As they reached the wide central pillar with the huge dwarf carved in it, Leon noticed that a moat of molten rock circled the central structure. This was the source of heat in Masterwork Halls. It seemed odd to him that tendrils of magma flowed upward from the pool. They snaked up and outlined some of the hard lines of the dwarven figure that was carved in the pillar. The odd flow of the molten rock was explained when Leon noticed the sculpted dwarf's arms, head, and axe held large red–

"Levigems!" Leon exclaimed.

"Yes! Levigems. They keep the magma movin' an' help some of our Craftsman guild. Right Duamé?" Jaq asked.

"Yeah, it keeps tha foundry under the forgeworks workin'." Duamé stated. Leon didn't know if he was imagining it or not, but his dwarven companion seemed to be more tight lipped than normal.

The entourage made their way along a relatively straight path through the stalagmite home structures. Some were simple conical hovels, while others were more complex. The complex structures had multiple floors with the tips of the rock cut off in places to allow airflow, and provide a vent for the aromas and smoke that came from their kitchens. A few dwarves passed in the wide street and stared with open mouths at the motley assemblage.

"Good bridge." Gezado commented, as they crossed the only stone structure that spanned the moat of magma surrounding the central pillar. At their close proximity they could see that the giant carved statue of the dwarf was intricate and detailed. A true wonder of art and talent.

The roar of the waterfall, and the tinking of the nearby hammers were quickly muffled as they entered an opening in the enormous dwarven figure. The opening they were brought through was between the base of its legs, and led into a wide domed room made of the large blocks. On the far side of the chamber was a raised platform where several dwarves sat in a row. There were six occupied seats and three that remained empty. Spread throughout the room were several more dwarves. Some stood guard while others occupied stone stools and tables. One elderly dwarf appeared to be passed out, collapsed and asleep, with his head facing the wall. His light snoring could barely be heard over the clamor of the dwarves on the platform. They sat in their more ornate stone chairs and did not seem to notice the presence of Leon's group. Instead they argued amongst themselves in a particularly vicious fashion.

"All dwarves here tiny, but loud." Gezado rumbled.

"I'm proposin' raisin' tha taxes in order ta make up fer yer lack o' production ya gnashgab!" An affluent looking dwarven woman yelled from the left. She railed at an angry looking male dwarf who sat next to her. His blond braids shook in rage.

He responded with equal volume, "Wot do ya expect? We haven't mined enough cause we haven't found enough! We're cursed I tell ya!"

"Dontcha give me that bunch o' bedrock nonsense 'bout curses an' tha like!" She responded with a wave of a dismissive, many ringed hand.

"Oi! Look alive, ya cumberground!" Yelled a dwarf with a darker complexion on the right side of the platform. "We got company!"

All who were assembled looked at Leon, the Queen and Princess, Gezado, and the others. Duamé turned towards Jaq with an exclamation of, "Feldspar!" and tapped the dwarf. Jaq stood unmoving, with his impish grin directed at Duamé.

"Over here, Onyxwill!" Jaq called with a wave. He occupied one of the seats in the center of the platform.

"Jaq! YOU'RE on tha military triad?" Duamé asked in disbelief.

Jaq Copperchin howled with laughter and slapped the pedestal in front of him. His badger tittered next to him, and the statue that bore a remarkable likeness to the geomancer crumbled next to them. Motes of energy snapped back to the younger dwarf, who chortled, "Been keepin' that under me hat this whole time! Ah, it was worth it! Yeah, boyo I'm leadin' tha geomancers here. Surprise!"

"Onyxwill?" Called out a different dwarf on the right. His visage was grizzled and his grey hair was pulled back and braided. He stood up next to an already empty seat and strode off the platform towards Duamé. Duamé, in turn, couldn't meet his eyes. A tense silence hung in the air as the older dwarf roughly grabbed Duamé and embraced him.

"Welcome back, lad." He said.

Duamé's voice wavered as he said, "Thank ye, Verne. I'm sor–"

"None o' that now," Verne interrupted, "Yer here. That's all that matters." After another clap on the arm, the older dwarf went back to his place among the dwarven leaders. This gave Leon an opportunity to try and be supportive, as he quietly asked Duamé, "Good to see your father again?"

"Ain't me father, meat shield. Don' see him here."

After making a few mental leaps Leon asked, "Your wife's?"

A simple nod was all the response that Leon got before Verne loudly pronounced, "Jaq, ya were sent ta figure out who tha army was tha' was approachin' us. Now ya seem ta have brought guests instead. Where is tha army?"

Jaq outlined the information that had been relayed to him by the others, and introduced Queen Chlorae and Princess Schalae. They approached the platform and Leon's heart broke as he listened to their plea.

"We have nowhere else to go. Agaprya never came to our aid. Please let us inhabit the lands above and I promise you the elves will be forever in your debt." The Queen finished.

Leon was disgusted with the dwarven response. Without so much as a word of welcome, the Commerce dwarves immediately began to question Queen Chlorae as to exactly what the elves could do for them. They touched on the benefits of various foods, additional taxes, and other inane details that had nothing to do with the root issue: the elves needed a new home.

Princess Schalae seemed to feel the same way as Leon, and with each question grew more agitated. Finally, she railed at the seven Nonagint dwarves who were present, "Look, can we live here or not?"

"Schalae!" The Queen hissed as the dwarves displayed looks of various levels of outrage and offense. While the Princess was admonished by her mother, the dwarven council traded insults as they argued amongst themselves. Even Gezado made the faint comment, "Must remember some of these for Entyrnet."

Finally, Verne slapped his podium and called for a vote. With seven out of nine dwarves present, Leon saw that one was missing from the Military triad, and that Duamé's father was missing from the Craftsmen. The vote carried, and Verne announced, "Tha elves are welcome ta stay!"

Sighs of relief came from Leon and his friends as Queen Chlorae issued a smile and a nod before allowing Gezado to take her place. After haltingly explaining that the trolls had plenty of treasure to trade and could work hard to earn their place, they too were allowed to remain.

"I see individuals that are neither elf, dwarf, nor troll! What about them?" Asked the vocal woman from the Commerce guild.

Gionna hobbled forward with help from Miala. Duamé announced, "I got tha honor o' presentin' Gionna Gærheart."

The elderly gnome took the admiration of those who were assembled in stride as she stated, "I'll save you all time. I have detailed knowledge of the workings of various offensive and defensive weaponry against the undead. Several prototypes and blueprints of how to make them are in my possession. Your defenses here are passable, but I have already seen areas of improvement on my way to this very chamber. My assistant here," she gestured to Miala, who fidgeted under all the attention, "Is a pyromancer of great power. She is quite valuable when it comes to fashioning some of the prototypes. She can also heat materials and metal to a temperature that I am sure your Craftsman guild would find interesting."

"Woah, really?" Verne asked. Duamé showed some of the triangular ingots that Miala had produced from his coins. Almost the entire room seemed interested. *Don't the dwarves have their own pyromancers?* Leon asked himself. That was something he would have to find out in the future.

The dwarves must have agreed on Gionna and Miala's usefulness, and granted them temporary citizenship while Leon was lost in thought. Almost all eyes were on him as he stepped forward to present himself to the dwarven council. Leon noticed Jaq start to fidget. Duamé gave him an almost imperceptible shake of his head, and Leon could guess why. They had to tread very lightly here. If the Nonagint learned of his being branded an outlaw, or of Leon's parentage, things would get very dicey. He thought of Adonai, and of what He would want him to do.

He wouldn't want me to lie, but how can I manage that?

"So then who is this?" The dwarf next to Verne asked.

"I was asked to help the elves fend off the horde. Since then I've escorted them here."

"He's... a warrior. Good in a fight." Jaq contributed.

"Are ya a mancer?" The commerce guild woman asked.

"Uh, no. I–" Leon cast an apologetic look to Duamé, who's eyes widened in silent protest. "I am a Judge."

Leon didn't know exactly what he expected the reaction from this pronouncement to be. However, the multitude of dwarves that laughed all around him was nowhere near the top of the list. Miala and the others began to shift uncomfortably, as Kelleren padded up to Leon and leaned into his side.

"A good jest ta be sure, lad." Verne said, still chuckling. "Really though, who are ya? A mercenary?"

"You could say that." Leon supplied.

"His name is Le–," Jaq began, but was interrupted by the other Craftsman dwarf who peered at Leon's spear with interest. "Wot kinda metal is that? Light blue, no striations. Haven't seen that kind in tha mines."

Words tumbled from Leon's lips and halfway through speaking Duamé grunted, and tried to indiscreetly tell Leon to stop.

"I was told, and believe it to be, aeonyte."

This time the laughter was even louder, and came from practically every dwarf. "Are ya sure he's not a jester? Or did ya tell him all our tall tales before ya got here, Duamé Onyxwill?" Verne asked.

"Aeonyte is a myth, just like Judges." The mining dwarf next to Verne stated.

"Now hold on there, Phonz. Ya can't prove that! After all, a Judge helped free us!" Jaq stated.

This devolved into more bickering, while Leon waited for them to determine his value to their society. However, it seemed that all they were inclined to do was argue. No wonder Princess Schalae had lost her cool!

The mining dwarf, Phonz, suggested that Leon remove his helmet so they could see 'What a real fake judge looks like'. Leon hoped that by humoring him, this would be over with more quickly. He lifted off the half helm that masked his facial features with impatience, and lightly tossed it to the floor, which caused a loud clang. Smoothing his hair back into place, Leon cocked his head and said, "Well? Satisfied? Or should I just stay outside with the elves?"

Verne huffed, "If yer a warrior, an' not mancer inclined, that would still fall under our Military guild. Ya don't need trainin' er discipline looks like, so he wouldn't be in yer purview, Clénoi."

The only other military dwarf on the platform didn't look thrilled by the announcement. She leaned forward, and the rustle of the tiny interlocking rings on her armor scraped against her stone podium. It was very intricate, and seemed to fit her in a way that allowed for the multitude of weapons she carried on her person. "Fine." she stated tersely.

A slurred voice yelled from behind Leon, "Ugh! Ya'll woke me up! I need another drink. Somebody get me an ale!"

Verne rolled his eyes. "Aw, get it yerself ya old coot! Then join tha conversation. We've been voting all day without ya."

Leon turned to see who he thought was Duamé's father. Instead he locked eyes with an older grey-haired dwarf whose beard was clumped together with snarls and tangles. The bags under his eyes paired with yellowish eye whites, and told of many recent nights likely spent passing out from heavy drink. Dread gripped Leon's heart, and he hoped that this particular dwarf was too drunk to say anything.

A heavily inebriated Admiral Silverspine issued a wet cough and blinked. He groaned and rubbed his eyes before shuffling over to a keg near a branching hallway. He refilled a mug, cradled his head with his free hand, and stepped up onto the platform where he plopped into the vacant Military guild seat.

Oh no. Leon thought.

"Alright, alright. I'm awake. Where's Ignys?" The Admiral asked before slurping loudly.

Jaq eyed Duamé as he said, "He's uh, workin'."

Duamé scoffed and muttered, "Course he is."

Jaq shoved the Admiral lightly. "Just say yes ta takin' this warrior inta yer guild an' we'll be done!"

Though Leon tried to turn his head away, he knew it was too late. The admiral's eyes were glued to him as he started to shake. What little color that had been in his face drained away. He slammed his mug down on his podium, which spilled ale everywhere, then stood up with a slight lurch and drunkenly yelled at Leon, "YOU! WOT ARE YA DOING HERE, EH?"

Confusion erupted everywhere. Other Nonagint members asked the admiral to clarify. Guard dwarves grabbed their weapon handles in concern. Even those who traveled with Leon asked him what was going on. Leon faintly heard Jaq ask, "Wait, ya know him?"

Slurring, the old dwarf continued, "COURSE I KNOW HIM! HE'S A RHISE! ER, HE–"

Whatever else Admiral Silverspine said was lost to Leon. Shouts and screams engulfed the room. Leon held his hands out in an attempt to explain himself and deescalate the situation, only to be tackled from behind and roughly brought to the stone floor.

The last thing that Leon saw before he was knocked unconscious was the disappointment on Duamé's face, and the horror on Miala's.

Chapter 14: The Prisoner

A dull ache throbbed in the back of Leon's head when he awoke. He groaned, and instinctively reached for the area where he had been hit to check if any blood was present. Chains clanked and jerked as they pulled taut, highlighting the limited range of movement available to him. He looked around and found himself in a cramped cell which was clearly made for smaller people. Stone walls surrounded him on all sides except for where one small opening held the bars and door they must have shoved him through.

A rank odor wafted from somewhere outside of the cell that they had him caged in. Leon tried to sit up and banged his already pounding head on the low ceiling. He cried out, and with his mouth open could almost taste the odor itself. Leon looked down and saw that his armor was gone, which left him clothed in only his undershirt and pants. His captors had even removed his necklace and boots. He hunched over, crossed his legs, and leaned forward. This movement displaced the few pieces of straw that were intended to grant a small amount of comfort in the tight space. Leon peered out of the cell and was greeted by a familiar sight.

"Hey you, you're finally awake!" Miala breathed with relief.

Her red hair was dimly lit by the torches that flanked the opening of a stairwell behind her. From what Leon could see, the prison seemed to be a long corridor that extended on either side of his cell. None of the other cells that he could see were occupied.

“I am so sorry.” Miala stated softly. She was flanked by two heavily armed dwarves who wore unfriendly expressions. They watched Miala as much as Leon while she slowly approached the cell bars. Leon tried to reach out to her but was stopped short by his chains. The cold metal manacles were bolted to the floor and bit into Leon as he struggled in frustration for a few seconds.

“Well, this stinks.” He stated.

“We all tried to explain and come to your defense. Gionna, Duamé, and I. Even the Queen and the Princess. They… they wouldn’t hear any of it.”

“What happens now?” Leon asked.

“I don’t know. Some members of the Nonagint were talking about holding some sort of trial. They were talking about things like executions, Leon!” Miala cried.

Leon’s thoughts were jumbled by the sudden turn of events, the nagging pain in his head, and how he may have messed up Adonai’s plan. *How can we possibly recover from this?*

“Well, let’s not… lose our heads.” Leon commented.

“Leon! This isn’t a joking matter!”

“Alright. Well, if there is a trial, then I will prove my innocence. I have nothing to do with, and want nothing to do with, Lucien Rhise. Once I can explain, everything will be fine.” Leon said in an effort to reassure himself as much as Miala. All the while he tried to calm his pounding heartbeat that could be felt in his throat. “When is it?”

“I don’t know, I will have to ask.” Miala admitted. “We will get through this, right Leon?”

He could see the worry that clouded her face. Truth be told, uncertainty plagued him as well, but what could be done from a dank cell?

Another guard came, and slid a metal plate containing several potato wedges inside the cell door. Leon noticed that he slid another plate into the cell on his left. He then pivoted and spoke in a flat tone, “Time’s up, lass.”

“No, please! He… he just woke up!”

"Ya can visit yer husband later." The dwarf said patiently. Miala's face flushed red, and not from her pyromancy. Leon's heart lodged firmly in his throat and stayed there.

"At least let me say goodbye for now!" She protested.

"Ugh. No tricks. Ya got one minute!" Came the hot retort.

Miala clasped the metal bars and leaned in as Leon mouthed, "Husband?"

"Well, how else do you think I got down here?" Miala said softly. "Everyone is behind you. We will keep trying to convince them of your innocence."

Leon scoffed, "Should be fairly easy. I didn't do anything wrong."

Miala reached through the bars in an attempt to grasp Leon's hands. Leon's chains brought him a handsbreadth away.

"Oi! None o' that! Yer outta here missy!" The guard shouted. Armor clanked as they escorted Miala and her grim expression out of the prison and Leon's sight.

Sighing, Leon reached for the plate of food and found the potato wedges to be better than the trail food he had eaten over the past several days. He munched on the lightly fried food and heard the other plate scrape across the floor in the cell next to him. Leon clearly heard the crunch and lip smacking of someone else eating beyond his line of sight. Entirely too soon the meal was over, and the same dwarven guard who had delivered the food came to retrieve both plates. A bemused look came over the dwarf's face as Leon thanked him for the meal then sat back in his cramped cell.

Leon silently prayed to Adonai and heard a slight cough come from the cell next to him, before a rough voice spoke, "Nice lookin' lass ya have."

This time Leon was amused. After his conversation with Miala and the mostly silent meal, he hadn't expected the occupant of the next cell to speak at all. Feeling the urge to be social, and hating the sense of aloneness that he felt, Leon responded, "Thank you. I am undeserving of her."

"Cause yer a Rhise?" The voice responded with snark.

"Formerly. My father disowned me right before I left."

"Disowned? Ha!" The voice barked. Leon could tell that the occupant was a dwarven male, but nothing beyond that. "One thing yer goin' ta learn shortly is that no self respectin' dwarf is gonna believe any word that comes from tha mouth of a Rhise. They're all snakes."

"Hey! My mother and sister are good people!" Leon retorted in anger. He did not dare to touch on the past resentment and hatred he had felt for Lucien. Leon had forgiven his father for his past abuse, and did not want to pick up the weight of hatred again. Instead he explained, "I grew up constantly disappointing my father. You would find that both he and my brother, Laric, are cut from the same cloth, while I would like to think I have more moral fiber."

The other prisoner grunted, "Don't try ta get my sympathy, Rhise."

"I'm not, I assure you." Leon said. "I… I don't even know exactly what Lucien did to the dwarves. He never said."

There was a small pause before the voice cracked, "My head ain't made o' pumice, lad."

"What?"

"Ugh. I don't got air flowin' through me head! It's an expression!"

Well, this is frustrating. Leon thought to himself. He knew that he couldn't get far in any conversation if one participant refused to listen. Regardless of what was said. Leon once again leaned back against the wall, which caused his cold manacle chains to scrape against his exposed skin. He sighed, closed his eyes, and tried to block out the residual pain in his head. Several minutes elapsed before the prisoner next to him spoke again.

"Ya really don't know wot Lucien Rhise did?"

Leon kept his eyes closed. There was nothing interesting to see, and having them shut seemed to ease his pain. "I haven't a clue. I know it was shortly after I was born. I also know that whatever it was caused him to fire all of his dwarven employees at the time. Then he went into the mining business himself."

"Cause he was a selfish, money-grubbin' pyrite!" Came the reply. The dwarven prisoner then launched into an explanation, and Leon paid rapt attention. "It may come as a surprise ta ya that almost twenty years ago, Lucien Rhise an' tha dwarves got along well. His father, Liam, set up a coordinated business with tha dwarves an' tha kingdom. He showed Lucien tha ropes, ya see."

"One day Lucien was helpin' tha minin' guild here at Masterwork Halls. They were findin' new ore veins an' coordinatin' shippin' ta Agaprya. We found a huge vein o' iron an' had a big party ta celebrate. Next mornin', he was gone. He made a deal with tha King, an' suddenly Agaprya wouldn't take hardly any o' our iron. We lost our major buyer."

"Soon enough, it hit our economy. Folks were outta work. Some went hungry. Others lost a lot more. Lives. Family. We haven't struck major ore veins since, try as we might. Lotta dwarves think Rhise cursed us somehow."

Leon was heartbroken by the tale. He had never really thought about the dwarven side of things. Never considered the ramifications of his father's expanded wealth and it's possible origins. As much resentment as he held towards his father, how much deeper was the simmering hatred that festered here at Masterwork Halls?

"I'm… sorry to hear that."

"Yer sorry? Sorry won't bring back lives. Won't bring back livelihood. Those are jus' empty words. They, like everythin' a Rhise says, mean nothing."

Leon knew he couldn't understand or fathom the depths of harm that had been done to the dwarven people. A mountain of troubles had weighed upon them ever since his father broke their trust. If Lucien could not be counted on to fix it, then Leon would have to find a way to do so. Leon felt a stirring in his heart, and knew that this was why Adonai had allowed him to be put here. There was a reason for him to have made the journey to Masterwork Halls, beyond merely escorting the elves and trolls.

He thought for a moment before he spoke, and chose his next words carefully. "I don't know how to fix the situation between the dwarves and the kingdom. Truthfully, I don't even know if there will be a kingdom a week from now. I don't know if you are aware, but a massive undead horde that attacked the Chimera lands and the Northern Elvenwood may be on their way here soon. Regardless of Lucien Rhise's actions, if I can help the dwarves, if I can fix the situation, I will."

"Even if it means yer life?" The other prisoner asked after a long silence.

Remembering his time in the navy, and the purpose he had there, Leon's conviction rose. "My life is not only my own. I have spent it defending others before, I would do so again."

The sound of shuffling feet and rustling came from the next cell. Just as Leon registered that he hadn't heard the clanking of manacles from where the dwarf was, he heard the other cell door squeak open.

Leon opened his eyes and looked out of his cell to see a dwarf with a dark complexion and white dreadlocked hair. His dreadlocks were pulled back and tied behind him, and he was not dressed in rags or prison clothes, but in a fine leather jerkin and pants that were dyed a dark red. This was no prisoner at all.

Though he had his suspicions, Leon felt the need for confirmation. "Who... Who are you?"

The old dwarf crossed his arms as he responded, "Tha name is Ignys Onyxwill. I believe ya know me son, Duamé. Our relationship has been rocky o' late, but he asked me ta take tha measure o' ya. When it comes ta tha trial, I'm inclined ta help ya, but it won't be easy."

Leon sat awestruck by the turn of events. He stared at the elder Onyxwill and slowly nodded in affirmation. "I would... greatly appreciate it."

"Good. Cause yer gonna need it." Ignys said before he turned and walked away up the nearby stone stairwell.

✦✦✦✦✦

Leon tried to settle his pounding heart. He focused on resting, as best he could, in the small dungeon cell. At some point he must have drifted off to sleep, because the pain in his head subsided, and the darkness that surrounded him lightened to grey.

The small, incandescent ball of light had grown to cover almost a quarter of his dreamscape's expanse. It almost touched the flat horizon, and gave off a continual warmth that reminded Leon of the wave of light that sometimes pulsed from it. It was ever present, and countered the discomfort he had felt in the prison cell.

So much had happened since he had last been here, and rather than wait for the angels to begin whatever lesson they had, Leon took control of the conversation. "Why did my father betray the dwarves?"

"The enemy is in your midst. You must keep the faith."

Lochemetel stepped next to Leon, also basking in the light. Her hair cascaded out of the helm that she wore, and her Aeonyte armor softly glowed. Her tone was conversational, and Leon tried to tamp down the slight frustration he felt from her evasion of his question. Instead, he decided to circle back to the question later.

"You're back… I wasn't sure when you would be…" He stated.

"I thank you for your concern. However, you should be more concerned about your circumstances. What follows is critical." She replied.

Leon hadn't really had many conversations with Lochemetel. Most of the time she spoke to him cryptically, or repeatedly knocked him on his rear in training.

"A different skirmish awaits you tomorrow. One among the Nonagint is not who they seem. You must find out who."

"What do you mean, 'not who they seem'?" Leon asked.

"Do you remember our conversation in the labyrinth?"

Leon thought back to the revelations that Lochemetel had given him, as well as the intentional glossing over and hiding of things that he found necessary to know for his well being. One revelation stood out amongst the others from their conversation.

“The nephilim spirits? How they try to possess people?” Leon guessed.

“Yes.”

“What? Is someone on the dwarven council possessed by a nephilim?”

“Yes.”

Shocked at her straightforward response, Leon blurted, “Why can’t you just tell me who? Why these games?”

“Because I cannot see who. Only possibilities. Just like the nephilim.”

Now Leon was confused. “I thought that you knew what was going to happen. You and Rohiel allude to as much all the time.”

Lochemetel turned to face Leon, her face was masked by both the helm and the light, but her eyes shone a bright blue just like the aeonyte metal. Her look penetrated into his very being as she stated, ***“Do you remember Rohiel’s explanation of your perception? The grape traveling across the table?”***

When Leon nodded she continued, ***“Those you cannot see, the malakim, mazzikim, nephilim, cherubim, ophanim, and others, are larger fruit traveling on the table. We can see more, but our perception is still limited. We are subject to the grooves and grain of the table just as you are. Some events we know are fixed. They are there, but clouded in mystery, even to us. We influence how we can, but we are not omniscient. Not omnipotent. Only Adonai is.”***

Leon thought he understood. He didn’t know about some of the beings Lochemetel named, but they were likely similar to the ones he did know of. After all, his perception was limited and he could not see the beings while awake. It didn’t require a huge mental leap to understand that if he needed Lochmetel and Roheil’s help to see things, they would have the ability to see more than him.

With a heavy sigh, Leon nodded. “So, find the nephilim possessed council member. Then what?”

“Stay faithful. Remember the tenets. Remember your training.”

“No pressure.”

"There is an enormous amount of press– Oh, you were joking."

The ball of light pulsed, and a wave enveloped Leon. It felt wonderful, and he could swear that he almost made out a whisper amongst the other noise.

"Are you ready?" Lochemetel asked.

"Do I have a choice?"

"There is always a choice. But you have been given instructions on how to make the right ones. It is up to you to follow them."

Leon thought back to another past conversation, one that was no less important. *"Lead with love, because love conquers all."*

"You are learning." Lochemetel said, and Leon could almost see a smile trying to peek through the glow that came from her.

When Leon awoke, it was to the clanging of his cell's bars. His head ached a little less, but that didn't stop him from having to cradle it due to the sound of the ringing metal as he squirmed out of the ball he had slept in.

"Wake up, Leon!" A gruff voice sounded.

Leon tried to snap to attention due to the pure reflex that came from years of being addressed by naval superiors. His reaction caused him to bang his head against the low ceiling, and yelp in front of Admiral Silverspine.

"Sir! I–" Leon began.

With one last metal clang against the bars the dwarf voiced his frustration. "Don't need ta call me 'sir' anymore, boyo. We need ta talk. I'm… I'm sorry I exploded at ya. Sorry I got ya in here."

The cleaned up version of the Admiral appeared just as imposing to Leon as he had on the first day they met. It looked as though he had taken his naval uniform, complete with leather straps, studs, pockets, and rings, and dyed it to be a different color than the Agapryan blue and black. The new deep earth tones of the uniform blended into the walls, while the polished metal accents and the double bladed axe that was slung across the Admiral's back reflected the torchlight. The light also reflected off of a metal cup that Admiral Silverspine offered Leon through the bars.

Leon retrieved it with hesitation, and sniffed. The dark liquid promised energy to his stiff and aching muscles. "Java. Thank you." He said, grateful for the sustenance. The Admiral grabbed another cup from a nearby table and drank from it with a grimace. "Can't stand tha stuff meself, but I needed ta make a change in me liquid intake. Part o' tha reason I came down here ta talk ta ya. Felt I needed ta make amends."

The bitter java tasted a little different to Leon, but was no less useful in perking him up. "I… forgive you, sir. Thank you for the drink. It doesn't have any… alcohol in it does it?"

Silverspine looked shamefaced as he said quietly, "As soon as I sobered up, an' realized tha situation, what I put ya in, I… I threw me flask an' tankard in tha lake. If I hadn't been… if I had just…"

Leon couldn't fathom that, with this confession from the Admiral, he would be the one on the council to worry about. *Eight left. Maybe? Not sure how this all works.* "It is okay, sir. You are forgiven, just as I am."

"Told ya not ta call me 'sir' anymore. A lot has changed since I last saw ya. Never thought I would, ta be honest. But then, I done told ya not ta go home didn't I?" He sighed and stated, "I ain't an admiral no more."

"What?" Leon exclaimed as he shuffled as far forward as his chains would allow.

"Had ta resign. Forced to, actually. By yer father."

"What? Why?"

"Whaddaya mean 'why'? Cause o' you! Cause he found out I didn't kill ya!"

Leon was sure he hadn't heard the former admiral right. Sure that he was still dreaming some nightmarish vision that would stop at any moment. Sure that Rohiel would appear, and talk to him about some mysterious wisdom that needed to be imparted. But it didn't happen. Time still moved forward and Leon felt–

Unsurprised. I am not surprised. Does my father's depravity know no bounds? Suddenly the reports from the heralds, that the *Dawnfire* had no survivors, made more sense. This was the reason for that narrative. Because, by all accounts, he had been dead to Lucien Rhise – until he had shown up at the engagement party.

But then why would Calvin tell me to go home?

Why didn't he just kill me at the engagement party?

Different theories and presumptions fought for the forefront of Leon's mind. He took a few moments to beat back the hatred towards his father which tried to resurface. He had already dealt with that. Now he was concerned, confused, and wanted nothing more than to distance himself from Lucien. Just like five years ago, when he stood in front of the same military admiral, and resolved to make the best name for himself that he could. With whatever time he had left.

Leon processed the information and nodded to Silverspine, who waited patiently for him to speak. "Who knows?"

"I told yer friends, who believe me. Ev'ryone else though, thought it was just drunken nonsense an' conspiracy, until shortly before ya'all got here."

"Why? What changed?" Leon asked.

"A herald report came. I'll let ya read it fer yerself." The dwarf pulled a scroll case from his belt and removed the rolled parchment. He handed it to Leon, then grabbed a torch from a sconce in the wall and held it closer to the bars so Leon could see better.

Engagement announced!
After a lengthy courtship, it has been announced that Princess Giselle will soon be wed to Lord Laric Rhise. His Royal Highness, King Garinth, will be abdicating the throne for the, soon to be, Crown Prince Laric Rhise. A bright future awaits Xaelon as the Rhise family joins the royal line and provides new hope to the future of the kingdom in this dark time. The wedding is planned to be held in Agaprya, as the

might of Xaelon and our forces will surely beat back the horde of invading undead.

Baron Haldis Halomir remembered!
A moving vigil was held for the Baron, who had faithfully served Xaelon for decades. His carriage appeared to have been assaulted by the undead on the way to his nuptuals with Lady Liara Rhise. The maiden was distraught by the news, and while she appreciates condolences, she will not be receiving visitors at Rhise manor until her brother's upcoming royal wedding.

Dreadnought ships welcomed!
As a dowry, the Rhise family provided three new Dreadnought class airships which now hover protectively over the skies of Agaprya. Fully crewed, and outfitted with the latest in cannons and war machines, these massive ships will surely provide a solid defense against the hordes. Have no fear citizens! You and your kingdom are safe against the undead. Remember to report any ill or dying individuals to the proper authorities.

Strongarm Smithies named royal outfitter!
Many in Agaprya have seen the telltale muscular arm and anvil emblem of the married smiths who now control practically every smithy in the capital. Claiming superior techniques and faster production, the Strongarm smithy has rapidly risen to become the dominant source of ironworks in the kingdom. Many smithies have sold their businesses to them, and have been taken under their employ. Strongarm has expanded their business multiple times over in the span of weeks. The royal family celebrates the success story of this enterprising couple, and will count on their business to continue to supply the kingdom.

Outlaw Leon's reward increased!

If you have seen or heard of any news regarding the outlaw known as Leon, please contact the authorities immediately! His crimes against the crown are unpardonable, and this criminal must be brought to justice. The reward for his capture has increased to five thousand golden eagles if deceased, and ten thousand golden eagles if captured alive. A fortune awaits anyone willing to come forth with credible information that aids in his capture.

Undead horde clashes at Bulwark Fortress!
While many in the kingdom were disheartened by the news of the massive horde entering Agapryan territory via the Chimera Lands, all were shocked at the conflagration that consumed the Northern Elvenwood. While we regret the sacrifice from the elves, their martyrdom saved the kingdom from a much worse fate! The remnants of the horde have turned south and begun to assault Bulwark Fortress. Their numbers are still great, however nothing will be able to withstand the might of the Agapryan military and airship naval forces. **For guaranteed meals and homes, please consider enlisting in our military today! Head to the War College or Naval Shipyards to start your adventure in defending the kingdom. Those who can prove mancer talents may be evaluated at the powerful Mancer Academy for more tutelage.**

New Judge rumor turns out to be a hoax!
While many have been duped by the fantastical rumors of a Judge sighted in the area, it should be noted that the royal family has not met with, nor confirmed the credibility of, such an individual. Such rumors, which could give hope to an individual, are officially labeled as false and not to be taken seriously. While the rumored Judge was last reported to be headed towards the Northern Elvenwood, all have seen the woods burn, and it is reasonable to assume the demise of such an individual. The tangible hope of the dreadnought airships, our strong military might, and the new King that is about to be crowned are real things to hope for.

It is important to note that any beliefs associated with the Judge rumors are unfounded and also not credible.

Leon screamed in frustration and threw the herald parchment back through the bars of the cell. Of course Laric was going to become king. Of course Halomir died under mysterious circumstances. Of course the horde hadn't been stopped by the fire. Of course he was still an outlaw. What hurt the most was that his belief in Adonai, and all of his efforts towards fulfilling his calling, had been refuted by a mere footnote.

If this was the narrative his former father pushed everyone to believe then Lucien and Laric were indeed on the verge of controlling the entire kingdom. At least until the hordes of Xhormas finally consumed every living thing and person. They must be stopped. All of them.

"So now ya see wot I mean when I say yer trial today ain't about yer citizenship. Dwarves ain't gonna welcome a Rhise here, related ta royalty er not." Silverspine explained, as he sipped his coffee.

"Then what is it about?" Leon wailed.

Silverspine sighed as he shook his head, "There's a lot o' gold offered fer ya. Enough ta be a spark fer tha Masterwork Halls economy. The council wants ta decide whether er not ta send tha next king tha criminal known as 'Leon' for tha whole reward, er just yer head outta spite."

Chapter 15: The Trial

An escort of several guards came for Leon a few hours later. They unlocked his door and manacles, then re-secured them after loosing him from the iron ring in the floor. He was quickly shoved up the stairs, and after a few turns found himself in the main cavern near the lake. Sunlight peeked through the opening where the waterfall fell. It shone along some of the water, illuminating a rising mist as it traveled.

Taken to the lake by the guards, Leon was allowed a quick bath. He was required to keep his manacles on, which made it difficult to swim. The water was extremely cold, but served its intended purpose well. After drying with a rough towel that had been supplied, a simple and tight fitting change of clothes were given to him before he was again escorted to the Nonagint chambers.

This time, the chamber was filled. Where dwarves weren't seated, they stood, crouched, or craned their necks to get a good look at the proceedings. A few elves, Commander Thorne and Qas included, chattered amongst each other as well. Whispers, grumbles, and a few dark laughs, accompanied Leon as he was escorted to his designated space before the platform that held the seated council members. An increased guard presence stood about the platform, and appeared to have the job of protecting both the council and Leon. More than a few murderous glares were cast in his direction from observers. Whether it was due to his family name, the burning down of their homes, his alleged crimes, or something else unknown, there were enough reasons for them to hate him.

Leon was marched to a centrally located chair, and deposited in it. He sat front and center to all of the Nonagint. Near the chair that Leon was forced to sit in were a few stone tables where his friends sat. Miala, Duamé and Gionna sat together with worried or pensive expressions. Even Kelleren whined a little.

The council members were all present for this meeting. Hostile looks came from everyone, save from Admiral Silverspine and Ignys. Their stares were more solemn, pensive. Leon looked at each and every one of them. He surmised by the wearers fancy jewelry and haughty expressions, that the commerce guild members made up the left side of the Nonagint. The military guild occupied the middle, and was made up of Silverspine, Jaq Copperchin, and a third female dwarf. She dressed as if in preparation for battle to occur at any moment. Jaq's frown towards Leon told of the change in his attitude towards him. Lastly, to the right, loomed the crafting guild. It consisted of Ignys Onyxwill, Duamé's father in law, Verne, and one more dwarf that rounded out the edge. According to Lochmetel, one of the nine dwarves was possessed. *But who?*

Verne took up an iron sphere the size of his palm, and struck it against his podium. An echoing clang reverberated throughout the room, which caused all conversations to cease. His cadence was slow and purposeful. "This meeting of tha Nonagint is called ta order. Because of tha momentous decision that is before us, we're scribin' tha meeting'. Any objections?" After a tense silence, which was broken only by the furious scribbling of a couple dwarves who were trying to keep up, he continued, "Silence is assent. I, Verne Granitehand am cedin' control of the trial ta Ignys Onyxwill. Bring out tha discerner."

A dwarven guard came from a side room with a small wooden stool that was placed before Leon, just out of his reach. Another placed a small, slightly transparent cube on top of it. Leon's brooding over the situation lessened somewhat.

Well, at least I can have the truth verified quickly instead of it taking all day. He thought.

“State yer full name fer tha record.” Ignys said, looking at Leon.

“Leon.” He said simply. A flash of green from the discerner immediately brought grumbling from a multitude of those present.

“Well tha discerner is obviously broken somehow! He’s a Rhise ain’t he?” The outspoken commerce guild woman shouted.

“Régi, ya make a good point, but it ain’t yer turn. So shut yer festerin’ gob, an’ wait!” Ignys retorted. He turned back to Leon and asked, “Aren’t ya a Rhise, lad?”

“I was. My father disowned me after I returned home and we argued about his style of family leadership.”

The flash of green again caused even more outbursts throughout the room, and Leon noticed some of the council member’s surly expressions start to waver. Verne pounded the iron sphere on the podium again to regain control of the room.

“I’m gonna need some java fer this.” Verne stated.

Leon’s chains clanked as he raised his hands and asked, “Wouldn’t it help, and save time, if I just explained what is really going on?”

After a mumbled assent from the council, Leon bared his entire story once again. This time to all who could hear. He shared about how he grew up in an abusive home, and left at fifteen to join the Naval Academy where he had met Admiral Silverspine. How he worked hard and advanced, only for it all to fall apart just like the *Dawnfire*. He shared everything that led up to his ousting from Rhise manor. The discerner never flashed red or yellow, and sparks of vindication came every time that Leon saw his words confirmed.

What frustrated him though, was that while addressing the Nonagint, he couldn’t figure out who was possessed by the nephilim. None of them looked out of the ordinary, and their unfriendly stares all seemed natural given the current situation. While he explained his history some of their expressed ire began to soften. Jaq’s flat expression morphed into his resting sly grin. Especially after Leon recounted the verbal fencing that had occurred between Laric and himself.

“I’m gonna interject here a minute.” The former admiral stated, after he rapped an orb of opaque white crystal on his podium.

“Go ahead, Kérik.” Ignys prompted.

That’s his first name? Leon thought to himself.

Kérik Silverspine retold how he met Leon five years ago, and corroborated his account of why he had enlisted and desired to maintain his anonymity. He confirmed how Leon wanted to distance himself from his father, and worked hard to eventually make his way up to the *Dawnfire*.

Leon then beat back the guilt he felt as he filled the aghast onlookers in on his account of the crash. Unashamedly, he gave the true facts of his journey back to Agaprya. He told of how he ended up watching Gelan die, before having to cut off his head to make sure he stayed dead. The flash of green from the discerner was met with gasps and groans.

These were paltry reactions compared to when Kérik Silverspine admitted that Lucien Rhise had ordered him to kill Leon.

“Plain as if he were orderin’ dinner. Told me outside tha prison that he didn’t care, even after I showed him tha dragon tooth an’ told him his son was a hero. Told me ta make sure that there were no survivors, that he didn’t have no ‘kingkiller’ son, er he would ruin me career an’ everythin’ I cared about. Granted, I was a little drunk at tha time, cause I knew I had ta tell King Garinth his son was dead later.” He turned to Leon and said. “May have affected me decision to leave ya alive. Course, if I could roll a boulder over yer dad’s plans I would jump at tha opportunity. Had no idea it would end up like this though.”

“So wait, yer tellin’ us that tha father o’ tha soon ta be king, ordered tha death o’ his other son?” Ignys asked slowly.

The affirmation went over like a bomb exploding in the room. It took several of the Nonagint members banging orbs against their podiums to get the people in the room to settle down. “OKAY, OKAY! We’ve established ya aren’t quite tha Rhise we thought ya were.” Ignys started. “While ya don’t seem ta swing tha hammer tha same way as Lucien, we still got some issues we gotta work out. If we were ta take ya in, an outlaw, regardless o' how innocent ya are, it could risk war with Agaprya. Especially if tha next king is yer deadbeat brother."

Ignys sighed before continuing, "Next is tha Query. Try ta answer as truthfully as possible. Tha discerner will tell us otherwise. "

Leon was half ready to jump up out of his seat and ask to be let go. Disheartened, he slumped back down as Ignys continued. Duamé's father turned to the three commerce guild members. "Yeema Opalbone. Yer up first. Remember, only one question each."

The bejeweled woman clasped her hands together as she leaned over her podium. Her snobbish, high pitched voice caused an annoying ring in Leon's ears. "Ya claim that ya are a Judge, an' that ya wield aeonyte. A mythical metal. Who gave ya such a title an' knowledge?"

Leon was fully prepared to defend his views of his family or father, but not of his faith. With the discerner there though, the truth was complicated. "Well," Leon started. "I was told I could be a Judge by an angel named Rohiel, and then an alukah named Rhoxmas called me a Judge before I killed it. As far as the aeonyte, I heard the term for the metal when a lich called it that."

Hearing how it sounded, Leon tried to follow his explanation up with more clarification, but was drowned out by the laughter from the many assembled. When the council restored order, another commerce dwarf, a wispy old man with teeth made of gold began to speak, "Yer claims seem crazy, laddie. Ever thought about convertin' yer worship ta somethin' more tangible?" He held up a small gold orb that he could hit his podium with.

Another question that wasn't related to the situation at hand. Trying to keep his frustration down, Leon grit his teeth, "Adonai has provided plenty of tangible evidence for myself and my friends to believe in Him. Belief, and following Him can ensure that you do not rise again as undead. That your spirit can rest forever with Him. Why would I want to follow anything else?"

More laughter came from the dwarves behind him as he glanced at his friends. They were clearly worried about how this was going. He motioned with his head towards the Nonagint. Miala seemed to get the hint and started to speak, "It's true! It's true! If we could just–"

"Order! Order!" Said the mining dwarf next to Verne. "Tha Nonagint is questioning tha Rhise! Er, former Rhise! Nobody else!"

This is bad. Leon thought. If he needed a simple majority of the Nonagint to vote in favor of him, it looked as though while he had addressed the situation of his family well, most of the assembled dwarves now thought him to be insane. *I have to try to turn this around somehow.*

The last commerce guild dwarf, was even older than the previous one. She thought for a moment before asking, "Your situation is precarious young one. Personal beliefs aside, we are a COMMERCE guild." She stated, glaring at the other two. "The reward for ya is quite substantial. Is there any collateral that ya have in yer possession, that ya can contribute ta Masterwork Halls ta offset yer bounty?"

Several of the council rapped their respective orbs on their podiums while other dwarves behind Leon slapped hands on their tables. A few shouted, "Good question!" which gave Leon time to formulate a response.

"I do not have my former family's funds nor do I want them. I would gladly give dues to Masterwork, to right any wrongs committed. In my possession I have my full set of plate and scale armor, made by master smith Duamé Onyxwill. Duamé, what would you value it at?"

"A thousand gold at least!" He yelled exuberantly. Leon knew that far exceeded what he paid for the chest, legs, helm, gauntlets, and boots, but was surprised when the discerner still turned green. Duamé honestly believed that to be the value, and Leon mouthed 'Thank you' before turning back to the council. Before he could continue, Gionna piped in and held up the other half of the blob of aeonyte he had given her.

"He also has this!" She exclaimed. She started to hobble over to Leon before a dwarven guard tried to block her with his outstretched arms. Without losing stride, she used the end of her cane to jab him in the stomach. Her assault caused the dwarven guard to collapse in place, as the breath had been forced from his lungs. Most of the other assembled dwarves laughed at him, and she deposited the aeonyte blob into Leon's chained hands with a wink before she shuffled back to her seat. A mumbled, "Respect your elders." passed from her lips to the winded guard on the ground.

"What is that?" The commerce guild member asked Leon.

He held it up as much as the manacles would allow. "This is aeonyte. We found it, and it is immensely powerful against the undead. It's worth is incalculable."

The same elderly council member asked, "Interestin'. May I see it please?"

"That's three questions from you!" Her counterpart, Yeema, protested.

"Oh, shut it ya dacite dalcop!" She retorted to more laughter.

"Yes, of course."

The dwarven guard Gionna had knocked the wind out of hustled over to Leon and conveyed the aeonyte to the elderly dwarf. She took a magnifying glass that she produced from somewhere on her person, and stared at it. Leon tried to provide information, "It glows under certain circumstances, and can turn the undead into salt on contact."

She raised a bushy eyebrow before having the guard carry it back to Leon. "Thank ya, young man. It is certainly a unique metal. It would be interestin' if our resident council member in charge o' minin' could find more o' it!"

The mining dwarf stood in outrage, "I keep tellin' all o' ya that Lucien Rhise cursed us! Nobody listens, especially ya Agnes!"

Agnes seemed to be the passive aggressive member of the council, and her age seemed to be accompanied by a quick wit. "Maybe it's just ya and yer workers that are cursed, Phonz. Ya seem perfectly fine in your lifestyle. Enough that ya could be a Commerce guild member if ya wanted."

Snickers and guffaws from the assembled dwarves accompanied the rapping of Ignys' orb. "Alright, alright! Settle down. Military guild is next. One question each."

The heavily armed female dwarf blurted a question before either of the others got a chance, "Is it true that ya killed a dragon, an' a giant?"

Leon flashed a grin. *Thank you Adonai for the simple questions.* "Yes. Although technically it was two giants, but not at the same time."

The green light from the discerner was all the confirmation that this councilmember needed as she sat back, her veiny muscled arms crossed. "I don't care about yer beliefs. I'll let ya train me troops any day."

To Leon, Jaq looked bored with the whole thing. Seeing it was his turn, he waggled his eyebrows and tugged at his goatee before asking, "We know from tha heralds that there is still an undead army out there knockin' about Bulwark. Assumin' they get here, would ya defend Masterwork Halls if we asked ya to?"

More thumps on surfaces accompanied the good question, as Leon answered a simple, "Yes."

Kérik Silverspine thought silently for a long time before he asked his question. "If ya were allowed ta go free, what would ya do in regards ta yer family?"

Well, he knew how to ask a question to garner favor and votes.

Leon shifted in his seat as he tried to address all the dwarves assembled. "I know Laric Rhise. He is more of a rake than kingship material. Lucien Rhise has also made enough shady decisions, least which was his attempt to murder me. If freed, I would do what I could to stop them from coming into more power. I would foil whatever schemes they have."

The dwarves assembled seemed to like this answer. After all, their animosity towards Lucien Rhise had not changed. Leon was concerned though, he still couldn't pinpoint who on the council may be possessed. *One of the commerce guild members maybe?*

The craftsmen guild was last to address Leon, and Ignys Onyxwill nodded at Verne before he spoke, “Ya have been honest with us as tha discerner shows. I think I speak fer all o’ us when I say we appreciate that. That bein’ said, yer father has lost tha respect an’ trust o’ every dwarf here. His actions towards us are unconscionable, an’ I want ta know YOUR feelings on dwarves.”

Leon breathed deeply before he replied, “I harbor no ill will towards any race.” He gestured noisily with the clanking manacles around him. “Dwarves, elves, trolls, all hold my respect. Of course, I would respect you all a bit more if you could let me go…” Leon trailed off, shaking the chains to chuckles.

Verne turned to the last dwarf in the line, the one who was the mining expert. Besides his argument with Agnes, he had remained silent and watched the exchange without any change to his expression. He maintained his silent thoughts until Verne prompted him, “Come on Jasperfoot! Let’s get this over with!”

The Nonagint member known as Phonz Jasperfoot sniffed loudly, and kept tugging at his dark braided beard. Finally he asked. “I wanna know more about this ‘Adonai’. Ya said ya learned about him from an ‘angel’. Where is it? I wanna talk ta it.”

Leon was caught off guard by the question. “Well, uh I typically talk to him when I, um, dream.”

Mumbles and snickers started after the discerner confirmed Leon’s statement. Phonz was quick to pick up on this thread. “Wait, ya dream these things up? How can ya know what yer talkin’ about is real?”

Verne tried to intervene at this point, “Oi! Only one question!”

But Leon’s friends were quick to try and come to his defense. Shouts of, “We’ve seen Rohiel!” and, “He talked to us!” came, before several orbs were smacked against podiums to restore order. As the room calmed down, another voice from the opposite side of the room piped up.

“He talks to himself when he thinks no one is listening.”

Leon caught a flash of green from the discerner as he turned to stare at Commander Thorne. The elven warrior stood amongst some of his seated brethren, and Leon felt the stab of betrayal from the elf who stared at him with an unreadable expression.

"Oh HO! Now we are gettin' somewhere!" Phonz stated. "An' who are ya?"

Commander Thorne walked his way around a few dwarven guards and introduced himself. He then launched into his accusation, "This man obviously thinks what he believes is true. No one is doubting his prowess as a warrior. I, however, have my doubts about his mental capabilities. I have observed this… Judge… talking to himself both in the Elvenwood, and on more than one occasion during our journey here. I do not doubt his intentions, but I do doubt his mind."

Leon strained against his chains as the discerner confirmed Thorne's beliefs. His friends also expressed outrage, and Qas was being restrained from launching herself at the commander by a few of her fellows. They were again quieted down by the Nonagint. Leon noticed the ones who repeatedly smashed their orbs against the podium were from the commerce guild and Phonz.

Well, great! He thought. If his conversations with Lochemetel were viewed as something unhinged, then it could complicate things. He didn't want to come off as a deranged madman, but the problem with the discerner was simple: it gave a confirmation on perceived truth. It couldn't actually tell what was the truth, only what was believed to be true by the one speaking.

Verne and Phonz were arguing, with the occasional chime from another member of the council. Phonz was making the case that he could continue to ask questions of anyone but Leon, while Verne was trying to wrest control of the situation back.

All the while Commander Thorne's remaining eye burned at Leon like the fire that had burned his home. He was upset, and Leon surmised that the elven warrior hadn't moved past the loss of the forest. Igniting the trees had been Leon's idea, and he held Leon responsible. If this was his retaliation for that, it was perfectly timed.

Verne threw his hands in the air and huffed, drawing Leon's attention back to him. Apparently he had just been outvoted on something, as Phonz addressed Leon's friends and the other elves. "Anyone else hear this boy talk ta himself? Speak up fer tha discerner!"

Those that traveled with Leon all spoke aloud their responses, with repeated 'no's turning it green.

Until a 'no' turned it red.

Until it came to Gionna.

"Oi! Ya DID hear him!" Phonz said, pointing at the genius gnome.

Gionna looked like she might burst into tears, but tried to clarify, "I… I think he might have been speaking to the other one! Lochemetel! I am not sure! I… I couldn't see it! I coul–"

Phonz Jasperfoot interrupted her, railing at Leon, "So really, if ya are hearin' voices when ya are asleep an' awake, can we really trust anythin' ya have ta say?"

Leon's temper flared, "I thought you weren't supposed to ask me any more questions."

Phonz replied, "Ha! Are ya talkin' ta me, or yer voices? Can't trust a Rhise. Even a crazy one. Call tha vote, Verne!"

In the end, too much doubt had been cast. Only three votes, from Kérik Silverspine, Ignys Onyxwill, and Verne Granitehand, were for Leon's freedom. Jaq looked shamefaced as Leon stared at him after his vote was cast. Phonz directed the guards to take Leon back to the prison to await his sentencing. Seeing the heartbroken faces of his friends, and the devastated Gionna, Leon thought of what he could do as he passed the smirking Commander Thorne. With a heavy sigh, still clutching the small blob of aeonyte in his fist, he knew what needed to be done. What he was called to do.

"I forgive you." He stated to the commander.

"And I will never forgive you." Retorted Thorne, as he glared balefully at Leon with his one good eye.

Thorne was too focused on Leon to see Qas approach from the side and pour every ounce of her strength into the punch she landed into his gut. The commander collapsed to the ground as order was called in the court behind Leon. All he could hear was the shouts of outrage and attempts to reestablish order as he was led back to his cell.

Chapter 16: The Aeonyte

Alone in his cell once again, Leon had the chance to reflect.

What if I am crazy? What if this has all been in my head? Maybe I'm still on the streets of Agaprya and have lost my mind? Maybe I died and am doomed to have hope ripped away from me every time I start to think things will get better?

Leon had already cried tears and entertained his doubts and fears about the trial and how it would go. Now as he sat chained and alone, he waited to hear what his sentence would be. He couldn't stop second guessing everything he thought he knew.

"Well, since people want to think I talk to myself, do either of you have anything that you want to say?" He asked aloud to Rohiel and Lochemetel. He hadn't really expected an answer, and silence was the only response he received.

And why would they respond? Lochemetel said that she couldn't contact me this way anymore. Plus, I failed. I couldn't get out of here. I couldn't convince Duamé to believe in Adonai. I couldn't figure out who the possessed council member was in time to outwit them. Though I'd bet this aeonyte that it is that Phonz Jasperfoot.

Leon stared at the piece of aeonyte that he had snuck into the cell. It's light blue surface was smooth and polished. It had been the only salvageable item in the Archives. There had to be something more to it, a reason why he had it. All of his journeys and struggles couldn't end here. There were too many counting on him.

The horde was still out there. His brother and father were still plotting and about to take over the kingdom – or whatever was left of it. Leon felt that he hadn't done enough. He hadn't spread the message of Adonai and His love enough. He thought of how every second could have been spent differently. *How can I save the world from here? Some Judge I am.*

Remembering Lochmetel's words in the Grove, Leon wondered if there were mazzikin around him, stoking the flames of his depression. In an effort to shake himself from his dark thoughts, he pondered the last time mazzikin may have plagued him. He thought back to the nephilim in the forest, and the words from the dragon Nachash Seraph.

It had asked him if he had ever heard Adonai's voice, or seen Adonai's face. Leon had spent the last month and a half fighting for a God that he had only heard of in dreams and visions – from beings whose perception far surpassed his own. With all of these thoughts rolling through his mind, Leon grasped the aeonyte blob tightly, shifted his hunched over body, closed his eyes, and spoke into the empty space that surrounded him.

"It's been a while since I've talked to you, but I think it's time that I ask something of you. I have risked life and limb for you. I have talked about you to my friends. I have seen your power when I needed it, and have needed it but not seen it. Now I'm questioning everything I ever thought I knew."

"Everything is falling apart, and yet here I am, still somehow hoping you will find a way to fix it all. I don't know what to do anymore, what to say anymore, what to be anymore. All I know right now is that I need to know that you are there, that you can fix this. Because you can, right? You can do anything!"

Leon's voice rose to a shout as he cried, "I need you! Please help me! Please be here!"

It began as a low rumble. A small flutter and shift in the ground, which caused Leon to brace his hands against the stone floor. As he brought his fist that held the aeonyte down to balance himself, shocked by the sudden unexpected movement, he saw with perfect clarity that the little piece of metal now produced a glowing light!

The shaking he felt through the floor increased in intensity, and Leon was violently thrown down to it. Crashing and destruction could be heard from outside the prison. Were it not for the bright light that glowed from the aeonyte blob in his hand, the successive underground booms would have made Leon fear for his safety. Deep in the earth, two successive cracks reverberated through what he thought must have been the entire mountain. The cacophony was punctuated by the sudden snaps that came from the cold manacles around his wrists, as they fell to the floor broken.

"I AM."

Overcome with emotion, tears streamed down his face as Leon bawled while the world all around him shook. These were not tears of terror or pain, but of pure joy – of belief. They were tears of a renewed dedication to Adonai, upon hearing the voice that provided a mere glimpse into His awesome power and might. With the aeonyte shining brightly in the midst of the chaos, Leon felt at peace in his situation – even while the world shook around him.

He watched his metal cell door warp under the power of the earthquake, and was awestruck when it, along with every other cell door, blew open so forcefully that they fell off the hinges that had snapped like twigs.

After the rumbling stopped, Leon heard shouts from outside the prison doors. Armed dwarven guards clambered down the stairs, fully prepared to beat back any prisoner who tried to escape amidst the madness. The guards were greeted by an unshackled, unchained, and unimpeded Leon. Instead of escaping, he lay on the floor and just looked up at the open-mouthed guards.

"Hey, what's up?" Leon laughed from the ground.

The guards moved to re-shackle him, and he started to laugh when every manacle that the dwarves tried to snap onto him broke apart when they touched wrists. "How are ya DOIN' THAT?" One of them yelled.

With much amusement, Leon explained who he thought was responsible, and offered to accompany them out of the prison to survey the damage and help with cleanup.

✦✦✦✦✦

Leon noticed a multitude of dwarves hurrying about as they scrambled to salvage their homes. Stalactites that had fallen from the ceiling of the cave skewered through many homes and halls. Cries of panic, and the ringing of many picks and hammers as they connected with stone, showed their determination to repair the cavern as quickly as possible. There appeared to be no shortage of workers anywhere, and it seemed as though dwarves of all ages contributed.

Leon was brought to just outside the bridge that spanned the magma moat. In its agitation, the moat bubbled and spat liquid rock that almost reached Leon's feet. The heat that shimmered from its surface obscured who was calling for him up ahead. He would not have been able to make out who it was had it not been for the distinctive red hair and Kelleren howling next to her.

"Leon! Leon over here!"

The two guards who accompanied Leon struggled to keep up with him due to their shorter stride. They reached him after Miala had already hugged him. As they began to protest a second thump against Leon's legs revealed a teary eyed Gionna. With an authoritative, "Back off, dearies!", she hugged Leon tighter.

Leon disengaged from Miala, then kneeled down to console Gionna Gærheart. She cried into Leon's clothes and wailed, "I'm so sorry, dearie! I didn't want to–"

"You have nothing to apologize for." Leon said, patting the small gnome on the back. Looking at them both, he asked excitedly, "Did you hear it? Did you hear him?"

"Hear what, the earthquake? Of course, dearie!" Gionna sniffed.

"No, not just that! Adonai! His voice!"

"Didn't saying you heard voices get you into this mess?" Miala asked with her hands on her hips. Her eyes widened as Kelleren woofed at her. Then Miala exploded. "What do you mean, 'You heard him too.'? You claim to hear bacon being cooked on the other side of the kingdom! Why, what did Adonai say?"

"I am." Leon said with a smile. He must have echoed what Kelleren spoke to her because Miala was no longer incredulous.

"Whatever does that me–" Gionna began to ask before she was interrupted.

"Oi! You! Judge! What are ya doin' out?" Yelled a familiar voice.

Leon turned and saw Verne and Ignys striding towards them from around a street corner. Duamé was behind them, accompanied by a few more elderly dwarves. Based on their dress and closeness, Leon figured that they were their extended family members.

Leon rose and held up his hands, "The earthquake. Is everyone alright?"

"DOES EV'RYHIN' LOOK 'ALRIGHT'?" Ignys roared. He turned to Duamé, "Does he always ask stupid questions?"

The younger Onyxwill smirked as he said, "Usually follows em' up with stupid statements too."

The guards who escorted Leon explained the miraculous chain breaking that had occurred when they tried to keep him imprisoned.

Kérik Silverspine and Jaq Copperchin hurried up from a different street and joined them as Jaq exclaimed, "Oh, everyone's gatherin' here then." He spotted Leon and his eyes grew wide. He took on a defensive posture before Silverspine laid a hand on his shoulder.

"Before fists start flyin', wot's tha situation?"

"Commerce guild triad is dead." Ignys stated gruffly. "Saw a stalactite fall an' crush their commune. I doubt anyone survived. Wot about tha trainin' grounds? Where's Clénoi?"

Jaq barked a laugh, "Gonna need more than a earthquake ta keep her down! She was pinned under a boulder before we got 'er out. She's trying ta assess tha damage ta tha grounds now. What about Phonz?"

“Can’t find em! Wot do we do with this guy?” Verne asked, gesturing wildly at Leon.

The guards had to explain their faulty manacles once again, after which Leon stated, “I want to help with the rebuilding effort. I can help. We all can.” He gestured to Miala and Gionna, who both nodded in assent.

As they surveyed the damage around them Jaq used his powers to fix some minor issues. Then some dwarves started to holler and shout from far off. The sound seemed to come from the lake area of the Halls.

Those that were gathered made their way to the lake. As they walked, more dwarves joined them, and soon it seemed as though the entire population was trying to head to the same place! Shouts of, “Did ya see it?” or, “Wot is that?” added to the mystery until Leon and the dwarven elders were able to get through to the edge of the steep slope that led to where the lake was.

The earthquake had dislodged a huge section of the cave opening’s ceiling, and most of the dislodged rock appeared to have fallen within the lake itself. Bright stars and a moonlit sky shone through the area that had previously been occupied by stalactites and half of the waterfall. The broken rubble and rock now divided the lake. What remained of the waterfall continued to feed one portion of the body of water, while the other was prevented from receiving any.

As the blocked-off portion of the lake lost the water it held, and its water source, a steep drop formed to the newly exposed lakebed. What Leon saw there stopped his heart.

How is this possible? He thought.

Miala clambered up next to Leon to get a good look, and her hands shot to cover her mouth as she gasped. Then Gionna arrived, huffing about her age and old joints before she also looked below. She cackled in delight, and threw up her hands in excitement.

Leon turned to address the remaining Nonagint. They stood with awestruck expressions before startled exclamations escaped from their mouths. A dark blur of a dwarf suddenly shouldered past them, and without stopping he roughly grabbed Leon and propelled them both over the edge of the lakebed.

Time seemed to slow as Leon stared into the enraged and snarling face of Phonz Jasperfoot. Almost everyone Leon cared about stood at the cliff's edge, having reached out too late to stop their descent. The shock of the encounter gave way to retaliation, as Leon grabbed ahold of Phonz's leather jerkin. Using their momentum, Leon pivoted so that Phonz was beneath him.

This proved advantageous when they both hit the smooth, wet, light-blue metallic lakebed.

Phonz's impact knocked him out cold. Leon, however, had landed on top of the smaller dwarf, which softened his own impact. He immediately reached out to steady himself, and his right hand, which held the piece of aeonyte, touched the ground.

The metal he held joined together with the larger vein of previously undiscovered aeonyte.

Light flashed as both his remnant piece, and the aeonyte within the lakebed, began to glow brightly. A familiar, though faint, warmth started to emanate from it. Leon gingerly rolled off the dwarf, and in the distance above saw the onlookers faces in the blue glow. All looked and stared in wonder until shouts erupted, and fingers began to point towards Phonz, which made Leon look in the dwarf's direction.

While Phonz's immobile body did not move, his dwarven silhouette blocked the light that shone from the floor. What manifested from the unconscious dwarf, in the space where the light would have been, caused a terrified Leon to immediately withdraw, as cries of horror filled the air above.

A shadowy figure, the likes of which Leon had seen in a dream, occupied the space. A nephilim spirit, with glowing red eyes, glared straight at him. It filled every available inch where the light had been blocked by Phonz's body. The spirit reached its clawed hand hungrily towards Leon. Then, when the claw touched the light, it recoiled. It held its shadowy, bat-like wings tightly against itself, as it roared at him. The sound rasped against his awake and cognizant mind.

Somehow, the light from the aeonyte shows the nephilim spirit? Shows what possessed Phonz Jasperfoot? Leon asked himself.

He felt woefully unprepared for such an encounter. Without Revelator or his armor Leon felt naked and exposed. While the nephilim spirit seemed to be imprisoned by the metal's light, Leon did not know how long it would stay that way. Still, he saw no way to injure the creature, much less detach it from Phonz.

His frantic search for a weapon, or anything to protect himself with, seemed to amuse the nephilim spirit. Cries of terror echoed from above as the nephilim spirit raised its voice to a warbling shout, "Hear me Xhormas! The true enemy is here! Let the horde come and consume! Consume them all!"

A prickle of fear and dread formed within Leon. That, paired with the cries from those assembled above, seemed to affect the light that glowed from the aeonyte vein. It dimmed significantly and almost winked out, but that did not seem to lessen its contrast against the shadow that emanated from the unmoving Phonz.

If it gets free, it will tear me apart! Leon thought.

Leon remembered the advice of his spiritual advisors, and pushed himself to move quickly with his faith in Adonai acting as his shield. He took a step forward and placed a hand on the aeonyte vein. As it pulsed brighter Leon shouted, "Fear not! For Adonai is with us! He can shake the very foundations of the earth! He can break every chain that holds us down. If Adonai is for us, then who can be against us?"

The light from the vein flared again, which caused the nephilim to recoil and huddle before once again roaring at Leon and those assembled. It tried to spread its fear, tried to exhort control, but even unarmed, Leon had power over darkness. Even weaponless, Leon still had courage.

A battle of wills began as Leon exerted his faith and confidence in Adonai over the fear and terror that the nephilim spirit tried to spread.

The dwarves, elves, trolls, and Leon's friends all saw the effects of his faith against the creature. Leon's faith caused the aeonyte to grow even brighter, until the spirit howled its objection at being confined in the light prison.

A shout of, “Hold it still!” came from above as Miala sent a streak of white fire down. It pulsed and went straight through the spirit’s head. A small puff of salt appeared where it’s screaming face had just been, and it winked out of existence with a bodily convulsion from the still unconscious Phonz.

The light from the vein of aeonyte extinguished as well. Once it was evident that the demonic nephilim was gone, a slow cheer began to spread amongst the onlookers. Leon looked to Miala, to his friends, then with aching muscles he sat back on the special metal that had reacted to his faith.

Act Three: The Hope

So do not fear, for I am with you; do not be dismayed, for I am your God. I will strengthen you and help you; I will uphold you with my righteous right hand. - Isaiah 41:10 NIV

Chapter 17: The Idea

It was later that evening, once everything had settled down somewhat, when Leon and his friends gathered near the Nonagint's meeting room. Work continued all around them to repair and rebuild the dwarven home. It seemed that since they lived underground, a good number of dwarves were awake at all hours of the day and night. This allowed them to clean up the debris from the earthquake faster than Leon thought possible.

Some of the sustained damage was severe. A communal area where the commerce dwarves resided was smashed to bits, ending the lives of quite a few who lived there. Duamé commented that their big homes were just too large a target for the stalactites to miss. Though Phonz had still not woken from his and Leon's confrontation, the council absolved Leon of any wrongdoing from both that and his earlier trial. Then they managed to carry Phonz's unconscious body up from the lakebed and to a makeshift medical area.

The trolls tried to be helpful; their four arms and muscular frames made light work of the debris that surrounded them. Gezado and Thur rested amongst them while Princess Schalae and the newly promoted Commander Qas also lounged nearby. After a private discussion with Queen Chlorae, Thorne had been demoted and relegated to overseeing the seeding of the new elven forest outside.

A few of the surviving council members attempted to maintain some semblance of order, but their meeting was constantly interrupted by random questions about Adonai, aeonyte, and concerns about the shadowy demon that had dwelt in Phonz.

As Leon finished explaining everything, a grave heaviness filled the room.

"That thing, that… nephilim… called to Xhormas and the horde... to come here." Gionna stated.

Ignys Onyxwill piped in, "From wot we know from tha herald, they're at Bulwark Fortress. Assumin' they head straight here, we got wot? Two weeks? Maybe a little bit more?"

Leon sighed, "That's if they were alive and needed to rest, eat, and sleep. These are undead. We have maybe a week. If we are lucky."

Queen Chlorae raised a hand, "How can we be certain that they are indeed headed here? Granted, I was not present when you encountered this nephilim, but can we trust what it said to be accurate?"

"With all due respect, your majesty, we can't afford to not take the threat seriously. It said 'the enemy is here'. It meant me." Leon stated. "We need to prepare a defense. We need to be ready for the horde."

"Why couldn't we just kick ya out?" Jaq asked as he tugged at his beard thoughtfully. "No offense, but if the horde is jus' after the Judge... Would ya leave if we asked ya? Draw away the horde?"

"Wot a load o' detritus!" Duamé replied. "Ain't no guarantee they would still leave us alone doin' that!"

Leon smiled warmly at his friend before responding to Jaq, "I would leave if asked. I would also do what I can to protect Masterwork Halls. Even after everything that has happened. But Duamé is right. You are assuming that the horde would leave you alone. If I did leave, it would mean that nothing would stop them from tearing this place apart."

Kérik stood from his chair and nodded, "Remember wot ya were taught lad. Ya got three options."

"Run, fight, or hide." Leon rose to his feet as well. "We can't run. We tried when they attacked the Elvenwood, and that only redirected them. The nephilim calling out to Xhormas eliminated any possibility of our being able to hide. That leaves the option to fight. We will make our stand here."

"Luckily, we got all that aeonyte down there ta use fer our defense." Duamé said with enthusiasm. "By tha way, I call finders keepers if anyone hasn't already."

"You weren't even the first person to find it!" Miala argued with Duamé.

"I can't seem ta find a point in time where I cared about that. Anyone called it yet?"

Silence was his answer until Gionna stated, "I think that if the vein of aeonyte belongs to anyone, it should be Leon, dearie."

Kelleren barked in what Leon assumed was agreement, which made Duamé relent. "It was worth a shot anyway. What are we gonna do with it? Make more spears? Weapons? Armor?"

"We would have ta see all tha properties of tha metal first. That'll take too much time away from preparing tha defenses." Ignys stated.

"Oh, well if it's data ya want dearie..." Gionna began, as she got out a stack of scrap parchment. She tapped her glasses frame until it rotated to a magnifying lens, and found the right scrap she was looking for. "Here ya go. I've spent a few nights examining aeonyte."

Ignys, Verne, Duamé, and the other dwarves jostled each other for the best position as they read through the inventor's notes. It took a few moments, but they mumbled through the document and conversed amongst themselves.

"No dross? How can it have no dross? It's raw, but already refined?"

"How can it be harder than steel an' weigh less?"

"Elvenwood capability o' transferrin' energy."

Ignys sat back and huffed. "That's all very well an' good, but we don't have tha time ta make armor fer everyone here."

"We could make weapons. Like tha spear, an' wand!" Duamé suggested.

Leon thought about this possibility. Something didn't seem right about trying to use the aeonyte for weaponry. Or even for armor, like the beautiful sets that Rohiel and Lochemetel wore. It didn't sit well with him, so Leon tried to find a way around it, "How much aeonyte is in that vein?"

Ignys Onyxwill barked a laugh, "Enough ta build a wall! Oi, we could build a wall! That's a simple structure, an' we'd make tha undead pay fer it every time they touch it!" A few of the others who were assembled rumbled their assent.

Leon grunted in consternation, as he tried to resolve his unsettled feeling. He looked to his friends for their opinions and support.

That was when he noticed Gionna Gærheart rustling through more of her notes.

She was unfolding a large parchment she had withdrawn from a pocket at her side. As she unfolded the one sheet, other scrap parchments fluttered down from it. She pointed an imperious finger at Jaq, "Can you bring me a few of those rocks over there to keep this flat, dearie?"

Jaq, who seemed disinterested in the conversation as of late, provided the stones she requested. Then he and his badger helped her gather everyone near. "I've been hanging onto this for a while, but I think it might be time. I thi–" She began.

"Time fer wot?" Jaq interrupted.

"Time for you to clear out your ears, and listen to me!" Gionna snapped.

"I don't hafta take orders from you, half-pint!" Jaq spat.

Laughter rumbled from Gezado as Gionna began to shift the lenses on her glasses and addressed the geomancer.

"Let me make a few things clear. I remember which way you voted during Leon's trial. I had to come to terms with my own unbelief in both him and Adonai. As should you. If the past day hasn't taught you anything about the danger we face, then you are the most foolish geomancer I've ever met. Now sit down, dearie, and pay attention!"

Jaq opened and shut his mouth in silence before he sat near the parchment. "Yea alright."

Gionna tapped her metallic cane on the floor and cackled, "I knew it was odd. Very odd that I wanted to go with you all to the forest, but looking back now, I understand why." She thrust her cane toward the design she had laid out on the floor. "We can build that."

Everyone leaned over to look at her design. Almost immediately objections began to arise.

"It's impossible. We don't have enough time!" Ignys said.

"You have thousands of dwarves here, yes? We have the labor force, and the tools, and the gumption. The only reason we can't do it is if we simply don't try dearie." Gionna countered.

Queen Chlorae contributed, "The elves can manipulate the wooden elements into whatever specifications you need. It is an intriguing idea."

"We don't even know if we have all tha material!" Verne protested.

Gionna reasoned with him, "We do. All the pieces are here. They just need to be assembled."

"I think… I think we could do it." Duamé stated.

"Ya haven't been here fer a few years, lad. Most have jus' hung up their tools! We can't build this!" His father responded, squashing Duamé's contribution.

Leon felt the urge to come to Duamé's defense, "I would listen to your son. Duamé built a whole business in Agaprya, in just a matter of weeks."

Everyone looked at Leon in confusion, Duamé included. "Wot ya talkin' 'bout, meat shield?" He asked.

Ignoring Duamé's nickname for him, Leon continued, "Didn't anyone else catch it in the herald?"

When nobody responded, Leon spoke again, "Strongarm Smithy. Their business has exploded since we left Agaprya. They've become the official royal supplier for ironworks."

Verne and Ignys cast outraged glares at Duamé. Verne, fuming, spoke slowly, "Ya showed humans how ta smith tha dwarven way?"

Duamé began to give a partial explanation, "I showed em a few tips, yeah! But–"

Before any further misunderstanding could occur, Leon tried to explain.

"From what I understand, Duamé is part owner. Lucien Rhise may control the iron that is supplied to the kingdom, but the tools and what is crafted from that iron is rapidly becoming Duamé's. The herald even spoke about them buying other smithies."

The awestruck look on Duamé's face gave way to pure exhilaration as he blurted, "They musta used tha buyout account!"

"Wot?" Ignys asked.

"If another smithy snooped around, tryin' ta get tha techniques, they'd come an' buy 'em out."

"Looks like it worked. You certainly have taken the sting out of my father's monopoly on ore supplies."

The two older dwarves' indignation gave way to incredulity as they hugged and patted Duamé on the back. Leon's friend gave him a strange look, and seemed to be on the verge of tears.

"Congratulations on your get rich quick scheme, dearie. Now, can we get back to the business of saving Masterwork Halls?" Gionna asked.

As Leon looked back at the blueprint the gnomish inventor had laid out, it felt right that they should do this. Leon was surprised that he had never seen it before. It was as Gionna had said, looking back at the decisions that were made, everything seemed to have fallen into place. Everything made sense. He felt a sense of peace, of rightness. This is what needed to happen. It was as clear as if he had heard Adonai's voice again.

After a long sigh, Leon assented, "Alright then, let's build us an airship."

Ignys shouted orders to a few subordinates who had been called over, and copies were made of Gionna's idea. Verne took charge of whatever crafting guild members Phonz was responsible for, and directed them to begin collecting the aeonyte from the lakebed. Duamé then took a hand in directing Jaq on some of the earthenworks that needed to be done.

As Leon watched them in action he could see why the Onyxwills and Granitehands were on the council. They were natural leaders. They were in their element as they instructed the dwarves who came to them with questions, while simultaneously managing all of their own assignments. They included Gionna in all of the decision making. Once the initial acceptance of the airship design occured, she handed a slew of other designs to the military and craftsman guild leaders. Leon saw a snippet of one that looked familiar, similar to the crossbow that she had back in her workshop. The others all looked like pure nonsense to him.

Duamé and Gionna were quick to get things going, as dwarves showed up from out of nowhere to help. Some of the dwarves went with the multi-armed trolls to dig the aeonyte vein out of the lakebed. Others left to spark forges and prepare them for work. More still were told to gather all of the scrap metal that they could find.

This last group was placed under Miala's direction. She took the sculptures, which were intricate works of art, and sadly ended their existence. With her wand in hand, she heated the metal, and recycled the materials into the ingot molds that were held underneath. Those ingots were then carried to the forges, to be remade into whatever was needed. With each piece of sacrificed art, Miala's sighs grew heavier. She pushed herself for hours, until her head hurt and her nose bled, just like that first night when they had camped out and discovered her talent.

Trying to be supportive, Leon followed her and Kelleren when she went for a walk. They paced around the hewn rock pathways, and Leon occasionally pushed aside manageable debris. Kelleren seemed to be interested in one particular rock that he found, and returned it whenever Miala threw it off into the distance.

Miala remained silent, clearly brooding over something. Leon figured it had to do with melting down the statues, and felt as though he should try to encourage her. "It will all be fine… you know… We are doing the right thing. You're doing the right thing."

"Would you just stop... trying to make it all okay? It's not okay! Nothing is fine! I don't even…" Miala trailed off.

"Even… what?"

"I… don't know!" Miala railed. "I feel like I don't know anything anymore."

Kelleren padded back up to them again, his claws clacking on the stone walkway. He deposited the rock he was playing fetch with in front of Miala, and whined before leaning his bulk into her. She gave a sad smile and rubbed Kelleren's chin before she sat down in exasperation. Leon tried to think of what else her problem could be. This time, however, instead of trying to console her, he just sat next to her.

He was exhausted. Not wanting to say anything, but not wanting to fall asleep either, Leon occasionally pinched himself to keep awake. *Why do all the intense conversations in my life seem to happen when I'm tired?* He asked himself.

Not having any answer to this internal question, Leon's thoughts were interrupted when Miala sighed, "I… don't like my powers."

Well I can't just say NOTHING to that! "Um, why is that?"

"All they do is destroy. Even when I thought I was creating something, I was just fooling myself. Like I told you before, all I do is burn things… Art, forests, …people."

Discomfort filled the air as Leon remembered Miala's revelation from the Archive in the light of what she had just confessed. "You defend others though. You defend yourself, and Kelleren too. I know I'm not supposed to pry but…"

Kelleren's ears perked up, and he flopped next to them, rolled on his back, and allowed Miala and Leon to scratch his belly. "I don't remember my parents." She said.

Like a jolt of java straight to his head, Leon's exhaustion disappeared, and he was immediately aware of how rare such a personal confession was from her. "I'm sorry to hear that." He replied.

"From what I was told, I was born and raised in Springfield. At a young age, too young for me to remember, our cottage caught on fire."

Miala said in an almost emotionless tone, while she kept scratching Kelleren. "Nobody could figure out the cause, but in the wreckage, there I was. Unharmed. I used to blame myself."

Kelleren brought his head up and nipped gently at Miala's hand. "I KNOW! That's why I said 'used to'!" She exclaimed. Her dog grunted and laid back down so he could continue being pampered. Miala's scratching seemed to cause Kelleren to kick his rear leg involuntarily.

"You… You can't blame yourself. You were just a child." Leon comforted her as best as he could. Kelleren glared between Miala and Leon.

"He's saying the dog equivalent of 'I told you so'." Miala smiled. "On some level, I agree with you. On another…"

"How… How did you come to be at the Academy then?" Leon asked, in an effort to help her by changing the subject. Instead, her smile disappeared, and she stopped rubbing Kelleren's belly. Leon was not privy to whatever silent mental exchange happened between them. All he could surmise was that Kelleren won the argument, because Miala sighed and turned to face him.

"My uncle also survived the fire. He took me and we moved to Agaprya. We stayed there for a while… Until I burned down our home there, too."

Leon knew the exhaustion she felt from the overuse of her powers was waning. He could feel a wave of heat as it began to radiate from her. Before he could ask her why that house had burnt down, she explained. "He had the same appetite that my former teacher, Mancer Psiente, had. Even my being his kin wasn't a deterrent."

Kelleren growled as Leon voiced his outrage. The sick desires that resided within some were beyond comprehension, yet in this fallen world they existed. He remembered images from his first vision, when Rohiel showed him the depravity of the living. Images of giants who thought they could just take whatever they wanted, visions of those who sought power so they could abuse others and get away with it. He didn't want to remember these things. They were things that should never happen.

“Miala, I–” Leon began, before she stopped him.

“There is a secret known only to some at the Mancer Academy. About how people become mancers. When I incinerated my former teacher due to his abuse I realized that the cycle, their secret, couldn’t be stopped. Not by myself. I fled before I could be silenced. Before I–” Tears streamed down her face, and she attempted to staunch them.

Leon tried to be as sympathetic as he could. He hesitated to give her any physical consolation. Her visceral reaction towards him in the dark of Rhoxmas’ lair made more sense now. He couldn’t fault her for it. *Why on earth wouldn’t she act defensively after all that she had been through?*

It seemed to have broken something inside of her. She had cut herself off from attachment, and refused to allow anyone but Kelleren in. She refused to allow herself to accept the feelings she carried for Leon, and by doing so she destined any relationship they could have to ashes.

“I think I now understand why you push me away.” Leon started.

“You see? The reason we can’t be together?” Miala asked as she cried.

Leon thought about how he would word his answer, before he settled on a simple, “No.”

Miala lifted her head with a look of confusion.

“You wanted to know about Adonai, and His love, before anyone else. Maybe that's because you were searching for a love that was right. That was true. Kelleren shows you love, but you can't close yourself off to the rest of the world and everyone else in it.”

Leon continued, “I know that you care about us. Otherwise you wouldn't be here. I hope that you care for me because… well, I care about you Miala. A lot.”

Tears threatened to fall down Leon's face as Miala suddenly embraced him. As they hugged each other she sobbed into his shoulder, and he could feel her tears soaking into his cloth shirt. He heard her muffled words as she spoke into his neck, “I care about you too.”

Later that night, after Miala and Kelleren had gone to bed to rest, Leon bathed in the remaining section of the lake. He washed away the troubles and concerns that had weighed on him. The priorities that remained included finding a place to sleep and locating Revelator and his armor.

Once he was done bathing, he focused on the sound of hammers striking metal and headed straight toward it in an open area near the lake. Gathered there were a multitude of dwarves. The dwarves were also joined by a smattering of trolls who had carried the aeonyte ore to nearby furnaces. Benches and pegboards were stacked with tools, and lined the work areas.

A line of workers transported the light blue metal to tables and anvils. Dwarven smiths would then pound the metal placed at their workstation into sheets. Once each sheet was fashioned to the correct size and thickness, it was stacked onto one of their well used carts. Then, when the carts were full, they were hauled off to somewhere Leon couldn't see. What he could see, however, was Ignys. He continued to direct the dwarves throughout the massive work area.

Trying to shout over the continual ringing, Leon yelled, “Do you know where my stuff is?”

“Wot?” Ignys called back.

“Do you know where my armor and spear are?”

“Wot?”

“Do you know where my armor and spear are?” Leon yelled again, over the din of the workers.

“No!” The dwarven leader hollered as he shook his head.

Leon shouted once again, “Is there anyplace that I can go to rest?”

With a hard stare, Ignys picked up a mallet and smashed a large gong. It must have been a signal known to those in the smithing area, and it caused the hammering all around them to cease – just as Leon yelled out, “I just don’t want to go back to jail!”

Snickering abounded amongst the dwarves. Ignys set his hammer down and pulled Leon away, allowing the workers to resume.

“What were ya askin’ ‘bout now?” The dwarf asked.

"I would like to go to sleep, but I don't know where to go, and laying my head on an anvil might not be the wisest choice." Leon stated without any trace of humor.

Ignys barked out a short laugh before he pointed to a wide, hollowed out stalagmite nearby. White smoke rose from it, and Leon was sure that it was not far enough from the hammering and tinking of the forging area to block out their sounds.

"Knock on tha door, tell Esper I sent ya, an' mind yer manners. Or this," Ignys pointed at his mallet, "Will go someplace unpleasant fer ya."

Leon commented with a chuckle, "Your son threatened me the exact same way… Granted with a larger hammer, but still…"

"Glad ta see me boy remembered wot I taught him. Off ya go Judge. I got work ta do."

"Thank you."

"No lad, thank you." Ignys replied, emphasizing his words. "Thank ya fer keepin' me boy safe. Fer standin' by him when he was lost. Fer helpin' ta get him back here. Ta his family."

"You are most welcome."

Leon kept an eye on the dwarven home as he approached it, and eventually saw its entrance. It was located just before a staggered stairwell, which led to other homes. While there was no yard in front of the massive stalagmite, a few small rows of tilled earth were lined against it for root vegetables and starches. Rows of squat carrot sprouts and potatoes ringed around the structure. At the entranceway an empty stone base stood, which must have once held a metallic statue that had been melted down to increase their supply. A small plaque that read, "The Oxynwill's," was still mounted to it.

Flint and feldspar! Duamé's home? Leon thought.

He knocked on the wooden door and after a few moments it was opened by someone Leon had hoped he would meet. "Are you Esper?" He asked.

An older dwarven woman, who had her long grey hair pulled tightly back, stood on the other side of the door. She looked quite matronly in her grease spotted apron. A broad smile lit up her round face as she exclaimed, "Oh! Ya must be Leon. Come in! Come in! Please!"

Uh, what?

Leon was a bit confused as he stepped into the hollowed out stalagmite. It was deceptively spacious inside. A few of the pale glowing crystals that adorned the cavern ceiling had been hung inside the home to provide a dim light. A nearby sitting area held a snoring Duamé. He shifted in his sleep as the front door of the home squeaked shut.

The main area held a kitchen and dining area, and the curved interior walls were well adorned with decorations. Another room, on the far side of the kitchen and dining areas, held a tightly wound stairwell that led to both an upper and lower level. Overall, the home felt warm and welcoming.

"Are ya hungry? I could get'cha sumthin' if ya like." Duamé's mother offered.

Deciding he was more tired than hungry, Leon started to politely decline until she wandered over to a small larder saying, "I'll just get ya a few things."

Platter after platter of preserved food was set in front of him at their small table, which was covered by a burlap cloth that had a floral pattern stitched into it. When she wasn't serving him food, she was tittering about and cleaning up around the household.

She's... so nice. So normal! Leon thought to himself.

One small feast later, when Leon felt he could not eat another bite or keep his eyes open much longer, he protested any more food. After insisting that he help clean up his own meal, Esper showed Leon down the spiral staircase, to his room. It was also lit by a crystal, and Gionna slept in a small kid sized bed which had flowers and tiny glowing crystals dotted above it. The girlish theme revealed to Leon that this space was not so much made for guests, but for a young girl. Probably Duamé's daughter.

He was shown to a bed that must have once been Duamé's. It was too small for Leon, but he didn't dare complain. He caught the faint smell of dust that permeated the room, which highlighted its lack of recent use. As Leon thanked Esper for the meal and room, she smiled and said in a kind voice, "If ya need more blankets just say tha word. Have a good night!"

Leon welcomed the goosefeather mattress. It was a luxury that he had never been allowed, even in Rhise manor. His father always said that he would get Leon a better bed, but never followed through. The softness of the mattress was an oddity for him, but that didn't stop him from falling asleep almost immediately.

Leon was awake just long enough to hear Esper complain upstairs, "Oh, where is that girl? She is goin' ta miss dinner!"

Chapter 18: The Groundwork

Leon awoke from a sound slumber to the unmistakable smell of bacon, and the sound of laughter in the main area above him. He clambered out of bed with aching joints and muscles, and managed to only trip twice on the dwarf sized steps he ascended. Once he arrived at the main level of the home, he found Gionna and Esper eating and laughing like two old friends. Duamé was also with them in the kitchen, and looked to be cleaning up after breakfast.

"Oh stop it! Ya didn't!" Esper crooned.

Gionna giggled as she continued her story. "I did, dearie! He had a head cold for a week, but it was worth it just to dunk him in that rain barrel after what he did!"

"Oh, me Ingys would have jus' stayed in tha barrel!" Esper replied as they cackled again.

Gionna noticed Leon's entrance and smiled, "Well good morning, dearie!"

"Good morning everyone. Is there an–" Before he could finish, a plate of food was conjured with speed. "Thank you."

Esper jumped in as soon as Leon took the offered food, "Did ya sleep well?"

"Yes ma'am. Thank you. What is everyone's plan today?" He asked, before biting into a still hot sausage link.

Gionna cleared her throat before starting, "I have to make sure the elves finish the airship frame. They said they have a way to speed up the process that I simply must see."

“Where is the airship being built?” Leon asked.

“Oh, right at the mouth of the cave, near the edge of the lake. That puffball Kérik said it’s the most defensible spot for it.”

Leon nodded, “I would trust his tactics. Puffball?”

Gionna smiled. “His mane of hair, dearie. First thing I always notice about him. You know he approached me many years ago? Back when he was an Academy graduate.”

Leon almost choked on the scrambled egg he had just taken a bite of. “Uh, what?”

“Oh yes! Apparently, he did it on a dare from one of his comrades. Course, I turned him down flat. Told the old puffball I was still getting over my second husband. Still, one wonders what might have been.” Gionna smiled at the thought.

Leon tried, and failed, to think of a younger Kérik Silverspine. Decked out in naval armor that wasn’t decorated, and following orders instead of giving them. Thoughts of the naval armor reminded Leon, “Oh, has anyone seen my gear? Ignys didn’t know where it was.”

“I got yer saltshaker an’ armor.” Duamé commented as he cleaned a plate. He nodded towards the corner where he had slept. “Yer spear is over there.”

Pausing his meal, Leon went over to the nook and found the spear inside. He felt more comfortable with Revelator back in his hands. He looked around, but couldn’t see the armor that Duamé made. Duamé must have seen him searching, because he commented, “Ya can have yer pointy stick. Tha armor may need another day or two. Gotta make a few repairs an’ adjustments.”

“Do ya need a saltshaker?” Esper asked innocently. “I think I have a spare…” She started to get up before her son stopped her.

“No, ma! It’s just a joke we have!”

“Oh, that’s nice.” There was a slight pause before she continued, “Esperella an’ I have lots o’ jokes. I wonder where she’s off ta this morning?”

Leon's confusion turned into bewilderment as Duamé said conversationally, "Don't ya remember ma? She's out playin' with a few wee friends. She will be back later."

"She always loves ta play with her friends. I hope she comes back soon so we can have some grandma time." Esper replied with a smile. Gionna started to talk about something with her, but Leon's head reeled. Duamé must have seen Leon's reaction, because the dwarf sped over to Leon and grabbed his arm in a vice grip. Duamé announced in a loud voice, "Uh, be right back ladies!" Wide eyed, he muttered to Leon, "Let's take a walk."

Outside, the ringing of the forging area seemed to keep pace with their brisk steps away from the home. Once out of earshot from the Onyxwill house, Duamé said, "I take it me pa didn't tell ya about me ma."

"What was that back there?" Leon asked. Something was seriously wrong, and knowing Duamé's history, it didn't add up.

They kept walking, and as Miala had done the day before, Duamé bared his soul to Leon. "Probably one o' tha other reasons I left. After Esperella died o' sickness, me ma kinda… lost some o' her marbles. Acted like she was still alive. Kept forgetting whenever we told her tha truth. Was like ripping a bandage off several times a day. Seein' her collapse over an' over again. Made me experience it all over again too. I got over me own spot o' madness. She never did."

"So, me dad, Verne, an' I all started ta lie ta her. Tell her Esperella was always elsewhere, but alive. Crazy thing is, it seemed ta work. Other families grew ta understand, an' keep their mouths shut. She rarely steps outside tha house anyhow."

Leon couldn't fathom the pain or heartbreak that would cause one to lose their mind and believe someone was alive, when they weren't. He knew of a couple lords or ladies who had stepped down from their roles when their minds addled, but Duamé was a friend. A comrade in arms. This hurt hit much closer to home, and was more relatable than mere hearsay. As much as he wanted to, Leon couldn't think of any way that he could help.

“I’m so sorry Duamé.”

Duamé’s response to Leon’s sympathy was almost visceral, “Don’t. Just don’t. I don’t need yer pity. I know…” He sighed before continuing, “I know ya don’t like lying, meat shield. Yer whole relationship with yer God an’ such. I just wanted ta make sure ya were in tha know an’ didn’t say something ta set her off. Apparently she had an’ episode recently.”

“What happened?” Leon asked, concerned.

“Jaq told me. Part o’ why he got on tha council. Tha last mancer leader here at Masterwork said something off color ‘bout me ma during a council meetin’. While everyone was in an’ uproar, Verne an’ me pa knocked tha tar outta him. Enough that tha next day tha fool resigned an’ left tha Halls, vacatin’ his seat.”

“Wow. That’s uh, fortunate for Jaq, and terrible for your mother. The whole situation is terrible.”

“Well thank ya fer statin’ tha obvious!” Duamé looked forlornly back to his family home as he huffed, “Sorry. I shouldn’t be takin’ it out on ya. Just wish things could've been different.”

Leon remembered the task he had been given by Rohiel and Lochemetel. He knew that there remained members of their troupe who had yet to accept Adonai. With approximately one week left until a massive, world ending horde of undead would show up at their doorstep, time was running out.

Maybe this is the opportunity to approach him again. Leon reasoned.

“Duamé, maybe… maybe things could be different.” He started.

The dwarf looked understandably confused, “Wot ya talkin’ about, meat shield?”

“Well, I would just think that maybe if you and she accepted Adonai that–”

Duamé didn’t even let him finish. Growling, he said, “I told ya before meat shield, don’t expect me ta be one o’ yer converts! Wot kind o’ a ‘God o’ love’ would do this ta me family? I would never follow someone like that!”

Leon had been thinking of how to respond to this rebuttal ever since the first time Duamé had spoken about his daughter on the road to Agaprya. It seemed like a lifetime ago, even though only a few short weeks had passed. Still, with the knowledge he gleaned, and the wisdom that had been imparted, Leon felt it necessary to correct his friend.

"That's just it. A 'God of love' wouldn't do that to a family. Adonai would want your family to be together. To grow. To love. To find happiness in following Him. Division and strife are not of Adonai. That comes from our own choices, and from the enemy we face. An enemy that would like nothing more than for you to blame Adonai for all your problems when it really comes from somewhere else."

Duamé was silent for a moment before he drawled, "Ya mean this 'Xhormas' character?"

"Yes Duamé! If he wants to turn this world into one full of undead, wouldn't it make sense that he wouldn't want your family to live in the first place? He would do everything he could to kill your hopes. Your dreams. Your happiness. You. Remember what Rohiel said? You could be with your daughter again! All you have to do is–"

Duamé cut him off with a wave, "I know wot ya rustin' want me ta do, an' I ain't got nothin' ta apologize fer. Especially ta a God I ain't ever met or who won't even speak ta me himself. Gotta try an' preach ta me through angels, and Judges, an' rustin' mythical metals."

Leon wanted to understand, but more so wanted Duamé to understand. Not wanting to push more right now, Leon held up his hands stopping the argument. Duamé rubbed his temples in frustration. "Ugh. Tha whole thing gives me a headache I swear. Me pa an' Verne seemed ta have patched things up since I left. If yer truth streak an' Adonai are gonna cause a problem, I can see if ya can stay with Verne an' tha Granitehands."

"No," Leon objected. While he wasn't happy about the outcome, he didn't feel it right to leave the Onyxwill household. "No, it's ok, Duamé. I'll stay with you guys."

“Hmph, ya just like me old bed…” After a pause Duamé added, “It’s tha comforter.”

Baffled by the odd remark, Leon was about to agree with Duamé when the dwarf continued, “Ya know, I think all comforters are better than quilts – but I don’t like makin’ blanket statements.”

It took Leon a few seconds to get the joke, then he burst out laughing. It amazed him to see how Duamé could permeate such a serious conversation with jokes. After a few more chuckles from the both of them, Duamé continued, “I gotta go work on yer armor. Ya go do wotever judges do in their downtime.”

Trying to bridge the gap between them, Leon offered, “Can I help with it?”

Duamé barked a laugh, “Can ya smith?”

“Well, no.”

“Then I would recommend ya stay away from tha hot metal, unless ya want to get branded on yer behi–”

“Alright! Alright!” Leon relented with a smile. Deciding to check on the elves instead, Leon asked, “Can you let the ladies know I’ll be checking on the elves?”

“Righto, meat shield.” Duamé responded as he headed back to the house. Leon detoured past the still noisy forges to the mountain’s interior lake.

He passed a few bustling dwarves, as well as a gaggle of playing children, before he descended a small slope. In the distance, near the exit of the halls, a group of industrious dwarves worked to reinforce the doors and guard towers. He followed the path to the right and saw lines of dwarves who washed clothes and gathered water at opposite ends of the lake.

Near the divide in the lakebed, where the aeonyte had been revealed, Leon found Jaq and a few other oddly dressed dwarves crouching down, with their hands pressed to the rock floor. Jaq’s badger watched intently from nearby, and Leon watched as the dwarven mancers shifted the very earth.

Loud pops and cracks accompanied their efforts, and a large seam in the earth widened. Rock and gravel pushed up on either side of the crack like a wave, creating a long troughlike ‘v’ in the earth. The effort appeared to be too much for one of the dwarven geomancers, who passed out cold and collapsed to the ground. Another dwarf seemed to be on standby, and emptied a bucket of water on the unconscious dwarf which awakened him with a splutter.

After the earth had been moved, two teams of elves laid thick branches at the divide’s lowest point. This resulted in the formation of the ship’s spine, though the branches were quite asymmetrical and not secured together at all.

An elven woman who seemed faintly familiar gave Leon a slight wave while she and the other elves knelt down. She was dressed in plain cloth pants and a loose fitting shirt that had its sleeves rolled. Leon began to hear the distinct sound of wood cracking and bending, as the stout branches visibly came together and entwined. The wooden joints also thickened and extended outward towards the sides. What would have taken years for a living tree to grow, took mere moments. Leon watched in amazement as veritable trunks grew to form the ribcage of a long airship.

“How wide again in the middle?” The familiar looking elven woman asked loudly. Her voice was strained as she concentrated.

“Five at tha beam, yer Majesty!” Verne hollered nearby.

Leon tried to process his shock as Queen Chlorae replied, “The what?”

“Tha middle! Its tha widest point o’ tha hull without tha wings. An’ eighteen fer tha length! Isn’t there an outline there? Oi, where is tha chalk outline o’ tha ship?”

The assembled elves grunted and groaned as one by one they stopped exerting their shaping efforts. The last elf to quit was the plain clothed queen, who suddenly collapsed into the arms of her tired retinue. Leon rushed over to help, and gathered her to her feet.

“Oh, fir trees! I did not see you there, Judge! I thought you were just watching.” The flustered Queen Chlorae exclaimed. She seemed out of breath, but accepted the cup of java that was passed to her with gratitude.

"What are you doing?" Leon asked with confusion and concern.

"Whatever do you mean?" She asked, conversationally.

"You… You're pushing yourself just like you did at the Grove, and you could collapse again!"

"I am not some sprig without roots to be easily torn from the ground, young Judge." She chided. The Queen drank her java and graciously gave the cup back to a nearby elf. Smiling, she continued, "Many leaders command imperiously, or say one thing only to practice its opposite. I've always believed in a simpler form of rule."

When Leon gestured for her to continue, she laid a gentle, motherly hand on his shoulder.

"Never ask anyone to do anything for you, that you wouldn't do for yourself if given the chance."

The Queen turned her attention to her elven retinue, and addressed their concerns with grace and poise despite her appearance. Leon heard her report to Verne Granitehand that they could resume their efforts once they ate a meal and a few more elves joined them. It seemed the elves had been quick to adopt the dwarven model of three worker shifts – which created a non-stop stream of production.

After being politely told that he was simply in the way, Verne suggested that Leon head to the dwarven training grounds. There he could help Kérik and the injured member of the military triad. Leon couldn't recall if he had ever learned her name. His mind had been occupied with other thoughts when he had been deluged with the council's rapid fire questions.

Cle-something? He tried to remember.

Leon headed towards the dwarven training area, which was near the back of the cavern. It was surrounded by more stalagmite housing, and proved to be a small amphitheater-like structure, similar to the chariot race arena in Agaprya. The training ground's recessed seating was partially filled with younger dwarves and surprisingly, a couple of trolls. They listened intently to Kérik Silverspine as he delivered a speech. Leon clambered over, and sat down in the spacious back row. Once settled, he listened to a familiar speech – one he had heard many years before.

Five years ago…

"Alright ya greenhorns, listen up!" Rear Admiral Silverspine shouted. His small stature did not detract from his commanding presence. Leon stood at attention, as did the other naval cadets whom he had gotten to know over the past few weeks. A myriad of races stood facing the dwarf, as he paced back and forth in front of the Cage. Leon stood next to a friend he had made on his first day. He was a short smart aleck named Dawes.

In the infamous Cage of the academy, an enemy soldier reached through the tight bars in vain. A bony skeleton, which was held together by the slightest amount of sinew, stood while the rear admiral paced in front of it. The bony arm tracked Silverspine, who stayed just out of its reach as he gave his lecture.

"Most o' ya seem ta think that yer settlin' inta some sorta routine now. Wake up early, run a lot, train a lot, an' eat a lot. Right?" A few of the cadets chuckled until the Rear Admiral's friendliness disappeared. "Now, yer schedule is gonna start ta include tactics. Learning wot we face. Wot tha enemy is. This," He said, as he pointed at the old, animated skeleton, "This is wot ya face. This is our enemy. Ya may think it ain't much, until ya meet a horde o' em. Until ya have been fightin' fer hours an' they haven't stopped comin'."

"Fightin' in tha Dead Wars ain't no picnic. Ya get tired? They don't. Ya need ta sleep an' eat? They don't. When ya swing yer sword so much ya feel ya can't lift it anymore, ol' boney here is ready ta choke tha life outta ya same as when ya lifted a sword fer tha first time. They don't feel pain, loss, remorse, er anythin' but tha need ta add ya ta their numbers."

While nobody present had the ease to respond to the Rear Admiral, the cold reality of the dwarf's words froze Leon's tongue in place.

Slaying undead wasn't really a priority for him like it was for Dawes, who had lost his whole family to a ravaging horde. While Leon would have liked to voice that he could fill any non-combat support roles the academy needed, he felt like he was already on thin ice due to the informal meeting he had with the Rear Admiral on his first day.

Silverspine continued his lecture, "Tha fact is, eventually if yer not careful, ya become one o' them. Unless tha crewmember by yer side is willin' ta take yer head off before ya turn. Nobody can avoid dying, all our lives end here." He gestured at the skeleton, "So if we are all goin' this way, it is yer duty, what ya signed on fer, ta take as many o' these rustin' undead with ya before ya go. So we're gonna train ya, and mold ya, ta run as many o' them inta that ground as ya can!"

Present Day...

The similarity to Kérik Silverspine's practiced speech ended when Leon heard him add, "An' ya got a week ta learn so unclog yer ears and listen good!"

Feeling that he wouldn't be helpful here either, Leon got up to leave. As he turned to exit the amphitheater, he heard the elderly dwarf shout, "O'maybe, ya should listen ta HIM!"

Armor clinked as heads turned, and Leon felt the multitudes of eyes upon his back. With a sigh he turned and saw hundreds staring straight at him. Revelator hadn't even needed to shine to draw their attention. The blasted whispers and mumbles that followed him wherever he went began in earnest as he stepped down to the center of the amphitheater and approached his former superior.

Leon felt exposed with so many eyes upon him, and wished he had his armor and helm to cover himself and hide his face. Flushed, Leon drew near to Kérik Silverspine and shook his hand while the former admiral gestured for him to address the crowd. Leon looked over the young dwarves and trolls. He even noticed a look of interest on the face of the dwarven woman at the front, who was a member of the

Nonagint. One of her arms was wrapped in a splint, but with the multitude of weapons she carried, it didn't detract from her ferocity.

Leon was becoming used to public speaking, and felt he had improved since he had first spoken to the village of Everbright. Without any further hesitation, he launched into an explanation of how to defend against shamblers, wretches, alukahs, and liches. He shared which tactics had worked when the elves fought against the horde and the undead chimeras. He talked about the dragon that the skeletal liches summoned over lake Xael, and how the undead were aligned with the menace. He described strategies such as disabling limbs before attempting a killing blow, engaging multiple enemies at once, and using some of the undead's mindlessness to their advantage.

It felt as though he lectured for hours. Some of the attendees left during his speech, while others filtered in. Occasionally, Kérik would interject to ask for further explanation, or add on to what Leon advised.

Partway through his lecture about how long it took for the deceased to rise again, an idea came to him. "Of course, if you want to avoid that happening in the first place, there is a very simple solution."

"Avoid wot, lad?" Kérik asked.

"Turning into undead. You could just stay dead, and your spirit would be at rest with Adonai forever." Leon stated with simplicity.

Seizing the opportunity, Leon shared what happened at the drained lake with Phonz and the nephilim spirit he had encountered. Then he circled back to the spiritual war between Adonai and Xhormas, and how belief in Adonai, along with true repentance, was an assurance of peace and protection from your body being subject to Xhormas' influence after death. The words tumbled from him. Leon felt with certainty that the best weapon in the Dead Wars was the capstone of his speech: belief in Adonai.

When questions were asked, he answered as best as he could. "Just ask some of the elves, they saw the power of Adonai firsthand. Some of their number did not rise as undead after the battles at both the

Elvenwood, and the bridge. The proof is there for those who are willing to look. Willing to believe."

Leon didn't pay attention to the size of the crowd that was coming or going, but taught until his throat was dry and he couldn't speak any more without coughing or clearing his throat. When he finally lifted his eyes to the seats of the amphitheater, the entire section in front of him was filled.

Dwarves were watching him with awestruck faces. Trolls were scratching their heads as they puzzled through what he had said. All listened to Leon's words, and saw as Revelator flicked on to signify that sundown had arrived. As Leon wrapped up his message, he pointed to the spearhead and said, "I have been told that dwarves worship minerals and that elves idolize nature. Adonai created them both. So why not worship the creator instead of the created?"

A sizable portion of the audience professed belief in Adonai after Leon's speech. The crowd dispersed for meals and their next rotation of shifts as Kérik Silverspine asked, "Can ya come back tomorrow ta speak again? Yer bringin' a much needed message o' hope with that horde approachin'. Especially now that yer tellin' us that we might be facin' dragons with em!"

Exhausted, Leon couldn't help but grin sheepishly as he agreed.

The next day there was a larger crowd. The audience was filled with not just those wanting to learn, but also with those who validated Leon's claims. In fact, many familiar faces joined the crowd. Queen Chlorae and Princess Schalae, Gezado and Thur, Ignys and his wife Esper, and Jaq were all present. Kérik once again introduced Leon, who spoke about tactics against the undead, then launched into the topic of Adonai. It was easier to speak about the second time, especially since he had the presence of mind to bring a skin of water with him. More questions were asked and answered, and as understanding grew, so did the crowd.

Feeling good about the work he had done for Adonai, and seeing that the frame of the airship in the distance had continued to grow day after day, Leon felt he had done well as he fell asleep in the bed he had borrowed from Duamé.

Chapter 19: The Attempt

Leon knew he was dreaming. Knew that he was asleep. But something was wrong. Instead of the typical grey expanse, he was surrounded by darkness. It was a darkness so thick and encompassing that he couldn't even see his own body. He tried to think of Revelator, and its shining light, to summon it. To pierce through the darkness. But it didn't work. Nothing worked. Nothing could be seen.

Then two large red-glowing eyes opened in front of him. Each eye was larger than his entire body, and cast just enough glow for Leon to see that his arms and legs were pulled taut.

A chilling voice, one that made Leon's skin crawl, growled in a raspy whisper around him, "Judge."

The fear Leon felt was almost palpable in his frozen state. He tried to move, but his muscles and limbs were locked in place and he found the only thing he maintained control of was his mouth. His teeth chattered ever so slightly as he addressed the being, "X-Xh-Xhormas."

"Yeeeesss." The fallen drawled as its eyes narrowed. "You see now, the futility of your actions. None can escape me. Not even you. Not even a Judge."

A dark tendril of shadow passed in front of its glowing red eyes and inched closer to Leon. As it grazed his cheek, Leon felt as though the side of his face had been soaked in ice water. He was freezing, and his teeth chattered even more. Leon felt like a small kid again. One who was subjected to the the torture and abuse of his elder brother and father. He could not escape or fight against this being. It had complete control over the situation, and all Leon felt he could do was grit his teeth and wait for the nightmare to end.

The cold, dark, eel-like tendril lifted Leon's chin as Xhormas spoke, "Ah. Your rebellious nature presents itself. You seek to defy me still? Knowing that I can crush you? That I could end your life this very moment if I wished?"

Leon wanted to respond, but the cold was too overpowering. He struggled with the effort, and it seemed to agitate Xhormas. Impatience grated through the deep timbre of Xhormas' voice as he said, "Speak! Why will you not speak, you worthless insect!"

I'm trying, so I can tell you to leave me alone! Leon thought.

"Hmph. I understand your defiance. After all, rebellion is something I know intimately."

"Wh-what do you want?" Leon managed to stutter out.

After a pause Xhormas growled, "Straight to the point then."

Its glowing red eyes grew larger, or perhaps they had gotten closer, as the ginormous shadow spoke.

"You have been cast out by your family. Your amorous interest wants to pursue nothing with you. You are preparing for a battle that you cannot win. Yet, I am willing to extend you and your friends mercy. Feel free to show your appreciation."

Baffled by Xhormas' knowledge of his situation, Leon said, "Th-thanks?"

"You may stay at that hovel, the stolen territory the dwarves call home, and all there may live in peace within the mountain. You would remain unassailed. Safe. All that is required is your obedience. All that you need to do is worship me."

Uh what? Leon railed internally. "Worship you? Look at what you have done! Look at all the people you've killed! How could I possibly–"

"Because you have no other options left. Worship me, and I will give you all that you could ever want and more. I could give you rest." Xhormas drawed out his words at the end, emphasizing the temptation.

Leon, however, wouldn't have it, "You just called me an insect a minute ago. I am pretty sure your real feelings towards me are clear."

"Your refusal will equate to your extinction. I would gladly have my forces consume your pitiful resistance. As insignificant as you are, I am giving you a chance to save yourself and your friends from my wrath. I offer you clemency. Is obedience such a high price?" Xhormas reasoned.

Well, great. Leon thought. *Here comes the guilt trip. Just like Mahomet, I can't trust him so how do I–*

Xhormas interrupted his musings, "What say you, Judge?"

Through the cold, the fear, and the frustration of Xhormas trying to back him into a corner, he was struck by a realization.

Xhormas can't hear me think?

Hey Xhormas, go take a salt bath! Leon thought.

When his adversary didn't react, Leon felt his brain go as hyperactive as Gionna's or Calvin's likely did when inspired. If Xhormas couldn't hear his thoughts, but Adonai could, then what power could this deity have by comparison? How could Xhormas possibly win with such a disadvantage?

The realization gave Leon enough boldness to snort, then laugh at the situation. At that same moment he started to feel his extremities.

"No."

The pervasive cold vanished as the tendril of darkness coiled and uncoiled in the glow of the fallen deity's eyes. "Then you consign all of the living to undeath. All who die are now on your head. A head that Nachash Seraph has assured me he will present as a gift after he digests the rest of you." Xhormas growled.

The threat, and revelation that Nachash Seraph survived the forest fire, rang hollow as Leon summoned up more courage. "You are a desperate being trying to win a war where you are completely outclassed. My allegiance is to Adonai, and–"

As soon as Leon said the Creator's name aloud, Xhormas issued an ear splitting hiss, and shot multiple tendrils towards Leon in the red glow. The shadowy appendages were about to pierce his head when a flash of light sparked in front him. A large glowing א appeared and the shadowy tendrils either crashed into or curved away from it. An altogether different voice, one whom Leon heard in a prison cell recently, reverberated through the nightmare.

"MINE."

The faint, frustrated, yell of Xhormas faded as Leon jerked awake. He was bathed in sweat and sat up on the bed to see that Revelator glowed in his hand. The Judge's Mark on it mirrored what had protected him in his dream.

Leon knew by the light of the spearhead that it was still early. He carefully climbed out of Duamé's old bed and made his way out of the Onyxwill home. Leon shuffled towards the lake with a change of clothes in hand. He was singularly focused on bathing and washing the last vestiges of fear from himself. As he passed the forges, smithies, and the staging area where the airship was being built, it appeared as though they were staffed by the same number of workers during nighttime hours as during the day.

The large wooden framework of the ship was complete thanks to a steady stream of elven hortimancers who had worked nonstop to grow and shape the vessel. Hundreds of other workers now swarmed the worksite as platforms were constructed for the decking. Sheets of aeonyte, and other building materials of various sizes, were brought over to the ship and assembled there. Walking by, Leon saw a few cannons being wheeled towards the warship, and teams of dwarves traversing the cave with cannonballs in hand ready to stock the onboard armory.

Leon made his way to a secluded spot near the waterfall to bathe. He ruminated on the nightmare and his interaction with Xhormas. There was no doubt that the undead army was headed their way, or that Nachash Seraph would want revenge for his maimed wing. With those thoughts, Leon found himself second guessing all of his recent decisions.

Is everything we are doing going to be enough?

The undead army, with all of their rage, would crash upon Masterwork Halls soon. In a mere matter of days they would be engaged in their last ditch effort to simply be allowed to live.

Leon finished his bath and changed into spare clothes before he headed back to the Onyxwill's for breakfast. His spear rested on a crag nearby and did not light again as he grabbed it. Daylight peeked through the mouth of the Halls as the night shift ended and the morning began.

The smell of eggs and bacon welcomed Leon as warmly as did the greetings of his friends. As he stepped inside the home he saw that everyone was present. Miala, Kelleren, Duamé, and Gionna all chowed down next to Ignys and his wife Esper. As Leon found a seat in the nook next to Miala, a plate awaited him.

Ignys leaned over to talk to him as he sat down. "Eat up quick. Got ta take ya ta tha smithy fer a bit before we meet with tha Nonagint. We got a mail carrier scheduled ta come sometime today, so that might be a thing. Especially since we've fallen in with tha infamous bandit!"

"It's not like Masterwork is declaring war on Xaelon." Leon responded in confusion.

"No lad, if Lucien Rhise is makin' a move on tha throne like we saw in tha last herald, then he's declarin' war on US." Ignys emphasized.

Gionna and Miala finished eating and rose to go help with assembly at the construction site. As she left, Miala met Leon's eyes in a lingering gaze which set his heart to fluttering. After breakfast was finished Leon, heard Duamé give a flimsy false excuse about where his daughter was, and why she couldn't play with Esper today. Just as quickly as Leon's heart had been set aflutter, it also broke.

The elderly dwarven woman took her son's excuse in stride, and with a knowing look from Ignys, he, Duamé and Leon all left for the smithies. It was quite loud and crowded next to the forges. Everyone bustled about the area with purpose. Those who weren't actually smithing were busy moving the smiths' creations and supplies. Crates of iron crossbow bolts or arrowheads were hauled off the site, while fresh iron or aeonyte ingots were brought over to be shaped into their predestined forms.

Ignys shouted to a nearby dwarf who appeared to possess an odd assortment of spare parts, "Take that over ta tha airship an' do whatever that genius gnome woman says with it!" Then he and Duamé headed to a workspace that was set a small distance apart from the others. It was larger than most, and had more tools hung from the nearby racks. They waved Leon over, and grabbed a familiar bundle off a nearby wall.

Leon smiled as he gazed upon his armor once more. It had been fully repaired and looked like new. The leather straps had to be replaced due to his skirmish with the satyrs, and the new ones had been dyed a high quality dark reddish brown. The scratches and gouges were gone, and its polished sheen reflected the slight stubble that had grown on Leon's tired face.

"We went ahead an' fixed all the damaged bits, an' gave it a good once over with the materials we had on hand." Ignys stated, as he held out an arming jacket to Leon.

As Leon put the jacket on he noted the comfort it gave him. He then strapped the rest of his armor in place and once more felt safe and protected. He stood from tightening the greaves on his shins, and was met by a wondrous sight.

It was a perfect circle, save for a small oval that had been cut out of one side. To Leon, the end result looked like a fattened 'c'. Duamé turned it to show that the straps on the rear side of the shield were positioned just right for Leon's hand to sit at the small section of missing material. During a fight he would still be able to hold his spear with both hands, and even rest Revelator inside it. The round shield had been mainly made from aeonyte, and bore a similar metal to his armor around the edges. Its pale blue exterior was a perfect match to Leon's spear, and it was lighter than what he remembered a traditional shield to be.

"You, you made this?" Leon breathed.

“Think o’ it as a ‘thank ya’.” Ignys said as he helped Leon strap the shield to his forearm. “Thank ya fer bringing me son back ta me. Thank ya fer giving us here at Masterwork Halls a task again. Fer bringing us outta our mire, an’ makin’ us work together instead o’ tearin’ at each other in tha Nonagint.”

Leon grasped the leather handle that wrapped around his thumb, and saw a familiar sight woven and embedded into it. It was the last piece of his missing equipment.

The bright red levigem that had once hung from his neck now rested in the palm of his hand. Leon would no longer have to struggle with his necklace, or the angle of the spear, to join them together and leap great distances. Duamé explained that it would now just be a matter of grasping the spear with both hands.

“Ta be clear though, I figured since yer a ‘meat shield’ it would help ya ta have an actual shield.” Duamé stated in his typical offhanded fashion.

“This is incredible!” Leon marveled at and maneuvered with the shield in hand, making adjustments for holding the spear in one hand a majority of the time.

“Ya might want ta talk ta Clénoi about tactics with a spear an’ shield. She’s our weapons master here an’ even with a broken arm, she could still knock us all flat.”

Leon flexed and felt the armor against him, then turned to Duamé and asked, “Is she at the amphitheater?”

Ignys nodded, “Ya. Trainin’ today. So none o’ yer sermons.”

“Sermons?”

“Don’t think we don’t see wot yer doin’.” Duamé commented. “Ya have done a great thing fer us here at Masterwork. Don’t push it with yer ‘Adonai’ stuff.”

“Duamé, I am just trying to help.”

At this point Ignys interjected, “Esper talked about yer preachin’ last night an’ seemed ta like it. But Duamé told me all about yer ‘God o’ love’, an’ I happen ta agree with him that it’s not our ‘metal on tha anvil’.”

Flabbergasted, Leon didn't know what to say. He didn't have an answer for their obstinate disbelief, but hoped that with only a few days left before the undead horde could show up, some sort of breakthrough would occur. In any case, Leon had to remember not to push too hard, especially after such an incredible gift.

"I… I understand. Do um, do we know when the mail carrier airship might arrive?" Leon asked, partially to change the topic.

Ignys peered at the sunlight that angled through the cavern opening, and where it shone in the Halls. "It's scheduled ta be here in a few more hours."

Leon nodded, thinking that he could train with this… weapons master dwarf in the interim. After profusely thanking the father and son team again, he headed towards the amphitheatre. Once there, he saw creatures of all sizes being put through training maneuvers and mock fights at different speeds. A troll sparred with three dwarves, while elves rolled around on the ground and tussled with each other. Several armored dwarves and soldiers walked through and directed it all. It took a few moments for Leon to look through the amphitheatre and spot the dwarf he was searching for. The earthen splint on her arm was what stood out from the rest.

Leon strode through the ranks of those preparing for war, and just like on the *Golem*, a few stopped what they were doing to stare at him. They stared at his new armor, spear, and shield. At the Judge who was supposed to save them all. His celebrity was not something that he wanted to focus on. Instead, Leon resolved to direct all the attention that he could towards Adonai.

He reached the area where Clénoi watched as a few dwarfs defended themselves against a mock charge. Even she raised an eyebrow as she appraised his new look. She appeared almost giddy as she asked, "New gear, eh? Looks nice! Shield an' spear are a good pair. Have ya fought with a shield before?"

Leon responded, "A few times."

With a smile, she reached back and drew a small dagger. "Well then, let's see what you know."

Surprised that she was willing to fight with her arm in a splint, Leon set his feet shoulder length apart, and in the typical 'L' stance. His shield clanged from the dagger that the dwarven weapon master threw. She ran towards him, drew another, and sliced and hacked with speed. Leon dodged what he could, and blocked what he couldn't. He stabbed and slashed with Revelator, careful to avoid her splint. A ring of onlookers gathered as he fenced with her.

The problem that he found was that she was not only fast, but a much smaller target than what he was used to. She stayed inside his spear range, which forced him to grip the spear closer to the tip. It also caused him to defend with the shield more often, as blows clanged off of it. Leon remembered his training, and braced with the shield set to reflect not just the object that hit it, but also the momentum behind it. Clénoi seemed to produce an almost endless amount of knives to throw at Leon, and the shield crafted by the Onyxwill's was certainly put through its paces.

Clénoi stepped well inside Leon's range, and was knocked back by a bash from Leon's shield. She had, however, managed to hook her heel behind Leon's leg. He was not able to react fast enough, and the dwarven woman pulled him off balance, causing him to stagger. Leon wasn't able to right himself before she recovered and dove towards his other leg. When she crashed into it, Leon fell to the side with an, "Ack!". Upon landing he immediately rolled.

The roll ended with Cleoni holding her short sword to Leon's throat. Many dwarves cheered as they watched the exchange end. She sheathed her sword and helped Leon sit up. "Good form, but ya used yer shield as a weapon too much. Ya can't just fling it around everywhere like a sword."

The blood pumped through Leon as he took in the advice. He looked around, and saw several onlookers exchange coins as they settled bets. After she allowed a few moments of the revelry, Clénoi shouted, "Alright ya lugs! Back ta practice! Square up!"

Time ticked by as Leon worked with Clénoi. He fixed his form and improved his use of the new shield. The lightweight shield proved to be a good counterbalance for Leon, as he learned that fighting with the spear and shield was different, though not as much as he had originally thought. She helped with his arm placement, and even though she only had one usable arm, still proved extremely agile. He felt the difference between training with her while awake, and with Lochemetel while asleep. By the time a horn sounded to signal the mail carrier's arrival, Leon's muscles ached with a familiarity of use.

He accompanied Clénoi as the Nonagint leaders converged at the Halls gate. They spoke briefly about what they might have to do once the ship landed, and some of their suggestions shocked him. Leon agreed that a few valid points were made: they couldn't know how pervasive Lucien's influence had become, and if he owned the Herald guild then whomever was on the ship couldn't be trusted.

As one they left the gates of Masterwork to watch the small airship descend. Like many old rowboats, this one had smaller levigems which skewered through its wings. The pilot maneuvered the small boat down near the gigantic exterior gate of the Halls, and as soon as it landed, a herald stepped from the boat and dusted himself off.

Unlike most heralds, this one was dressed in puffery that was windswept. Even the herald's hair had been blown into an unkempt state, and he huffed about his appearance. The frills of high fashion looked ridiculous to Leon. After years of simply attempting to stay alive, anything other than a uniform looked unimportant. Still, Leon had to admit that watching those who were wrapped up in such trivial matters, while he worried about life and limb, amused him.

Kérik Silverspine came forward and deposited a sack that jingled into the mail carrier. He peered at the pilot and grunted softly as he came back towards Leon and the other dwarves. An almost imperceptible shake of his head signalled a lack of recognition. The herald squawked as he looked around, "Um, didn't there used to be more of you?"

"Yes, yes there was." Verne commented flatly.

After an uncomfortable silence, the herald shrugged and continued, "Well, alright then."

He pulled out a small scroll case that had a red ribbon tied around it. As he slipped the ribbon off, Gionna and Princess Schalae crested a small hill in the path where thousands of new trees were beginning to grow. Many of the elves flitted about the young trees, and tender young shoots and stalks promised a rich, lush forest in a few years. Some of the trees were already shoulder and head high, which was incredible to see. As Gionna and the Princess approached, the herald began to speak his news.

"It is with great pleasure that I announce the royal wedding between Princess Giselle and Lord Laric Rhise will be held in one week's time. King Garinth is pleased by his ability to retire and let youth and strength issue in a new chapter for Xaelon."

Leon could easily see the opinionated, biased, blowhard's message through the report he conveyed. *Laric and Lucien are making their move.*

"–and the might of the kingdom's army and air capability will surely prevail against the undead hordes." The herald finished, before moving on to another article. "The bandit known as 'Leon' is still at large, and is considered extremely… dangerous…" The flush that grew under Leon's armor and helm was telling, as he watched the herald trail off his pronouncement to look straight at him.

"Ya probably shoulda stayed in tha halls, Judge." Verne sighed before he called, "Now!"

A swarm of dwarves, along with Princess Schalae, all ran and clambered onto the small mail carrier – effectively cutting off any chance of escape for the herald and pilot. Leon would have helped had he not felt so touched by the gesture of support the dwarves and elves had just shown him. Gezado must have hidden behind the entrance doors to the halls, because he lumbered up and put a large foot and a couple of his hands onto the airship, which effectively pinned it to the ground. With a rumbled, "You going nowhere," the troll stared at the petrified pilot who held his hands up in surrender.

The herald mirrored that gesture while the few dwarves present waved hammers and axes threateningly at him. “P-please! Don’t hurt me!” He squealed.

Gionna gingerly tapped her cane up to him and said, “Don’t worry, dearie, we won’t.” Then she snatched the herald message away. She tapped her glasses until what looked like bifocals rotated in front of her eyes, and proceeded to scan through the rest of the scroll.

“Standard rubbish. This is why I don’t listen to heralds anymore. No news, just propaganda.” She announced, as she rolled up the scroll and handed it back to the spluttering herald. She tapped her glasses again until the lens with the tiny suspended discerner cube was in front of her eye. She tried to question the herald, while Leon’s attention was drawn over to the former admiral and the pilot.

“I don’t recognize ya lad, but I’m askin’ ya ta get yer beehind outta there slowly.” Silverspine said, as he hefted his double bladed axe in his hands. The pilot silently acquiesced. With raised, dirt-stained hands he stepped from the airship as Silverspine stepped on.

“Wot are ya doin’ Kérik?” Verne asked with concern.

Kérik Silverspine pulled a few leather straps from a side pocket and fashioned a harness to keep himself on the ship. “Goin’ on a scoutin’ expedition. Gotta see how far away tha horde is. Oi! Princess. Got any scouts with good eyes on em?”

“Ex-excuse me!” The herald tried to protest.

“We’ve heard enough outta ya. Quiet!” Verne admonished.

A few elven scouts clambered aboard at Princess Schalae’s direction, while everyone’s eyes watched the former admiral maneuver the mail carrier upward.

A sharp sting of pain lanced through Leon’s side as he was roughly jostled and brought to the ground. Revelator rolled away from him, and he heard several shouts and a few screams dimly through the pain that was overwhelming him. Leon tried to turn halfway over, but was hindered by something he couldn’t quite reach, which stuck out from his lower back. The effort caused another jolt of pain to lance through him, as he spasmed on the ground. Blood stained his fingertips as he looked up towards movement.

Gezado stepped on and subdued the pilot of the mail carrier. He struggled and screamed as the troll viciously brought his huge axe down on him. It thudded into the pilot, just as Leon's head lost strength and collided with the soft grass below. A distant voice yelled, "Leon! No!" before his vision went black.

Chapter 20: The Recovery

The familiar grey expanse greeted Leon as he lay on the ground in the dream. The flat smooth blade that had protruded from his lower back was gone, which allowed him to stand. He was in the same worn clothes he had been given while in the prison. Neither Revelator nor his armor were visible. All of his pain was gone, and all Leon could feel was the warmth of the gigantic ball of light that floated in the sky. While Leon enjoyed its familiar warmth, he was concerned.

Concerned for his friends. Concerned for his family. Concerned for the residents of the Halls, and the imminent battle that would take place. Due to his worry, he yelled out in the expanse.

"Rohiel! Lochemetel! Adonai!"

The pulse that came from the ball of light in the air was massive. It blew past and through Leon, causing his hair to whip in the wind it generated. He shielded his eyes from both the wind and luminescence. When he lowered his forearm, the two angels who had guided and trained him stood in front of him. They were both armored in their elaborate aeonyte. Rohiel's face was obscured by the light that emanated from him and Lochemetel's was covered by her helm. Despite his inability to see their features, Leon knew they were staring at him.

"What… What happened? One moment I was there and the next…" Leon trailed off as Rohiel silently extended an arm out to his side.

An image materialized which showed Leon as he lay on a stone slab, dressed in the same clothes, surrounded by a few of the Nonagint, as well as Schalae, Gionna, and Miala. Much to Leon's astonishment, Miala held Revelator. As he watched himself in the vision, it looked as though Schalae and a few of the other dwarves and elves were ministering to him. A cloth bandage had been wrapped around his midsection, and bore a dark red stain next to his spine. The stain looked big. Much too big.

Gionna spoke to those who were assembled around the interior of a large stalagmite home. Her eyes were red ringed, as if she had been crying. "It seemed the pilot was new, based on the information gathered from the herald's interrogation. He began flying the mail carrier a week ago, long enough to know how to fly it, but not long enough to wash the dirt stains from his nails. That was the key."

"After we analyzed the dirt, paired with the build of the pilot, it became evident that he was a miner by trade, and not a professional pilot. The dirt is not indigenous to Masterwork Halls, and if I had to guess, I would say that it is likely closer in makeup to the soil found around the Levigem mines to the southeast. Between his being human, a miner, and our soil analysis, we can safely assume who ordered the assassination attempt. It would be asinine to assume that he was the only person commissioned to carry out the attempt. Who knows how many of these mail carrier pilots are possibly Lucien's men…"

The image of the meeting disintegrated and blew away in a gentle breeze. Awestruck, Leon looked at the two angels and threw up his hands. "So what? That's it? I'm dead? This… This can't be it! What about the others? About Duamé? I never got the chance to…"

Once again Rohiel extended a hand, and the room rematerialized. This time Duamé was there. He sat in a small chair, next to the stone slab that Leon's body was on. A few tallow candles were lit, which provided just enough light for Leon to see by. He saw that Duamé was also crying.

"Boyo, I don't know how it happened, it... Well okay, I know how it happened, but it was jus' tha strangest thing. She just... remembered."

Duamé looked up and slapped the stone table Leon was on. "She remembered everythin'! Tha whole flintin' thing! Me leavin', me pa an' I tellin' her Esperella was out when she really wasn't. She just said, 'Ya shouldn't lie about such a horrible thin' anymore, an' that Esperella was playin' up there with Adonai! Ever since she heard ya talkin' about Adonai she got better. Ever since... since she accepted Him at tha amphitheatre."

Watching the one sided exchange, Leon felt as his heart leapt into his throat. He waited for Duamé to say the words he wanted to hear. His friend continued talking as if Leon could respond. "I know, ya would tell me a giant-sized 'I told ya so' if ya could. If ya could wake up, we could use yer help. We only got a shiny, dolomitie day left till they arrive according ta Silverspine. Even so, I'll..."

Princess Schalae entered at that moment, "I need to change the bandage again, Duamé. Miala wants to try with Revelator again, to see if healing will work this ti–"

"Alright, alright! Jus' gimme a minute!" The dwarf huffed an explosive breath as he stood from his seat. He laid a gentle hand on Leon as he said, "I'll protect em for ya. I'll protect her. Don't need no Adonai ta do so. Jus' need me a new hammer an' me stubbornness, right?"

The image disappeared like the first, and Leon fell to his knees in despair. So much was left unfinished. So much left undone. Duamé hadn't accepted Adonai. The horde needed to be defeated. Lucien and Laric needed to be stopped. Xhormas needed to be stopped!

"Let me go back! Please! I need to go back!" Leon cried to Rohiel and Lochemetel. He pounded the grey floor of the expanse with his fists due to his frustration at their silence. Finally, looking up at them both, Leon yelled, "Answer me!"

The light pulsed again and Leon's concerns disappeared in a sense of comfort. His troubles turned to calmness, and the heaviness of his worries and cares were wiped away like tears from his eyes.

"Why would you want to leave this place?" Rohiel asked, breaking the peace of the silence.

As Leon still knelt on the floor, he remembered his friends who were about to face the horde. He thought of those he had met in the Halls, at the Bridge, in the Grove, in Agaprya, even in Everbright, which seemed like a lifetime ago. Their faces bubbled to the surface of his mind as he remembered each and every one. The last face he thought of was framed by fiery red hair, and Leon's heart yearned to be with her again.

"For them. So that they could enjoy the peace of this place, like I do." He responded.

Rohiel reached out and lifted Leon to his feet before he said, ***"Greater love has no one than this, that someone lay down his life for his friends."***

A question formed across Leon's mind as he remembered all the tests he had gone through with Rohiel. All the lessons about wisdom and knowledge that he had to learn and remember.

"I'm not… dead, am I?"

Rohiel clarified after a pause, ***"...No. Only comatose. Only Adonai can raise the dead back to life."***

The angel walked behind Leon, and between one step and the next he disappeared without any further elaboration. A wave of light pulsed once again, this time bearing a slight heaviness as Leon looked at himself. His recently remade armor materialized over himself. It was unblemished and accompanied by his new shield on one arm, while Revelator formed in his other hand.

He turned and saw Lochemetel similarly dressed. In addition to her usual armor, she also had an aeonyte shield strapped to her arm. "Let me guess. 'I must learn'?" Leon asked.

"No." Lochemetel replied, as she tapped her spear and shield together. ***"You must win."***

Surprised by her response, Leon launched himself towards his angelic sparring partner while she simultaneously ran towards him as well. They stabbed and sliced at each other, causing their spears to bounce and slide off of their opponent's shield. Lochemetel was as fast as ever, but Leon felt that he managed to hold his own a little longer with each skirmish. He knew some of her attack patterns well, while new patterns emerged as she used her shield to obscure what her next move was.

Lochemetel landed a few blows and then swept Leon's legs out from under him. He acknowledged his temporary defeat, before he got up and nodded again. Almost immediately they launched into another skirmish. They parried and thrust, and the boundless energy of the expanse never allowed Leon to tire or feel the pang of exhaustion.

No matter how Leon thought he might gain an advantage, or which angle he chose to attack, Lochemetel proved unbeatable. Her responses were short, effective, and would have been brutal if Leon had been an undead. Whenever Leon defended himself, he could usually last three to four blocks or parries before she would slap him with the flat of her blade, or shove him to the ground.

During one exchange she thrust her spear as she usually did, but then swung it sharply down like a sword, before finally shoving Leon away with her shield. She had performed this same maneuver a few times during their spar, which usually indicated that she wanted Leon to learn how to counter it before she moved on to another sequence. On many occasions Leon had felt satisfied with just knowing how to defend himself. Now he had another mission – he had to win.

After he fell flat on his back once again, Leon quickly got up and nodded. As he approached Lochemetel he kept his spearhead behind his outstretched shield before he thrusted. This was one tactic he had quickly learned from her. His opponent would be unable to know exactly where the thrust might come from. When he did stab, he was careful not to overextend. She knocked his spear aside then sliced downward with her own while he sidestepped. Leon jumped over her spear's low sweep, and crashed his shield into her upraised one. They both pushed and shoved each other away.

She then thrust her spear again, and this time rather than knocking it away, Leon leaned out of it's path. He caught it's shaft, and trapped it within the opening of his shield with his own spear. For a split second his eyes met Lochemetel's. Then he grasped her golden spear with his shield hand, and turned. The bodily momentum threw them both to the side, and she lost control as Leon skittered his spear down the length of hers. The angel stayed out of his spear's reach, and relinquished hers for the first time since Leon had begun sparring with her.

Leon seized the moment, and let her spear clatter to the smooth grey floor. He tapped his spear against the Levigem held in the palm of his hand, and leapt toward her. Lochemetel righted herself just as Leon barrelled into her upraised shield. His mass still managed to knock her down as they careened across the floor of the expanse.

As they slid to a stop, Leon was on top of her armored form, and Revelator's spearhead was pressed against her neck.

A smile played across her helmeted chin, as Leon stood and held out a hand to help her up. Lochemetel grabbed his shield hand and hoisted herself up. Then she turned Leon's hand upward to show the levigem embedded in the leather.

"Wisdom is better than jewels." Lochemetel said as she placed a finger on the levigem. Then she walked over and picked up her golden spear with her back to him.

"Are you ready to return?" She asked.

"To there, yes. To here," Leon replied after a moment, "Not until I have saved as many as I can."

As one last wave of light started to pass over Leon Lochemetel spoke again.

"Then go give them heaven, Judge."

A high pitched tone hovered just on the edge of Leon's hearing as he opened his eyes. The cool stone table he awoke on was the same one he had seen in his vision. It appeared to be some sort of medical recovery area. The smell of incense hung in the air which masked the scent of perpetual illness. A faint snoring came from one bed over where Phonz still laid unconscious. The light that gently illuminated the room didn't come from either candles or glowing crystals in the ceiling. Instead, it came from Revelator, which both Miala and Schalae gripped.

The high pitched noise also came from the glowing spear, and faded as Schalae withdrew her hand from Leon's side. She was dressed in her dark bark armor, and Kelleren sat nearby matching her in his dog version of the bark armor. As Leon's eyes shifted to Miala, she hurried to him.

"Leon!" She cried, as she embraced him. Kelleren woofed softly as Princess Schalae let go of the spear, which silenced the tone in the air.

"Gopher wood! Gently!" The princess admonished. She got an earthenware cup and passed it to a grateful Leon. "Drink slowly."

The water had an odd taste to it, but Leon drank it anyway while the elven princess looked over his bandages. After she ran her slender fingers over a sensitive spot on Leon's lower back, Princess Schalae announced her prognosis, "Well, it seems that your healing accelerated with the light from the spear and the resonance that occurred. A scar has formed, but how do you feel?"

"I feel… good. Great even." Leon exclaimed, as he sat further up and turned and twisted. A small pull of the skin on his lower back was the only remnant of the injury that laid him out. "How long was I, um, out?"

"Three days." Miala said gravely.

Leon bolted upright. "What? But that means–"

Miala interrupted him, "It means that you need to get in your armor and get some food in you. The horde of undead has been sighted from the mountain, and we need our Judge."

Leon felt no pain as he stepped from the table. He looked around the room and saw his arming jacket and armor. The aeonyte shield lay neatly on top of the pile, and Leon scrambled to put it all on.

Schalae and Miala scrounged a couple loaves of bread from the larder before the princess excused herself to join and prepare with the elves. He just about inhaled the food while he got dressed in his armor. Donning his helmet, he glanced at Miala who treated him with a warm silent smile. An awkward silence passed between them, which caused Kelleren to utter a doggy groan and curl up between them.

As Leon tied the last leather cord of his greaves over his black boots, he glanced up to see Miala watching him. Revelator still shone as she gripped it in one of her hands. Curious, he asked, "Any dreams since you took it up?"

A small smile played over her mouth as she replied, "Less recurring nightmares, but no visions like you talk about."

"Fair enough." Leon said as he stooped down to Kelleren and scratched behind his ears. The involuntary thump of his leg against the floor caused Leon to laugh before he walked to Miala and grasped Revelator with her. The sound resumed and the spearlight grew brighter. It suddenly cut off when she let go.

"So, what did I miss?" Leon asked, before adding with a smile, "Besides you?"

Miala made a face and Kelleren groaned again. "That was moderately horrible." She replied, hiding a grin behind her hand.

"Too much?"

"Way too much. But to answer your question, you should come outside."

They walked out of the medical stalagmite and Leon noticed that a number of dwarves walked the streets of stone. A few were garbed in military gear, like chainmail or plate armor, while others wore padded clothes or whatever protective gear they had on hand. Various weapons, both blunt and bladed, could be seen, and a grim determination filled the air. Everyone moved towards the lake and the cave opening where the waterfall normally fell. At some point during his recovery the waterfall must have been diverted, as a cloudy sky now showed through the opening. A small flash of lightning in the distance preceded the distant rumble of thunder.

Leon began to see the more heavily armed dwarves, a few elves, and an occasional troll which stood a head above the multitude of warriors. He followed Miala as they weaved their way through the gathering crowd, until they reached their destination next to the lake.

With the contribution of thousands of dwarves, elves, trolls, a gnome, and a week of working around the clock, the airship had been completed. It showcased hard lines and angles, was longer and slightly wider than the *Dawnfire* had been, and was completely covered in aeonyte. Four large levigems protruded from the hull of the ship, two on either side. There appeared to be two lower decks, within the ship, and a top deck. The Nonagint, and the rest of his friends, stood and watched his approach from the top deck railing. Underneath them, ten cannons poked from the side of the ship – double the armament that the *Dawnfire* had possessed. After he climbed the gangplank to the top deck, Leon shook Ignys' proffered hand.

"Where did you get the levigems?" Leon breathed in reverence.

"We pried some off tha statue. Tha mail carrier's levigems seemed ta be enough ta keep our flow goin' when we replaced 'em." Ignys replied as he patted the airship.

Leon looked behind Duamé's father and saw several contraptions on the ship which caught his attention. Spaced along the top deck railing were some sort of turrets that dwarves and elves stood at. Their dress identified them as being mancers, either geomancer or hortimancer – depending on their race. These mancer turrets had a thick, forearm sized elvenwood rods at their tops, instead of crossbows.

Spread along the railings as well were crossbow turrets like the one in Gionna's workshop. These had two strings and one large trigger. While Leon inspected one of the contraptions he heard a voice from behind him, "I realized that in order to resolve my jamming issue I just needed two bows to work with each other. One bow fires, which in turn redraws the string on the other. Much more efficient! I don't know why I didn't come to Masterwork Halls and figure it out sooner!"

Leon smiled and turned around so he could bend down to allow Gionna Gærheart to hug him. "Welcome back to us, dearie."

"It's good to be back." He responded. He looked up to see the remaining Nonagint, Queen Chlorae, Princess Schalae, Duamé, Miala, and Kelleren all watching him in their various war gear.

Kérik Silverspine took the opportunity to shout, "Captain on deck!" All of those at the turrets gave short salutes. It took a moment for Leon to realize whom they meant by 'Captain'. As Kérik stepped closer he asked, "How are ya feelin', lad?"

"Not worthy of the honor."

"Well, don't go thinkin' ya can be tha first ta fly this ship, cause I already called it." Silverspine said as he shook Leon's hand.

"I'd be honored to have you as my 'first mate' then sir. You could pilot it… Most of the time." Leon reasoned.

Kérik winced as he said, "Ya gotta name her, lad. Can't call it 'it'. Grates against me granite that does."

Leon hadn't given any thought to naming the ship. It was probably evident on his face as Kérik clapped his shoulder and said, "Think about it. Meanwhile, we got some time before we square off with tha horde, lemme show ya around."

Their high-profile entourage followed Silverspine and Gionna as they highlighted the particulars of the airship. The middle level held a substantial gundeck. There was a row of ten cannons on each side, with a couple reserve cannons and ballistae at the front. Each gunport appeared to have their cannons on tracks for maneuverability and pivoting ease. Ammunition was stored in boxes, next to each individual cannon. Everyone followed the direction of Gionna's cane, as she waved it towards the stores of iron balls, canister shot, and ballista arrows. There were also coils of chains, and box upon box of crossbow bolt 'cartridges'.

The rear of the ship was occupied by a multipurpose room – one that could be used for storage if necessary. The bottom deck held sleeping areas, a kitchen and galley, and two privies. There was also a reinforced room with a door at the far end. Ignys chuckled before he entered it.

"What's back there?" Leon asked.

Gionna sighed before she replied, "A necessary aberration it seems."

Ignys opened the door to reveal a small room with multiple eyelets and tools hung all around. Several thin sheets of aeonyte were stacked in a corner, and the back of the room had a fireplace with a flume that led upward. All of this circled an anvil that had been centrally placed in the middle of the room.

Leon was dumbstruck. "You built a forge. On an airship?"

Duamé snickered, "Ah, we built a forge on a dwarven airship. Tha first of it's kind. We may have ta make repairs ta all this metal, an luckily, I got me an assistant who's pretty handy."

"That would be me." Miala said as she raised a hand, "I guess we got our 'traveling smithy' after all."

"She's learnin', but she keeps givin' me these blasted headaches." Duamé said as he rubbed his head.

"What are these if I may ask?" Queen Chlorae gestured towards a pipe opening that came from the ceiling. The length of pipe joined with a few others outside of the room. There seemed to be a pipe with an opening in every room.

"These are speaking pipes. They run all through the ship and converge at the ship's wheel." Gionna replied. "My house in Agaprya has a similar setup. All of my successful inventions went into this ship, your majesty."

The old gnomish inventor sighed and looked around, "This is it. My life's work. My masterpiece. I cannot tell you all how wonderful it feels to have brought my vision to life. I can safely say that this is what I was meant to design."

"Well, let's hope it works." Verne commented.

With a smile Gionna tapped her cane to the floor. "It will, dearie. It will."

A low horn that came from inside Masterwork Halls echoed throughout the ship. Deep and sonorous, it was followed by a shout from Jaq Copperchin on the top deck. "Everyone had better get up top. They're here!"

The entourage began to file up the stairwell, but Princess Schalae lagged behind a bit. She turned and asked Duamé, "Have you been getting a lot of headaches lately?" Her lips pursed in thought.

Duamé rubbed his temple some more as he nodded. "Yea, now that ya mention it. All tha time now."

Schalae pressed further, "Do you remember when they started?"

"No. I'd like ta say it was after I met 'meat shield' over here." Duamé said as he thumbed at Leon.

Leon thought he could help diagnose the issue, "Didn't you start complaining about headaches after you put on the ring? Did we ever figure out where it came from and what it does?"

Duamé looked at Leon with an awestruck expression before he pulled off his gloves and exposed the triple braided ring of elvenwood, iron, and rust. Then, as he waved it in Leon's face, he asked, "Are ya tellin me I got on a ring o' headaches?"

When nobody answered him as they climbed the last set of stairs to the top deck, Leon surmised, "Maybe. We always figured it could be cursed. Because of where we found it, it would make–"

Duamé clanked the hand with the ring against the railing of the ship while he tried to force it off. It seemed unwilling to budge. After a few moments of effort he said, "Must be me big breakfast holdin' it on. I'll get it off later."

Another horn blasted, louder than the first, and they all looked out of the mountain's opening to see their adversaries. The top deck of the airship was high enough to provide an excellent vantage point for looking out of the cavern opening and down to the river gorge on their right. To their left was the sparsely growing forest of trees that the elves hoped to nurture into a new forest. Directly in front of them was the wide road that led up to Masterwork Halls.

Leon could see none of it. Instead, a sea of undead covered it all.

"Have a look, Judge." Kérik Silverspine handed Leon a spyglass. As he peered through, he saw with more clarity the countless shamblers and wretches, from both Xaelon and lands more distant, that covered the landscape. A few wore the tattered remains of Xaelon armor. Whether they were undead from Bulwark Fortress, Hookvale, or some other place within the country, Leon could not tell.

Chimeras and an occasional giant were randomly spread throughout the undead army. The now depopulated Chimera Lands had provided centaurs, satyrs, and other gaunt creatures for the horde. Both chimeric gryphons, as well as a few dragons, flew among them, and made up the aerial portion of their fighting force. The light of glowing red eyes led the way for each and every one of them to advance on the Halls.

A sound came from them as they approached. They repeated a chant that Leon had heard once before, in a dream. A chill ran through him as he listened to the undead speak as they moved closer to Masterwork Halls. Even from far away he could tell that the multitude of desiccated voices spoke one word over and over again.

"Xhormas. Xhormas. Xhormas."

Clénoi, who had been silent until now, looked through another spyglass before she passed it along. Then, in her most conversational tone she remarked, "Should be a good scrap." Then she cupped a hand to her mouth and shouted down, "Seal tha main doors!"

Dwarven geomancers near the main entrance of the Halls heard the signal, and pressed their hands to the cavern wall. When they did, two giant slabs of rock that were located to either side of the enormous entryway to Masterwork Halls shifted. They fell towards each other and collided with a resounding 'boom', that marked the finality of their action. The only entrance into or out of the Halls was now the opening where the waterfall normally fell.

"I'm gonna go inspect tha seal." Jaq said before he hustled down the gangplank. A few of the Nonagint members, along with Duamé, shouted for him to be careful. Jaq stopped and flashed them a sly grin before his badger tittered at him to get moving.

Clénoi drew her short sword, turned away from the opening in the mountain, and walked to the railing of the airship. She gazed out at the thousands of living who were ready to fight for their homes and lives, then she raised her sword up over her head.

"For the Halls!"

"THE HALLS!" Came the reply from the masses.

"Yer turn." She said, as she turned to Leon.

"Wait, what?"

"Ya spoke ta many o' them at tha amphitheater. I know how ya like ta talk… Time ta inspire yer troops, Judge." She responded, with a gesture towards the Halls.

Leon certainly didn't want to give the impression that he loved to talk. Yet Clénoi made sense, and he stepped towards the railing unsure of what to say.

Give me the words, Adonai. He thought.

Leon could feel the eyes of all the assembled warriors on him. Many dwarves and elves looked determined, but also nervous. Everyone knew the stakes, and the odds of survival. They had spent the past week building a symbol of defiance against the undead. They had gambled on a ship that all of their hopes now rested on. Thunder rolled outside again as Leon cleared his throat. As Revelator shined, he held the spearhead high for all to see. He remembered words that had been spoken to him before, and began.

"Do not fear! Stand firm! Trust in Adonai, and He will–"

A serpentine hiss interrupted Leon. One that was so loud it sounded as though it came from just outside. "WATCH YOU ALL DIE."

Nachash Seraph, and his army, had arrived.

Chapter 21: The Assault

Leon felt the fear that the massive dragon's voice instilled, and pointedly decided to ignore it. Instead, he focused on the feeling of annoyance Nacash Seraph's interruption caused him, and shouted, "Ready for me to take the other wing, serpent?"

A loud snarling hiss echoed from outside. It shook dust from the ceiling, which caused a few to cough during the dragon's reply. "YOUR IMPUDENCCCE ISSS AMUSSSING. RESSSISSSTANCCCE ISSS A WORTHLESSSS EFFORT."

"So then, you brought your entire army to surrender? Fantastic. If you could just dispose of yourselves that would be incredibly convenient." Leon responded, drawing snickers from among the defenders.

"I SSSEE YOUR… PROJECT. A WORTHY EFFORT, BUT IT WILL ULTIMATELY PROVE FRUITLESSSS."

Leon saw the way his words emboldened his comrades against the unseen mazzikin around them. "I encourage you to come and stick your head inside, so our 'project' can add a few additional holes to that oversized skull of yours!"

Laughter echoed from those that were assembled, which enraged Nachash Seraph. The roar that ensued made Leon grip the railing of the airship, as it felt like the entire cavern trembled.

"SSSLAY THEM ALL."

Screeches, yells, and roars from outside met the defiant shouts of those inside Masterwork Halls. Two short horn blasts signalled that the defenders should give each other additional room for their weapons, as bows and crossbows were lifted and aimed toward the cavern opening. Leon felt a slight tremble from within the airship as ports opened and cannons were aimed toward the exposed opening in the mountain.

Leon looked out on the massive horde, and tried to divine what strategy that Nachash Seraph would employ. During their battle in the forest, ground forces had been sent first, and the gryphons had been deployed after – once the defender's positions in the trees had been revealed. Now there were hundreds of gryphons and a few dragons to worry about at the onset, but from a much more defensible position. The cavern opening was large and off the ground, which allowed Leon to see the cloud of gryphons that swarmed as the undead horde moved closer to the mountain.

"They'll attack with the gryphons first!" Leon shouted, just as the swarm of large, dead, half-bird, half-lions converged and surged towards the opening. As they crossed the mine's threshold, Leon shouted amongst others to fire.

Arrows, bolts, and cannonballs met a veritable wall of the flying, undead gryphons. They either exploded mid-air in fur and feathers, or fell to the pit that had been made from the earthquake and subsequent mining of aeonyte. A few careened down into the hull of the airship, and the aeonyte in that area flashed upon their impacts. The bodies of the dead gryphons fell amongst the ever growing pile of salt grains. It appeared that the aeonyte hull of the ship had the same effect on the undead as Revelator.

Far more gryphons survived the initial blast than were stilled, and Leon heard frantic shouts of 'reload' and 'fire at will' before the undead gryphons flew into the cavern and began their assault on its defenders. Leon swung and cut one into two salty segments before a loud roar caught his attention.

Chagrin ran through Leon as two dragons followed the griffins and barrelled through the opening. The dragons swooped in and opened their claws – not to rend limbs, but to release what they carried. Armored undead dropped down and began to wreak havoc and death all around them. The dragons then wheeled around and flew directly above the grounded airship and out of the cavern again. Leon presumed they went to gather more forces to deposit within the cavern.

"I gotta git ta me station!" Duamé shouted, as he crushed the head of a gryphon on the wooden deck of the ship. He nodded at Leon as he ran off to the forges.

Leon was humbly reminded of the fact that he dealt with a foe who was millennia older than him, and had an overwhelming amount of more battle experience than him. Their strategy was sound, and had already worked to disrupt the defenses of Masterwork Halls. While a general melee broke out to bring down the undead forces around the ship, an unfamiliar sight and sound thrummed from on the ship.

Elven and dwarven mancers pointed their large turrets, which lined the airship, and fired. An odd detail didn't escape Leon's notice. Green bolts of energy emanated from the elven turrets while brown spheres came from the dwarven ones, and he saw that a few of those missiles were tinged with a white glow. Those magical bolts that impaled the dead flesh turned it to salt, and the undead gryphons dropped, unmoving, to the cavern floor.

A shout from the gun deck relayed that the cannons were reloaded. Then Silverspine yelled to Leon, "I'll direct em! Give us tha word!" He cut off a gryphon's claw, then with another swing it's undead head went sailing as he cleared the way to the stairwell. He swung himself down the stairs just as Leon saw the dragons making their way back to the opening.

"Get ready!" Leon shouted, as he ducked under another gryphon that clawed at Miala. She retaliated and its head and torso were incinerated. The dragons were making their way towards the entrance while Leon thought fast. He saw that they had more undead clasped in their claws, ready to be dropped inside. Just as the giant lizards were about to reach the lip of the opening, he screamed, "Fire!"

Leon clearly saw five cannonballs converge on one of the dragons as it poked its head in. Three of the balls crunched into it, causing it to collapse outside the mouth of the cave.

Another dragon took a hit to one of its wings, but soared up and over the others as it careened inside. Leon sought to intercept it while it was still within his range.

Without too much thought Leon ran towards the dragon, slamming his levigem and Revelator together. He launched himself from the airship railing, and with his spear extended he careened towards the flying beast.

The dragon had begun to rain fire down amongst the defenders as it unloaded its cargo. Preoccupied with its mission, it didn't see Revelator's shining speartip coming until it was too late. A couple of turret blasts knocked into its wing and side at the same time Leon's blade sank into its eye. Salt immediately encrusted the wound, and it's head changed from a scaly green to white. With its fiery breath extinguished, the beast's bulk started to fall, carrying Leon down with it. Fortunately it appeared as though the impact would crush the undead it had recently dropped.

As he landed, Leon brought the edge of his new shield down onto the head of a shambler. It crunched, proving the aeonyte shield also had a salting effect on the undead. Leon withdrew Revelator from the salted dragon and, amidst off hand comments from his fellow defenders, helped deal with the undead who had survived in the area.

"Thank you, Judge!"

"Ha! Show-off!"

"They are trying ta break down tha doors! To tha doors!" A dwarf shouted before he ran off. Leon followed those who split off from the fighting force, and ran towards the new crisis.

Many had already gathered at the sealed entrance door and Leon realized he needed a faster way to get there. He didn't want to risk jumping and being hit by a stray missile mid-air so he raced ahead on foot. Another gryphon came at him with it's razor claws outstretched. They scraped against the edges of his raised shield, which produced a hair-raising tone. The undead monstrosity warbled at Leon as it's claws began to dissolve into salt. Unfortunately, that didn't stop the gryphon's efforts. It forced Leon off balance, and closer to a line of undead assaulters. He worried that he would lose his position and be thrust into the midst of the enemy.

A moment later a bellow sounded and a blur rushed into the space the large gryphon had occupied. Gezado charged through the ranks with his axes whirling. His leather armor was spotless as no undead seemed to be able to match his speed and reach. A large great axe was held in two hands on one side, while he chopped down the tackled gryphon with the hatchets held by his other two. The ferocity of an entyrnet troll, as it fought with all four arms, was mesmerizing to watch. Leon had to tear his eyes from the troll leader who had rushed to his defense.

"Go, Judge! Go!" Gezado yelled.

Leon ran his spear through another undead before he continued to run past the airship on his way to the entryway doors. The defenders in this area were sparser. Leon saw that a few were already winded and catching their breaths before they returned to the battle. The light of Revelator showed Leon faces that were tired, but as they looked upon its light a few of the defenders stood and followed him. No words were spoken, but a renewed vigor built behind him as a small force started to form. They crashed into the fray near the sealed doors, and joined in the defense efforts.

Long dead skeletons and wretches fell under the onslaught of the dwarves and elves who accompanied Leon. He chose to take on the more dangerous opponents that came across his path. There were fully armored undead who hacked at all those around them, and undead centaurs and ogres who sought to snuff out the light that emanated from Revelator. The Judge of Xaelon salted the ground as they all fell under his spear. While the defenders around him rushed forward to confront more undead, Leon saw a pair of gryphons fly past him overhead.

As he watched the gryphons, he saw that more crossbow turrets had been mounted atop the nearby defense towers. They fired at the gryphons who harassed the entryway defenders. The beasts worked together in a well executed plan. One would draw the fire of the crossbows, while the other would wing its way from another direction, and assault the turret operators. Leon watched in horror as a few dwarves fell from a tower.

"Quickly, up the tower!" He shouted to several of the dwarves and elves behind him. Though Revelator pointed toward the ground level door of the tower, Leon spotted an easier way for him to climb the tall defensive structure. He joined the levigem and spear together once more, and immediately felt lighter. The tower was comparable in size to most giants, but he felt certain that with his faith, and belief, he would accomplish the feat. With a silent prayer to Adonai, he jumped.

At the apex of the jump Leon touched down on top of the tower. He had no time to celebrate his success though, because the two undead gryphons finished savaging the tower's defenders and turned towards him. Leon blocked one claw swipe with his shield while simultaneously stabbing at the other gryphon. The undead creature shied away from his shining blade, and clacked it's beak at him in response. His back was pressed to the crenellated edge of the tower, and he sidestepped along it to keep only one of the beasts in front of him. When it rushed at him he ducked and thrust his shield up, which made the bulky chimera go over the edge. Salt grains rained along the edges of the shield – evidence of its effect on the rotting flesh.

As he confronted the remaining chimera, the creature nipped at Leon with it's razor sharp beak. It drew inside his spear's range, which allowed for the perfect opportunity to bash its skull with his shield. After a few sprays of salt, from the hits against its head, Leon chuckled at the inspiration he had for a name.

"HA! It's... A... Shield-shaker!" He spoke with each continued impact against the beast. The undead chimera finally ceased moving, at his feet.

A small contingent of dwarves clambered up the stairwell to the already cleared tower top. The dwarves cast cursory looks at the undead gryphon. Then they secured the area and rushed to the two crossbow turrets, prepared to fire at other enemies.

Leon looked down towards the sealed entrance and the battle that was being waged there. A group of undead, presumably deposited by the dragons, still fought with ferocity in a growing circle. The occasional dwarf or elf had risen and added to their numbers, but the ground around them was littered with unmoving bodies.

A boom and a flash of nearby movement caught Leon's attention. As Leon looked toward the commotion, he saw that Jaq was trading blows with another dwarf! Chunks of rock and earth erupted from the ground around them as Jaq swung his crystal tipped staff around like a club. The red-eyed dwarf gestured in wide arcs which caused rocks to launch at Jaq. The two moved constantly as they threw each other about the area.

Rocks crumbled down around the main door with each successive boom that sounded. The undead horde were trying to breach the doors, which would grant them another entry point. If the undead could attack on two fronts, then the defender's chances of survival would drastically decrease.

"Cover the front doors! Don't let the undead through!" Leon shouted to the defenders on the tower. A few nods of assent were given in response as he turned back to the situation at hand. He saw a pocket of undead who fought near Jaq and the lich. Elves and dwarves were working diligently to hold them back.

That would be his landing point.

Leon tapped Revelator against the gem in his palm and leapt from the tower towards a relatively sparse area. Bolts of light came from the airship turrets and arced overhead as they impacted against the dwindling number of gryphons within the cavern. When Leon landed, it was among the elves who fought with graceful movements and long, leaf-thin blades. The clang of metal against metal, bone, or bark armor sounded around him.

The light from Revelator showed skeletons, rotting corpses, and armored humanoids that all wielded whatever weapons or armor they could. These red eyed assailants crashed against the elven and dwarven lines. Leon joined the fray near Jaq and a few other dwarven geomancers who defended themselves against the undead. Another boom sounded, and a crack appeared in the stone that blocked the doors.

Leon flanked and impaled the lich dwarf. With a flash it turned to a pillar of salt that collapsed under its own weight. "Oi, that one was mine, Judge!" Jaq complained as his badger, Honey, wound herself into a ball on his shoulder. She growled at Leon, before Jaq exclaimed, "Git down!"

Leon dove to the side and looked back as a large orcish shambler brought its huge mace down where Leon had just stood. Jaq grunted and brought his fist in the air in an uppercut motion. A much larger fisted arm that was made of stone exploded from the ground in response. With a bone shattering crack it connected with the orc shambler and sent it flying up and into the wall of the dimly lit cavern.

"Thanks!" Leon said as he scrambled up.

"Don't mention it!" Jaq replied as he shook off his fatigue.

"They're trying to break through!" Leon yelled as another crack formed in the rock wall.

"Ya, tell me something I don't know!"

"Can you fix it?" Leon asked.

Jaq looked up at the door which shuddered again, before he looked back at Leon and shouted, "Cover us!"

Leon turned and saw a couple of elves cut down which allowed two shamblers and a wretch to break through their defensive line. They ran straight for Leon, who met the shamblers with both his spear and shield. As he impaled the second shambler, the wretch's needle sharp claws raked at Leon's arm. He hoped that his armor would do the job it was intended for, and that the needle-like claws wouldn't pierce his skin. He knew that the wretch's toxin had the power to dull his senses. He grunted with the frustration of having been hit, as he backhanded the wretch in the face with his shield. A follow up stab with the spear was enough to finish it off, and Leon chanced a look behind himself to see the status of the doorway.

Jaq and two other dwarven geomancers pressed their hands to the wall of stone and earth. Ripples of gravel and rock built on top of and around the door. Leon felt the very ground beneath him sink slightly from the displacement of the rock around them. The sound of the horde as it tried to get through the doors grew fainter. Jaq and the other geomancers exhaled and took a moment to rest, while Leon turned back to see a familiar figure approach him.

"No! Not you!" Leon lamented when he saw the red glow that came from former Commander Thorne's remaining eye. The elf was encased in black bark armor that had an amber stained hole in its chest. He snarled at Leon and raised a huge two handed sword in challenge. Leon barely had time to register the loss of the great warrior before Thorne rushed at him with a hollow rasp.

The elf's thin greatsword clanged against Leon's shield like a gong as he attacked in a rage that had continued beyond life. He swung his weapon at Leon without hesitation, and it rapped again and again against the upraised shield. Leon looked for an opening but Thorne was fast, and had carried all of his tactical knowledge and skill over into his undeath. The elf sidestepped a stab only to swing at Leon once more. He fought with the frenzy of a rabid animal.

Leon knew he would have to time his counter attack just right. He braced against Thorne's next strike, and pushed back with his shield. His shove caused Thorne to stagger, which gave him the opening to try and stab the elf with Revelator. Thorne turned his stagger into a whirl and knocked the spear aside before he resumed his assault.

It took Leon a split second to realize that Thorne's reaction time, on his side where his eye was blinded, was slightly slower. That second cost him. An upward swing of the leaf thin greatsword caught the edge of Leon's helmet. Leon pulled back, which allowed the tip to catch the edge of the helm, and rip it forcefully from his head. It clattered to the ground and into the melee several steps away.

Thorne stepped close after he once again knocked Leon's spear aside. Leon stepped forward into the next attack with his shield. Then he rammed his exposed head into the elven commander's. The elf staggered back from the impact of the unconventional tactic, and Leon followed up with a punch from his shield hand. A spray of salt flew into the air as the elven commander's neck snapped. Thorne's head twisted enough from the blow that his one good eye faced a screaming Leon. That red eye saw with clarity the moment Revelator's speartip pierced through it.

Thorne's head turned white and his body fell. A small salt pile was all that was all that remained of the commander. Emotionally numb from dispatching Thorne, and from the battle as a whole, Leon looked for his next opponent. Another boom reverberated behind him, and he turned to see an exhausted Jaq help two other geomancers up. "Is that door going to hold?" Leon asked as he pointed to it with the spear.

Jaq shook his head and yelled back, "Probably not. We've got minutes at this rate!"

"Can you collapse the tunnel? On the other side?" Leon asked.

"Ya want ta cause a cave-in? With us in here?" Blustered one of Jaq's companions.

"Do you have a better idea?" Leon countered.

"How would we ever leave again?" Jaq exploded back.

"In that!" Leon shouted, and pointed at the airship.

After a pause, and another boom, Jaq nodded his agreement and wearily turned back to the sealed doors. He placed his hand and the crystal on his staff against the smooth stone. He then mumbled something to the mancers next to him, which Leon couldn't hear. Whatever it was, it made them both lay their hands on his shoulders. After a moment, Jaq screamed and stomped one foot down.

The effort of the movement caused Jaq to collapse. His fall into exhaustion was perfectly timed with the cacophonous sound of rock cracking and crashing. His two companions helped get Jaq up as tremors shook the ground. The badger, Honey, leapt down from Jaq's cowl and chittered at them before it ran off towards the forging area. The two mancers turned as they continued to hold Jaq up by his shoulders. Then one of them shouted over the din, "Let's get outta here!"

Leon and the dwarves lurched around on the shaking earth, and tried to rally the other defenders. They directed their troops to move towards the forging area, closer to the towers and the airship. All of those nearby fell back to the defensive towers near the doors. Even there, billows of falling dust choked those who breathed. More rumbling shook Leon's feet as a few stalactites fell behind him. They crashed and impaled both the ground and any foe who was too slow. With a pang of loss, Leon realized he left his fallen helmet behind under the rubble.

Leon led the two mancers and the unconscious Jaq to the forge area near the airship. There, several lightly armored members of the crafting guild stood ready at their workstations. Ignys and Duamé stood by anvils, with hammers and mauls in hand. Several hundred other dwarves stood with them. The tools these dwarves wielded were not for repairs of weapons or armor, but for fighting the enemy if and when the defensive lines broke.

Based on the number of undead that had begun to swarm around the edges of the airship, and towards the forging area, those tools were about to be needed.

Chapter 22: The Defense

The hordes of undead kept coming. First they came around the airship in ones and twos, then they spotted the living, and ran in droves to engage them. Crossbow bolts and multicolored lights came from behind the airship turrets and slammed into some of them. Some stumbled, or turned and ran towards the airship. Others just dropped, unmoving, where they were.

Leon found Duamé and Ignys, and stood beside them as the elder dwarf grumbled, "Seems to be going well so far."

"How do you figure that?" Leon asked.

"Well, we're not all dead yet." Ignys replied.

The first few shamblers came within range of the waiting blacksmiths. If there was one thing that these dwarves knew, it was how to work around an anvil and forge with the tools they had. Anvils were used to trip opponents. Hammers were used to crush skulls and limbs. While Leon dealt with his own undead foes, he occasionally spotted the father and son next to each other, using the familiar space to their advantage.

Ignys fought with a large, dark, metallic mallet in one hand, and tongs in the other. He used the tongs to capture or deflect whatever weapon was brought against him. Then a quick slam with the hammer was all it took to disable his enemy or shatter their weapon. The short and forceful arm movements required by their trade allowed the dwarven smiths to execute their foes with brutal efficiency.

Duamé seemed to revel in the use of his new maul. He swung it in wide arcs over his workstation, and Leon saw more than one undead be thrown against the pegboard wall. The hanging tools and pegs would catch the and pin the undead, which allowed them to be finished with one downward swing. A pile of shamblers began to accumulate on the floor as their unlife came to an end.

The deep horn inside the hall reverberated three short blasts before the sound was cut off. Leon knew that in Xaelon it would have meant undead were approaching, but that seemed blatantly obvious now. What else it could stand for he didn't know, but he did hear several dwarves groan around him as they continued to fight. The piles of deceased created tripping hazards, and the sharp metal edges of their weapons were a danger if stepped on, so the defenders were forced to continually revamp their battle lines and give ground where they could. They edged back in such a way that allowed themselves to use the permanently dead bodies to their advantage.

Within a matter of seconds, a lithe figure with two curved swords cut a path towards Leon. Princess Schalae stabbed and sliced her way through two wretches as her hair whirled all about her. Blood spotted her bark armor, but thankfully none was amber in color. "They broke in through the other line!" She shouted around them.

"They're in tha city?" Ignys asked.

"All those who can't fight are still in the meeting hall, but they're headed there!"

"Duamé, we are movin' ta tha meeting hall bridge!" Ignys roared.

"Right!" Duamé responded as he bashed a shambler, "Just stay here Judge!"

"I can help!" Leon protested.

"You're needed here!" Ignys replied, before he ran off. Duamé ran after his father, prepared to defend the defenseless.

Schalae took the father and son's place in the defensive line against the shamblers and wretches that kept coming. Her constant movement throughout the area allowed her to cut down not just her own opponents, but also ones that the nearby dwarves were facing.

“How did they get through?” Leon yelled to her above the battle din.

“There are so many undead that they have filled the hole at the waterfall where the aeonyte was mined! Once that was full they just poured in by climbing on top of each other!” she replied.

Leon stabbed and sliced in a continuous motion with Revelator. He bashed and beat against the enemy with his shield. Fatigue started to make itself known, but necessity and survival held it at bay. He knew he had to keep going. He imagined that he was back in the grey expanse with boundless energy, and training with Lochemetel. Whether it was from the light of Revelator rejuvenating him, or due to every friend that he knew he had to protect, Leon continued to fight through his exhaustion.

After cutting down a large undead centaur, a loud bovine bellow made Leon turn his head just in time to see a muscular minotaur stamp it’s leg and charge. The chimera bowled a nearby blacksmith over with its wide horns before it reared upright. It then drew a massive sword from a back harness and carved through the defenders wherever it’s glowing red eyes turned. Schalae and Leon exchanged a brief look before Leon said, “I’ll go high!”

The princess didn't respond, she simply dashed toward the minotaur who had knocked over an anvil with one of its wide swings. She dove within its range, dodging both sword and horn, before she slid under its wide stance and sliced through its legs. The creature fell to its knees, and tried to twist its bulky undead body to attack her. At that moment, Leon leapt and lodged Revelator’s blade into the minotaurs neck. Salt spread from the wound as the nearby defenders cheered and pressed harder against their enemy.

Princess Schalae cut down more of the undead, then bodily shoved their remains next to the bulky minotaur carcass. After she repeated the process a few times Leon realized what she was doing. He began to help build a barrier on the other side of the minotaur’s mass with his own dispatched bodies. Their makeshift wall continued to spread as more of the glowing red eyes went dark with every strike and shove.

The blacksmiths that were around them saw an opportunity to build something, and joined in their effort.

It was then that Leon first noticed hardly any of the bodies piled on the wall were from the defenders. He turned another centaur to salt and stepped back to look around. While some of their forces had fallen, they had not risen. Dwarves and elves lay sporadically in repose, noticeably different from the undead who were ravaging them.

First there was Anissa, in the Archives. Then Vyn. Then the elves at the bridge. Now here. Those who had placed their faith in Adonai were at peace. The effect it had on the battle was contrary to what Leon had known his entire life. This massive horde they fought was not growing nearly as much as it normally would when it consumed a population. With this realization, Leon's faith bolstered and hope grew within him.

Lightning flashed outside the cavern and thunder rolled. For a moment, Leon couldn't understand why the light from outside lingered, until he realized there was a pronounced circular glow in front of him. The shield that Duamé and Ignys made glowed like Revelator. Leon had just long enough to register this development, before a shambler came within his range. He shouted in exhilaration as he blocked a sword strike, then cut down the undead attacker.

Faith was the key. Faith was what made the aeonyte shine. In Rhoxmas' cave. At Everbright. Even as he struggled with the nephilim who had possessed Phonz. The aeonyte shined every night that he held onto his faith. As he looked at the airship, Leon realized how they could turn the tide of the battle. He saw how the symbol of hope that had been crafted by Masterwork Halls could help the dwarves believe, and boost their morale.

He just had to figure out how to get there while the undead poured into the cavern on the other side of it.

"Schalae!" Leon yelled.

"Still here!" She replied from the other end of the wall they were building.

"We have to get back to the airship!"

"Why? Wait, why is your shield–" She started to ask.

"I have an idea!" Leon exclaimed.

"How do we get there?" Princess Schalae asked, as she cut through an undead satyr.

Leon looked at the dwarves and elves who still fought around him. He knew that they couldn't just hop over the newly constructed wall and press the attacking undead back. Leaping over the ranks of the horde would also be too risky.

If only I could communicate with them somehow! Leon thought as he cut low. He knocked over a skeleton and its head bounced away, which tripped a shambler, who then knocked its head into a nearby anvil. A small ringing sound was punctuated by a nearby smith who brought his hammer down on the shambler. After the fiend was dispatched, the smith gave Leon a thumbs up before resuming his fight.

Leon looked past the smith and saw the gong that Ignys had used with him days ago.

"Schalae, cover me!" Leon yelled as he ran over to the gong. He nearly tripped over an anvil himself as he and the Princess made their way to the device. Leon hurriedly took up a nearby mallet, and smashed it against the gong. Its distinctive tinny crash was thankfully quite loud and obnoxious. With a flurry of inspiration, Leon waved Revelator high in the air. Its glow shined in a short arc above him before he went back to smashing the gong.

"Oi, what's goin' on with that nonsense?" Jaq groaned from nearby in between the gong's sound. The two geomancers who guarded him looked visibly relieved.

During the first few minutes of clanging the gong and waving Revelator, Leon saw no response from the airship. Then, the turrets on the closer side of the airship seemed to change their firing patterns. Bursts of light rained on the short, bare field between the forging area and the airship. After a few moments of this, Leon could see the dim outline of a figure jump from the ship's top deck to ground level.

Halfway through their jump, the figure burst into flame which revealed their identity to him.

As Miala Mytherin landed, Leon saw a small dome of flame explode from her. She was a living torch as entered the space where undead walked, and ran towards the forging area. The shamblers and wretches that stopped to deal with her were, in actuality, dealt with themselves.

A bright ribbon of white fire shot from the wand that she held. She whirled it around her like a whip, and whatever undead skin or armor it touched was reduced to ash. Undead limbs and bodies were bisected where they stood, and piles formed as she continued to spin the wand in a circle around her. A single tendril of flame displayed both the power and potential of the pyromancer, as she advanced and cleared the way for them.

It was beautiful, and terrifying.

Leon knew that this was the opening they needed.

"Everyone! To the airship! Get around it as closely as possible!" He yelled. He whirled Revelator above his head one more time before he helped Jaq to his feet, and the defenders fought their way towards Miala. Dwarves, elves, and a few trolls rallied and ran around their created wall onto the path that led to Nonagint hall in one direction, and the airship in the other.

Leon saw Gezado as he still fought diligently alongside several other trolls nearby. Schalae disarmed and destroyed any who came against her. Even Jaq, exhausted as he was, proved able to knock an occasional undead to stillness with his staff. The defenders carved their way to Miala. With one last flick of her whip, its flame extinguished.

"You seemed to want something?" Miala asked.

"You did it! We need to get everyone onto, or close to, the airship!" Leon replied. He then looked around and asked. "Where's Kelleren?"

"Guarding Gionna. Where's Duamé?"

Leon speared a shambler before he replied, "Guarding the Nonagint hall with Ignys."

"I'm fine if anyone wants to know!" Jaq inserted.

They, along with the multitude of other defenders, slowly but surely secured the clearing against the rampaging undead. They employed the same tactics that had been used in the forging area, and a defensive line was established with every undead they overcame. Leon lost count of how many he had faced. An undead Xaelon guard. A fallen elf. Even undead who wielded strange weapons and wore tattered clothes from distant lands. All were felled by either Revelator, or his shield.

Occasionally, there would be a small break in the fighting. Oftentimes it came after a barrage was fired from the airship's cannons at the cavern opening. Any defender who had the strength, hoisted and heaved the defeated undead to strengthen their new wall. The entire process was repeated with each wave of undead that came at them.

Soon, the undead began to go around the walls, instead of over them. The defenders set up chokepoints at the gaps, so the horde could not overwhelm those who fought to defend their very lives.

A shout that came from the top of the airship almost broke Leon's concentration. "Leon! Ugh, Leon!"

Leon looked up and saw Kérik Silverspine as he leaned over the railing. With the light that came from Revelator, Leon was able to see that his former superior's puffball hair was sprinkled with blood, but otherwise, he looked unharmed.

"Git yer bright behind up here!" Silverspine shouted from over the railing.

Leon glanced over towards the bow of the ship. "Lower the gangplank! We'll clear the way!"

Kérik looked back to the entrance of the cavern and darted away from the railing. Leon turned back to the fight and after a minute he heard the clatter of a long wooden walkway, as it hit the stone floor a short distance behind him. Luckily, it came down within the area that they were defending. Leon and a few others clambered up the wide ramp. Schalae also assisted an injured elf up to the ship. Leon lent a hand to help her, and then took a quick look around the cavern from the higher vantage point.

Unmoving bodies littered the entire area as thousands of defenders continued to fight. Thunder rolled once again outside, perfectly timed with the rumble in Leon's stomach. The evidence of their stalwart resistance surrounded him. The turrets had performed exceptionally well, and collapsing the doors to Masterwork Halls had proven genius. The parked airship provided a good barrier for the undead to have to get around, but through their sheer numbers they managed. The undead no longer seemed interested in getting to the rear of the cavern, but instead they crowded around the airship.

A dwarf screamed hoarsely from below, as he whirled about with his two handed maul. It took a moment for Leon to realize that the dwarf was Duamé. Somehow he had made it back to the defensive line, and he looked a little worse for wear. Leon lept from the gangplank back down into the fray and both he and Miala cut through the undead that surrounded their friend. Between the efforts of all three of them, enough shamblers were defeated to pull Duamé back from the front line. The dwarf calmed down enough to stop swinging, which allowed Leon and Miala to help him stumble up the gangplank and onto the top deck.

As soon as Leon stepped on the top deck, Kérik Silverspine rushed over to him and pointed outside. Leon's attention was split between the sight, and his effort to hear what his friend was saying. Duamé was half rambling and half sobbing to Miala. Leon caught just a few of his words, and his heart broke for his friend.

But the dread that crept into Leon's heart could not be stopped as he looked outside and saw more gryphons in the distance. Along with those beasts flew more dragons, and beneath them even more undead marched. There were enough undead to cover the entire exterior of the mountain.

Nachash Seraph's huge, worm-like bulk, could be seen approaching the entrance of the cavern with his undead minions.

Leon's hopes crashed as he saw the serpent's next wave of forces. He looked down from the railing closest to the entrance, and saw the massive pit that had once held half of the lake and the aeonyte vein. Now it was filled with a mass of undead and their red glowing eyes. Those that couldn't get out were simply trampled on by the fresh forces of undead that arrived. Even if he got the aeonyte on the ship to shine, even if his plan worked, what could they do against the sheer numbers of the horde?

There is just no way we can win. Leon thought.

Chapter 23: The Star

"What are we going to do?" Kérik asked Leon, as he pointed to the oncoming forces.

Leon tried to shift his mentality. Tried to not give in. He forced himself to respond to his former mentor. "What is the condition of the cannon stores? What is the status of those manning the turrets?"

"We lost a few hands, an' had ta improvise!" Verne stated from nearby, as crossbow bolts thrummed from the turret at his hands. Leon saw the older dwarf do a double take as he looked at Duamé, who continued to sob. "Wot happened?" He asked, as he rushed from the turret to see to his son-in-law.

Kérik grunted angrily and ran to take Verne's place at the turret. He fired at a few large targets before yelling, "Go below decks ta see Gionna about wot we got!"

A giant's upper half appeared at the cavern opening before a tinny shout from inside the airship yelled, "Fire!"

A couple of cannons shot their loud, heavy payload and obliterated the nephilim giant's torso as it fell outside. Leon took the opportunity to run past his crying friend and, as much as he wanted to console him, went below decks. A mass of dwarves, Gionna, and Kelleren were there, and any who were not busy reloading watched for targets outside.

"What's the situation?" Leon asked Gionna as he tiptoed around the busy dwarves.

"Bad! Our stores are getting low, so we are shooting at the bigger threats!" She informed him as she looked out a porthole. Her glasses were slightly askew, and her purple and grey ponytails were frizzed, which complimented her frazzled appearance. Kelleren looked as though he was absolutely miserable to Leon, and whined at him while he laid down and covered his tan ears.

Leon felt that it wouldn't be right to give the dog false hope, as they were still immeasurably outnumbered. All he could do was give a reassuring scratch on the dog's head, as Gionna stated, "Do what you can out there! We will do what we can in here!"

"Mind if I borrow Kelleren? He should be with Miala." Leon asked. The dog immediately sat up and wagged his tail. Gionna nodded and pushed up her glasses, which just slid right back down the bridge of her sweaty nose.

Kelleren barked and raced up the stairs as Leon followed. He saw that the top deck was growing more populated by the second. Queen Chlorae had been joined by her daughter at a wand turret, and both were being guarded by Qas. Verne cried right alongside Duamé, and Miala held her dog while tears ran down her own face as she looked outside.

All comforted each other as best as they could while Leon approached Duamé. The dwarf was quiet with his thoughts, and glanced at Leon before he looked back outside at the opposing army. The dwarf sniffed and rubbed his nose with a forearm, which only smeared the grime that was there. After a moment, he said to Leon, "Me family is gone."

Leon's heart wrenched again as he laid a comforting hand on Duamé's shoulder. "I'm so sorry, Duamé."

"I got ta see me mum again. In her right mind. Before she – before they died."

"What happened?" Leon asked.

"They held off tha undead at tha bridge is wot happened! Me ma an' pa died from their wounds, but not until they stopped every one o' them that was attacking tha Nonagint hall. They saved everybody in there, an'– an'..." Duamé trailed off as he grabbed at Leon's armor.

"They didn't turn. I couldn't do it. Couldn't end someone I loved. But it didn't matter, boyo. They never turned!"

Cannons from below decks fired once more, causing a thunderous cacophony of iron. Duamé pounded his fists against the deck of the ship in what Leon assumed was a way to vent his pain. He pounded out his frustration and grief until his leather gloves split and ripped open. Then he spoke again.

"I'm– I'm sorry. Leon." Duamé sniffed. "Sorry I kept ya at arms length. Sorry I kept makin' fun o' ya. I'm just sorry."

"You know," Leon said as he helped Duamé to his feet, "I do believe that this is the first time you've called me by my actual name."

Duamé barked a mournful laugh as he replied, "Don't get used ta it... meat shield."

"If you both are quite done, we've got more incoming!" Kérik roared as he slapped another box of bolts into his turret.

Leon approached the railing and saw that there were quite a number of giants headed towards the cavern entrance now. Nachash Seraph was right behind them, and circling in the air above the maimed dragon was another cloud of gryphons and dragons. Leon stared, and knew his adversary was waiting for their chance to enter the cavern and destroy whatever resistance remained. Duamé silently joined him at the railing.

"Duamé, I appreciate your apology."

"Thank ye, la–"

"But I am not the only one you should apologize to." Leon interrupted. He hoped that Duamé would finally accept the truth.

"Fire!" Gionna yelled from below. The cannons barked again, and added to the projectiles that had been launched against the giants at the cavern's opening. Most fell from the initial blast, and others were brought down by the turrets. Leon, however, looked past the giants and saw that Nachash Seraph was nowhere in sight.

“Gionna, RELOAD NOW!” Leon screamed. *If we don’t have a salvo ready against the serpent then–*

“IT ISSS TIME.” Hissed Nachash Seraph, as his massive head and feathered multicolored frill rose into view. The enormity of his head and frill took up almost the entire cavern entrance. Cries of terror filled the air as the serpent’s forked tongue flicked between it’s rows of serrated teeth.

Kérik yelled, and a few others shot at the serpent, but Nachash didn’t even seem to register the blows.

Miala ignited one hand with white hot flame, then she grabbed Leon’s shoulder with the other and leaned in to say, “I love you, Leon.”

The only words he had to respond with, as he pointed Revelator at Nachash Seraph in defiance, were, “I love you too, Miala.”

The serpent’s head moved closer and it’s mouth grew wide in a reptilian smile. “VENGENCCCE ISSS–”

“I’m sorry, Adonai!” Duamé cried out, as he smashed his fist onto the railing.

Light and sound seemed to explode from everywhere, all at once. Leon felt blinded for a moment and held his shield up to block the bright flash. When he lowered the shield from his face he saw that Duamé’s ring glowed through his split leather gloves.

Nachash Seraph’s jaw was clenched shut, and flames licked through the gaps of his huge draconic teeth. The gigantic dragon appeared to be convulsing over the pit full of undead, as it’s body hung halfway out of the cavern. He was pinned in place by a white hot finger of lightning that skewered him from outside the mountain. The bolt then forked into the pit, and onto the side of the airship.

A hum of electricity hung in the air, and Leon’s sweat plastered hair stood on end. Through the tumultuous noise, a divine voice, which he had only recently heard, thundered, ***“MINE!”***

The voice of Adonai echoed throughout the cavern of Masterwork Halls as thunder continued to roar louder than a hundred gongs. Through the noise Leon felt his tired muscles rejuvenate, and a renewed vigor filled him until he thought he might burst. It was similar to the feeling he experienced in the grey expanse, and for a moment Leon almost felt weightless.

Smoke started to rise from Nachash Seraph's head as his rainbow-feathered frill caught on fire. Leon watched as the undead in the pit below turned to dust. As the lightning danced through the dragon, and onto the side of the airship, near its aft, it scored the ship but did not electrocute anyone there. It did, however, drive the cannon crew, and Gionna, up the stairs. They stared, slack jawed, as Adonai's divine judgement seared the dragon for much longer than any normal lightning bolt would have lasted. It's cacophonous power was both incredible and undeniable.

Moreso, the entire aeonyte hull of the ship began to radiate a faint glow. What Leon had hoped to accomplish with his faith, had instead occurred due to Adonai's intervention in reaction to Duamé. Just like Revelator or the shield, as the lightning impacted across the ship's hull, it's surface began to shine. It looked much like the light that glowed in Leon's dreams. Now, made real, it was an even more spectacular sight.

Leon caught wisps of movement from the corner of his eyes, which made him look over and watch as winged creatures flew from the cave and fled into the distance. Their ghostly, implike visages could only be seen for a brief moment, before they left the radiance of the airship. That moment, though short, had allowed Leon to recognize the outline of hundreds of mazzikin, as they were chased from the cavern by malakim. *A war on two fronts,* he thought.

Cracks started to appear in Nachash Seraph's head as the red light in the dragon's eyes extinguished. A clap of thunder punctuated the last vestige of lightning, then the dragon's broken husk fell into the sizzling ash heap in front of the airship. Leon looked out of the cavern opening, and saw yet another image that he couldn't comprehend. The undead army fled from the engagement. The cloud of gryphons and dragons, the giants, the chimeras, all the wretches, shamblers, liches and alukahs, ran south – away from the immeasurable power of Adonai.

As Leon looked back into the Halls, he saw that the undead who were still trapped in the cave were also attempting to escape from the surviving defenders. The glow from the airship allowed Leon to see that the energy and exuberance he felt was not just his own, but shared among all the living. Leon leapt back into the fight, with his companions close behind. As the minutes ticked by, and each additional undead fell, a growing chant could be heard throughout the cavern. It echoed and rebutted the name of the fallen god that had been chanted by the undead horde. This chant continued until the very last undead within Masterwork Halls was felled.

"Ad-on-ai! Ad-on-ai!"

After the battle was over, the smell of death was poignant. Cloth rags were tied over noses, as many used their remaining muscle and willpower to dispose of the dead. Defenders turned into gatherers and mourners. Desiccated bodies of the undead were either tossed into the pit, or the lava around the Nonagint halls, and their remains were burnt.

Metallic weapons and armor were taken from the undead army and gathered in piles near the forges, per Verne's direction. Some of their horde had obviously been from Xaelon or the Chimera Lands. Others had weapons and armor that were exotic, and their desert garb or tropical outfits displayed just how far they had traveled. Masterwork Hall's dwindling material stores were no longer an issue, but the solution had been a grim one. On occasion, Leon saw some of their comrades break down into sobs before continuing with their work.

Verne, Kérik, and Jaq seemed to be the only surviving members of the Nonagint. Clénoi's still form was found near Ignys and Esper. They all rested at peace, having used their ability to defend the infirm and the young, who had been locked away from the main hall. The remaining dwarves and elves who had been stationed there all agreed that they fought valiantly. Even Esper had apparently run from the safety of those who were protected, and had taken up a sword to help. Phonz still remained comatose in the stalagmite that served as a medical facility.

Overall, approximately a third of those at Masterwork Halls had lost their lives in the battle. All who remained were aware that if Adonai had not intervened, their destruction would have been complete. Evidence of his power was displayed through the husk of Nachash Seraph, as it laid amongst the ash pile of undead in the pit. It was also evident in the faint, ever present glow of the airship, and the giant א that had been scored into its side. The lightning from Adonai had not only defeated the dragon, but also left the Judge's mark for all to see.

Still full of Adonai's boundless energy, Leon worked to deposit the forms of the undead into the pit. His friends gathered near him to help. Miala built upon the fire that was already burning in the pit, ensuring that it would thoroughly consume the dead, while Duamé wordlessly helped Leon carry the undead bodies over. Soon Gezado came over to assist with the larger corpses. Then Jaq, Verne, Kérik and Gionna pitched in. Even Queen Chlorae, Schalae, and Qas congregated to help Leon, assess their losses, and discuss what would come next.

At one point, Leon lost count of how many he had thrown into the pit. Whether friend or foe, each one had a name, a face, a life, or even an unlife that had ultimately been extinguished here. As he tossed a long dead goblin skeleton into the fiery pile, Kérik was the first to speak.

"Ain't ever seen undead retreat from anything, before." He commented.

Leon had thought about that as well, and added his own thoughts, "They were headed south. Toward Agaprya."

"Why did they leave? Why not finish their attack?" Princess Schalae asked.

“Adonai intervened.” Leon replied simply. “He destroyed Nachash Seraph, and would have probably wiped out the whole army if they had continued. Once their commander was defeated, they fled.”

“Then why are they headed towards Agaprya?” Miala asked. “Lifebread village, to the east, is closer. Or, if they were afraid, they could have just scattered.”

They pondered this as they worked in silence for a few minutes. Then Kérik sighed and turned to Leon, “Boyo, I covered this in yer training. When ya know yer going ta lose, but gotta fight anyway, wot do ya do?”

The answer came to Leon in a mere second, “You cause as much damage to the winning side as possible.”

“Right. They’re headed ta Agaprya ta destroy it. They couldn’t defeat us an’ Adonai here, so they are headed ta where Adonai isn’t.” Kérik finished.

Leon stared at the pit full of burning undead. “They mean to consume enough of the world so that we can’t rebuild. So we can’t come back.”

“Then what do we do?” Queen Chlorae asked.

Leon thought for a moment, then finally looked up at the airship before he replied.

“We counterattack. Bring Adonai to them.”

Kérik pumped a fist as if he had wanted that answer. Others agreed in different ways, with the exception of one.

“We are dangerously low on munitions.” Gionna stated. “Don’t get me wrong, I feel fantastic at the moment for some inexplicable reason… But, at some point we will all feel our years and our scars again. We have plenty of dead that need to be added to the pyre, and unfinished business to attend to here, before we assault the undead on what would likely be a suicide mission.”

Leon felt her point was valid, but countered, “We have Adonai. He is all that we need.”

“I would file explosives and projectiles in the necessary category as well.” Gionna retorted.

“Now hold on here,” Verne said after he tossed a pauldron on top of a pile of scrap metal, “We basically built that airship fer free. In fact, a lot o’ us paid for it with our lives. Now ya want ta up an’ leave with it? That is, after ya want us ta make more cannonballs an’ crossbow bolts fer ya?”

“We are actually running low on arrowheads too.” Princess Schalae commented as she joined in.

Verne also has a point. Leon thought. *Have I asked for too much from Masterwork Halls?*

Since he purchased his armor from Duamé, he had no money. Leon had no idea how to respond to Verne. As he was about to say something, Miala reached into her robe and pulled out a few bags of coins. She tossed them over to the pile of metal that Verne was collecting. As she started to verbalize the amount she offered, Duamé piped in.

“Give ‘em my share too.”

“What?” Exclaimed several of them in unison.

The miserly dwarf reiterated to Miala, “Everythin’ I got.” Then Leon's friend whirled on his father in law.

“I'm callin’ in every favor. Every copper crow ya owed my old man. Every worker that we can spare, ta work as soon as they can, fer as long as they can.”

Verne walked around Miala, added Duamé’s contribution to the other coin sacks, and laid a hand on his shoulder. “Are ya sure, lad?”

“I'm leaving Masterwork again. Probably fer that last time. An’ I am gonna bring tha fight ta them. Fer all we lost. Fer our families. Fer me family. Fer Esperella. I could use tha help.”

Verne hugged Duamé fiercely, causing some to look away. A few teared up at the exchange, and Verne looked at Leon once they were done, “Take good care o’ him. He’s family.”

“I will.” Leon replied, before an idea struck him. “You know…”

They all turned to the Judge they had come to rely on as he said,

“Esperella is a great name.”

✦✦✦✦✦

It was much later that evening when Revelator shone along with the shield Leon held. He stood on the top deck of the ship, and stared out at all who were once more assembled. While there were fewer than there had been before, those that remained stood in front of him with resolve. They stood triumphant over their victory, and expectant of what he would say.

"I will make this brief. I ask for volunteers to join me on this airship. We will pursue the horde, and hopefully overcome them before they reach Agaprya. There will be much danger, and I cannot guarantee your return to the Halls."

"Almost everyone here has lost something to the undead. To Xhormas. Whether it be a home, family, or a future once thought promised. All of our losses have brought us here – to a place and an opportunity for us to strike back. To end this war. And while I would not fault you, should you choose to create a new life out of what you can here, the threat is still out there, and it needs to be dealt with."

"If you wish to come, then come. If you feel led to stay, then stay. In the end though, when we leave to fight, know that we fight for you. For Agaprya. For Xaelon. For Adonai. Here, on this Star of Hope, the *Esperella*, we will make our stand."

Cheers abounded amongst the crowd as Verne stepped forward after Leon. "All ya Craftsman Guild dwarves! We got another job! We're taking this scrap an' makin' every cannonball, bolt, an' arrowhead that we can. Fire up them forges! Time ta take tha enemy's weapons an' turn em against 'em! This, is a PAID rush job!"

The cheers from the crafting guild dwarves seemed to be every bit as loud as everyone else's.

Chapter 24: The Hidden

Leon expected his dreams to be invaded by the expanse that night, and they were. After his exhaustive effort during the battle, the grey, flat, and featureless place greeted him almost immediately when his eyes closed.

He also noticed that few other guests were present.

Leon saw the shocked expressions of Miala, Duamé, Princess Schalae, and Gionna Gærheart. All of them, including Leon, were dressed in the gear they had worn for the battle. They all looked around in wonder before they met Leon's eyes. Exclamations arose as Leon approached them. "You– you're really here! All of you!"

"Is this where you go when you dream?" Miala asked.

"It's kinda boring." Duamé commented.

Leon looked about and couldn't find the small sun that emitted the light bursts anywhere. Then Gionna cried out and pointed upward.

The ball of light hung high overhead, and pulsed over them. It bathed the entire landscape in iridescence, and washed them all with warmth.

"Oh… Oh that's lovely." breathed Gionna. The others all assented similar feelings.

"You have brought Adonai worship back to the world."

Rohiel and Lochemetel materialized from the wave of light in front of them. Their glow and aeonyte armor left most speechless. Duamé, however, stepped forward and rubbed the back of his head, "Sorry fer, uh, trying ta punch ya." He said to Rohiel.

The angel's head was obscured by light, and while Leon couldn't see it, he could see that Rohiel's head had shifted slightly, and he addressed the dwarf in a humorous tone, ***"You are forgiven of course."***

"Nachash Seraph is no more, but his horde remains." Lochemetel said, as she stepped forward. ***"You must engage them, or all will be lost."***

"That was the plan." Leon stated.

"You cannot tarry too long." Lochemetel warned.

"We won't." Miala replied, as she crossed her arms.

Lochemetel strode over to Miala, and leaned over to whisper in her ear. Leon couldn't hear her words, but whatever it was that his sparring partner said made Miala hug the angel and say, "Thank you."

"Why, uh…" Duamé started to ask, "Why us? Why'd it take me acceptin' Adonai fer him ta intervene?"

Rohiel slowly walked in front of each of them as he responded, ***"There are many different aspects of Adonai's love. Love for a people. For a family. For a friend. For a beloved. For a child. There is no fear in love, but perfect love casts out fear. I said before that each of you must align yourselves to His purposes for you. When you do, when you love, He responds."***

There was a glorious silence as everyone puzzled through Rohiel's words. The angel stepped in front of Leon and laid a hand on his shoulder.

"Lead them, Judge Leon."

A light wave pulsed from above, and just before it reached them Rohiel spoke again, ***"Prepare yourselves. You must be ready."***

As the warmth washed through him, Leon awoke.

The next two days passed quickly, and Leon clambered out of Duamé's small yet comfortable bed. He huddled together with his friends over breakfast, still recounting aspects of the dream they had shared, as well as the previous day's work in supplying the *Esperella.*

A knock sounded at the door, and Duamé hollered for whomever it was to enter.

Verne Granitehand stepped into the stalagmite home and made a beeline straight for Duamé.

"Lemme see yer hand." He stated gravely. Leon and Miala shot up from their chairs as Kelleren woofed. They all stared in shock as Verne inspected the ring on Duamé's hand that was braided with elvenwood, iron, and aeonyte. After a few moments Verne nodded and asked, "Can ye take it off?"

"Do you know what it is? What it does?" Leon asked, as Duamé wiggled the ring off and handed it to Verne.

The elder dwarf held it up to a glowing crystal to see it more clearly, before stating, "Nope. But I know who it belongs to. Come with me."

Leon, Miala, Duamé, Gionna, and Kelleren followed Verne out of the home as he walked with haste. The possibilities of who owned the ring were endless. They hadn't anticipated finding them, much less discovering that the owner lived at Masterwork Halls.

After a few twists and turns, Verne led them to the medical center. They entered, and Leon was greeted by the sight of an awakened and cognizant Phonz, who was drinking soup. Verne gestured to the group, conveying that the formerly possessed dwarf meant no harm. "I'd better let him tell ya hisself."

"Oi, that's them isn't it!" Phonz said feebly from the slab of rock that was his bed. He set his cup down on a bedside table and sat up some more. "Please come closer, I do so wish ta apologize fer me behavior. Wasn't… wasn't quite meself, ya know?"

As Leon and the others shuffled closer, Verne held out the ring they had carried for what felt like so long. As Phonz saw it, the older dwarf crooned in delight and snatched it up. He jammed it on his finger and sighed in apparent relaxation before he said, "Thank ye, Verne. Strange how I lost it. Strange times though."

"Ya ain't gettin' a headache by wearin' it?" Duamé asked.

"Oh, dolomite! No, of course not! I am just glad it was found!" Phonz replied. Then he squinted his eyes at Leon and asked innocently, "Didn't I push you down a cliff?"

Leon had no idea what to say to such a ridiculous question. "I bounced back."

"Yes, well sorry about that. Haven't exactly been swinging me own pick for the past twenty years it seems. That thing, it really didn't like ya!"

Leon was confused enough to be rendered speechless. Duamé started to ask about the ring again, but was interrupted, "Can ya maybe tell them what ya told me?" Verne asked Phonz.

"Well, tha way I understand it, is I haven't been meself tha last twenty years. Could see everythin' tha thing was doin an' sayin', but couldn't stop it. Wasn't in control ya see." Phonz wheezed at that revelation, and sipped at some more soup before he continued.

"Last time I remember being in control, we were headin' inta tha Amalek tower with Lucien Rhise."

"Wait, what?" Leon's heart lurched as he felt his pulse quicken. *Did my father have something to do with this?*

Verne Granitehand blew up at the older dwarf. "Feldspar! Phonz ya knew better than ta go in there! Why on earth–"

"Well, he made a good case, an' I felt it from tha Diviner that there was something in there!"

"Tha what? Diviner? Wot's that?" Duamé asked.

"Oh! This!" Phonz said exuberantly, as he waved the braided ring on his hand about. "Been passed through my family for generations. Helps me sense where ore veins are."

Dread crept into Leon's thoughts, and his throat became very dry as Duamé breathed, "So that's what it does?"

Twenty years ago, when he was just a newborn, his father had made his fortune by discovering iron ore to the southeast. They were near his family's existing levigem mines. But they had found the ring in Rhoxmas' treasure horde! *Surely he couldn't have...*

"So you're saying my father stole the ring?" Leon asked.

At this, Phonz's eyes grew wide as he peered at Leon again. "Yer one o' Lucien's boys? Funny, I don't see it. But no, wasn't him who took my ring, it was tha other feller. Tha one we found in tha tower. In tha mausoleum we uncovered."

Verne gestured wildly as he spoke, "Wait, wait, wait! Ya found someone in a mausoleum, in a tower ya weren't supposed ta be in ta begin with, tha stole yer ring an' ran off?"

Phonz cleared his throat and tried to clarify, "It's, it's all a little bit fuzzy here. I'm... trying ta remember it right. Maybe, maybe if I see it again?"

Leon and his companions agreed to meet Verne and Phonz outside of the monolithic trio of towers that had been made by giants. This allowed him, along with the rest of his friends, time to gather their armor and weapons. They geared up in preparation to confront anything that they might find in the supposedly cursed and haunted towers.

After they had gotten ready, they walked briskly through the teams of dwarves and trolls that carted food and ammunition aboard the *Esperella.* Barrels of crossbow bolts were rolled up ramps and into the cargo hold. Cannonballs and canister shot were hoisted into the gun deck and stored. A few large entyrnet trolls carried sacks of delicate explosives, which had been repurposed from the mining guild. Everyone had worked together over the past two days in a frantic rush to get the airship ready for its assault against the horde.

Leon and his friends strolled past it all, and soon met with Phonz and Verne outside the huge carved monolithic towers. Phonz carried a stout walking stick and a dwarven lantern that held a glowing crystal. He seemed energetic and visibly excited to solve this mystery. Leon felt that he was close, so close, to finding out a secret that had been hidden from him his entire life.

“I still can’t believe that ya broke the rules an’ went into a tower without telling anyone.” Verne grumbled.

Phonz cackled before he responded, “This is why yer a smith an’ not a miner! Ya don’t understand tha excitement o’ being tha first ta find something new. Tha thrill o’ discovery!”

“An’ look where it got us.“ Verne said, as he turned to face Leon and the group that had arrived. “Are ya ready ta sort out this mess?“

After everyone agreed, Verne headed to the leftmost tower, which was closest to the cavern opening. They passed through a roped off area and Verne waved off a couple of dwarven guards with a grumbled, “Nonagint business.”

They clambered their way up to its entrance, near the cavern wall, which was quite simply a hole in the tower. Old wooden boards had been nailed together to block it off, but were easily removed. The smell of dust and old, undisturbed air wafted out from the opening as they all crept inside. Leon noticed Revelator flick its soft glow on as he crossed the threshold. At this point the spear’s reaction no longer surprised him. Even though it was daytime, the spear seemed to react to giant ruins, and giants, in general.

Between the glow of Phonz’s lantern, and Revelator’s lit spearhead, the group could see well enough as they continued down a wide but short corridor, and into the hollow interior of the tower. Huge blocks formed steps that spiraled both upward and downward along the tower’s wall. The space had numerous cobwebs that stretched along the oversized tables and chairs which were designed to hold much larger bodies. A few coughs were emitted from some, and Kelleren sneezed from the dust that covered everything. Still, the dust ridden air was slightly easier to breathe than the air filled with death and decay that they had been breathing for the past two days.

Phonz led them to the stairwell that led downward, and Leon helped Gionna down each of the large steps which proved difficult even for him. Eventually, they made it to the lower floor, which was bare of furniture but had several passageways that branched outward like spokes on a wheel.

"Where do these lead off to?" Miala asked.

"We don't know. Tha towers have always been off limits. Haunted." Verne stated, with a pointed stare at Phonz.

"Oh, stuff it! I thought I sensed more iron down here after our big find! Lucien an' I were in no danger! We thought… We thought there were no such things as… ghosts." Phonz said the last bit softly, as he shone the lantern down a southern passage. "Here! It was this way!"

They all congregated and followed Phonz a short distance down the highly arched hall. The tower had clearly been made for the giants, and soon doorways began to appear on either side. While the hallway continued off into the distance, Phonz turned and gestured with a hand at the broken wood that made up the bottom of a large door. They scrambled inside and saw a small room with a ceiling that sloped downward from the entrance. There was ancient, foreign writing along the walls, but the center of the room held a sarcophagus with a shattered stone lid.

"Phonz. Wot is this? What happened?" Verne asked.

The older dwarf was mumbling to himself loudly, "We– we broke into tha tomb here. We heard somethin'. A voice maybe? We got in here an' I got knocked out after something burst through tha sarcophagus. When I came round he was whispering over me. Tellin' me things. Maybe not me, but tha… thing."

"Lord Rhise?" Leon asked.

Phonz clarified, "No, tha other guy! Tha one that came out o' tha sarcophagus!"

There was a heavy pause in the air as everyone understood the implications.

"So, my father… was in league with the undead you found here?" Leon couldn't believe it. His father was building airships to use against the undead.

Why would he align himself with them?

"I don't… I don't think tha feller was dead. No red eyes, ya see. No decomposition at all! Ya would never have thought it! Especially when he spoke. An' then… well, me memory gets foggy at that bit! Wasn't in control o' meself anymore."

"It talked to you both? What did it say?" Leon asked with urgency.

"I don't remember!" Phonz wailed, as his voice echoed throughout the barren room.

"Do you at least remember what it looked like?" Gionna asked.

Phonz stuttered through a description that became more and more detailed as he went on. Leon continued to listen, and his dread turned into horror as a sickening feeling developed in the pit of his stomach. With every descriptive word uttered, the mouth watering ill feeling grew. It moved up his throat, and escalated to the point where he retched into the exposed coffin while everyone watched him with concern.

Leon didn't have all the answers yet. Questions still abounded in his mind as to why, and how, it had all been done. A new urgency came over him to not just save Agaprya and defeat the horde, but to return home as soon as possible.

Adonai, protect my mother and sister! He prayed silently.

"Ya alright, Leon?" Duamé asked.

Leon spat the remnants from his mouth as he said, "I– I can't believe it. I have to–"

"Do you know him? The person?" Miala asked.

Leon yelled in a rage, "OF COURSE I KNOW HIM! HE'S–"

Epilogue: The Missing

Meanwhile…

"Hang it all Silas, where are you?" Lucien growled in anger.

Almost everything had gone according to plan. The plan that had been thoroughly and painstakingly created and agreed-upon so long ago. Now, because of Leon and that blasted undead horde, everything was on the verge of falling apart.

Leon was supposed to have died in the dragon attack on the *Dawnfire*.

When that failed, he should have died at the hand of that blasted Admiral Silverspine.

After that also failed, the horde that assaulted the forest should have ended him.

Lucien had been hopeful when he saw the smoke that rose from the Elvenwood. However, even then, rumors and scouting reports from the pilots and heralds on mail carriers suggested that he had escaped with the elves. It made no difference now. The horde that left Masterwork Halls, and headed rapidly towards Agaprya, must have finally put an end to the troublesome boy.

The undead horde's movements made no sense to Lucien. While he did not have a mind for tactics, it was strange to see the way they moved across the land. They consumed the Chimera Lands, were burned in the Elvenwood forest, then turned southward and smashed into Bulwark Fortress. After that, they destroyed Hookvale, then assaulted the farther away Masterwork Halls instead of Agaprya. Now though, panic had begun to set into Agaprya as the horde moved towards it. They were a mere day away, and due to their direction of attack they blocked any chance of easy escape to Last Bastion in the northeast.

Lucien smiled to himself with the knowledge that King Garinth's last acts were forced to be those of a coward. He had ordered the evacuation of Agaprya. The vulnerable would be evacuated via airship. They would first fly east, and then north towards Last Bastion, to avoid the horde. The military would hold Agaprya for as long as they could. Lucien was glad to be a fly on the wall during the King's argument with his electrical pet, Elmira. He insisted she cut her ties with the Mancer Academy, and denied her request to defend the city with the other experienced mancers. Instead, she was instructed to continue to serve as the royal guard. Soon enough that service would include Laric.

That said, the plan had still gone awry.

The plan required Silas to bring Ladies Erika and Liara, as well as the rest of the staff and guards of Rhise Manor, on the next transport to Agaprya. Then they would all head to Last Bastion together for the coronation ceremony. They were supposed to display a united front. Erika, in her current state, would garner sympathy, while Lucien's business empire would show strength.

After Laric's elevation, Silas repeatedly conveyed confidence that the undead threat would be defeated and go away. *Where then, is my wife and daughter?* Lucien railed internally.

Lately, everything about his business partner had turned his stomach. Since he had shared with the seneschal that his associates had failed, and that Leon was alive, Silas had been more off kilter than usual. Lucien had always permitted Silas his eccentricities and beliefs. After all, he had certainly shown his value in the past. His latest behavior, though, was quite out of character for him.

His son turned to him as soon as he stepped on the transport ship, and asked with an imperious tone, "Father, where are Mother and

Liara?" Lucien felt his son must be practicing his royal speech, because days earlier he would never have addressed him in such a manner.

Still, it was a valid question, and Lucien wondered where they were as well. The royal airship transport that was scheduled to take King Garinth and Princess Giselle was ready. Lucien and Laric accompanied them, along with all of the necessary toadies and fawners. They would head to Last Bastion as soon as they could, before the undead horde came too close. That time was at hand, but three key figures were missing.

"We must assume that Senechal Silas will meet us at Last Bastion, with my wife and your sister." Lucien reassured both himself and Laric, as he patted his son's shoulder.

They could wait no longer. After two messages had been sent to Silas, demanding he stick to the plan and come to Agaprya, a missive had returned which made no sense. Lucien thought he was smart enough to know when he was on the bad end of a business deal, but Silas' guidance had never led him astray before. This response from Silas was confusing though… It contained instructions that were so vile, so incomprehensible, and were completely contrary to everything that they had worked for. It caused Lucien to wonder if Silas had been drunk at the time he wrote the note.

"In case we fail?" Lucien read.

They wouldn't fail as long as everyone stuck to the plan! That's why Silas should already be here!

The captain of the royal transport, the orcish woman Ashera Urk, hollered that it was time for them to leave. Lucien scanned the horizon from the gangplank of the ship one last time. The comfort of watching his massive dreadnoughts as they circled the city gave way to the discomfort of the knowledge that his wife and daughter would not be joining him. He now knew he would not see them on the horizon, rushing to meet them before their departure.

Lucien wanted his wife by his side, even though she could neither move nor speak, while the crux of his plan came to fruition. He wanted his daughter to celebrate their family's elevation with him, regardless of how awkward their relationship was. Their absence pained him, and reminded him of the seneschal's message. Lucien ran his fingers over the confusing parchment message in his pocket, as he climbed aboard the transport *Golem*.

His plan was coming together on one end, but unraveling at another. He looked at the note from Silas again. It had been his only acknowledgement of Lucien's existence in the past two days.

Who was this... this 'Xhormas' that Silas wrote about anyway?

Bible Verses

Used for The Rhise of Hope

Now the giants were upon the earth in those days; and after that when the sons of God were wont to go in to the daughters of men, they bore to them, those were the giants of old, the men of renown.
- Genesis 6:4 (LXX)

Be sober-minded; be watchful. Your adversary the devil prowls around like a roaring lion, seeking someone to devour.
- 1 Peter 5:8 (ESV)

Have I not commanded you? Be strong and courageous. Do not be frightened, and do not be dismayed, for the Lord your God is with you wherever you go."
- Joshua 1:9 (ESV)

So do not fear, for I am with you; do not be dismayed, for I am your God. I will strengthen you and help you; I will uphold you with my righteous right hand.
- Isaiah 41:10 (NIV)

What then shall we say to these things? If God is for us, who can be against us?
- Romans 8:31 (ESV)

Arise, O Lord! Confront him, subdue him! Deliver my soul from the wicked by your sword.
- Psalm 17:13 (ESV)

No weapon forged against you will prevail, and you will refute every tongue that accuses you. This is the heritage of the servants of the Lord, and this is their vindication from me," declares the Lord.
- Isaiah 54:17 (NIV)

For the life of the flesh is in the blood: and I have given it to you upon the altar to make an atonement for your souls: for it is the blood that maketh an atonement for the soul.
- Leviticus 17:11 (ESV)

"And do not fear those who kill the body, but are unable to kill the soul; but rather fear Him who is able to destroy both soul and body in hell."
- Matthew 10:28 (ESV)

Beloved, never avenge yourselves, but leave it to the wrath of God, for it is written, "Vengeance is mine, I will repay, says the Lord."
- Romans 12:19 (ESV)

"Now may the God of peace Himself sanctify you entirely; and may your spirit and soul and body be preserved complete, without blame at the coming of our Lord Jesus Christ. Faithful is He who calls you, and He also will bring it to pass."
- 1 Thessalonians 5:23 (ESV)

But the fruit of the Spirit is love, joy, peace, patience, kindness, goodness, faithfulness, gentleness, self-control; against such things there is no law.
- Galatians 5:22-23 (ESV)

There is no fear in love, but perfect love casts out fear.
- 1 John 4a (ESV)

Now faith is the assurance of things hoped for, the conviction of things

not seen.
- Hebrews 11:1 (ESV)

God is a Spirit: and they that worship him must worship him in spirit and in truth.
- John 4:24 (ESV)

Jesus Christ is the same yesterday and today and forever.
- Hebrews 13:8 (ESV)

And God created great whales, and every living creature that moveth, which the waters brought forth abundantly, after their kind, and every winged fowl after his kind: and God saw that it was good.
- Genesis 1:21 (ESV)

And God said, Let us make man in our image, after our likeness: and let them have dominion over the fish of the sea, and over the fowl of the air, and over the cattle, and over all the earth, and over every creeping thing that creepeth upon the earth.
- Genesis 1:26 (ESV)

If a house is divided against itself, it cannot stand.
- Mark 3:25 (ESV)

Acquiring wisdom is much better than gold, and acquiring understanding is better than silver.
- Proverbs 16:16 (CEB)

To the only wise God be glory forevermore through Jesus Christ! Amen.
- Romans 16:27 (ESV)

The fear of the Lord is the beginning of wisdom, and the knowledge of the Holy One is insight.

- Proverbs 9:10 (ESV)

For by grace you have been saved through faith. And this is not your own doing; it is the gift of God,
- Ephesians 2:8 (ESV)

For I know the plans I have for you," declares the Lord, "plans to prosper you and not to harm you, plans to give you hope and a future.
- Jeremiah 29:11 (NIV)

Every good gift and every perfect gift is from above, coming down from the Father of lights with whom there is no variation or shadow due to change.
- James 1:17 (ESV)

And these signs shall follow them that believe; In my name shall they cast out devils; they shall speak with new tongues; They shall take up serpents; and if they drink any deadly thing, it shall not hurt them; they shall lay hands on the sick, and they shall recover. So then after the Lord had spoken unto them, he was received up into heaven, and sat on the right hand of God. And they went forth, and preached everywhere, the Lord working with them, and confirming the word with signs following. Amen.
- Mark 16:17 (KJV)

Suddenly, there was a massive earthquake, and the prison was shaken to its foundations. All the doors immediately flew open, and the chains of every prisoner fell off!
- Acts 16:26 (NLT)

Have I not commanded you? Be strong and courageous. Do not be frightened, and do not be dismayed, for the Lord your God is with you wherever you go."
- Joshua 1:9 (ESV)

For wisdom is better than jewels, and all that you may desire cannot compare with her.
- Proverbs 8:11 (ESV)

The way of a fool is right in his own eyes, but a wise man listens to advice.
- Proverbs 12:15 (ESV)

Greater love has no one than this, that someone lay down his life for his friends.
- John 15:13 (ESV)

Acknowledgements

I would like to thank you, the reader, for bearing with all the twists and turns that I put you through. There may have been a few times that maniacal laughter spouted from me while I was writing, but that was tampered quickly by the strange looks from my family. Hopefully I weaved an entertaining enough tale to make up for it.

I also would like to thank my writer's group! You are amazing and even if we can't all meet at once some of the time, we still are able to hold each other accountable. To all the fellow writers out there, find yourself a group of people you can laugh and grow with. It makes a world of difference for me!

Thank you to Pastor Derrick Rawlings of Freedom Worship Center in Warrenton, Va. Your guidance as a teacher is invaluable. Thank you to those at SkywatchTv studios for your content as well.

I can't express enough thanks to my family, both immediate and extended, for sticking with me throughout this process. It's been a long time coming, but we are over the hill and in the final stretch (For this trilogy).

Finally, and most importantly, thank you to God for appointing me with the task of writing this series. Thank you Jesus for choosing me of all people, and for your unending grace and mercy!

Author Bio

Max B. Sternberg lives in Virginia with his wonderful wife and two incredible boys. When he is not working, or filling his time with the activities of a husband and dad, he enjoys delving deeper into biblical scripture and telling dad jokes. He strives to live his life as best he can – in all areas – for Jesus. Max believes that humor, mixed with truth, and tied together in a relatable way, can be an amazing way to reach people for the Lord. It is his sincere hope that readers will find his imaginings, paired together with biblical truth, inspirational for a deeper relationship with Christ.

The Rhise of Hope is his second literary work, and one other book in the series is planned for upcoming release in 2022.

www.ingramcontent.com/pod-product-compliance
Lightning Source LLC
Chambersburg PA
CBHW030422310726
48979CB00009B/1577/J
* 9 7 8 1 7 3 6 9 9 8 9 5 3 *